THE HALL OF HORROR

The lift halted. It had become so cold that their breath volleyed like cannon smoke, and even the warmer-blooded Hhronka were starting to shiver.

The doors parted. "Here are the only true Hhronka on Teffht."

Despite an iron control, A.H. felt a wetness on his cheeks as he looked into the crinkled, transparent bags.

This wasn't just slavery; it was cannibalism...

Other Avon Books by
Michael Lindsay Williams

MARTIAN SPRING

FTL:FURTHER THAN LIFE

MICHAEL LINDSAY WILLIAMS

AVON
PUBLISHERS OF BARD, CAMELOT, DISCUS AND FLARE BOOKS

FTL: FURTHER THAN LIFE is an original publication of Avon Books.
This work has never before appeared in book form. This work is a novel.
Any similarity to actual persons or events is purely coincidental.

AVON BOOKS
A division of
The Hearst Corporation
1790 Broadway
New York, New York 10019

Copyright © 1987 by Michael Lindsay Williams
Published by arrangement with the author
Library of Congress Catalog Card Number: 86-91029
ISBN: 0-380-89632-X

First Avon Printing: March 1987

AVON TRADEMARK REG. U.S. PAT. OFF. AND IN OTHER COUNTRIES, MARCA
REGISTRADA, HECHO EN U.S.A.

Printed in the U.S.A.

K-R 10 9 8 7 6 5 4 3 2 1

FTL: FURTHER THAN LIFE

Chapter 1

...in the middle, as though waking from deep sleep...

As he fell off the edge of the high red cliff, the avian felt the rubber band of gravity tug him downward. For an instant he was weightless, giddy with genetic fear, then the hot updraft bathed him and lifted him by his outstretching wings. The jerky strains in his chest and shoulder muscles alternated...right...left... as ground detail rapidly miniaturized and he fought to keep his wings horizontal against the rising buffets. Then the thermal carried him high into the laminar flow, and he hung, balancing with quick movements of wings and tailvanes, perpendicular to the cliff like a tethered kite.

Twisting his neck, he looked far down to watch first his mate and then their two offspring trot from the dusty ledge into the air. When all three had risen safely alongside, he called joyfully for them to follow. Giving several deep breaststrokes, he slid forward, drew his wings in slightly, twisted his tailvanes, and, losing altitude, glided out over the sun-splashed rain-forest canopy. The knitted tops of the blue-green, red, and yellow vegetation spread like a nubby ocean to the sharply curving horizon. The craggy mesa from which they'd flown was the only shoal in sight.

The avian appreciated both the parts and the synergistic

1

whole of the complex beauty he saw, and that this consciousness was framed by his pleasure in the simple movements of his limbs. Often his seesawing nonchalant glide took him into the turbulent air just above the uneven canopy, and he had to row back above it with swinging beats. He felt the stab in the spinal tendon he'd torn in a recent fall and the elastic wrench in his limb and thoracic muscles as the stuttering air drag sought to dash him against some crest of the forest's wave. He sucked the cooling wind-stream past his face into him, and it breathed him to life. As always, thoughts of food, sex, family, and even self were swept from him by the triumph and the unsullied joy of being airborne.

He could hear a similar amnesiac victory in the wind-tattered cries of his family. Pulling through the thin fluid of atmosphere, floating free, all sound telescoped to whisper, air-centered, the macrocosm's coordinates origined at their temporarily unfettered beings—as though reality itself tapered away from them toward diluting infinity . . . they conquered everything!

With ripening ebullience he saw the familiar cleft appear in the forest's roof far below. Calling loudly, he flexed, then tucked his wings to his sides and plummeted. Feeling the wind's pressure increase on his face, hearing its whistle alarm, he watched the maw beneath the giant aqua cauliflower umbrellas gape darkly. At the lowest possible height, he popped out his wings and splayed his tailvanes to catch the slam of friction, curving into the leafy cavern at blurring speed. His mate and young followed more slowly.

The clump of taller trees formed a nave that braided through an arboreal cathedral. Alternately he glanced at the jackstraw matting of the lower branches hiding the forest floor and the turquoise mosaic of sky flickering through the boughs of the archway. He playfully flapped up and down, over and under thick aquamarine branches that reached out for him from enfilades of trunks with smooth leafless fingers. The stale-tea smell of the forest curled about him. The first bend in the nave brought isolation from his family. Were the avian to worship a god, he would have done so here, for he was filled with a peace and awe unique to the spot. Not even the raucous hoots and frightened slitherings of the small upper tree dwellers could breach his feeling as their reluctant eyes witnessed this explosive intrusion.

He breathed cool damp reverence, thought of absolutely

nothing. Then the dogleg gantlet ended in an open apse; he blipped into full sunlight and started.

The quarter–Earth-sized sun's low angle and the tonsured fringe of nightly clouds told him the time was short to seek out the great clearing's safety. He swooped an upward spiral to wait for his family. They burst out single-file, separated by loud taunting cries, playing tag. He called. Their surprised faces rotated to him and then to the sun. Immediately they too climbed for perspective altitude, and all four chased the setting star.

As the canopy rolled toward and beneath them like an embossed sheet, it lost the yellow-red highlights, becoming flat and shadow-tucked. They watched the ochre bubble spill onto the lumpy horizon, and flapped faster. The upper arc shimmered its corona of xanthous needles in farewell, shrank to a point, and clicked off. Instantly the sky's fused color bands became spectral, red pinned at the horizon by the orange afterglow, with violet directly overhead. The opaque hues blurred translucent, revealing the larger star-points. The canopy grew details again, then gradually submerged with the oozing blackness. They were as quiet as the dead day.

Then the night glow of the great clearing blinked its aurora, ahead and slightly to the right. Tension rippled away with their calls, and they began to glide and lose height toward it. Above the smeared-together treetops the glare brightened in premature sunrise. In an instant the straight border of the clearing stepped below the forest top; they banked and circled in singly. The strip of open ground between the house and the high forest wall was slashed with light, the house having sensed twilight and turned on the floods.

He saw the smooth turf rise and with practiced eye watched the grid lattice grow. Quickly he twisted his wings vertical and backstroked to slow his forward motion as he bent the twin-coil-spring back-support with its vaned stirrup cups and brought down his legs to a perfect standup landing. The avian became a man once again.

Alcyon Hermes Krieder tugged his arms out of the sweat-slick plastec sleeves of the two-section jointed wings, slapped the harness belly buckle, and shucked his wingpack. Breathing deeply, he touched the switches on his wide grav belt to resume one-g weight, reluctantly feeling the ground press his feet harder. As the pituitary opiate created by the day's flying ebbed with its euphoria, he sensed a tiredness beyond the physical.

Medicine, proper diet, and exercise could slow time's effects but not stop them. He and Joan were in their late fifties and, barring accident, at the midpoint in life. Tonight, however, A.H. felt crow's-feet metastasizing both body and mind. Beneath his sodden orange onesuit, the chafed skin at his shoulders, crotch, and just above his elbows where the wing-pack joined to him seemed to sting more than usual. It would take an irritatingly inconvenient time healing, longer than twenty years ago, certainly. Every major muscle ached, in tune with the lumbar tendon pulled weeks ago. His bladder threatened to explode and kill him like that Roman emperor; "walnut bladder" was the most recent addition to his list of untreatable defects. As he looked up into the gray-lit sky to watch Joan and the children, he noticed the loose ends of vitreous floaters, protein strands jarred free from his retinae, swimming like bugs across his once-perfect vision. And the cochlear buzz he had also learned to selectively ignore insisted on overwhelming the warm-up serenade of the nocturnals in the forest.

Yes; as he'd got older he'd become more sensitive to, but less tolerant of, nearly everything. When young he had been the master, his body the uncomplaining slave. But now it made ever-greater demands on his time and attention, assuming a separate identity whose total character was compassed by the rapidly oscillating poles of disgruntlement and gratification. He actually seemed to feel Mars turning under his feet, slowing an infinitesimal bit with each rotation, just as he was.

He pulled off helmet and goggles, snorted a soft mucus plug back from the isthmus where his deviated septum narrowed his left nostril, and spat out his habitual pebble of hardened chewing gum. Joan came down into the crossed cones of light with comparable skill, equally grateful to dump her gear and gasp away her oxygen debt. Without helmet, her thick wavy hair straggled damply onto her shoulders. It had once been obsessingly auburn, now was silver-combed. The statuesque, well-exercised body was hourglass yet, but drooped like slightly softened tallow; his mind traced the tiny watersheds that lined her full white breasts, gibbous with dark areolae. As he watched her gather her equipment, he saw her as an aging dancer: grace without quickness, tautness with tightness, pride without arrogance.

Still he regarded her as beautiful. It wasn't possible for him to separate the mask from its bearer. She understood so much, not just emotionally, but logically and scientifically as well. She worked hard at this, too. With understanding came appreciation. With appreciation came the tolerance that had been the fulcrum of their relationship. When they angered, disappointed, or saddened each other, it was with defensible disagreement, not lack of comprehension.

Poe was wrong, he thought wryly, sure this would offend her literate nature. The most tragic event possible is not the death of a beautiful woman. It's the life of a beautiful woman who is stupid.

Joan shined him a sweaty smile from her handsome, broad face. A thin red goggle line encircled her thick brows and straight, blunt nose, giving her the semblance of a full-lipped owl. Her expression graphed more than pleasure, relief, or companionship. Its kaleidoscopic nakedness reminded him of the faces of stiff-backed debutantes he'd seen in photos from the 1800s. Trapped and crushed by puritanism that would last another century, they had dared to reveal themselves—the living, sensual, yearning beings within the high collars and ankle-length dresses—if only to the camera's asexual eye. Sin once removed. As always, this look, revealed to him alone, sought to transport him from the melancholy she saw in turn.

True, his mood was, at least partly, a response to his physiological state. And while there were no physical rewards for getting older, there were emotional and mental ones. This day had been rare, dream-pieced, thus the more precious. A person might live a full lifetime and have but a handful of such memories.

And so he insisted on free flying with them every week. Good therapy. The shared joy bound them closely again and temporarily shut out the dulling restiveness that inevitably nibbled at him.

(A little more desperate than the mass of men, and less quietly so. But perhaps he had that right, that duty. In Their *desired* image created They him.)

Prometheus Carl already had most of his father's large frame, dark coloring, and thin, hybrid Aryan-Amerind features. He also possessed one other of A.H.'s qualities, potentially of far greater consequence. He dropped into the spots far too swiftly for a standup stall. Playing fighter pilot again, showing off. His speed forced him to run stumbling after touchdown, slapping air with his wings to keep balance, nearly falling. He quickly opened his harness and studied his equipment to cover. A.H. twisted away with his smile to see Renata come in with mirror repetition of her mother's style. She also resembled Joan in her copper hair that streamed from her helmet like hot exhaust, full figure stretching her yellow onesuit.

"Hey, Ace!" she teased as she tugged her harness loose. "Next time better let me land first so I can foam the grid!"

Petulantly P.C. crooned, "Sybling ribaldry could be very flattening to you, dear sister."

"Uh oh." She placed her full upper lip between her teeth. "Let's not touch him off, people, please."

"Uh oh. Forewarned is short-armed, people, please," he imitated snidely.

Palming her ears, Renata cried, "No! You're not going to be Pun Punk again, are you?"

"Not if you promise not to play Faerie Princess," he anted. "Besides, those were more malaprops than puns."

"Very, very *mala,* then."

A.H. watched his children with ambivalence. Within their actions, words, their very essences, he could see the outlines of the adults to come, the full potential, physical and psychological, of the dehydrated toadstool-embryo being in each, awaiting time's watering. They resembled A.H. and Joan, but they were/ would be totally new and unique individuals, truly reflecting the genetic amphimixis of their parents' gametes.

He was as intermittently proud and ashamed of his children as most others who accepted parental responsibility fully. He had striven to give them all the tools he knew to live successfully, or at least to be content. But the tools were *his,* and worked best in *his* environment. As he had become bitterly aware, environments always change. Eventually they would have to find their own way. Till then his children's failures were partly his fault—and they realized this, too. It was an inescapable cycle, for they would one day commit the same duty to their own children. Didn't this make parentage innately fraudulent? And could his pride ever wash his special guilt over P.C.?

"Folks," he interrupted in his learned peacemaker role. "Let's banter toward the showers. I for one would like to finish dinner before *Mass* starts."

P.C. depicted amazement. "You're really watching that? I borrowed Sagan's *Contact* for tonight!"

Chin up, Renata said, "Bernstein's *Mass* is an American

classic. They perform it live only once a year. It's high culture —something you sorely require—and you can see that dross anytime."

Joan hooked A.H.'s arm. "There's a holo in both your rooms. Watch what you want. Papa and I are going to retire early."

His response fell short of her smile, even though he ignored their self-conscious smirks. She whispered across his shoulder, "Unless you're too tired to retire, that is."

How he longed, needed, to yield to her coaxing, to be buoyed with her and hold the day's warmth. Starting to the house, he said, "Just now my only properly working distensible organ is my bladder."

"Dog on a long walk again?" He nodded.

"Flying enlarging your glands again?" he returned. She nodded.

They hung their wingpacks in the shed against the east wall of the flagstone house. The design followed that of the native Hhronkan dwellings: a giant egg of wood and stone, crested with a lobular string of sleep rooms, many window-walls, and a garden–patio with pond at one end. A green-blue vine like fugitive kudzu covered most of the roof, blending it almost invisibly into the rolling marain of the clearing, and reducing cooling costs this near the Martian equator.

P.C. trotted to the side door; the house accepted his palm on the I.D. plate, and the lock bolts clacked. He turned with index fingers up. "Life is like watermelon seeds: the part that keeps it going is the part we always spit out. Eh?"

Together they pointed thumbs down, and he finished glumly, "At least it wasn't mala-propped."

As they entered the living room, the radio sensors registered their approved presence, activating lights and venting. The spongy tan carpet continued smoothly up and over several scattered floor evaginations shaped like curving chaise longue chairs. These and the stalactite globe-lamps were the only concessions to Hhronkan decor; the rest was relaxed colonial.

A.H. went directly to the rear toilet, and Joan stepped up to the kitchen circle on the right. The two teenagers spontaneously combusted toward the wooden spiral stairs bracketed to the balcony that cantilevered over the rear of the living room. Shoving P.C. off balance, Renata hit the first tread three paces ahead. He countered by switching off his grav belt and leaping five meters to the balcony railing. Clutching the wrought-iron slats, he chinned and arched over to land flat-footed in front of her as she left the top step.

Throwing out his arms to block her, he exulted: "Faster than a speeding pullet! More powerful than a loco commode! Able to leap ta-a-all balconies in a single bound—"

Wincing with each phrase, Renata lifted his belt with both hands and bounced him backward several feet across the catwalk, where he landed on his buttocks and slid agape over the polished planking.

Giggling, she said, "Remember, chim*pun*see, four-tenths g makes even Pooperman just another Fart Sent!"

"Low-ass Pain!" he called at her as she receded primly down the hallway.

Looking up, A.H. caught the end; he shook his head to Joan with a smile, a brittle veneer to cover the resurgent mood. P.C.'s buffoonery—it was as desperate a pretense as his own forced cheerfulness—and far more habitual. Another topic they'd come to avoid.

"Adults one minute; children the next. God, the entropy increase! If only we could transfer that energy."

She smiled back from the slit leading to the center of the kitchen carousel, its halves now closed around her. Pearl in clam. "I was just about to say that. Hard to believe they'll soon be degree'd."

He walked up and squeezed through the passage to her, as if physical closeness could buffer him from his own feelings. She swiveled the stool to open several bright-enameled doors and worry the crackling contents.

"Damn machines will never taste-test to *my* standards! I'll reprogram *again* tomorrow."

He tapped the menu indicator. Turkey, yams, squash-corn, salad, wheat bread, and an appetizer of Wlaatan *varduun,* a native aquatic form resembling miniature whales. With their nonterrestrial proteins there was little nutritional value, but they had a great taste.

"Mmm. High protein and carbohydrate; good for flying days. I'm ever grateful you've a—traditional?—hobby." They exchanged smirks. He read the many nuances in her face.

So much was communicated by expression, touch, and vocal pause and inflection that had nothing to do with the words. That was true even with strangers, but . . .

It had been over twenty years since they'd met. Each had certainly impressed the other that night, but not in a totally positive way. He had known many women, most of them only in the biblical sense. They had become something of a habit to him, like bowel movements: not necessarily pleasant, but pleasantly necessary. Without exception they had disappointed him. But, rife with cynicism, he had lived as an elective outcast, largely a self-fulfillment of prophecy. Yet Joan had been and was overwhelmingly different; he had seen that immediately from both her conversation and its subliminal counterparts. She had suffered less confusion of identity or vagueness of purpose than most people. Her intelligence, education, and humor had been honed by a sense of self-worth that was well balanced by an honest humility. And she had seen similar rarity in him. But his addiction to mutual masturbation and hers to emotional security had botched any chance of a smooth beginning.

So their relationship had been slowly forged, as much by outside influences and coincidence as by personal attributes. But once formed, it had proved durable, could not just fade within. They had invested much of themselves and had grown together through time. Yet he felt a twinge of fear. This restiveness could not continue; it had already worked between them for too long.

He saw that she was aware of his struggle to keep the day's lightness, that she would continue her cajoling to help him, as she always did.

"Sauternes or dry?" She shook, then nodded, her head with his. "Montovani, Kliegel, or Joel?" he asked as they both shook heads three times and smiled. No soothing of savage breasts tonight. He'd almost said it, but that would have been too blatant a nonchalance. Deceit must be more delicately balanced.

She lowered an oven door, and the smell of the sweet potatoes was like fresh chrysanthemums; it vied with the fragile odor of her sweat. Swallowing the wetness in his mouth, he touched an hour's extension into the main panel. As she curved to him in query, he pushed under her armpits and cupped her bosom, feeling its weight through the taut bra. Perhaps this time it could be more than a placation; it might be a return to a deeper joining.

"If we move apace we can bathe *twice* before dinner . . . my, my they are bigger."

She was surprised by his aggressiveness but fell in gamely. Reaching behind her, she raised thick brows. "Yours too."

Suddenly he felt a tingling at the base of his skull, a cold-morning shiver at his neck running down his body, erecting every hair. Came the muffled touch of identity and that increasing gestalt of knowledge, the impaling of gossamer veils by steel spikes. His individuality broken, he lost control. The tightly clenched hope left him, and he surrendered to the blurring of the forces within. Yet the sense of loss was diluted by the intrigue of this rare visitation . . . and need.

"What's —" Joan began as she felt him stiffen further.

The grumbling chatter of a Hhronkan grav flyer landed on the pad near the house. "It's Shree Shronk."

Her brightening didn't quite cover her disappointment. Still she held her own hope. "How nice! Just in time. *Varduun* is a favorite of —"

"He has news. He wants to join in a Total Projection."

She smiled uselessly. "What for?"

He shook his head. Ten years ago, when he and Shree had still been codirectors of Mars, each administering his own species's affairs, they had been necessarily close. But since elections had finally begun and they'd retired, the social visits had declined. There would always be a gulf, it seemed. Hhronkans and humans were similar, at times complementary, but not identical. There would always be subtleties not understood, even between *baasa*. As time had passed, these had seemed to become more important and had made meetings less comfortable for him. And in the twenty years they'd known each other Shree had performed only three Total Projections. This ultimate merging was needed only for eidetic sharing of memory. He could think of nothing currently important enough to require use of this identity-dissolving, exhausting technique. Nothing that couldn't be satisfactorily transmitted through first level *baas* or even word of mouth.

"You'd better put dinner and baths on hold."

Reluctantly they drifted from each other as the house, polite as ever, announced over the panel speaker, "Visitor at front door." The little TV plate set high in the carousel glowed with a slightly overhead shot of the illuminated stoop.

A monster stood there, uncomfortably blinking into the camera pickup lens. It had taken years for A.H. to accept his initial revulsion of the Hhronkan visage, and that acceptance had finally freed him of the prejudice. But the disparities remained. The hairless beige cannonball head displayed bilateral symmetry. Yet there were no external ears, only small pores high on each temple. More noticeable was the lack of a nose; a wrinkled rimmed opening at the face's center dilated and contracted with each whistling breath. The two eyes bracing this and set below a single bulging brow ridge were startlingly unhuman. Gray scleras with purple irises that slitted horizontally, cateyes rotated ninety degrees. The lashless lids blinked with irritating infrequency, continuously staring as though mirroring disbelief. Only the mouth seemed familiar: wide, full-lipped, femininely sensual, but opening to reveal the scalloped, bony chewing ridges.

A.H. spoke in practiced tone: "Dim lights; open front door."

Interior illumination dropped by half, to what the being would find more natural. The panels opposite the one they'd entered after flying clicked apart. The thin figure stooped slightly to pass the jamb and met them as they left the gaping kitchen.

It stood there, a tan-gray giant made of snakes. Krieder was tall, but Shree Shronk was two heads taller. His two arms were cobras, each with four heads; his two legs were pythons ending in four-toed, clawless bird feet. There were no sharp angles or joints in the beige body. When he moved, it was with the curling sinusoid motion of snakes, which thrust moving rows of bumps through his diamond-wrinkled skin—fingertips within a balloon, revealing the endoskeleton of short ligamented bars of bone. His featureless tan torso and gray-accented labia-flapped groin were hidden by the wraparound, belted, bright yellow robe. Its short length and wide sleeves allowed maximum flexibility for his supple movements. Now he stood stiffly, eyes fixed downward on them, so cocooned with tension that they remained silent.

Looping up a warm knobby palm to each of their chests, he pressed lightly with the callus-tipped nailless fingers, two opposable thumbs bracketing two middle digits. "Give as you require." The bass voice resonated from far behind the mouth, formed within the muscular respiratory tube that functioned as his larynx and lent a hollow trembling quality to his speech.

The greeting was standard, but they both sensed the lack of personal warmth, the shared joy he usually engendered. Even the human inflection he'd learned to employ was missing. Tonight he was totally business untainted by pleasure. Typically Hhronkan, never mixing the two, any more than they did craft and engineering. They never attempted, as humans did, to make their art practical or their machines lovely. The dimorphisms could be disconcerting.

"Uh . . . as you require," mumbled Joan, stepping up and returning the touch, inured to the intimacy of it and to the pronounced quadruple heart pulse that staccatoed beneath her hand.

A.H. only looked up at the staring eyes, sensing the tightly contracted Self, like squeezing a marble ball. For the first time in many years he regretted Shree's *baasa* ethics. They could have lightly merged at once and exchanged the information necessary to relieve his dread. Instead, they'd use clumsy words and slowly build the proper environment to initiate the infinitely more intense Projection.

Usually he couldn't help but agree with Shree. They had little right, less need, to pry into another's privacy under ordinary circumstances. Besides, minds had evolved in isolation, and the intimacy even of light merging could be unsettling, to him at least. The residue of foreign thoughts shadowed his own for days afterward. He used his *baas* power like a bee's stinger.

He became aware of the renewed wetness in his armpits, the old-leather aroma of Shree, Joan's discomfort, and the presences on the balcony. P.C. gripped the rail, a stone gargoyle; but Renata, damp hair hanging like vines, grinned and shouted.

"Shree! I thought I heard your flyer!" She started to the spiral stairs; Shree's upturning face instantly wreathed with an embossed black ring. The color eddied into his lucid flesh like hot black coffee dumped into cold milk. The ring shrank inward to his mouth and vanished, then the skin returned to beige and went glass smooth.

As with terran fish and cephalopods, the transparent outer skin of the Hhronka possessed a layer of chromatophores that spread out or contracted by voluntary/involuntary nervous command to show more or less pigment. Resultant color ranged black, gray, and white; and three-dimensional skin patterns could be added to these dynamic face/body displays. Hhronkan dermis lacked appropriate musculature to provide human expression. The tightening and smoothing of the dermal muscles "hid the skin" from further display. This black ring denoted emphatic negation.

In shock she stopped with a double take, and her innocent chagrin prodded A.H. "Shree and I will go to the patio. Please don't disturb us."

Joan nodded as he led across the living room to the north window-wall, touched open one of the convey glass panels, and stepped into the cooling evening breeze. Turning back, he was trapped by an uninvited recognition. Shree bobbed toward him by curling one snake-leg ahead, clutching the rug with its bird foot and straightening both legs as he shifted his body forward, then curling the rear leg ahead, while curving both legs inward, to repeat the next pace. Suddenly the fore–aft bowlegged stride was a *reality;* Shree himself (bobbing serpentinely past him, cat-eyes staring, nasal pore dilating, hidden skin loosening again, becoming soft beige with its grayed shadings, face with brow ridge like some bald, time-warped Neanderthal) was an utterly strange reality.

They *made* me, those post-Millenium Frankensteins. Knit my carefully chosen gametes' genes as one knits yarn, with purpose. Mine and so many, many others. And only I—except for one other now lost to time (I, Alcyon of the Pleides; he the lost Plead)—was a success...with Shree's help. Where were all those others now? Scattered like sterile seeds, abandoned, worthless. Had it been wrong? I am the *product;* how can I judge? Yet their world made the experiment illegal, through fear and its handmaiden, morality. So they pursued us, humiliated us, even killed us. Still, here I am today on Mars, "Wlaata," the Cradle, to the Hhronka, its own children. And now I will join my mind and soul to one of them, a being born 30,000 years ago! I am awed by my capacity to internalize.

In the muzzy starlight they moved under a corkscrew tree near the pond. A.H. plopped into a wrought-iron sling chair while Shree settled on a curving plastec chaise that fit his hipless frame better. A.H. involuntarily sensed the patio around him. The muted hiss-twitter-hoot of the nocturnals, the splash of the terran fish in the pond, the cold-damp of the hard iron frame embracing him, the humps of cobblestones beneath his tennies, the stale-tea smell on the slight breeze, the hollow rasp of Shree's nasal breath.

"I am sorry for my harshness with little Renata, but her joyous greeting would have broken my concentration and set back our merge. Please explain to her."

The soft foghorn voice dropped from the tree's shadow, framing his dread. "Why is this Projection necessary?"

Shree respired a bubble of expectation around them. "Umar and Droom have solved the gravity equations."

Of course! *This* was important enough for almost any consideration. Umar al-Askari was an Iranian mathematician, one of Earth's finest; Droom Kreethar had been Primary Guardian of one of the two buried Hhronkan Repositories; Shree had been Primary Guardian of the other. Though she wasn't the Hhronkan's best mathmind, her ability to form a partial merge with Umar had yielded important results. One was the improved gravflux belt he now wore. Formerly, the equipment would have been too bulky and energy-consuming for personal portability. So humans on Mars had spent a great deal of time in centrifuge rooms, and still many had suffered long-term low-g effects. Now they each wore the belts and needed only to recharge them daily and replace the grav lattice periodically. Yet such accomplishment would be negligible against the ultimate unified field theory relating gravity, EM, and the nuclear forces in a rigorous way.

"You mean the complete, final solution?" he asked at the shadow. Again he felt Shree's Self field pulsing with concentrating energy. This sunburst of power drew him inexorably into imitation.

"All the things we've discussed are now possible?"

"In time."

"The ftl technique too?"

"Yes."

"How soon?" The Hhronka usually viewed time more languidly than humans. Their civilization was a quarter-billion years old; their life span nearly double a human's. Yet tonight Shree was encrusted with anxiety. Now he knew why.

"Within one year." Or 1.8 terran years.

"You really want to try for Tau Ceti . . . Kmeaa, to search for the lost Hhronkan expeditions! But why the Total Projection? What memory do you want to share?"

"I wish you to remember my wife Feeahra with me and also to recall a newscast I discovered accidentally several years ago, one recorded during the last Thaw time after I had gone to the Long Sleep."

Each of the 1024 Guardians in each of the two Repositories

chose one mate with whom to produce one embryo for inclusion among their assigned groups of 512 Children.

A.H. thought of Shree's own son, Tweeol, who had often accompanied his father on visits. Quiet, shy even by Hhronkan norm, he and P.C. had grown through the last of their childhood together and had remained close. They shared the budding talents of their fathers' inherited *baas*—and a bittersweet dilemma given them unintentionally.

As their ancestors had 214 times before, these Guardians and their Children would normally have survived Mars's 60,000-year Freeze cycle, caused by its axial obliquity, in impeded animation and been reawakened at the start of the next 600-year Thaw. But human intervention in terraforming Mars had broken the Freeze and their Sleep midcycle. Now 2,048 sprouting villages covered Mars, each under guidance of its Guardian. And the first Thaw generation was already being born of the Children themselves.

A heroic feat for any group, human or Hhronkan. Perhaps the Guardians deserved the near-deification granted them by their city-families.

"It is necessary that you comprehend, emotionally as well as factually, certain things about the Hhronka and what truly happened then. I have not told you everything about the Kmeaan tragedy. There was no need at the time." He seemed to rush on in apology. "It is true there was considerable evidence that Kmeaa had a family of planets, but there are nearer systems with similar data. We would never have sent groups of sleeping Children and Guardians based solely on this. There was more ...much more." His sibilant voice hushed to a whisper and faltered. "And there were not just two groups sent sequentially; there was a third. The newscast is from that time and will explain. Decisions will soon be made regarding the ftl technique. Your people have the resources to construct the craft, but will want to try for a closer star. And they will not be willing to send as large an expedition as we *must* have. They may even require an unmanned probe be tested first. This would only waste time! I will need your help to make your people understand what we must do!"

He'd never known Shree to be so intense, to pump emotion into his speech to impress him. It pricked his curiosity more than the request for a Projection. Even before he began, his assent was mutually acknowledged. Still he spoke the litany, smoothing the rough dry sands of individuality between them.

"I wish to know your need. If it is true and just, let me help."

"I will take it gratefully and respond in kind."

The first step was to form a simple merge. The night sounds blared, then receded in A.H.'s mind as he built up energy within his central nervous system. Heart, lungs leaped to the demand; blood surged. Neurons increased metabolic rate several times. What in other humans and Hhronka was a mere flame became a furnace. From deep bloomed the familiar but disused kernel of power. It was well controlled; the control *baas,* was all. With it he channeled the energy into the field whose nature was as yet not understood, even by the Hhronka, but whose physical existence was denoted by them with the label "Self," a component of the mind.

Again came the tingle at the base of his neck, but now he was its source. It spread up to englobe his head. His identity core seemed the center of a gossamer web scintillating outward spherically . . . outward he pumped it . . . stretching toward infinity . . . it blipped and faltered as his own inward sense impressions shot through the shimmering web like radials of spilling black paint. His weariness, the stuttering twist of his long-empty stomach, the hot sticky flush of his sweated skin, the meaty smell of his soiled crotch, the darting itch of his encrusted scalp—and his residuum of fear at the next step. He struggled to shed these distractions.

Shree's brightly glittering Self brushed his, not spikes now but water spreading into the dry sands. Physical sensation was instantly flayed from his web. Their Selfs entwined like drifting smokes. Each sensed the interference in his own field caused by the other's and interpreted that feedback as thoughts, words, sentences, essays, emotions. Bubbles of meaning burst in their minds' pools. The exchanges came with familiar ease, as though moist wax ear plugs had been withdrawn and too-faint sounds were now audible. What they learned was merely a small part of whatever was uppermost in the other's mind, and "truth" had no absolute value in these gestalts. Now they altered their Selfs' upper-level patterns until they pulsed to one of compromise; salient thoughts were two echoes coalescing into one. Yet the single web still had two nodes of identity, north and south poles of a single mindfield.

A.H. had awakened Shree in the middle of a 60,000-year

sleep. By accident he had merged with the Hhronkan Repository's sentient computer and opened the otherwise impenetrable building. Slowly he had established with Shree a poor contact sufficient to teach him English, since A.H.'s larynx could never completely mimic Hhronkan. Then Shree had helped A.H. release himself from his own prison of childhood guilt and employ his *baas* fully. Ten years of subsequent training and he was good. But Shree would always be the naturally evolved teacher, he the manufactured pupil. Shree sunk the common web's tendrils deeper, white-hot needles into A.H.'s mind. He screamed his terror as he felt the roots of his very being torn free, braided with the alien parts that were not *him*. The poles drew together, fused . . .

. . . a chaotic potpourri of human–Hhronkan thoughts, snagging like random flies in the single-node web . . . noncorporeal identity fades . . . only recognition of existence whirls in black freefall. Then Shree remembers . . . and within their shared mind . . . the distant past lives once more . . .

Chapter 2

It is a typically gorgeous, equatorial, spring day. The cloudless air reeks of the pungent musty odors freed from the forest ground by the night's rain. The Narrow Sea has never been more picturesque, its pale blue-green water curving over the northern horizon, and its jagged tree-coated south bank stretching down from our hill, zigzagging left and right into cerulean infinity.

The many vine-roofed houses at the town's edges below can barely be distinguished in their cunning patterns of clearings. We have seen the children there, playing in the sunlight. We luxuriate in the unlimited sense of freedom here. Lying on the damp, plant-quilted ground, we feel renewed life at the joined center of our beings, their roots reaching up into the sky and down into the sweet-sour soil of Wlaata. We can almost sense the planet spinning. I withdraw my light merge with her, parting us.

Feeahra too has never been more beautiful. Her smooth face is near perfect in the yellow sun's glare. The delicate roundness of her brow fits well the small contours of her cheeks. No eyes are as deep in color or emotion as hers, no lips as fully shaped and inviting as they tremble in self-consciousness at my open inspection. And no body could be as sinuous and fluid in motion, nor as desirable by seduction, nor as enticing from her skin's rippling display when we join in love. I behold the loveliness beneath the flesh as well, filling it from within, radiating warmly to my joy.

My genital labia became firm with lust, but this forces me to think again of the topic of our argument. She wishes to bear a child, even though I must leave them both behind in the Long Sleep. I have already promised her it is our embryo that will go among my Children, but this is not enough.

"Would you condemn our child to the Terminal Generation? To be one of millions sterilized at birth, going through life themselves childless? To watch with hopeless despair as Wlaata becomes unsupportive of life? To grow old and, if unfortunate, be one of the last few remaining in a dead world of ice storms and scant preserved food? Finally, when the air itself freezes, to be forced to live underground and never to stand naked under the sun and stars?"

As I finish mercilessly, she displays the violent white-black flashes of horror. She moves close to me to touch and embrace. Quavering.

"When you are gone to the Sleep, I will be here, always loving you, always remembering you and knowing you and our child lie so close..."

Her flickering display is saying much beyond words, a poignant whole of loneliness, longing, and despair. She actually sheds tears, something I have never seen outside my core-family. Attempting to assuage her premature grief, I love-breathe with her; but the response is mutually too arousing, and I separate our mouths, exhaling her sweet air.

Her hot wet face and vigorous Self, with which she knows I will merge, reproach me before her words. "Your duty, always your duty...

"Yes. My duty to the Hhronka and to my Children. I am the only *baasa* to qualify as Primary Guardian; I alone who can link with Leeowm Waa and make it capable of true creative thought in its machine duties. This is the purpose of my life! You have known of it, and so our future, from the beginning."

Her eyes and breath-pore open wide in anguish, then her skin hides further display in smoothness. "And what of your duty to me? Oh, Shree! I can not look at a life without you, or at least without our child, growing beside me, part of you staying after you have gone. I did not seek love with you; it happened because of what we are to each other. Must I pay so high a price for this fate?"

She grips my arms tightly, drawing to me to share the spice of her passion. Her skin moves against mine in a rhythmic cunning pattern she knows is irresistible to me.

"Please, my love! Unsheath yourself to me. There is so little time left before conception is forbidden."

My arguments are sound, but my heart has ever been my skin's betrayer. I too dread our separation. Yet another death to endure before my own, for I shall leave part of me with her regardless of whether I take or leave our child. Can there be for me as well a higher price than this? As we entwine, I cannot remember a time so full of hopeless sadness or hopeless love . . .

. . . again the whirling freefall of nonidentity . . . the reborn memory . . .

The tiny scene buoys in the air before me. Oddly, the holoimage reminds me of a human toy described by Krieder, a bubble of water placed over a modeled winter's landscape. Shaking it floats clouds of minute white flakes to create a brief counterfeit snowstorm to delight a child or bemuse an adult. Since this image was recorded, the soughing storm is surrogate as well, but its desolation is real for me.

White, white snow drives down from a dull ribbed sky to mix with the dirty ochre drifting across the cracked, scarred tarmac and terminal building that crown an endless rocky plain. All life has been swept away, but not before placing representative progeny into the frozen ground. Plants have sent tap roots deep; pregnant animals have buried themselves alive, often aided by their mates, to be firstmeal for their awakening young. The ultimate sacrifice.

A sub-clustered crowd huddles on the paving at left from my perspective. One of the larger orbital shuttles is being prepared in the midst of its attendant vehicles on my right. What can its mission be so near the Freeze? We should have withdrawn all our artificial satellites and off-planet operations by now. Occasionally an individual fissions from its cluster and moves toward the shiny outstretched liftwalk into the shuttle's underside. This is *not* a robot mission! The small crowd is evidently composed solely of family and acquaintances of the departees. There are no cheers, no music flares of salute, not even a display wall. I am granted an uncomfortable overlay of hope and hopelessness. Sudden chill! I suspect the goal of this flight.

Leeowm Waa told me this newscast was made only twenty-three years before the end of the Thaw time and seven years after the Day of Ensealment of the Repositories and the start of my Sleep. It is the final record in the Kmeaan file. I become certain of the departure's meaning; but why then, and why at all? Although cross-indexed into several other files, this is the first time I have seen this record. All the better; it is depressing fare.

This near the Freeze, the polar and temperate regions are now uninhabitably cold, and the atmosphere measurably lighter as it begins to freeze out there. By now our scientists have distributed the many megatons of designed industrial wastes across Wlaata's low-lying areas, to be mixed into the soil by the millennia of duststorms to come, ensuring the proper melting of the permafrost in the next Thaw.

The remainder of the Terminal Generation have packed together underground in the equatorial zone, for even here wet and dry snow now falls year-round. I feel empathy for them; how we despise enclosed places. If only we had the resources to allow all our people the Sleep. Now for them there is nothing to do but wait, to remember and yearn for the open surface and ... wait. Suddenly I admire my people anew and feel guilty pride that they trusted me with the fruition of all they might have been. Yet we have both striven to our limits to see that trust realized. Is not such courage, such sacrifice, proof that we Hhronka deserve to survive and continue?

Above the wind's dead breath, the resigned yet determined tone of the unseen announcer matches my matrix of emotions as the crowd steadily thins.

"It is difficult for us to accept that the day of departure for the third Kmeaan expedition is already here, and even more improbable that nearly a century and a half has passed since first we received the signals from Kmeaa. Encoded in simple binary language, they described an advanced civilization living on that star's third satellite. With the complex technical data came instructions for creating an image of the Kmeaans themselves, a creature even less hhronkoid than the animal-savages on Sciinlo, our sunward heavier-gravity neighbor."

The colorless, stubby, three-digited, pebble-skinned being

takes the place of the launch scene. The narration is reviewing well-known information. News is the oracle. Fact will outweigh rumor. This wasn't made for the now long-dead Terminal audience. It is for the Children, that they might know the past correctly. The only honest history is the simple recording of it.

Droom Kreethar said the technical data of the Kmeaans has proved a great boon to her work on a unified theory for the four causal forces of nature. One result is the improved grav belts the humans wear here and that also allow us finally to visit Sciinlo in person, though unfortunately this comes too late for us to migrate there as intended. Apparently the Kmeaans solved the unification riddle, though they didn't explain this solution completely in their signals. Another mystery.

I wonder what the narrator's reaction would be to learn that in only half a Freeze period the "animal-savages" have advanced enough to both terraform Wlaata, if accidentally, and artificially produce a functioning *baasa,* one I grew to call friend. The dying landscape returns.

"We have all puzzled over why such a technologically adept species would only send information and invitation to visit, yet not visit themselves. But it was an invitation we welcomed. The joy of meeting another intelligent people would be enough; but the chance also to find other planets more hospitable than our own, to export some of us and avoid the total loss in the Freeze of all we build—"

The aged voice breaks, momentarily overwhelmed by the inevitable horror to come. I thought myself inured to this.

"Two consecutive expeditions were sent, with adults, children, and embryos sleeping in impeded animation for the sixty-eight-year journey. Two times we waited for the seven-light-year signal of success at journey's end to return. None came. Not from our people, nor from the Kmeaans, despite our repeated queries. The sacrifice had been made; we would send no more."

How the word *Kmeaa* itself always conjured mixed sadness and wonder in the people of my Thaw time, and in me.

"But then, only four years ago, a piece of message was detected."

I am stunned; a seam in the Kmeaan mystery at last! If only it had come before my Ensealment!

"It definitely originated from the second expedition since it was specially encoded. Most of the brief transmission was ruined by interference, but three words were certain: 'further than life.' That was all, but enough. Their only prior message, months earlier, spoke of having awakened in good health and of entering the Kmeaan system. Therefore, 337 of us have volunteered to again seek there the fate of so many of our people."

An unknown death in far space or a known death on Wlaata —a poor choice. I pity them—and envy them.

"Whether these final travelers will awaken safely at the Kmeaan system and find a kinder world, as we hope those who went before them have, none can say. But we wish them well."

Another cluster fissions; this time a woman and her...yes, young daughter move toward the shuttle. Unusual now for a child...Feeahra! Her buoyant walk. Despite their heavy robes in the cold, I know her and our child, Affeel! Touch the remote, still and enlarge the image. Life-size they hang before me. I too cannot move or speak.

Feeahra, you are older, a full woman and lovelier. Affeel reflects your charm in miniature, as I knew she would. Grim resolve, befitting pioneers, firms your display. Of course you would have gone on such a journey, to give our child at least a chance for a full life. Did you succeed?

My Fee, the irony! I blink away the wetness (I have not wept since we said farewell) to see you clearly, from all sides now. This recorded you frames our ages nearly equal, yet I still live, while you—Does your dust drift in space, to congeal someday into a star? Or is it mingled in some world's soil to grow a living thing?

How I miss your gentle strength! How well you finished the uncompleted me! How worthy you were of life and sentience. My duty to my Children had to come first, but now that is almost done. And I would give all I am or will be to twine with you but one more time upon the night hills of Wlaata! It is too late. So much of life is lost through time's random net, so high a price. Must I suffer this *again?* They fade to memory. But I vow: now my destiny is to learn your destiny.

A.H.'s consciousness burst into being and shrunk-fit back into his body. Sweat-soaked, hard-breathing, exhausted, he slumped in his chair, adjusting to the new surroundings. How odd to be in this heavy angular corpse! How alarming to find his body flexing only certain ways, his hearing better, his vision worse, his skin an immobile hairy parchment hung over too-long bones. For the last minutes he'd *been* Shree; for the fourth time he'd been Hhronkan. For the first time, he truly understood!

He had known of Feeahra and of Shree's loyalty to his role. And he'd always questioned how being "parent" to 512 Children could ever compensate for the loss of adult love. It hadn't. Such was the sacrificing nature of the Guardians. Or at least it was a tribute to their appreciation and acceptance of their reality. What they had done had been of absolute necessity for survival of their kind. How many humans could so subsume their personal lives? Perhaps the same proportion as within the Hhronka. Perhaps that had also been a limiting factor in the Repository strategy as much as energy, material, or psychology.

Also surprising was the depth of emotion he'd shared with the giant Hhronkan. That these beings possessed strong feelings was well known. But their reserve, in private and public life, was legendary. He had shared such personal revelations with Shree only a handful of times, this creature who had both endangered his life and saved it, who had shown him the truth of his own past. Next to Joan, Shree had once been his closest friend. Yes, had been. Despite any kind of differences, species or otherwise, they should have remained so. The fault was his . . . in both cases.

Similarly exhausted, the Hhronkan lay in the tree's shadow, submitting to the short period required to resume disconnected identities. Finally his gasping also slowed and he whispered, "Now you understand why we Hhronka must go to Kmeaa, why I will go with them. I regret forcing you to internalize my heart's sense."

It was still like talking to himself. "I appreciate the chance to understand, as always. I'll help any way I can, and . . . I too will join the expedition."

It just tumbled out like a confession, driven by something deeper than Shree's shared urgency. Softly, the being spoke his name in a human tone conveying expectation, empathy, and protest, a masterful accomplishment for a Hhronkan.

"No, Shree, it's more than your Projection. I have my own reasons. You know me . . . have known me. Remember?"

Shree curled into the starlight that poured pale phosphorescence onto his upper surfaces. A.H. looked up to see Phobos's dot shoot out from behind the round head.

"The heart is the navigator in you too, Krieder; but always

the head must be the pilot. You have much to discuss with your family. The danger, the time dilation—it may truly be a one-way journey. Consider well. The Council of Cities is already negotiating with Earth for one of your space habitats. We will move it to Wlaata's orbit for refitting. We could leave in nine months."

A.H. felt warmth swell, a retying of old bonds. "We have an adage: 'The longest journey always begins with the first step.' I believe we've just taken that step a second time."

Shree stood unmoving a moment then looped a palm down to his chest. His deep monotone was edged with humor: "Of course, we left-handed Hhronka have a mirror saying: 'The longest step begins the first journey.' I also hope we can make this second journey together."

He turned quickly and blended with the tree-strewn gloom at the patio's end. A.H. sat staring at his dark convex twin in the house's window-wall. He saw the metaphor: he was one being existing in two states at once, unable to cross the barrier between. He was immobilized at another of his life's major fault lines. As with first love and its end, or loss of true friendship, and return to loneliness or the death of parents and remembrance of the security they'd granted, pattern and substance were forever changed. New knowledge and feeling prevented any return to the old; fear of the unknown retarded advance. Most people past age eighteen found it impossible to again overcome such fear and hung within their own Schwarzchild radii, caught like light inside the boundary of a black hole. For the rest of life they were cloaked in changing body, costume, and affectation, but were unaltered deep inside where the trapped juvenile cowered. A neoteny of tragic waste. He had always been pushed across the barriers by forces outside his control. But this was completely a choice situation—and not his alone, he remembered with sudden guilt.

Then the turbine on Shree's flyer screeched alive, and the autolike two-seater rose slantwise above the far side of the house. He could just catch the faint blue exhaust of the thruster pods above the cockpit canopy and the dull orange of the buoying grav mesh on the vehicle's underside. Then the brilliant lights came on fore and aft. It angled above the forest's height, screamed, and shrank west toward Shree City.

The returning quiet was complete as the frightened nocturnals also hung between old and new situations. His reflection incinerated, the living room momentarily illuminated, and Joan came out through it, still in her onesuit, her hair clasped behind her neck. She dragged another sling chair alongside his, clattering its iron frame over the stones. The familiar language of their companionship filled the silence between them as he shaped his revelation to her, his plea.

For several minutes she sat patiently looking up at the beclouding sky. "One of the Muslim caliphs in Spain about A.D. 1000 once said, 'I have now reigned about fifty years in victory or peace, beloved by my subjects, dreaded by my enemies, and respected by my allies. Riches and honors, power and pleasure have waited on my call, nor does any earthly blessing appear to have been wanting to my felicity. In this situation I have diligently numbered the days of pure and genuine happiness which have fallen to my lot: they amount to fourteen.' This has been one of those days, hasn't it? Not just what happened but the way we all felt about it, together."

He nodded, leaning forward slightly so she could see his smile. The convergence of their thought was also an effect of aging with each other, though she was more literate in expressing it. Cool night breezes, let down from the gathering rain fronts over the forest, alternately brought and dissipated the lap of her insistent, controlled breathing.

Her question begged his sincerity. "Why have you stayed here on Mars and never returned to Earth?"

She could still totally surprise him, too. "You mean after my co-directorship?" She just stared thoughtfully at the cumulus and pantomiming flashes spreading across the stars. "I could have; we could have. The kids certainly liked it well enough that one visit, but—"

He twisted to stare at the starlit facets of her face, felt his jaw muscles harden quite on their own. "Would you really go back to *that*, being one of Selye's caged rats? The unnecessary crowding, the chaos everywhere. Oh, there's the *appearance* of variety, the shock and charm of the old and new crammed together, a thousand different folkways per square kilometer. Yes, yes. But it's only facade. It all *looks* different, but to me it *feels* exactly the same! The manic need to conform within a region, and every region's getting denser all the time.

"Probably that's one cause of so-called human nature, though I've always believed it's whatever we pretend it is. Regardless, it's buried here—or was, anyway. Maybe as long as we're kept off balance by newness or given enough elbow room by limited isolation, our Hydes stay harmless inside our Jekylls. The Hhronka surely think so. At least we don't have to listen to our neighbors' toilets flushing through pressboard walls!"

He leaned back, quelling irritation at her distracting probe, realizing his reaction was overblown to squelch his fear. She dropped her chin and swung her head a bit side to side.

"No, A.H., I wouldn't want you to bear any such pressure. My father suffered that all his life. He had the best of intentions, but no will. My clearest memories of him are the times he'd load me and a few hundred pounds of food into the back of one of our store's pickups and drive around giving it all away to families on dole. We'd come home really warm inside."

She reached both hands urgently to his face. "I can still feel his Sunday whiskers scratch when he hugged me, his cheeks red-splotched, grinning; made me feel as good as he did. But it taught me that no one gets enough just giving. That's one reason he drank. The life back there took a good man and made him first a drunk, then a Jesus-freak, both of which made him ridiculous. I loved my father, but I never liked him much."

Revelations and origins. It often seemed that only in making the revelations did the origins become real.

He nodded at her rancor. "I never had the pleasure *or* pain of knowing my parents—or gamete donors, in my case. But my teacher, Franklin, was the same as a father, and more. When they killed him for trying to reveal the antigenics experiments, I was only eight. But I knew what love was, what we'd meant to each other. Enough to mistake myself and my ability as the cause of his death. If Shree hadn't helped me to see the truth, I probably would've self-destructed long before now. Certainly you and I would not have made it; guilt and love don't sleep well in anyone's bed. I suppose that's partly the reason he's been a father to both of us, huh?"

They looked across understanding and hesitance at each other. Her chin came back up out of shadow into the glow matching the silver in her hair. "You're missing the point. My father and you have a lot in common."

An even more unexpected gulf, stopping his reaching hand. He thought of Shree and his long-dead Feeahra, the gulf no hand could cross.

Her resonant contralto spoke in capitals. "It takes two conditions to sustain our, or any, relationship: we have to be *in* love, at least occasionally, and we have to be content, in ourselves and in each other. You haven't been content in a long time. It's grown obvious to us all, especially since you retired." She pressed both palms against the invisible barrier between them. "It's as though you're wrapped in polyfilm, always holding back part of yourself; we don't share deep down, the way we once did—the way my father and I once did. I know you're trying to break through, even tonight. But—"

Now he saw the hurt and anger in her stiff posture, the tightness in her shadowed face. Cold guilt clenched his gut, and he knew the impotence of being trapped by himself.

"P.C. eavesdropped. We know all about the Kmeaan expedition. And please don't say anything to him. If I had the ability, I'd have done it, too."

He let his face down into one palm and pulled his chin back up through the vee of its thumb and forefinger, rubbing at fatigue and shame. "I'm sorry. It's something I *have* to do," he whispered.

"Perhaps, but you've made us feel so . . . *unimportant* to you!"

Starlight rebounded from the tear sheen in her eyes. "A.H., I came to Mars for the same reasons you did, partly hiding from myself, partly wanting something better. We all run from some things and to others. Are you running from us?"

Revelation and origin. The challenge broke his paralysis. She *had* to understand; that was the best he could do for her. Why was it always necessary to hurt someone to get anything he really wanted?

"It's not that simple. When Shree and I were co-directors, we were making a *difference*. Now, even my *baas* is useless without political authority! And you know just what chance I have of ever being elected to any office. Oh, I'm the local celeb, all right, up there on the pedestal, safely powerless. But no one wants an official they might be unable to lie to; our representative democracy wouldn't last a week on total honesty."

At first he'd disregarded the few sidelong looks and reticence of those who gestured casually toward him from the crowds, fascination tinged with revulsion. But over the years it seemed they'd all duplicated the pattern. No matter that he'd explained a thousand times his ethics and limits. Did everyone in this self-centered species think they had something *worth* hiding? Feelings long absent had begun to haunt him again.

He broke the friable sarcasm out of his voice. "I suppose I have withdrawn from you, and from life here. It's getting just like Earth, in the human communities; more and more I see the dismay in the Hhronka around us. I thought by ignoring the changes I could keep from caring too much, could tolerate it all. Instead, it looks like I've been selling out to everything I hate."

He drew up straight in the chair. "But I won't let the rest of my life go for nothing! And I don't mean you're nothing. You three will always be important to me, but this is important, too. Shree will need me out there! We may be contacting another sentience; my *baas* could prove as vital as it was when I woke Shree. Remember?"

Her damp snuff accused him. "You are still not being totally honest with me or yourself. And you *must* be now, for a decision like this."

He let her breathe away some of the anger. How useless it was trying to muffle the pain he caused. "What do you think?"

Her voice became a lecturing monotone: "You've always expected too much, especially of yourself. It comes from giving too much, too often. You're always saying, 'If everyone did what they're supposed to do.' Well, they never will. We all break the rules sometimes—even our own rules. No one can foresee things well enough to make a rule that *never* needs breaking. Not even the Hhronka, though they're better at it. That's probably why you've stayed here. There are simply fewer people to disappoint you. And Hhronkan society is closer to part of your ideal since it fails less at ideals, but it's so *very* narrow. You can't have it both ways. It is admirable to want equality, justice, honesty, and total individuality . . . to work for them, to give of yourself—and damned rare. That's one reason I love you. But you—we all—have to *take* as well. And how can you take when you've totally isolated yourself, even from us!

"Tolerating failure requires acceptance. I think you can't accept the future here or on Earth because you've never accepted your past. Shree helped you over the guilt, but not the bitterness, the resentment, for what they did to Franklin and for the witch-hunt you and the other *nhumbies* went through."

His heart froze and breathing pinched at her words, truth he already knew but had held at a tolerable intellectual distance.

Those haunting feelings that lurched just beyond emotion's reach were echoes of the vehement passions that had oppressed his early life. He realized for the first time that, though he couldn't shed them, he could control them, and with definite purpose. Hate could be a powerful wellspring of sustaining energy.

She lowered her eyes to him, features and voice in supplication. "That's past now. Everyone has to eventually surrender, make peace."

His ire spouted. "Really! Do I? Does—should anyone? Isn't that tacit approval? Doesn't that make you an accomplice in everything that's wrong? I left Earth to get away from a people whose only moral is 'What's good for me?'; whose only ethic is 'Don't get caught!' My leaving was collusion enough because I was only running away. And I've failed even at that. All I've done is prove I can be one of them if I let myself. Well, I might have to *accept* being in a species so egocentric that it puts its pets above its own kind, but I'll never be *resigned* to it!"

Her smooth-faced shock at his acid burst dredged the horror he felt beneath the surface. Intellectually he'd fought this battle so many times. For him, there seemed no solution to the emotional dilemma, though she'd found one herself. How could he help her to see that he didn't necessarily *want* a solution?

He slumped back into the hard womb of the chair, conscious of its iron simile for life itself, rigid in both its support and its denial of what you wanted. "I'm not running this time, or ever again. Not if I hold tight and keep alive what I believe. I may not be able to change things here, but I may out there. That's my one last dream. Don't you have any more dreams?"

She looked back at the sky. "Only one. Perhaps my need to keep what I found here—the only time I ever have—to share it with you the rest of our lives, buried my need to dream further. But that's what happened to the Hhronka, isn't it? They were simply surviving from Thaw to Thaw, resigned to extinction when Mars eventually freezes forever. So I'm losing what I want most, my life with you. Perhaps there's more Hyde in you than in me."

Understanding, appreciation, tolerance. Again she had revealed something new about each of them. Again she had fulfilled his faith, his trust, even though it placed her across a gulf they might never be able to bridge.

Through a capitulating smile, he said, "I hope not." He stretched out his hand once more, but she waved it down.

"It's all right. It's all right," she consoled.

Soon she took in a breath and let it shudder out.

"At least you've made *our* decision easier." He saw the shadows under her Giocondic smile. "After all, everyone we love is going."

She lifted her hand to his. Tightly he took her sinewy smooth fingers with their squared nails—the touch of friendship, not desperation—a second time this day. Her hand was cold at first, but it grew warmer as they sat closely and stared up at the sky even after the rain began to fall.

Chapter 3

No matter how she concentrated, Droom Kreethar could not keep her nose from falling off. The damp, wrinkled, chamois-soft lining of her own nasal sphincter had poor sensitivity, and she had to remember to keep it clamped onto the mushroom stump of the false proboscis shoved into it. But, as with rubbing the belly while patting the head, her attention would eventually stray, and the piece of soft plastic would work loose and squirt out like a seed.

This only renewed her umbrage at having to disguise herself as a human female every time she left her apartments in the upper levels of New Teheran. Again she tugged peevishly at the too-tight cowled headpiece of her black pleated *burka* and ex-haled hard against the ridiculous veil as though it were a moth that had fluttered too close to her mouth. At least the coarse neck-to-ankle dress with hood, required by *purda*, the law of concealment, conveniently hid her slender jointless body and bald earless head. It also helped to disguise the lithe bobbing walk as her kneeless legs bowed fore–aft.

She closed the door to her entryway as her other gloved hand went automatically to the wide belt under the robe. The wrig-gling fingers (one false) perused the control panel over her ab-domen, checking the settings and remaining charge. If the body-shaped bubble of warped space-time ever failed, she would suddenly feel Earth's pull go from her native .4g to 1g and her weight would jump 2.5 times, leaving her virtually paralyzed, pinned wherever she collapsed.

She went along the narrow dim corridor of enameled stone, trying to ignore the usual miasma of dank concrete and claustrophobia that threatened to choke her. Emerging gratefully into a broad enclosed boulevard, Droom joined the bilateral flow of black and gray corpuscles that attempted to fill the unadorned vessel. The corridor squeezed through a mitral arch—typically Persian, pointed and falsely supported by tapered pillars on both sides—and expanded into a huge ventricular arcade. Add sand and an open sky and exchange wood stalls for the lunaluminum ones, and the bazaar within, though it sold only luxuries, would have copied any other during the last thousand years. She passed quickly through the clattering bedlam of buyers and sellers and entered another passage.

The skylights and occasional windows had become black mirrors in the early evening, giving a multiple perspective of the systaltic crowd. The robed people and their reflected twins furtively showed their dusky faces to her on both sides and upside-down overhead. Again she noted with distaste the habitual expressions of self-conscious penitence for things done and undone, for things yet only thought, the continual insecurity and self-examination.

Had she ever known such a tightrope walker's fear, the strain of the delicate balance between what was demanded of her and what she felt it was possible for her to do? Between self and societal image? Unlikely! She was Hhronkan, and the Hhronka had long ago matured beyond allowing emotions to create baseless insecurity, even in childhood.

The snare of memory. Little Anyaa, one of her 512 Children (could she truly have been her own biologic child as well?), always reaching up to her, straining to be touched. Her little body lithely agitated, arms looping back and forth, entire skin flickering with dark fluid smears of distress as her mouth and nasal pore dilated–contracted rapidly in supplication. Droom, disbelieving it, patiently chiding her and glancing at groups of her other, more serene, Children in embarrassment as she again explained about her role as Guardian, her necessary impartiality. The caretaker machines would hold her, feed her; go to one of them; she could but supervise, lecture, guide.

Not once in Anyaa's brief life had Droom ever held her with affection, as—

"Allahu akbar, hayya ala khayr el-amal." The voice of the muezzin over the speakers accordioned out the first word to end on a high pitch, dropped the second, then rushed the rest of the sentence to anchor his call to prayer.

"God is greater; hurry to the best act," Droom translated the Arabic derisively to herself. The flow quickened in response to this electromagnetic epinephrine, and she went into an unoccupied lift to tap the promenade level switch.

"Your god is greater than my patience, certainly."

Of all the humans (billions!) in existence, why did their finest mathmind, at least the one with whom her Self could form a partial merge, have to be a Shi'ite Muslim, and an Iranian into the mix! This had been discovered by accident during her one extensive tour of Earth several years ago. She'd sworn never to return. However, Umar was equally adamant about not leaving New Teheran. So, to quote an old human (Bacon?) gibe she knew he would resent: "If the hill will not go to Muhammad, Muhammad will go to the hill."

She would have smiled if she'd had the muscles for it. Instead, an embossed wave of white rosettes arose round her thick-lipped mouth and spread outward over her face, a bouquet of wry humor equivalent to the human facial contortions she had finally learned to read.

Such an utterly intractable people! Their strictly regulated lives often obstruct every effort to get things done in a timely and efficient way. And their beliefs! This "Allah" they are so certain exists, a supreme, omnipotent, virtuous being who created and controls all. Really, such childishness! Why can't they and the other human theists simply admit the universe is an indifferent collection of energy, matter, and entropy, governed by natural laws we've yet to discover totally, and get on with the business of discovering them? No, they spend their brief lives lying away their fears to each other and to themselves, even about the inevitability of their own deaths and the end of their identities. We Hhronka surely would never have survived if we had allowed such fear and petty selfishness, the truest form of self-deceit, to—

She checked her familiar tirade—one that was at least partly wrong. She mustn't allow her role as a scientist to seduce her into generalizing about everything. Also the lift doors had clacked aside, and it was impossible to buoy ire within her whenever she stood on this open promenade.

She loosed her veil, bobbed out from under the low portico onto the unoccupied deck, and went to grasp the rail at the edge of the platform. From here most of the roof of New Teheran was dimly visible. It was a giant, shattered, dark crystal, only planes and angles staircasing away on all sides. Nowhere were the voids of the city open to the sky or outside air, and through tens of thousands of rectangles white, yellow, and blue light checkerboarded to give the crystal a spangled glitter that counterpointed the star-dusted sky.

The slippery-gritty feel of the wet rail impressed itself on her. She looked out farther to the sea dimpling far below the two visible edges of the city. The thin piercing odor of the salty ocean (an interesting smell, like one's own sweat or feces; Wlaata's seas stank of iron) reaffirmed that it surrounded the city. For New Teheran was a floating world.

Iran had already become an ideological island during the last century. Its people, with their language, dress, customs, and very gene pool rooted in the Persian past, had always been isolated from their Arabian, Turkish, and Hindu-Indian neighbors. Even the spread of Islam in the seventh and eighth centuries had failed to homogenize them with religion. The Shi'ite sect, the largest minority in Islam, attained dominance in Iran alone, finally becoming the state religion. This served only to aggravate continuous border skirmishes into wars with Syraq, Turkey, and the USSR, through its latest republic, Afghanistan.

But it was economics, that most elementary of all social forces, that caused a physical split as well. When alternate power sources began to shrink the demand for oil, the Iranians' source of wealth shrank with it. They spent the last of their petrodollars to construct self-sufficient seaborne cities in kilometer-square sections and launched them into the Arabian Sea. Finishing only a decade ago, they had linked to form the titanic complex that had become New Teheran, an ark that drew its energy and food entirely from the sea. This total independence permitted them to both leave behind their enemies and unwanted minorities and to follow an existence prescribed in its every aspect by their religion, without outside interference or intrusion—especially by an alien such as she.

Reluctantly Droom had to admit there were, after all, similarities between these humans and the Hhronka. At first the primitive Hhronka had emulated the other Wlaatan animals by burying themselves with unborn progeny in the future perma-frost. But in one Thaw period their exponentially budding science had enabled them to construct underground Repositories to hold (so few...) selected embryos in impeded animation—far safer than being freeze-dried—to survive and reestablish their civilization on the storm-destroyed surface with materials deposited in the buried buildings.

This had given a jump-start recovery from the Freezes. But it hadn't freed them of the horrible necessity of choosing whose children would pass on to the next Thaw and who would be left childless to die when the planet's next chill solidified the air into the ground. Perhaps that was why the Hhronka made self-sacrifice their central virtue, she thought. Could it have been otherwise when each person of the Terminal Generation must resolve to be sterilized and die, leaving no child behind, their bid for immortality denied? But, within the limits of Hhronkan technology, there had been no other solution. Even subterranean cities were ruled out by their *ooural,* genetically inherited claustrophobia, which in New Teheran drove her here each night to breathe deeply of the openness and stars. Was it the artificial selection of the Children that had done this, and more, to them? She was certain this was true.

Over the 115 Freeze-Thaws, virtue had not been goal enough. Imperceptibly her people had lost their need to learn, to grow, to dream; their struggle had become a stagnant action merely to survive as they had been surviving. Unchanging and unchanged life, just what these humans sought. They too had built this city to survive and to escape and to preserve.

But, she suspected, this was not sufficient for them either. Most other humans instinctively sensed the necessity of reach-ing out, at any cost. Fortunate then that humans had come to live on Wlaata. Droom herself had at last been convinced that the wisest course was to join these often irrational beings and grow together with them. Pursuit of this goal had kept her here for three years.

The perfect unification of nature's forces still lay in the com-plete solution of descriptive equations that had baffled the Hhronka and all of their computers, despite the Kmeaan boost. Thus she had returned to New Teheran to work with Umar al-Askari. He was a leader in the human effort, but more impor-tant, he and Droom were, to each other alone, borderline *baasa.*

When close, they could merge a part of their Selfs synergistically to form a new mental entity that possessed mathematical abilities orders of magnitude greater than either had separately.

And during those times when we are merged, scrutinizing the equations, and we realize another step toward the solution, when I see the face of nature dissolve away a little more to ultimate truth—for those few moments of joy I would endure *anything!*

"Why are you not at prayer? And why are you here without chaperon?" spoke a peremptory voice in Persian Farsi.

The *muhtasibs* stood in a line at the opened lift like three additional pillars to the portico, their dark robes fluttering. She recognized two of these moral police; they had taken notice of her differentness (had her stride alone been sufficient?) some weeks ago and had been attempting to follow her, without success till now. Typical of them not to simply approach her but to wait and catch her in some transgression.

"And why are *you* not?"

Their faces showed surprise as her deep voice rasped up from her trachea. The unfamiliar one in the middle, the largest, came forward in a two-step dance of anger. "You will come with us to the *qadi* for judgment, now!" His companions passed him on either side, and he lurched to reform the line.

As with humans, the Hhronka had many modes of behavior, but two were of major import. Those who prescribed to the Meethlah ethic were nonviolent except when left no other choice and would never take the life of any intelligent being under any circumstances. The Orrtaan Hhronka were not so disposed. Droom was Orrtaan. One hand darted under the dress to touch the grav belt controls, lightening her. The line faltered a bit as it approached and they saw that the transgressor stood almost as tall as their tallest. Then their arms swept up.

Now her nosepiece chose to eject itself as though a tiny missile to defend her from the attackers. They halted like a chorus line to see it fall at their feet. Their astonishment shifted to horror as the breeze lifted the free front of her cowl to reveal her brow ridge.

"Allah preserve!" whispered one.

"A jinn!" screeched another.

She continued the choreograph by springing low over them, enshrouding the pirouetting turbaned head of the taller in her skirt. Her long arms sky-hooked a chin on either side and jerked

them backward. As she came down she followed through with
the forward arc of each arm, and the two smaller men slammed
into the deck, flipping like sprung mousetraps to lie still. The
third was quicker, her touch having abridged his horror. Before
she could turn to face him, he leaped onto her. As she glimpsed
him descending like a blanket, she momentarily forgot and
braced to be crushed. But as enough of the massive body con-
tacted her low-g bubble, it filmed him as well, and he became
six-tenths lighter. He was but a stiff cape on her rounded
shoulders, his arms scissoring her thick neck. She bobbed under
the concrete portico and launched like a shuttle. His head made
a hollow thunk like slapping a ball.

"I believe you would score that two strikes and one spare,"
she gasped as she dumped him. But the comment was merely
bluster to cover the shaking hollowness within. She had never
struck a human before. Quickly she palpitated them. Strong
pulses, regular breathing; the damage was minimal.

This had not been necessary. She could have revealed herself
to them, though it would have compromised her position here.
Had her antipathy for these beings truly ripened at last?

Umar Muhammad al-Askari felt the smooth weave of his
tighten across his buttocks and shoulders as he again touched
his forehead to the carpet.

"I bear witness that there is no god but God and Muhammad
is the Apostle of God, and Ali is his comrade," he murmured,
beginning the evening-night prayers. His mouth filled automati-
cally with the words of the seven rak'ahs but he smelled the
acetate residue of the polycloth rug. His mind partially freed
itself from the ritual and remembered the slick talc feel and
mummy fume of hot dry sand . . .

He was seven. His tall stately mother (delicately handsome
behind her veil) held his excitement-damp hand in her firm dry
one as she took him for the first time to the Meydan-e-Shah in
his native city of Isfahan. His wonder-blanked mind sponged
the place with the eagerness of a child left alone too often. A
child who had survived this by creating a world composed only
of himself, his few toys, his tiny house, its adjacent dusty
streets, and the imaginary companions from stories. Now he
knew the delightful terror of learning that the real world beyond
was more complex, mysterious, beautiful, and ugly than any he
could have imagined.

Many centuries before, the city had been the capital of the Seljuq Empire, and the huge courtyard and encircling buildings commemorated glories forever past. They left the warm dark of the mortar-scarred Lotfallah Mosque on the east side of the empty flagstone rectangle and were enwrapped in the hot cotton of the sun. Within her shadow, he drew the thicker air into his chest and stared around his mother's dark skirt into the fragrant magnetic confusion of the bazaar sprawling on the north side. They would not visit there today; they had little money, as always.

Instead they continued across the griddle surface toward the Ali Qapu, the Lofty Gate, its pillared arch windowing only the parqueted wall of a building beyond. Suddenly he stopped and was lifted by his mother's inertia. He saw the horses: large, dark, muscular, the foamy white aromatic sweat lubricating bridle and harness... rolling elastic swiftness of their swaying backs turning beneath him at his knees' pressure... jolting halts... He saw the helmeted men swinging the long clacking mallets as they rippled over the grass like calling centaurs. He knew that through the gate, to the right, down the steps, was the grandstand from which he could see them, hear their chinking bits and plunking hooves. He knew the long-forgotten surges of sudden screaming triumphs.

Jerking his hand free he dashed forward yelling joyfully. "The horses! I want to see the horses!"

His mother's vain calls dopplered behind as he passed the arch, ran along the ochre-bricked wall of the imperial audience hall, and slowed to take the top step. He had to watch each cracked cement tread in order to go so fast and almost collided with a huge, startled old man wearing incongruous riding boots. His robes entangled him briefly like drapery. On the first landing he looked up at the skinny V's of bench rows and roofed box seats fanning away left. He ran along the one even with the landing, not seeing the peeling paint and rusted stanchions, not seeing the horses, not seeing his mother rushing to him as he stood there disconsolate. For he now knew that there were no horses, would never be any here again.

She knelt to him and grasped his small pointed shoulders, concern overlaying puzzlement in her eyes. "Umar, how did you know they used to play polo here? I'm sure I've never told you," she said quietly.

He snuffled and twisted in her palms. "I don't know. I just

remembered, I guess," he replied in the soprano misery of a child without the answer.

Only puzzlement remained as she settled onto the bench behind him with a sigh. "Polo hasn't been allowed in Iran for nearly a century, since the Ayotollah Khomeini founded the Second Islamic Republic."

He stood in silence, looking at the splotched field as the memory of the horses faded.

"Mother, who was my father?"

He saw the crinkling surprise spill over her veil and knew why he'd hesitated to ask. She chose her words and built an altar for their self-respect.

"Your father was of the house of Askari, and you are the son of our *mut'ah.*"

Mut'ah, a temporary marriage, sanctioned by their religion and its law. But he knew in his mother's life there had been many, many. He would not hurt her further, but bolster their pride instead.

"It is from the house of Askari that the Hidden Imam came, the Mahdi, who will one day return to our sight to fill the earth with equity and justice," he said with the adult firmness of the *mullah* from whom he'd first heard this. And his mother's face flooded with an admiration and awe that, until the moment of her death, she'd never shown to him again . . .

This was the earliest coherent memory in Umar's mind. He was aware that it was very unusual to have memory start at the late age of seven, and this disturbed him, especially since the memory always came to him during prayer.

He was completing the final prayer unit when his apartment door swung open and Droom bobbed quickly in to reclose it with a backward push. She paid him only a glance, then went across the rectangular room, exploding out of her disguise, trailing it behind her. She hastily drew out the end of a long black cord from her belt and plugged it into a low wall outlet. Only then did she relax, remove the contacts that hid her slitted purple irises, and view his ascetic quarters.

It still intrigued her that, with modern materials and methods, these people had managed to create a decor superficially identical to the centuries-old one she'd seen in Persian history files. The intricately designed rugs (the only decoration), simple furniture (real wood since he was of the professional class), and padded couch were betrayed only by the fluorescent lamps, the electric kitchen alcove, and of course the large flat write-screen on which they worked each night.

She pulled the stikseams open on her boots and flicked them off with wriggles of her bird feet, enjoying the freedom, watching Umar finish. He was not large; she towered over him as most Hhronkans did most humans. His narrow, pointed shoulders and round head added to his slight qualities, which seemed to be straining with rapid movements upward against gravity. But she never thought of this when looking at his face. The dark crop-bearded Aryan features and small black eyes beamed a calm intensity that superseded other observations. He was the exceptional Teheranian, secure within himself, as though some unfailing psychic compass guided him. The only time she felt his doubt was during their merged gropes toward the solution. Oddly, this discomfited her. No one should be that certain *all* the time. It often gave her an unfocused eerie feeling.

He did the final genuflection and rose to face her, the open sleeves of the *chal'at* sliding down over his clasped smooth hands. "And couldn't you wait until I had done the prayers?" His soft baritone was calm and disciplined as always.

Her elbowless arms snaked in an S-curve of regret. "I am sorry, but my power reserve was depleted and had to be recharged at once."

Umar merely nodded. This was surely a reasonable action under such circumstances. However, there would be little use in further verbalizing his acceptance and understanding of this. Three years of working with Droom had taught him that the elaborate ritual deference and politeness of the *tar'of* was as wasted on and irritating to her as it was with most non-Shi'ite humans. Now he smelled the leather odor of her and turned to the apartment control board by the kitchen.

Touching the vent switch, he asked over the sudden gasp of air, "Your tea the usual way?" Turning to catch her smoke-ring "nod" as it opened outward over her face, he could not prevent his eyes sliding down her naked beige body. Her total lack of hair still startled him, as did her pubic flaps and absence of breasts or navel. He touched the white china teapot's fluted handle on and saw her peripherally as she reclined onto the couch. The bone slats of skeleton protruded rhythmically. He couldn't tire of seeing her and internalizing the reality of her existence and what it might mean to him, to Islam, and to all mankind.

She resented his subliminal look of shock and assumed shame at her nudity. Normally she would have ignored this. From the start of their relationship both had in unspoken agreement avoided potentially emotional areas and stuck to the job. With time these areas had unintentionally become well delineated anyway, yet they had maintained this extension of their personalities. But tonight Droom was prompted by the *muhtasib* incident.

"Would you please explain to me the *purda* and its meaning in your religion?"

He paused in assembling the pot, tea bag, and lid to realize that she'd at least read the involuntary part of his expression when he'd looked at her. She was finally getting good. But to wait so long for such a question! Nevertheless, his duty was to reply. Perhaps it was a beginning. He brought the tray to the low table by the side of the couch, poured, and sat cross-legged on the rug opposite her. She readily cradled her cup in pad-tipped fingers and drew in the fuzzy flat taste. The hot tea held the very aroma of Wlaata's forests and was a far better euphoric than alcohol, which acted also as an emetic on Hhronkan physiology.

It still amazed him to see her pick up an object with either side of her ambiprehensile hands, the two outer digits functioning as opposable thumbs, though she preferred the inner palm of her left, of course.

He spoke steadily through the vapors of his two-ounce glass. "God in His infinite wisdom has created many material and mental pleasures for us: food and drink, beautiful shelter, comfortable dress, and friendship, wealth, influence, reputation. Sex and its attraction is also an attribute endowed upon us to both preserve our kind and to be enjoyed. However, while all these pleasures have been created for man, man is not created for all these pleasures, especially in excess. The primary goal for humans, and all intelligent existence, is attainment of wisdom."

Droom watched his eyes darting as though following the random path of a ball of perfect elasticity about the room, occasionally touching her. She expanded and fingered her sore nasal sphincter absently as she agreed with the reasonableness of his statement. Most Hhronka felt much the same about physical pleasures.

"When anything interferes with this pursuit to the extent that one becomes subservient to it, it is sin in the eye of God. Sex outside of legitimate marriage is such a sin. Yet it is self-evident that permanent marriage cannot fulfill the instinctive sexual desires of everyone. This explains the success of prostitution throughout the non-Muslim world, and even to a lesser extent within it. We Shi'ite Muslims have sought to ease this problem partly with the *mut'ah,* the temporary marriage with mutually agreed time limit and dower."

A look (pain?) shot across his face that Droom had never seen there before, but it was gone, perhaps even before he himself had felt it. She was still often frustrated by human expression and its uses. Even if the emotion symbolically represented by the subtle, plastic, three-dimensional shifts of face and hairy coverings was interpretable, it might not be genuine. Humans continually lied with their expressions. To be sure, both species dissembled at times with their words, but Hhronka never added false displays to this sham. It was considered an ultimate in bad manners, and it was unnecessary. Not only could display always be either controlled to beige neutrality or hidden behind glass-smoothness without hurt or question, but also lying in general wasn't integral to Hhronkan social interaction. One displayed what one truly felt or thought, a mutual understanding, the very purpose of communication, passed.

But what humans called "white lies," and therefore certainly "black" ones as well, were indispensable to daily function between them. With the deceptive words they: smiled when sad, showed interest when bored, wept to show joy . . . and sorrow (!), and covered hatred or wrath with a number of innocuous constructs. It could be quite confusing, and it seemed to confuse the users themselves—as trying to manage two sets of emotions, that felt and that displayed, eventually must. Often it seemed that human speakers bore expressions they just could *not* intend since they did not complement their words and were nonsense in any context imaginable . . . as was this look from Umar.

Almost spasmodically he took one of the cubes of coarsely refined sugar from the saucer, placed it on his tongue tip, and sucked the scalding tea through it.

"The exposed parts of a woman's body can be unnecessarily exciting and tempt beyond self-control. Thus she covers them, except in her husband's presence."

She replaced the empty cup and rasped, "Nearly all human cultures have antinudity laws—or at least folkways. Even we

Hhronka usually dress, either from tradition or modesty, though there is more humility than shame in it. But why is it your women must cover so much of the body?"

Encouraged, he poured her another cup, shifting his weight off his prodding slippers as he did so and dabbing at her spilled drops with a cloth napkin. "We think the higher rates of sex-related crimes in non-Muslim areas, where women do not cover, prove the argument. And there is provision for a woman to conceal only to the extent that she perceives she is causing undue response in the men about her. And perhaps we of Islam, secure in our knowledge of God's Will, are simply sexier."

His wry grin was such a unique event that she automatically responded with clouds of rotating white rosettes over her whole face. Though he'd seen the display before, it broadened his.

"And why must it be the woman who conceals herself? Why not men? Surely both sexes are attractive to each other!"

Question, answer. They were all there, like post boxes. Just take out the correct one. "Because in our society men are the aggressors in such situations; a woman would never betray her modesty no matter how attracted to a man. Also men do more physical work than women, even here in our automated city. Such costume would be impractical."

She ingested this with a sip of tea and remained silent as she thought of the indifference of her people to these matters. Sex still operated, but not with such volatile results.

"Of course, in your situation here, concealment is merely to prevent any disruption and protect you from idle curiosity."

She decided not to relate tonight's disruption. "Yes. What human could ever be sexually aroused by me?"

Again they displayed humor, then he was the solemn relayer of secrets. "You must realize that the existence of another intelligent species came as no surprise to Muslims. And we consider you Hhronka as merely another group of *ummi,* people without Scripture, to whom the Truth has yet to be revealed or transmitted. God willing, I might be an instrument for your people's learning. That is one reason you were allowed here by the council of *mullahs.* God has commanded tolerance and the pursuit of knowledge of all worlds. So I also supported your coming to Teheran. Our learning can go both ways."

Although intrigued by these frank revelations and their deeper puzzles, she had no wish to arouse a proselytizing facet in him and was glad she'd never broached this topic before.

"In pursuit of knowledge, are you ready to begin?"

"Of course," Umar answered affably, also having decided this was enough for now.

He cleared the tray as Droom went to the write-screen on the rear wall and called up their program files. Holding one of the remotes, she lay back on the couch. Umar palmed open his wall safe, removed a copy of their data files, and inserted the flat plug into the screen's slot. His open robe and small turban came off as he settled lightly onto floor cushions near the couch.

They had merged many times; there was little preliminary. In half a minute both were relaxed and reaching out for each other mentally like mating sea stars. Neither felt the psychosomatic sensations or reticence of Shree or A.H. Rather, a filmy net seemed to drift down over both their heads. Each felt the centripetal tug that drew them to their mutual mental center of gravity, and each sensed only a momentary hesitancy at the abdication of total individuality. Then their currents swam together.

Umar saw thick white and purple paints being slowly stirred and spun dizzily on a giant turntable. Droom simply blanked her upper mind and passed through the discomfort like a door into summer.

But their minds were only partially joined, and the synergy affected only those parts dealing with such abilities as math reasoning. The "I" of their minds split. One partition retreated to a niche and perched, dangling legs and observing as though the other partition were an identical twin performing on stage below. The performers merged to create a mathematically adept idiot savant. Droom-spectator sensed tonight's merge was deeper, the composite mind stronger, than ever before. Perhaps it was the stimulation of the incident on the city roof or their talk's intimacy. For Umar-spectator the sensation was merely a lessening of the usual schizophrenia of the merge—similar to the way he felt when goaded by his lusts but chided by his ethics. Only now the antagonism was between the it–them savant and the symbols that littered the write-screen.

As always Droom remained on the couch pointing and tapping the black plastic remote to call up desired sequences. The screen image flicked sideways, then blurred up and down like a microfiche in a hand-operated reader. The rows of English, Greek, and Latin letters slid by, propped up with alphanumeric coefficients, superscripts, and subscripts, held apart by pluses and minuses, grouped and subgrouped by three kinds of parentheses, harnessed like teams of draught animals into integrals by the stretched-up S on the left, and bisected by the logic bridge of the equals sign.

When the savant felt the need for visual explication, Umar quickly rose and plucked the light pen from its holder. Squiggling carefully, he walked the new statements across the cleared screen in luminous tracings. If corrections were needed he touched the pen to the change while Droom blanked with the remote. When finished, the screen's contents were converted to neat typescript and indexed into the growing data file.

Strangely, it was during these times that Umar, as merge spectator or working alone, felt both content and resentful. Even before age eleven, when his mother had had the effrontery to die and leave him totally alone, he'd realized his differentness. Secreted in a public boarding school and forgotten by embarrassed relatives, his mental abilities and strict seriousness had soon set him apart, subverting his few attempts at relationships. At first his math talent was simply there unbidden, an additional mark of Cain to draw the sidelong whispers and taunts of his fellows. But later it had become both a buffer against the continuing envy and derision, and a weapon to express his righteous anger at their sin. It was their pride, not his. His talent was a gift from Allah, and he would use it to His glory alone. Let those who did not agree with His will be judged by Him. As master mathematician he could continue to tolerate his isolation and the repugnance of his fellow man.

The savant reviewed the recent work: the leads and dead ends, the unexpected identities and resultant substitutions, the crisscrossed symmetry transformations and cancellations, the multiplex layering of tensor indices and gauge functions—all aimed at extricating elegant simplicity from overlapped complexity.

A century and a half ago, theoretical physics had spanned both relativity and quantum mechanics. The exact geometry of relativity described the classical macroscopic universe in terms of curved space-time, the constancy of light's velocity, and the equating of mass with energy. But on the subatomic level its predictability failed utterly, giving events an infinite probability of occurrence with infinite energy of interaction. This miniscule world was better described by Bohr's quantum mechanics, which identified atomic matter particles as discrete groups of field waves or quanta, surrendering deterministic classical measurement for probability distributions. Then relativity and quantum mechanics were unified by the quantum field theory.

Using this mathematical method and the fundamental logic of symmetry as a framework, the elementary particles and basic forces, with the glaring exception of gravity, had been unified under the superstructures of broader models, such as the Georgi and Glashow SU(5) symmetry. Partial confirmations of these theories came with the observation of neutrinos and the decay of protons to pure radiation. However, the attempts to bring gravitation into these schemes had not yet been successful.

As the savant worked, Umar-spectator sighed to himself. Poor Einstein. Despite the spectacular accuracy of the macroscopic predictions of his General Relativity—"theory of gravitation" was a far better name—he missed the quantum theory blossoming because of a stubborn confusion. Heisenberg's Uncertainty is only a statistical admission of the impossibility of an exact and constant measurement in the subatomic world, where measurement itself disturbs the system. It has no sense of "uncertainty" of cause and effect, which Einstein correctly does not accept. So he tries vainly for thirty years to unify electromagnetism and his geometrical gravitation, without quantum mechanics, and vouches, "God does not play dice." To which Bohr replies, "Stop telling God what to do!" And later Hawking adds, "Not only does God play dice, but also he throws the dice where they cannot be seen."

How ironic that Einstein originally got the analogy from the American philosopher, Emerson, a favorite of his, who says, "The Dice of God are always loaded." Then again, why should a philosopher have any better, or poorer, vision of God's Nature than a mathematician?

(Umar-spectator halted to realize that he had shifted to present tense in thinking of these dead men, as did most mathematicians. Indeed, it was a form of immortality bestowed on all great people by their successors and students. An immortality of living thought and emotion, as children were of the flesh and the spirit.)

Truly, there was a close relationship between philosophy and science. He remembered what a more recent American philosopher, Sklar, said: "You can't do very good philosophy unless you get your science right. But you can't do science in full self-conscious understanding, unless you realize how much it depends upon philosophical modes of reasoning as well."

Then he thought also of the irony of Einstein's "cosmological constant" and recalled Sklar's warning to "be extremely wary of adopting the position that the scientific results are a given." Another *apparent* error had been Einstein's introduction of a constant into his gravitational equations that set a finite size to the universe. He did this to agree with the pre-Hubble wisdom of a nonexpanding cosmos, and later regretted it bitterly. Yes, reciprocity of idea and experiment was First Law.

Work on later theories seeking to combine the flexible symmetry of quantum models with the experimental truths of Einstein's gravitation had derived a cosmological constant. (Umar-spectator mused idly over authoring *Einstein Freed From Every Flaw.*)

Bastard child of astronomers and particle physicists, the most recurrent form had been named omega, the ratio of actual cosmic density to the threshold density necessary to determine closure. Although several sources of hot and cold nonluminous matter had been proposed—and a few discovered—the cosmic density and so the value of omega remained undecided. It might be a cyclic universe if omega were greater than one, or open to eternal expansion if the ratio were less than unity, or if the densities were equal then expansion would also continue, but slowing toward zero asymptotically, granting the universe a maximum but never-attained size.

One major obstacle dogged the most successful unification schemes, termed supergravity theories, as it had Einstein's own attempt. Infinite probabilities in some interactions involving gravitons could not be removed as they had been in those excluding gravity. And interactions with infinite probability at infinite energy made no sense. What was lacking, after almost a century and a half of attempts, was a theory from which could be derived the general proof for finite probabilities in *all* possible gravity interactions. It was on this theory and proof that Umar and Droom had worked for the past three years.

But tonight Droom-spectator was unusually insistent. In a rare departure from norm, she wiped the screen and curled sinuously up from the couch like a two-legged octopus, then shoved the remote into Umar's left hand while plucking the pen from his right, and went to the screen. At these times, Droom-spectator directed the actual work, shifting their mental center of gravity toward herself, and Umar-spectator merely lent mental power to the merge. Then Umar-spectator felt like a telefactored puppet, a high school geometry student parroting an instructor on stylized proofs but unable to strike out on his own creatively. His ego did not suffer from this. Allah's gifts could also be limited. But he felt that without his active contribution full power could never be used by the savant. The effort was normally wasted.

Yet now, as the matrices of curving symbols began to drain from the pen, Umar-spectator also realized a change. It was like seeing the face of a stranger for the first time; now the stranger had spoken—and the way the face looked was forever familiar because personality had overlaid feature. The symbol-strings were new of course, but he began to predict the next statement to be written. It made better sense than ever before. He felt the synergistic surge in the savant. It was proceeding with the fluency that all successful theoretical work required.

Mathematics was a toolbox. For specific jobs there were one or more specific tools. They were applied in sequence to compound the letters of reason into the words and descriptive sentences of logic—no . . . *no.* That was not correct at all, only a popular analogy. In truth, there was little similarity between sentences and math. It was *not* another language; it went much deeper. It was simply not possible to sensibly talk about many mathematical ideas in words, any more than quantum ideas like "spin" or "rotation" of particles—which were also conceptualized as bundles of waves!

Beyond a certain level, there were only the operator and operand symbols and the nonverbal relationships they represented. Yet these "slithy toves"—either verbal or symbolic—could also transport thought far from simple explanatory pragmatism to a rarified view of perfection, as the Universe *should* be but wasn't because it was far more intricate, and stranger, than this imagined description. And even this chaste distillation was forever whored to reality by Gödel flaws, internal inconsistencies, an entropy of the creating mind as inevitable as that of the reality itself.

Indeed, math was *reasonable,* but it wasn't always *logical.* This was why computers were of limited value in theoretical work. They eased tedious calculation, but there were no sequential principles with which to program the machines to take one step beyond those taken already. Even with amazing sophistication, representing "mind" to some, they were incapable of those intuitive educated guesses that were sometimes correct and still the sole province of organic intelligence. There was more to mind than complex memory and calculation.

The savant was working on one equation set, paring away identical terms, canceling variables—and suddenly a constant of cosmological significance appeared. The composite mind was not capable of consternation, but its components were. Umar looked into Droom's eyes, like looking into a mirror in the partially merged state. For a physical constant to occur at this point, it must have some deep meaning, not be an artifact of error.

This constant was intimately connected to the symmetry between the graviton and the other elementary force-carrying particles, in effect assigning a parameter to the cosmos. But was it size? Rate of expansion? Density? Or some quality unknown and unguessed? Droom-spectator led, thrusting the constant into the grand cosmology structured by their theory, testing the fit like a puzzle.

Once, the startling call to morning prayer erupted over the room's speaker, but the savant continued with dual-minded purpose. As with most significant discoveries, it came not with a bang, but in whispers.

It was already part of symmetry theory that phase transition temperatures existed for the force carriers: gravitons, and intermediate bosons, photons, and gluons too. Cosmologically this was interpreted as postulating the existence in the first instant after the Big Bang of a single kind of elementary particle and force. As the universe cooled, phase transitions occurred that broke this supersymmetry. Subfamilies of particles and associated forces were "frozen" out from each other at different threshold temperatures and the higher symmetries forever lost. Therefore, the current cosmos was a phase in which only the symmetries of quantum chromodynamics of gluons and electrodynamics of photons remained, again with gravitons conspicuously absent from the theory.

Under these symmetries, the compositing particles of matter, such as quarks, shunted from one form to another, creating their complex interactions at entropy's cost. But no definite phase transition mechanisms nor temperatures for all of them had yet fit any theory.

This new constant gave the phase transition temperature for gravitons. And the solutions this derived in their theory gave the phase temperatures for the other force carriers, as well as clues to the mechanisms of transition. Not all questions about elementary particles, such as their relative masses, nor many other fundamental constants and interactions were answered. Perhaps a total absolute resolution of every question could *never* be found—for all the correct questions might never be asked. But their theory pointed the way for the continuing effort.

And it implied the final closure of symmetry, completing that of the Big Bang, and the life span of the universe with its surprising ultimate destiny. For, although it meant omega was one, there would come no endless asymptotic expansion.

In the far distant future, when the background temperature of space cooled sufficiently toward absolute zero from its present $2.7^\circ K$, gravitons would cease to be pure kinetic energy, gaining a large mass, as photons had before them. Since total energy must be conserved, this meant the effective range of gravity would decrease from infinity to a few thousand kilometers. Their theory predicted this final phase would occur at the same time the average outward expansion of the universe would exactly equal the inward average gravitational pull. Robbed of gravity's infinite range, massive bodies would curve space-time far less drastically. A general cosmic contraction could never take place. Rather, planets would fly away from their suns, along with their families of comets and asteroids. Galaxies too would disintegrate, and clusters of galaxies disperse.

The cosmos would eventually become static, neither closed nor open, frozen into an oscillating Brownian homogeneity until entropy dimmed all stars, emptied all black holes, and decayed all matter to slowly vanishing energy. Not a retreat to chaos, but to the final order of total uniformity and kinetic death.

And it also gave them the means to complete the general proof for finite probabilities of graviton interactions.

Umar felt the rubber-band snap as the merge was reflexively broken by Droom. He looked down, embarrassed. His chambered nautilus of concentration had muted his damp triumph from him. But Droom hadn't noticed his projected emotion either; she was flickering black-white in a victory of her own.

"At last...we've finished," he murmured as he collapsed onto the cushions. "Praise God."

"No," said Droom. Her skin went glass-smooth and beige. "It has just begun."

Chapter 4

P.C. awoke already aware of his spiny hard-on and the bedcover tent it erected over him. Disconcertingly, it lacked connection with his asexual dream. Then he noticed the wood-hewn panels of his room in the Krieder house . . . back on Mars! Since this was impossible, he jerked his gaze down and around the room. As he watched the familiar walls slide past, the dead grasp of the loosely tucked sheet and blanket strained to hold him. Yet he moved not a muscle! His naked body felt like die-stamped lead statuary, stiff as his phallus. He suddenly *floated* up and free from the twisted hump of warm covers, drifting planklike across the room to dock headfirst, faceup against the back of a padded armchair!

His amazement revolved back to the intensity of his mastlike erection. It was *so* good, so wickedly strong! Now he found he could clutch it with his right hand and rock it around like a "joystick." Chim-*pun*-see; he was alone, so this displeased him. The feeling of raw sexual power surged. Then he saw the hump on the bed begin to quiver. It jiggled as though something still struggled beneath to free itself. On the floor a thrown pair of pants shimmied and drew into a knot, as though an Invisible Man sought to dress in them. The holo remote on the night table did a flip and thudded onto the carpet. The hump on the bed moved toward him.

Just as it sped up and rammed his feet, he understood. Not poltergeists; it was *him!* He had the power! By will alone he was moving objects. He merely glanced at and urged the pants and flat black box; they shot to him as if on clotheslines. Simultaneously, he felt energy flush through his conduit corpse like an epinephrine wave. Overhead the Hhronkan, globe-tipped, stalactite lamp reflected the predawn light leaking through the window across the bed. Impulsively he wanted the fixture to glow, without really believing he could cause it to. Playfully he tested. Short dendrites of blue sprouted at the inverted spike's base, then the globe filled with lightning and exploded loudly, showering bits of glass like fossilized snow. He laughed in complete triumph. Oh, the power he possessed . . . the incredible *power!*

Suddenly he awoke from his dream of awakening with a spiny hard-on and was instantly aware of its real tent and that this was not his room on Mars. He right-angled and stared in confusion a moment. Yes, a dream within a dream. The remote lay unmolested on the stand. The Invisible Man had abandoned the pants and fled, no doubt panicked by the threat of his old nemesis, the fossilized snow—but the fixture hung whole from the smooth white ceiling. With a broken sigh he threw off the covers and lay back to automatically masturbate the phallus into submission. His breathing had begun to deepen and the pleasant images to form their violent rhythms when the significance struck.

Telekinesis. He'd never shown even the rudiments of any ability to move objects, including electrons, any more than his father had. He smiled with rueful satisfaction. At least he'd *dreamed* of having one power his father didn't have; for a few subjective minutes he'd been unarguably superior!

The smile soaked into his face. The erection also withdrew, and he quickly went through the room's coolness to the sanctuary of the shower stall in the bath alcove. He was child of a deified hero, the man—his artigenic origins now chauvinistically dismissed—who single-handedly had established "peaceful relations with the Martians." How could he ever hope to fulfill A.H.'s greater expectations for him? From him? This insecurity had finally festered into a mutual reticence neither attempted to overcome.

As he let the warm needles wash away his guilt, P.C. reaffirmed the absolution. It's only a dose of a neo-post-pubescent, filial rivalry." His face shaped the proper bittersweetness. "But the knowing, the damned trite psycho-logic, doesn't help how I *feel.*"

The chance of widening the gap and lessening the love they did have was too great; it would be, until the youth proved himself to himself. Caught between extremes, he used humor to camouflage vacillation. Each smile he shared with A.H. sustained their caring; a laugh went far in shunting away the fear.

When he emerged fetuslike and saw he had only minutes to meet Twee, he urinated and shaved too quickly, drawing a neat inch slice in the soft skin under his adam's apple that bled stubbornly. The denim pants and short-sleeved pullover seemed loose, scratchy, and reeked of stale dryer. His concave grousing belly told him he'd enjoy breakfast for a change as he slid aside the glass door to the second-story balcony. He heard the building's sensors click off all power and strode to the concrete platform's end, reaching left over the railing to grab a rung of the ladder leading up the outer wall. Hopping onto the honeycombed glass panels he crossed the roof to his wingpack. It lay unanchored since there was never a wind here, only eternal steady breezes.

Reluctantly, he dropped prone and pushed his stiffness and the cold, pebbled surface away from his chest forty-five times. He 'coptered his arms several seconds to vent his lungs and dekink his breast muscles then held the pack's form-fit plastec frame above his head and dropped it onto his back like a scuba rig.

The nylon chest, waist, and crotch straps joined in a quick-release belly buckle. A stirrup cup clipped around the heel of each sneaker and splayed their vane-fans with foot motion. The cups hung from two sleeved coil springs that attached to the frame's lower end over his buttocks, ran down the back of each leg, and stiffened his body as keel in flight. He tugged on the round helmet and pulled down the upper faceplate. Finally he slid each arm down the elastic sleeve beneath the proximal section of each jointed wing and gripped the handle anchored under each distal section. The rig was colored sunlit honey, with the scalloped trailing edges of the curving two-meter-long wings dripping coral as though they bled. Four years ago he'd thought this impressive; now it seemed a bit juvenile. Holding the wings just off the roof, he clopped to the edge above the balcony and again responded to the view with a smile.

The house sat atop a terraced hill sloping down a hundred meters to a ribbon of rocky stream and was mirrored by another hill beyond. Up both slopes stepped banks of houses, rectangular modules of glass, steel, concrete, and aluminum. The smoke gray of the bare lunar-soil brick and stucco stood out where it wasn't painted, as most of the residences were. An entire spectrum of colors checked the hillsides, mimicking the autumnal shades of the grassy belt and the maples, elms, and other deciduants that flowed along the stream. Leaf mold and damp grass odors rose on the slight breeze. Each dwelling had its own high-walled courtyard, which was often the roof of at least one room of the house below. Maximum privacy and freedom in minimum space. It could have been a home cluster in San Francisco on Earth or, save the terran plants, in a Hhronkan city in the Tharsus Mountains on Wlaata. But it was on neither world.

P.C. twisted backward and saw where the blue-gray band of sky touched the ridge of his hill twenty meters behind the house. He could walk across this gap, hopping the utility lines that filled it, and pound its cold surface. Left and right along the stream, in the clear distance, the strip of park and houses curved upward through arched holes in the sky. The world was circular. The world was roofed by gridded glass along which slid stardust.

Wheels. For eons genus *Homo* had been enslaved to gravity and friction without them. For millennia they had known the freedom and power of riding on them. Now they felt the triumph and irony of voyaging from their parent solar system for the first time riding in one. The claustrophobic Hhronka were not similarly amused.

It was an early Stanford torus, one of the first SPS factories constructed by a lunar-mass-driver-catcher system. With a 1000-meter diameter its circumference was 3.2 km, and its 200-meter-thick rim spun to give .6 g average at the dwelling level. The compromise pull gave semicomfort to both its occupying species. It had housed over 6000 people at its peak; now only 542 beings rode in it. With bureaucratic austerity it had originally been labelled "SPS-27." Then it had become one of the 'ponics stations in the interim between the World Dust Bowls of '21 and '38 and the development of nonsoil agriculture on Earth. Finally a dissident Jogger group had purchased it as a refuge (its park strip did make the perfect running track), renaming it *The Breaking Wind* in satirical whimsy. But age had begun to weaken its structure, and repair costs had over-whelmed athletic orgasm. It had been abandoned to time and the scrappers nine years earlier.

So Shree and A.H. had been able to obtain it at a bargain: 1) half the personnel would be human, at A.H.'s insistence, to improve social and genetic viability should return to Sol fail; 2) the nine terran regional space agencies that chose to sponsor the expedition would tow it to Wlaata's orbit, at Shree's insistence, to even cost-sharing; 3) the Hhronka would refurbish its frame, repair the MHD power plants, and replace the obsolete deuterium-tritium thrusters with their own radiation-free deuterium-helium-3 fusion engines, at everyone's insistence.

Earth's response to the Hhronkan destination request surprised even A.H. Acting as coordinating negotiator, he had timed his announcement to quickly follow the general ballyhoo over the ftl discovery. At first he had received either silence or the pointed self-serving questions he and Shree had expected from the regional authorities. Secretly he had been flattered to find his reputation still held the power to stir even this reply. But neither he nor Shree had expected the media to capitalize so intensively on the "lost expedition" mythos. Within ten days every being of both species, except for the mentally incompetent, had been inundated with the few facts and many speculations. In twenty days, A.H. had managed to have the newsrec he'd shared in Shree's Total Projection 'cast throughout the system. In thirty days anyone not for "Krieder's Hhronkan Rescue" was judged to be on the evolutionary scale just below slime molds. In six weeks the contract for *The Breaking Wind* was signed.

It had caused him to reevaluate humanity's ability to internalize.

The Hhronka had kept the original layout of alternating residential–recreational, administration-commercial, and agri-manufactural sections on the rim. But the differences in species' personality and maintenance requirements was recognized by segregating the rim into human and Hhronkan halves, the latter having been completely rebuilt with native materials and designs. The colony frame itself had been changed to solve the acceleration–nonacceleration dilemma. While the huge thrusters, clustered at one end of the long axle through the hub, exhausted material, the wheel could not be spun without spiraling everything into the rim's "rear" sky-wall since inertia's vector then pointed back along their course—the central reason cylindrical craft had been rejected. So the six spokes had been hinged at midpoint and realigned parallel to the hub, and to the acceleration, at the journey's start. This meant the rim also had to be sectioned into six sealed arc pieces, one centered by each spoke. During acceleration the outer ends of each curving rim section experienced an "uphill" pull, but only machinery and supplies were stored here. And with so few crew and sleeping animals, the central "level" portions of each arc section held them comfortably. Like a partially folded umbrella frame the *Wind* had been boosted at .6 g to 10 percent of light speed, then with engines shut down it had been reopened and spun.

A shout echoed, and P.C. looked across the greenbelt valley to a house in the lowest tier. From within the graveled courtyard his mother waved and grinned. He lifted his right wing in reply. It was still a long voyage to Sol's heliopause. With plenty of dwelling space, each crewbeing or family had a house well separated from other occupied ones, something needed by the Hhronka and desired by the humans, especially P.C.

Above them the glass arch grew a sunrise. Large banks of lights brightened, and the exterior chevron shield plates rotated completely together like venetian blinds, cutting off the sliding starfield. This far from Sol they had packed away the mirror disc that had ridden the axle end opposite the thrusters. Closer in it had bounced sunlight to the hub mirrors and then into the rim through the roof arch. Through the closing slits the only parts of the wheel to be seen were the globular hub, the roots of its protruding axle, and two complete spokes. They appeared to hang over the ground like the crotch and legs of some enormous tailed giant. One thirty-five-meter-wide leg pierced the roof and thrust into the greenbelt 150 meters to his right; its lift doors, ports, and windows were blemishes in the white skin. Inside the rim to his left he could see only the base of the other leg, the upper portion being cut from view by the curve of roof. It centered the next rim section, the first of the three Hhronkan arcs. Its nearer border was marked by the lattice checkerboards of the twin bulkheads placed there to seal the ends of both sections airtight when separated during acceleration. Now the many squares they comprised stood open in their support frames for air flow. This also added a defense against total loss of atmosphere in case of hull puncture.

P.C. launched toward this grid. Backing several paces, he tested the shoulder ball sockets with a few strokes of the wings, tucked them in, then ran hard for the edge. His swan dive peaked too quickly, and through a pulse of fear he snapped out the wings to pull back and down. He fell to within a body length of the downhill neighbor's courtyard wall before gaining sufficient lift. His shame and unusual fatigue made him suddenly wish for his grav belt. But they all had to conserve energy and grav material.

Icarus in reverse, he had to climb higher for safety, closer to spin center. Near the rim's arch, he'd weigh almost 13 percent less. He stiffened his spine, pointed his toes to spread his tail-vanes, and pumped hard. In a glimpse he saw his mother watching him. She'd probably recognize his difficulty and nag him again to use the underground tram "like everybody else." "Everybody else," including Joan and A.H., used wingpacks whenever feasible, for the fun and exercise.

At last it got easier, the air got warmer, and the brushed pattern of the titanium-steel ribbing beams could be clearly seen. Then the polyresin reinforcing strands within the glass panels themselves stood out. He leveled off gratefully and glided back down a bit to avoid hitting a light bank. Sweat cooled him, and people's morning sounds, funneled by the arch's shape, whispered up around him. Coriolis torquing had negligible effect on the physics of objects in so small a wheelie, but it had added significantly to the psychologoical misery of its passengers, including himself. How apropo that this force, named for its French discoverer, explained why Earth's toilets flushed clockwise in the northern hemisphere and vice versa. (This, of course, ignored the stranger, less comforting reasoning of Mach's principle, the interaction of the water with the mass in the rest of the universe.) Human semicircular canals and Hhronkan equi-liths remained sensitive to this deflection-of-spinning in *Wind*. In addition, all solid surfaces constantly trembled with the violence of elastic recoil. And any change in radial position over about fifty feet from spin center was readily noted by its accompanying inertial "weight" change. The river of stars overhead had completed the total disorientation at journey's start.

P.C. often had the queasy impression he saw *through* the park's stream at a twin star flow beneath instead of beholding a mere reflection. So was accentuated the fact he rode on a celestial carousel ... without firm solidity anywhere. The combination had caused an alarming true weight loss and the flushing of many toilets before time and some drugs had ushered in acclimatization. And still he felt relief whenever he flew and lessened all these primal signals.

He'd already covered half the distance to the bulkhead and lined up with one of the uppermost ports in the opened grid. Now the roofs and courtyards of the houses below formed a checkerboard too. As he approached, he took a few fast pumps, locked the wings out flat, and glided into the four-meter-square hole. The stream of warm channeled air he joined made it feel like swimming underwater. The thick amber mold-panel with its large hinges, lock bars, and motor arms was lipped with a heavy black airseal strip that mated to that of the bulkhead frame when closed. After flipping through the black interspace, he saw this construction reflected on the Hhronkan side.

As soon as he entered the agricultural section, he felt Twee's expanded Self brush his own. Shree's son was already in the air, circling the spoke ahead. P.C. could just see the blue satellite speck revolving across the white cylinder in a lazy glide. On many mornings the two flew a lap around the entire colony rim, then landed for breakfast at one of the communal dining halls before starting their shift on the thruster crew. But he was far too tired for that today ... no need explain to Twee. Unlike their fathers, they had spent most of their lives communicating through *baas*.

Twee had been conceived over 30,000 years ago. His embryo had lain under impeded animation, growing infinitesimally slowly in the Meethlah Repository until only twenty-one years ago. Then came the decision to coexist with the humans, and Rebirth for all the Children had begun. P.C. had been born a year later, yet he called Twee "Loomna," or "old one" in Hhronkan. Unlike their fathers, they held no *baasa* ethics with each other. From early childhood each had felt the other's strong mental touch and had merged Selfs whenever they could— whenever they were out of their fathers' presence and not separated by sufficient distance or objects. It had come as naturally and inexorably as learning to talk to others with their mouths. A.H. and Shree had attempted to stop them, warning about the consequences of overmerging. The fathers believed they'd succeeded, but instead they had simply forced the sons to be secretive about it—as with their inevitable experiments with alcohol, tobacco, sex, and other drugs. (Twee becoming drunk on iced tea yet vomiting on one gulp of beer had taught them both that there were, truly, physiological differences between them.)

They had grown closer in the last two decades, unlike their fathers, even closer than identical twins could ever be. Their joining had become almost as overlapped as that of a Total Projection. They too could create a single mind. Therein lay the danger their parents had feared, for their personalities began to merge as well. While still children, they had almost lost individuality to become one schizoid being in two bodies. Fortunately their periodic separations had enabled them to sense the danger and, following the self-preservation instincts of all individually sentient beings, contrive a means to escape it. Each had deliberately chosen character traits, in keeping with his own species, that by agreement only one would ever display. The cultivation of these distinct constructed images into the minds of those about them had created the desired feedback, and the chosen traits were truly grafted into each Self's personality to form a kernel of isolation for each. P.C. used humor when around others to express one facet of identity; and later in life this had come to serve double duty in preserving his relationship with his father. Twee used an emotional device that P.C. would not, dare not, mimic. Yet, of course, they continued to share much, beyond careers as propulsionists. Indeed, they were neither human nor Hhronkan, but hybrids of both, an oddness symbolic of their species' cooperation and therefore tolerated by both peoples.

As P.C. flapped and glided high above the aeroponic lattices, their Selfs slipped together as easily as a tired foot and a worn slipper. As with A.H. and Shree, *baas* was accomplished by mutual field interference and feedback, was largely subverbal, and was extremely rapid. In words it would have been:

P.C. tele'd :: I'm tired and hungry this morning. Let's skip the lap and go eat!

Twee replied :: Now who is the Loomna? Hhronkan or human food?

P.C. was close enough to see the easy grace with which Twee articulated his own wingpack, its design mutated to suit his jointless anatomy. He also saw the lined gray display pattern of teasing condescension on Twee's face. The emotional set of the second question, the accompanying field pulses of which gave P.C. the irritating secondary feeling of being petted on the head, held more of courtesy than sincerity. One trait chosen for Twee by his own physiology was his dislike of human foods. P.C. pulsed reluctant assent; he'd have to make up at lunch for the nonnutritive Wlaatan "proteins." But at least he liked the tastes, and since the Hhronka ate only breakfast and supper, getting to a human commissary for lunch would be politely easy.

Although each house held its own kitchen, commercial area restaurants had been expanded to accommodate large crew segments. The mealtime camaraderie was deemed necessary by both peoples to sustain unity and a sense of both the scientific and Hhronkan aspects of the mission. Both species often exchanged visitors at evening meal, as good politics. However, alone at breakfast each felt free to discuss matters, uninhibited by the other's presence. This morning Droom was characteristically expressing herself as though any other presence would be no hindrance at all.

As the only Guardians on the mission, She and Shree sat isolated by the typical deference of their people. They faced each other at one end of a long low wooden table thrust into a thicket of young blue-green iceheart trees. The Hhronkan rim sections were designed to present an open-air feeling whenever possible, to dissuade them they were actually trapped inside an airtight wheel spinning away from their home world, perhaps forever. The height of the glass roof helped on its own. And this dining hall was plant-infiltrated, walless, and had a dirt floor— a picnic glade with furniture.

Droom wore the traditional Orrtaan costume of knee-length trousers and sleeveless vest of light blue broadcloth-textured material, food-splotched by this and former meals. Shree was robed as usual, and both were shoeless. Of course, the Hhronkan crew was evenly divided into Orrtaan and Meethlah, and several tens of both sat interspersed at least thirty paces away. This philosophical difference did not extend to the social level; only in emergencies involving potential killing would roles be assigned by ethic.

Droom also wore a dark-barred display on her cheeks equivalent to a human scowl as she flexed up from the ground-level chaise next to the table. "But humans can live packed like *kwerrli* worms in a burrow! We Hhronka need the open surface of a planet to escape from our *ooural!*" Her black-starred display relayed deep anger.

Shree paused and hid his skin, permitting her to do the same so both could retreat from their pique. Their faces at last became finely lined and soft again. "Comfort was not a priority basis for the decision against using the Sleep on this voyage. And our prior expeditions had no choice, with a sixty-eight-year travel time."

Droom absently rubbed the rim of her nasal pore with a food-smeared second finger, still haunted by the ghost of her missile—nosepiece. "We might need the Sleep in the future, depending on what we find at Kmeaa."

Shree countered her nonchalant display by wrapping his arms around his upper torso in the lecture mode. "We can construct the necessary mechanisms at any time from the stores on board. It simply was not desirable to remain dormant. We need interaction with the humans. Half of them have never even visited Wlaata before; we must develop a close rapport before we reach Kmeaa. Success of our actions there—or afterward—may depend on such unity. Why have you never questioned this before?"

In response to the dark query circles on his cheeks, black waves of distress rippled over Droom's face as she lifted up again. "I have never been entombed awake before! Was not my live burial in the Orrtaan Repository sacrifice enough?"

She was sufficiently loud to draw several glances from nearby diners, who quickly reversed at her look. Once again their faces became glass smooth. Shree picked with a tonglike *ulff* at his fruit section, studied the remains of the enormous meal just eaten, and palmed the bulge in his torso it created. The English and sarcastic tone he used would be understood only by her.

"We have *all* been 'entombed' only a few weeks. The ftl translation point lies only two weeks away. Surely the Orrtaan Primary can tolerate this old enemy a little longer. Or perhaps you have found a new enemy more worthy—"

"Hope of the Children!" She also resorted to English and its inflection. "You have finally begun to think like them as well!"

In futility he stared into her unblinking cat-eyes, ignoring the repeated nearby stares. She brusquely shoved a curved melon wedge between her chewing ridges and bit. The other point flipped up into her nasal pore and lodged a blob of green pulp there. Without pause she exhaled the bit onto the table's grained surface with the rest of her plate's fallout and continued munching and talking.

(Shree doggedly balanced brief shame with the fact that the often-begrimed petulant chaos enveloping Droom harbored one of his people's most creative and loyal minds. In defense of her incredible dwelling, which Shree had compared to a giant three-dimensional puzzle constructed of waste, she had said, "It is not a matter of laziness, but of priorities and energy limits. Besides, *I* know where everything is!")

"In the past we Hhronka have had too little freedom from the exigencies of mere survival for the luxury of enmity. Our maximum cooperation was required to ensure meeting the exact parameters of life during the Thaws and preparations for the next Freeze. But no more. With a practical means for relatively rapid interstellar travel, we *will* colonize other systems. The last Rebirth has taken place, a fact I fear not all Hhronka have yet accepted. Eventually, if not on this mission, we will be meeting other peoples. We must begin to choose wisely whom we will and will not trust.

"We have never *had* to rely on humans before. And I am not alone in sometimes feeling that the only trustworthy hum is a dead human. We have both had good cause to feel that way. What actions might require their cooperation on this mission?"

With sadness Shree replied, "You have lived among humans, but you still do not understand them." Seeing her rising rebuttal, he hurried on, forming curving number symbols in gray patterns on his forehead as he itemized. "There is a finite set of possible outcomes for the prior expeditions. First, they may never have arrived safely at the Kmeaan planet. We know from their early transmissions that all three did get to the system, and that the last got close enough to discover seven planets. But then they all may have encountered some natural obstacle, perhaps a radiation belt, and were totally destroyed. In this case the mystery will never be solved."

Both pulsed darkly, then Droom whispered, "And we will be the fourth to be lost."

"Perhaps. All the better reason for completing our improvements on this colony's electro-magnetic shielding fields. A second possibility is that they all arrived at the Kmeaan planet, but the natives had already been destroyed or had destroyed themselves somehow. This would surely explain why only one set of messages ever came from them; their technological base was removed or so severely damaged that it could never recover. Then when our expeditions arrived a similar fate, say a plague or residual radiation, overwhelmed them. We may find primitive remnants, too backward to construct an interstellar transmitter. And this is where the humans could be of immense aid. Both they and their technology are extremely flexible, adaptable to new situations—something we Hhronka have not encountered for—"

"There is no need to prove human adaptability to me, Primary. You are a keen theoretician and would have done well as a Technician. But you are ignoring the last piece of message from the third expedition: 'further than life.' We have no satisfactory explanation of it. Could it be that in fact all our people arrived safely, met these Kmeaans as intended, and then were deliberately *prevented* from making further transmission? What if that last message were one of desperation and warning, cut short by the Kmeaans?"

The dark sinusoid pattern flooding his face told of attempts to discard this possibility in horror. "Why would any sentient species expend such effort to contact others and aid them in crossing the vast distance only to betray and imprison them? That would be an act of purest insanity!"

Her white smoke-ring jetted out. "Yes, it would be! It is unpalatable but possible. These beings may have been, may be, more unstable even than humans." The blip of white just below her eyes meant mild sarcasm. "And what if the Kmeaans *have* harmed, even destroyed, our people. What will we do then?"

Shree's distress pattern was finally hidden by glassy skin. "I am Primary of the Meethlah. I will never condone the murder of any sentient beings, not even for just retribution. Besides, our weapons and numbers preclude attacking an entire population."

To spare him, her face too became tan glass. "You forget the humans' weapons and that we Orrtaan are not so constrained."

His discomfort was blooming so great that he changed topic. "News is the oracle. We are arguing in ignorance. And all this is meaningless if we do not survive the journey ourselves."

The umbrage of her gray stippled display colored her monotone. *"If?* The mathematics is correct! *Our* technicians have installed the device! We *shall* translate to just beyond Kmeea's heliopause as Umar and I have explained. I assure you I am not gambling any lives to prove it!"

At Umar's name white rosettes danced over his face. "You must admit, then, to human usefulness."

"I have never argued over their *usefulness,* Shree."

Encouraged by her familiarity, Shree said, "Droom, in truth, I have always found it difficult to judge humans because of my relationship with Krieder. He is so like us. From the very beginning he has always tried to do the correct thing for all."

She held back the last bit of conviviality. "Yes. It is unfortunate that they all have such a difficult time determining *what* is correct."

Twee and P.C. had demerged and tightly contracted their mindfields long before entering the hall. But approaching behind Droom, P.C. caught this final sentence and was certain of its referents. "Garping about us poor humans, again, Primary?" he chided softly.

The Hhronkan did not use skin smears to show chagrin. She briefly shut her nasal pore like a string purse and shaped her mouth into an O. "Yes, P.C. Krieder, I was, though you were not intended to hear this," she replied with typically painful honesty.

Twee stared a moment across the table at Shree, then sat beside P.C. to Droom's right. Neither Hhronkan showed sign of noticing the slight, but merely nodded at them.

Twee and P.C. also shared the problem of their relationships to their fathers but for different reasons. As one of Shree's 512 children, Tweeol had been reared with absolute impartiality by the Primary Guardian. The other 2047 Guardians never knew their own offspring, a seeming cruelty designed to ensure such impartiality. But though the *baasa* father had quickly found his *baasa* son, Shree had insisted on maintaining Twee's relationship according to plan. By the time the Children had been ten years old and Shree had felt it fair to hold Twee closely, it was too late to matter to him. The artificial isolation from so near a parent had frustrated his child's gift of love, and he had found another target for it. They remained close, but simple trust and deep warmth were forever abridged. Shree was stoic about it, usually. "The price of love is always high," his Feeahra had said. As he watched the two youths dig into the fragrant hot bins in the table, he once again felt the pain of that price.

Without display, he said to Droom, "I do not know what the humans would do if your conjecture proves true and we

Hhronka decided to act as you suggest. But I know what Krieder would say: 'We *will* take prisoners.'"

The human dining halls were designed directly opposite to those of the Hhronka, at least the architects seemed to have suffered agoraphobia rather than claustrophobia. The low false ceiling was aided in breaking up the volume by high mazelike walls, planters, and split levels, and was low-lit to present a womblike coziness to help anyone discomfited by the thought to forget that their metal–glass world was the only refuge of life for hundreds of millions of miles.

This morning the rest of the Krieders and Umar were clumped around one side of a long table in an alcove. Opposite sat Captain Mowry and several of his bridge crew. A.H. was relieved that this group's authority extended only over the flight to Tau Ceti. The Hhronka weren't interested in sharing this command aspect and contributed only part of the engineering crew on their thrusters. Mowry's people came from European regions; though most people on the colony dressed casually, several of this crew actually wore regional military uniforms with decors attached. It implied a chauvinistic divisive attitude he felt was better left behind on this uncertain journey. Also, he had rapidly developed a dislike for the captain. The tall thin man was younger than A.H. but already had silver-gray hair. He added to his own idea of authority image by wearing a pullover knit sweater with starred epaulets, oddly mimicking a terran sub commander. But it was his streaked Vandyke that had alienated A.H. initially. He was von Bok reincarnated, the director of Mars's human colony when the dormant Hhronkan had been found. The man had attempted to betray and destroy them for their superior technology, and had paid with his life after nearly succeeding. A.H. knew the comparison was superficial, but Mowry's behavior often supported the prejudice. The captain's very expression reminded him of von Bok's, the scant smile of someone who has just told himself a smug joke not to be shared.

They were finishing breakfast when Mowry's morning wit chose Umar as target. Distinctive in his robes and turban, he was an easy choice to provide an ego-stimulant to match the food's caloric high.

Shoving back an immaculate plate, the captain leaned forward and asked into the digestive lull, "Umar, I've become curious about you. You are the only Mohammedan in the contingent. I'm sure we'd all be interested to know more about your beliefs and if they've had any bearing on your joining us. For instance, do you hope to find the Kmeaans worshiping Allah?"

Umar had spent the past months acclimatizing himself to a non-Muslim society. Although he'd visited other parts of Earth, he'd never lived long enough in one place to become familiar with the daily milieu in the life-styles. The lack of a cohesive theme, as religion gave New Teheran, bothered him only slightly since he had always been a solitary man, even in prayer. Indeed, he found the more secular dialogues stimulating. But some superficial aspects of Western culture still irked him, especially the exposure of women, and especially that of Renata. At first the form-fit clothing and bared arms, legs, faces, and hair of the crew's females had been as easy to ignore as their equivalence in role with the males. He simply gave everyone the same cool courtesy when necessary and volunteered nothing. After all, as he'd explained to Droom, this was a source of temptation he well understood. Its very existence within him gave continual proof that *purda*'s concealment was justified, redoubling his moral resistence.

As with many zealots, he believed his recognition gave him eternal immunity. He was, of course, incorrect. So his frustration had been the greater when he found it increasingly difficult to keep his gaze from straying to Renata's suddenly "naked," youthful body, to remain inert to her soft woman's smell, to refuse to enter into the eye-contact play she challenged. But it was her strong resonant voice and its intelligent content that had first chinked his righteous armor. Since he founded his own worth largely on mental prowess, he couldn't help but respect hers. And for him, respect must be the basis of all love, including the sexual variety, an event yet unknown to him.

But Renata was no virgin. True to her cultural guideposts she'd experienced the ultimate early enough to realize it wasn't and had long ago matured beyond the sex-drugs-possessions goal-triad of most Western youth. She and P.C. shared A.H.'s exploratory itch, though theirs came more from the curiosity of youth than the frustration of middle age. She also had degree'd in a frontier science, agriponics, and daily tended the food and recycling vegetation of the human sections. She had always chosen her sexual partners carefully—down to the pan-veneral pretest—and appearance was naturally part of the pleasure.

Umar's swarthy robed reticence had touched her romantic vein at once. Her favorite hobby was old cinema, so old some had no audio. He brought to mind Rhett Butler, the pirate–entrepreneur in *Gone With the Wind.* Here was this character's dignified charm, admixed with the restrained desire of Rudy Valentino in *The Sheik.* Her few tries at provoking conversation in order to probe the man's mentality, also important, had been politely rebuffed. Though he occasionally gave her visual messages, he almost shyly refused to let them be bilateral. So she was delighted by Mowry's jab and the prospects of Umar's revealing reply.

The Iranian's face lit with an animation none of them had seen in all the time on board *Wind,* and his lecturing tone couldn't quite cover the joy with which he approached every aspect of his topic. He responded to them all, looking from face to face, even Renata's.

"Any religion is a complex subject, impossible to describe coherently in one session—especially Islam, which is almost totally unknown to Westerners, and to you, whom I have gathered are all unbelievers."

He abridged their surprise and incipient protest. "Oh, please. Feel neither embarrassed nor defensive. God has commanded tolerance of all uninstructed people. My only goal is to do what you have asked: explain what a Muslim believes and how it can affect his outlook. In fact our fundamental tenets are close to those of the Judeo-Christian, which you no doubt do know: the one, all-powerful, Lord of the worlds; the immortal soul; evil, embodied by Satan, and good miracles; revelation of divine knowledge through Prophets; the last day of judgment; heaven and hell. We believe in all these. A Muslim is one who follows Islam; 'Muhammadan' is never correct. The Arabic word *Islam* implies surrender to God's will, but the religion of Islam is the practice of faith and obedience, the habit of obligation to be guided and disciplined into conformity with that Will, which is the entire reason for human existence."

Across the table he saw the poorly controlled tremors of derision and amusement in the captain and a few of those sitting and standing behind him. The Krieders seemed merely interested. But he took a sip of cooling tea and continued without apparent notice. "The physical document for this Will is the *Qur'an,* which literally means *recital.* These sacred truths were revealed by the angel of God to Muhammad—may God bless the Prophet and the peace of God be upon him—over a period of several years, recited by him to his hearers, and recorded into 114 titled chapters. Noah, Abrahim, Moses, and Jesus were all such Prophets. This is why Jews and Christians are among the peoples of the Book. There were other Prophets but Muhammad was the last."

At the repeated holy invocation of blessing, a few listeners turned away to hide smiles, but again he seemed to take no note.

"However, the *Qur'an* is not the only source of law, of *Shari'ah*, the Way. There is also the *Hadith*, or tradition, the example of the lives and words of Muhammad and His contemporary and subsequent followers, as recorded and handed down through the generations. Thirdly there is *Qiyas*, analogy of situations similar to, but not directly covered by, the previous two sources. Finally there is *Ijma*, consensus of the community. But this last is prescribed to only by Sunni Muslims, the majority sect; Shi'ite Muslims find Islamic truth through the Imamate. I will hold on differentiating these two major divisions.

"There are five basic religious duties, called the pillars of Din, for every Muslim. First is the *shahada*, witnessing that 'There is no God but Allah; Muhammad is the apostle of God.' We Shi'ites add the phrase 'and Ali is his companion.' Second is *salat*, daily prayers; Sunnis pray five times a day: dawn, midday, midafternoon, sunset, and after nightfall; Shi'ites pray only three times, combining dawn–midday and sunset–night."

"Aren't you supposed to face Mecca, too?" asked Renata teasingly. "How do you do that on a revolving wheelie?"

Umar took the gibe as softly as intended and merely smiled back, locking eyes only for a heart-jump moment. Yes, an unusual, clever girl, if brash. "Facing Mecca is a unifying act of devotion for Islam, but it is not imperative. Allah has answered this through the *Qur'an*. I quote *Sura*, or Chapter 2, 'The Cow': 'The east and west are Allah's. He guides whom He will to the right path.' 'Righteousness does not consist in whether you face the east or the west.' "

Renata just pursed her thick lips and nodded, impressed by his astuteness.

"The third pillar is *zakat*, almsgiving of a fixed percent of one's wealth to the poor. Fourth is the fast of Ramadan; during this month we do not eat or drink in daylight hours. And finally is the *Hajj*, the pilgrimage to Mecca and nearby shrines once during life. Of course there are more specific rituals and duties, but these vary with sect. The most important other universal doctrine is social service. Submission to God cannot stop with the intellect, but must include the spirit, the heart, as well. True Muslims do not merely build a facade of ritual habit around themselves and continue with self-centered lives. We seek together as a community 'to enjoin good and forbid evil' as the *Qur'an* says. This means we actively contribute time, acts, and money to helping those in need, to recognize their rights as well as our own. The necessity of identification of the government of the state with Islam is part of this recognition and its attainment."

Now the sublimated derision some listeners had shown earlier was gone, though Mowry's amusement remained obvious. Most others were taken by his sincerity, even Renata. A.H. could see they felt here was a "good" person, in the selfless sense the altruistic Hhronka used the term, and that Umar lived as he spoke. They could see it in his gaze, clear and open. However, A.H. was past ready for this "lesson" to be over. He had apprehended Umar's attitude long before this breakfast seminar. Call him sanctimonious, chauvinist, Muslim, Christian, Jew, Jesus-freak, Krishna, born-again charismatic, shaker, Holy Roller, Jogger, or Cosmist. He'd seen extremists excuse the most egregious atrocities against people, laws, and nature in the name of religious rectitude. For him religion would always be a product manufactured from fear and a refusal to accept reality as it appeared to be. As a nhumbie he had suffered from the fears of such people. But even if he were wrong, even if he were a "believer," he'd always be wary of those who combined Umar's intelligence with fanaticism. There was no more dangerous human being than one totally certain he was doing the will of "his God," and was therefore error-free.

"What's a she-ite?" asked Renata, her rapt attention only aggravating her father's discomfort. "I've always associated the name with all the violence and wars in the Mideast at the turn of the century and, of course, with New Teheran."

Umar's manner at once grew more somber, his tone more grave. The teacher was replaced by the eulogist. "A Shi'ite is a Muslim who prescribes to the Shi-ah sect, the largest minority of Islam. *Shi'ah* is Arabic, meaning literally 'partisans'; here, the partisans of Ali. Let me tell you of the tragic events after the death of Muhammad—may God bless the Prophet and the peace of God be upon him—so you will understand this schism.

"Long before the Prophet's death, his cousin and son-in-law, Ali, had gained many adherents by virtue of his exemplary service both in battle and in the furtherance of Islam. For instance, in A.D. 622, when the unbelievers of Mecca who opposed the Prophet's growing political power sought to assassinate him, it was Ali who slept in his place as decoy and allowed the successful emigration from Mecca to Medina, the very survival of Islam itself. And at Ghadir Khuum, the Prophet proclaimed Ali the guardian of the people of Islam.

"Yet despite this recognition there were others, politically and militarily powerful, who opposed Ali's succession, seeing a loss of their own influence. On the day the Prophet died, in A.D. 623, even as Ali and the close relatives and companions were preparing for the funeral service, this group met in the city mosque and elected the first caliph. Indeed, there was immediate need for this successor, a symbolic leader who with divine sanction would be the executant of sacred Law. Naturally, the *shi'ah* of Ali protested the election of a caliph from this group, but the act had already been accomplished. To preserve unity and peace, Ali acquiesced. However, to consolidate their authority, the majority group held that the caliph had been elected by 'consensus of the community,' which by numbers alone, they claimed, would be infallible, and *Ijma* became the fourth source of law for Sunni Islam.

"Initially, three caliphs ruled by election; then, popular support, along with disgust at the scandals of the murdered third caliph, placed Ali into the leadership. Still opposition remained, and Ali was himself murdered after only five years, in A.D. 661. The *shi'ah* could do nothing to prevent the return of the Sunni caliphs, though they resisted. In 669 Ali's eldest son was also killed. Finally, in 680, Ali's youngest son, Husain, the youngest grandson of the Prophet, was tricked into ambush and massacred with nearly all his wives and children at Karbala. It is this horror that caused the irrevocable split of Shi'ite Islam."

Umar paused to breathe deep and stare into his audience's eyes. For him it could have happened yesterday. "Oddly, an Englishman, Cragg, has expressed it best. 'It was one of those occasions in history where mingling anger and pity, wrought into the cult of suffering, evoked a staunch refusal to forget or, by forgetfulness, to conspire with the injustices of fate and leave

the spilled blood silent in the sand.' It was similar to the senti-
ment aroused by the assassination of Jesus, or his Holiness the
Ayatollah Khomeini, or even Kennedy, if you will. Martyrs all.
It is Husain's martyrdom that is commemorated on the tenth day
of the month of Muharram, when the faithful parade, pray, and
inflict wounds upon themselves in sympathy to his passion. And
it is from the Shi'ite conviction that both the caliphate and religious authority belonged to Ali and his descendants that belief in
the Imamate sprang. Ali himself, as blood descendant of the
Prophet, was preserved from error and sin. This lineal infallibil-
ity is considered by Shi'ites as the source of derived truth,
rather than Sunni consensus of the community.

"This is embodied in the Imam, a spiritual leader appointed
by God and the Prophet; he must be a descendant of Ali and be
able to prove the appointment by performing a miracle when
asked. There have been twelve Imams, beginning with one son
of Husain, who survived the Karbala massacre. The twelfth
Imam was Muhammad al-Askari, born in 868 in Samarrah. In
939, by Divine Command he went into occultation and will
remain hidden until God wills him to reappear and bring justice
into the world. He is known in the *Hadith* as the Mahdi.

"It was the persecution by our enemies last century that
forced Shi'ites to acts of self-defense called 'terrorism.' We
were vastly outnumbered, being systematically exterminated by
every country that surrounded us. It was to escape this pogrom
that we finally built New Teheran and fled into the sea."

All his audience, including A.H., were mesmerized, speechless by his cadence and his words. Joan dared break the silence.

"I assume you are a Shi'ite and also related to this Imam?"
The slight dusting of satire squeezed into her tone. A defensive
look bolted across his face but was quickly replaced by his usual
calm demeanor.

"We are of the same house."

A.H. coughed and snorted to clear both the tension and his
partly clogged left nostril. He saw that no one considered the
situation amusing anymore. Still he had to ask "Why did you
come on this mission and take the chance of isolating yourself
forever from other Muslims?"

Suddenly animated, Umar said, "God has commanded attainment of scientific knowledge as one route to wisdom. Another is the mystic inner revelation, such as that of the Sufi
gnostics. The *Qur'an* says, 'If you have power to penetrate the

confines of heaven and earth, then penetrate them!' God is *Rabb-al-Alamin,* 'the Lord of the worlds,' all worlds. By learning the signs of God's handiwork in both microcosm and macrocosm we may better guide our own behavior. Besides, whether I personally return or not, my knowledge gained will be radioed back and not be lost.

"Also, the fifth Imam has said, 'God, since creating the world, has created seven kinds none of whom were of the race of Adam. He created them from the surface of the earth and set each being one after another with its kind upon the earth. Then He created Adam.' I believe the Hhronka are one of those seven other sentients, and I am certain we shall find another in the Kmeaan system. This will be God's word confirmed."

He looked at the slack jaws before him and smiled sadly, the admix of pity and envy the wise always feel for the ignorant. "I must return to my work on the ftl calculation. But I shall be happy to continue this discussion at any time. Good day."

As he walked out of the hall Mowry and several bridge people at last laughed nervously. The captain quickly rose and left without a word.

"Well, how's that for the opium of the people?" Joan whispered to A.H. with a rueful grin.

His brows soared in consternation. "I suppose it's no different from any other religion: benevolent intentions yielding the occasional atrocity, granting its believers the strength to face life's grimmer aspects. In fact, it *sounds* more reasonable and compassionate than most in some ways, but . . . his intensity!"

He aimed this last at Renata, anxious over her reaction and daring to step out of neutrality.

Joan was nodding emphatically. "That's the point; *he* does believe it."

Renata stared after the robed man. "Yes. Totally."

Chapter 5

Umar allowed his eyes to leave the wall for an instant and saw an infinity of Renatas. To both sides, behind and before, above and below, he was englobed by dwindling lines of repeated her, crouched ready to spring, from the first full-sized one to the last visible miniature at the vanishing point of each curving line. And he also stretched outward in shrinking lineal multitudes, each him perfectly redundant in motion, simultaneously copying each action as he performed it.

All the Umar-lines lifted their heads to watch the many blue balls rebound in six directions within the six-sided box. Yet he now ignored all the twin players as well as the other surrogate spheres, concentrating on the only one that he, the proto-Umar, could physically strike. He watched it come off the front wall, hit the floor, below which an upside-down duplicate of this room lay, and bounce high above his head into the rear wall. Spinning around, he lined his body up with the ball's calculated future path back toward him and cocked his backhand. But it had good spin and struck the rear wall at a slower speed than he'd guessed, falling at a steeper angle toward the floor. He lunged forward one pace at it, got his racket between the ball and the floor–wall juncture, and flipped with his wrist. The contact was soft, but it hit the strings squarely and arced to the floor near the front wall. Renata, four paces away, had no chance to return it to the front wall before second bounce. It was his point.

After his revelation of Islam and his beliefs, Umar had got more notice but less attention, which fit perfectly with his expectation. Conversion of unbelievers was rarely easy. Therefore he'd been surprised by Renata's invitation to play R-ball—and by his own delight at it. A week after the breakfast they'd nearly collided in a corridor turn in the courthouse, both on the way to a game. She had dared him to a five-game match soon, and the expectant stares of their male partners had urged him to accept, to refute the bounding rumors of his Muslim bigotry and male chauvinism. But deep inside there had been a tingle of excitement too.

He exercised for health and mental clarity; she played for the fun and emotional release. It showed in their styles. He attacked the ball with ferocity and energy, seeking to set up power shots. She let the palm-sized blue rubber sphere come to her, with a minimum of movement and maximum of time to plan her shot's placement. Only she would admit that spectators might view it as his brawn against her brain. But Umar had insisted on an hour early enough to ensure privacy. The tie score of two games each had so far favored neither approach.

R-ball was a derivative of racquetball (a "spin-off," said P.C.). The court dimensions and most game rules were the same, but the difficulty was orders of magnitude greater. The walls, ceiling, and floor were finished in a smudge-proof polymer that gave glass-mirror reflection. The parallel lines of reflected images of mirrored courts and their moving contents adjacent to the actual one could be distracting even to the most experienced, who used the reflections to advantage also. There were no right-angle junctures where most planes joined. Instead, starting a half meter from such junctures, the walls curved smoothly into each other and the ceiling. And the joining of the front wall and floor was curved, but the side and rear walls formed right angles with the floor.

With these curves, any crotch shots, pinch shots, tight banking, or zee shots were impossible off the front wall. But if the ball went in just right, its path would be bent into an arc following the curve, and it would shoot around the corner to emerge along the opposite plane. Yet the ball's elasticity made it very difficult to use this trick; a skilled player could gain from this maneuver, but great accuracy was needed. Otherwise the ball simply rebounded randomly out of the curve. This configuration did make rollouts easy; if the ball was hit down gently into the front wall's curve, it would come out bounceless across the floor for a score. To compensate, it was legal to pick up such a rollout with the racket. The R-ball racket frame had a tapered, sharp-edged rim to facilitate these "scoops."

Altogether the game required far more movement and skill than racquetball; after becoming expert at *that* game, one then entered R-ball at the novice level.

Enclosed court games were a natural in New Teheran, and Umar had played since childhood, as had Renata. They both wore the obligatory dark shoes, shorts, and shirt, kneepads, and safety goggles. Umar eschewed a headband and wore a matching navy terry wrap on his right wrist, playing his carbon-fiber racket with his gloveless left hand. She wore an olive band to hold back her otherwise loose copper hair and used a plas-calf glove to help her right-handed grip.

The colony had only .68 g at the courthouse level in this rec complex. So they had handicap weight belts to give 1 g effect and prevent leaping two body lengths after high shots. In a volume this size Coriolis force was negligible, but the ball traveled differently at this weight anyway.

This was game five, the decider for their match. Umar returned to the white server's box at midcourt as the ball he'd hit bounced in. Feeling confident from the easy point, he stood on the hard tacky soles of his inverted twin's feet and bent to race him to the ball. Gathering cool air into a hollow chest, he waited for the panel set flush in the top of the rear wall to light with the score, indicating the referee-comp was ready for his serve. Instead it blushed a red "Reset." The sensor network embedded in the court's surfaces had scrambled its test input and would take a few moments to clear. He stood akimbo and looked up at the ceiling's myriad tiny perforations through which even lighting shone and echoes were captured. A soft tone gonged; white numbers lit in the panel.

"Eighteen, seventeen," announced the voice calmly.

He wiped a browful of warm wet with his wristband. Three points to the win. Then he turned the leather handle to put the drier side into his damp palm and spun his left wrist inside the nylon loop to twist it. Renata was as flushed and aromatically soaked as he, the area around her mouth dewed white, the hair wetted to a light blood color on top and at the temples where it passed under the band. With a gasp of smile she nodded and pointed at the front wall with her racket while rocking weight from one knee to the other at center-rear court.

He still couldn't understand how he'd allowed her to force him into a catch-up situation all morning. Perhaps he'd been overconfident; the first game had gone to her with surprising speed. Then he had awakened and played in earnest. They had alternated wins the next three games, and he simply could not find the cause for his on–off response to her play. Maybe his speed and strength were even with her finesse and strategy, but it also seemed that whenever he concentrated well he took points steadily.

Bending at waist and knees, he set his serve position and held out the ball, tasting coppery dryness. He dropped it, stepped his right foot forward, and cocked back.

Into the pause Renata said, "I've been reading the *Qur'an.*" His forward wrist snap was completely off and the serve bounced from the front wall to fall back within the server's box. The white rectangle glowed around him, and the asexual voice said, "Short," as the panel lit with the word. He retrieved the ball after two fumbled tries and looked back to her, shocked by her interruption and puzzled as to what his response should be.

"That is very commendable. Any difficulty with the text?" he replied noncommittally, bouncing the ball.

She straightened and smiled archly. "Well, I was concerned over that part about woman's inferiority to man, beating them and such. Do you really believe that's true for *all* women, and is it fair?"

He'd expected the question eventually, but not in the middle of this game. Off guard, he had to compose himself before grasping his pigeonholed justification. It was difficult. If ever he'd known a female who seemed many men's equal, it was this one. But then he'd known so few.

"You refer to Suras Two and Four. But recall the entire Wisdom, please: 'Women shall with justice have rights similar to those exercised against them, although men have a status above women.' And also: 'Men have authority over women because Allah has made the one superior to the others, and because they spend their wealth to maintain them. Good women are obedient. They guard their unseen parts because Allah has guarded them. As for those from whom you fear disobedience, admonish them and send them to beds apart and beat them.' This is God's will; He has designed it so, and we can but accept."

She decided not to rebut this, yet her tone grew more insistent. "OK. But what about all that waste over the 'rewards of Paradise,' the 'bashful, dark-eyed virgins' that will 'dwell' with the righteous? Isn't this just a bit too tilted toward the male? Surely it's not God's will to give men a superior afterlife too! What's a *woman's* reward for righteousness?"

Again Umar responded haltingly, falling into the litany slowly. "The . . . the *Qur'an* was revealed at a time and to a people. For understanding and acceptance, its wisdom often had to be couched in analogous terms, much as Jesus' parables. Arabia was then a land of scattered nomads, dozens of independent tribes, male dominated, riddled with superstition and belief in pagan pseudo-deities. To ensure success and the spread of Islam, the language of revelation had to appeal to all, both literate and illiterate. Indeed, it is the fact of the beauty and moving quality of the *Qur'an's* literature that is one of the proofs of its divine origin, for the prophet was himself unlettered."

To her derisive head shake, he quickly added, "But you also must realize that the Muslim society has evolved just as much as the Christian or Hebrew since the seventh century. More. And though it is also oriented around the male, it is not dominated completely by him. Women have respect and courtesy; they live with dignity and safety—unless their own actions change reputation. No woman has ever been attacked in New Teheran, few in *any* Islamic region. Nor do we cheapen their sex by using it to sell everything from chewing gum to politicians. They would never be abandoned in age, poverty, or illness because their usefulness to the public is ended. Our women are not mere property. Can women in your society say this?"

It was her turn to be surprised, and when nothing issued from her opening mouth, he stumbled on, waxing adroit. "Women do not just run the house and stay pregnant—shoeless, and tied in the kitchen, as you say! They can and do inherit wealth, manage businesses, and have much influence in the lives of their families—"

The ref-comp binged the warning: he had to serve in ten seconds or lose it. She nodded apologetically at the front wall again, and he stepped into a rushed zee-ball. Slamming it slantwise into the right side of the front wall, but keeping it out of the corner curve, he sent it ricocheting into the right side wall. It bounced back diagonally across the court toward the rear of the left side wall, where it was meant to drop too closely into the square corner to be picked up by her. But his aim was off, and it fell directly into her backhand. Her smash drove the sphere into the left end of the front wall's lower curve, where it rolled down into the arc and shot back out along the floor only inches from the left side wall.

Caught with his weight on the right foot, he shifted in reverse and tried for the scoop, but it was too fast. In desperation he dove ahead of its roll, racket outstretched, wrist bent. Still he arrived late, skidded into the side wall after the ball went by. Renata's serve.

"Good try!" she yelled triumphantly over the ref's "Sideout."

He lay there a second before rolling over and nodding back diffidently. It was after they'd assumed service positions again, and he stood massaging his bruised left shoulder, that he realized two things:

1. His game was varying directly with his concentration, and inversely with his *seeing* Renata, not just looking at her. Umar had felt lust many times in life, but he'd never before had a fleshy target for it, alone, available, and not behaving as had the few women his prominent position had allowed him to meet.

2. He was sure she knew this and was using it and her question about Islam to distract him—merely to win a game! Umar also had known righteous anger.

He stood there, balanced between the lust and the indignation, sensing the heat flickering within and without his body as if it were the flame of a candle. He watched the sliding bands of muscle in her slender legs that went up, up into the olive shorts that tightly wrapped her double-handful buttocks, that locked into her almost too-narrow waist. The bong sounded. "Seventeen, eighteen." She turned to check his readiness. He saw the slim, muscled arms, the uplifting, grapefruit bosom, the way the sunset hair caped her slightly sloping shoulders, the flushed, smooth face whose full lips, reddened further, stood out livid against the white contrast, how the transparent goggles formed a wet-looking line around her cogent, wide, dark eyes. He inclined his head.

She served a simple high lob, bounced off the upper front wall to come down vertically into the right rear corner. He was there when it fell, scraped it off the wall with a tremendous backhand and sent it blurring along the right side wall. Its speed was so great that it continued completely around the front wall to the opposite side wall still pinned about halfway up. Renata was backing up from the server's box, watching for the ball's fall. Umar was moving, too, trying to get left to center-rear-court rally position in case she returned it. He glanced at the sphere, and they converged.

Since he was somewhat crouched and turned and she was upraised, she collided into his right hip and rolled backward and sideways over it, spinning a whole turn to land faceup. Umar was also spun by the impact, crossed ankles, and fell to her left with his legs tangled under hers.

It was the sensation that instantly tipped his balance. Her warm sweat was sweet-sour on his damp right flank; the impact was hard-muscular yet soft-fleshy. It acted like a touch-switch to his pent desire; his self-control exploded into willfull action. He rolled over, lifted himself onto her with his right hand as his left went around to her right buttock, clumsily grasping, kneading, drawing her against him. He rammed his phallus bulge into the soft warm trough where her legs joined, felt the femoral muscles tighten in umbrage. The resistance urged him to clutch his right hand to her firm left breast as if he would rip it out through the elastic brassiere. He *had* to stop the jiggling wallow of the right one as it sagged out over her arm. He used his mouth, bit hard. This pain finally initiated her overt reaction. Up came her left knee between his, just sharp enough for him to wince and release his mouth and right hand.

He jerked up to see her jarred but unfrightened face.

"That's what I call one *hell* of a hinder!" she said lightly, trying to smile.

Already he had regained the flood within himself, had recognized that while she wasn't a chaste Muslim, neither was she a trollop. It redoubled his mortification. Redness deepened his dusky skin down to his collar. She was reminded of Hhronkan distress displays. He pushed away quickly, rose, backed away a step with the racket still dangling by its loop from its supplicant palm, silent with horror.

"Please, please . . . forgive me!" he managed at last.

Back in control, she settled on amusement. Through her grin she said, "No, Umar. Please forgive *yourself!*"

He groped at the door sensor; the panel drew back, and he darted through as she lay back on the floor in laughter. Poor

Umar! The Sheik and Rhett, both destroyed by her simple flirting!

And in the outer corridor stood Tweeol. He watched Umar running away in terror of himself; he heard her giddy elation. And his skin became smooth, smooth as glass.

The dwelling A.H. and Joan chose to share was directly across the park strip from P.C.'s and down several units from Renata's. All the units were modifications of a basic design: two-story with bedrooms on the upper floor. But A.H. had chosen the ground-level salon–dining room to double as a writing studio because it abutted the kitchen, and composing and recomposing accelerated his appetite. They had brought some of their colonial furniture despite the weight. "Coming back or not," he'd vowed, "I will never again eat off glass and aluminum." The oak, six-place, gate-leg table nearly filled the small space. It held two plate terminals, one with a printer attachment, and several low stacks of pages. They sat on opposite sides, each before a plate, now propped up on their stands to facilitate touch. He read as she idled.

"Yeah, yeah. I like it; it's ready," he mumbled around his clenched wad of sugarless gum. With his between-meal treatment and meticulous brushing and flossing after eating, he treated his teeth like gold so one day they wouldn't be. He'd suffered dentist's invasions throughout childhood, and modern science could do anything except cure the Pleistocene sweettooth he'd inherited. He dropped the slippery gray sheet of celluloid onto a pile and tapped the storage switch on the cool touchboard in the plate's lower half. The glowing script on the upper screen faded.

Joan stopped swinging a crossed leg. "I still think you should just read it off the screen. That's how everyone else will read it. Why not wait till it's finished and print it all at once? This single-page editing takes too much time."

He smiled for leniency with the ends of his lips. Her acquiescent eye-roll acknowledged it. He liked books. And he loved the *idea* of books, of real paper, stitching, and glue, of a treasure ready to hold not only in the mind but also in the hand— dollars of gold, pieces of eight. But books had gone the way of currency long ago. Now they were luxuries for the wealthy collector, like petrol-powered cars or leather shoes. Joan had been content to sell her collection of imaginative fiction and rely on tape copies. But he'd brought the few volumes he owned, and he intended to bind these loose sheets when *Martian Spring* was done and add it to his hoard. There might even be offers from the few shelf-book publishers to turn out a collectors' edition.

As important, he needed this positive reinforcement before committing his text to comp memory. Although he enjoyed reading and critiquing the ideas of others, he was revulsed by any critical scrutiny of his own work. It wasn't simply the forest-and-trees problem. His mental constructs always seemed so superior to the filthy words that gave them communicable reality. As though the symbols in electronic memory or on paper were but pale representations of what he'd thought and felt, that they tainted the purity, lessened the impact, and sullied the worth of his ideas—the inevitable agony of all writers, surely.

He considered a sip from the untouched glass of iced scotch at his elbow. It was the only drug his aging endocrine system could yet metabolize into a comfortable, often creative high without knocking him on his ass. But that too was a gamble each time. Would it be jewel-hinged Delany wisdom or corkhead waste? He didn't need the gamble, today for sure. They'd all be taking a far greater risk soon enough. Perhaps it was this imminence that had honed his productivity this morning. After all, some people screwed best in public stairwells.

"Time is a commodity we shouldn't—" He cut her off at her look of anxiety and nodded in apology for reminding her. Quickly he spat his gum into a palm, knuckled a switch, and spoke at the pickup dot.

"During my first talks with Shree Shronk, when his English facility, aided by our *baas,* had risen sufficiently, I probed the nature of Hhronkan society. I was certain the outcome of our species' encounter would depend not only on our natures, but also on their independent expression. Our coexistence would succeed relative to the degree of similarity in how each people dealt with its own kind. There are such societal comparisons between the Hhronka and the pre-Communist Chinese. In both, primary responsibility for behavioral, educational, ethical, and criminal disciplines is lodged with the family clan, termed 'core-family' by the Hhronka. But in place of an imperial Chinese aristocracy, broader decisions in Hhronkan society are made at the city, province, and planet levels by a true democracy of individuals. This gives each Hhronkan a dual identity: core-family member and world citizen.

"I want to emphasize that these beings possess electronic voting hardware not much more sophisticated than our own. But for them it works. Every elective issue is voted on by an average of 98.4 percent of eligible citizens. And I believe this success is due to the influence of Mars's physical environment. The core system no doubt originally arose from and was reinforced during each Thaw by the independence of the growing Guardians' cities and the resulting closeness and intermarriages within each during succeeding generations just after the Thaws began. Each Guardian, faced with the impossible task of guiding thousands of young beings, assigned his authority to the Children [he altered tone to interject, "Capitalize children"] themselves, who in turn spread it among their own children, and so on. The death of the Guardian in a city signaled loss of the ultimate judge, and the people assigned this role through election. Over many Thaws, this and other practical procedures became custom, then law.

"The Hhronka consider their own individual lives to be as important as we do, but they also feel a duty to their entire people matched only rarely by humans. Strong cohesion was engendered by the fact of the coming Freezes and the complete obliteration of their physical culture, except for that preserved in the Repositories. We humans are accustomed to believing that though we die, our works remain, which has always proved a source of competition among us. But the average Hhronkan knew that no matter what he created it would be totally lost within six hundred years. Thus the preciousness and fragility of the inter-Thaw links of the 2,048 Guardians and their million-plus wards. To fail in cooperating with the exact needs balancing their comp-directed economy, or to alter their society even minimally, became almost sacrilegious to them. This, coupled with the sobering knowledge of Mars's eventual permanent freeze, led to complete stagnation, even in scientific research. Now, of course, we humans like to think our conjoining has revitalized them, and this mutual expedition is one proof of that.

"This is the reverse of the stability in Chinese culture, which arose from the lack of change in physical environment or any continual unabsorbed exterior pressure, such as invasion. In addition, the orientation with the past and ancestor worship in the Chinese as opposed to the Hhronkan concern with the future and devotion to the Children of the next Repositories points up fundamental differences in the personality ranges of our two peoples. Stop."

Joan looked up from her screen with pique smoothing her forehead. "You're going to get some arguments about that Chinese bit from terran historians. Why are you getting into this at all?" She waved at the text glowing before her on the screen. "Williams's monograph covers Hhronkan society in greater detail. We agreed this is supposed to be our personal recounting of the events just prior to and after the Hhronka were first discovered and how we figured in their decision not to fuse us right off the globe. That's what people want to know. Why play sociologist?"

He pulled in one corner of his mouth, rubbed his right palm over his chin, feeling its stubble, and propped his elbow on the table so talking made his head bob up and down. "I don't want *Martian Spring* to become more proof of Sturgeon's Law, or just another 'How We Did It' romance, the way Shiguchi's Saturn moons mission was pandered. Ever finish *Threading the Rings?* See? This has got to become a classic, so it and Williams's *The Hhronka: Portrait of Suspended Love* are always used and thought of together."

Immortality. Everyone wanted it, no matter how deeply they buried and ignored the instinct consciously. Most hoped for its actualization through their children, as the Hhronka did, others through their works. It was one sure motivation for most writers, including himself. Those with the talent left verbal monuments that they hoped would transcend history. Those without talent or children often sought permanence by leaving *some* mark of identity, even irrational ones. Thus some crimes, Guinness stunts, or graffiti—the epigrams of existence placed for all to see. Even unsigned on toilet walls, these authors were comforted by the lasting memory of their humor or hostility there, no matter how temporary in reality. Those without wit— and the young, to whom death was only another unknown terror, along with maturity—could grant but the bare minimum of their initials, the mere cipher of an existence barely appreciated even by themselves.

Joan stared a moment, then smiled tartly. "'Blest be the art that can immortalize.'" Truly, she read him—like a book. And secretly she was very pleased that A.H. was intent on writing again. Back on Wlaata he'd not done any in over a year before they'd left. It was a sign that this journey was innervating him and their closeness as hoped.

His grin spread sarcastically. "How well you know me, my dear." He lifted his brows in query to her quoting tone.

"William Cowper."

"Never heard of him," he taunted. "Try this one: 'Some, for renown, on scraps of learning dote, and think they grow immortal as they quote.'"

"You've been reading again," she chided.

"Edward Young," he replied in triumph. Haughtily he added, "Anyway, it is essential for all writers to be familiar with past important or relevant works. And if I have written better than other authors, it is because I have peered between the legs of giants."

Her mouth gaped in mock horror. "Sir Newton would never have approved of plagiarism!"

Though they both recognized their forced lightness, they laughed, pointed pistol fingers, and echoed, "Gotcha."

Suddenly from behind A.H., P.C. burst through from the kitchen. "But don't forget: Brevity is the troll of wit!"

They jumped in their seats but smiled back as he continued nervously. "Copying my act again, huh? Reproduction without royalty is nasty business, even for parents."

All three were aware his humor had fallen flat. A.H. and Joan exchanged looks of reluctant capitulation to what was finally at hand. But P.C., long ready for the adventure, still struggled to console them.

With a baseless chuckle he said, "I feel like the guy who walked into the fireworks factory with a lit candle: everyone's being *very* friendly, but I know I'm not welcome."

"Thanks, son, but...it's time," A.H. said kindly. They stood and touched off the terminals.

Fidgeting with impatience, P.C. said hopefully, "Captain Mowry agreed you can watch from the bridge, though there shouldn't be anything to see. Rennie's already there with the others."

A.H. nodded and turned from the table to lay an arm onto the youth's shoulder. He flinched, then accepted the contact. A.H. ignored the hesitancy, and the three went into the courtyard and onto the spongy grass of the greenbelt. There was a moldy hay smell that joined with the sound of the stream's gurgling. He was still sorry the bird embryos slept with the other organisms.

Joan, opposite A.H., slipped an arm around her son's waist. "Let's not take the tram; let's use our spoke lift and go around the hub to the bridge."

They wheeled from the tram station stairs near the stream and followed its course two hundred meters to the concrete apron, where it circumnavigated the base of the giant's leg. It was a white tower lurching up through the unshuttered glass roof to the hub's bulge, from which two other legs strode out to the rim left and right a sixth of the way 'round from them. The large lift slid smoothly upward toward spin center, its speed slowing to give gradual weight reduction to match decreasing centrifugal effect. The with-spin face of the car was transparent, and they looked out through periodic ports in the spoke. The rim world shrank at their feet; the car passed through the roof, and they were greeted by the diamond-point starfield spinning toward and past them on either side. The rim looked slimmer than expected from the gallery windows in the hub's cushioned equator passageway. In nearly null g, they bounded along handholds through the next spoke junction and then climbed a radial corridor away from the rim's spin plane to the bridge.

This deck encircled the "north" axle with its nonrotating docking lock; the "south" axle held the thrusters. To overcome the acceleration–nonacceleration dilemma simply, the bridge's floor lay parallel to the wheel's spin plane so that during acceleration the floor stayed "the floor." Now the slight centrifugal tug made the inner wall seem uphill. Crews working at stations on the winking banks of monitoring and command modules that lined both curving walls had to strap into chairs to prevent drifting to the outer wall. The bridge's angular motion was so slow they could easily move opposite to this tug or keep stationary.

The others were braced against the white-padded rails in an observation bay in the outer wall. The captain saw the newcomers approaching and nodded at a crew member to start the final count.

Renata said to Umar, "But I still don't see why we had to bring the *Wind* so far from the sun before we could translate."

A.H. stifled anxiety as he watched the dark man remove a fingertip from between his lips. Everyone had noted the Muslim's change in the last weeks. His calm self-assurance and alacrity to discuss and explain religion or other matters had diminished. In their place was an increasing reticence in courtesy and speech, and a nervousness expressed by the continuous chewing of his cuticles. At times he seemed to be consuming himself, starting with his fingers. And Renata's presence only aggravated these symptoms. His infatuation was now obvious to them all, but instead of having a positive effect on the man, it reminded A.H. of moth and flame. His daughter remained intrigued, perhaps flattered by her unintended power, and A.H. maintained a studied silence, trusting her judgment.

When she addressed him, Umar stared at her, looked away, and hesitated. Droom jumped into the embarrassed pause. "Remember our objective is to create a temporary spherical field of super-dense gravity around the ship, just under that necessary to make a black hole. And we use the total conversion of gray material to do this."

Crews had spent the last ten days installing thin plates of the bronzelike ceramic into a ring of insulated refrigeration units on the outer circumference of the rim's hull.

"In ordinary use, such as on belts or flyers, gravity flux is created by applying a specially modulated, rapidly pulsed EM field to the material in a way that induces the quark bags of the crystal's nuclei to overlap."

"Halt!" interrupted Renata. "I'm a biologist; on physics I am slightly light. The neutrons and protons are composed of triplets of quarks held together by gluons, right?"

"Yes. It is analogous to three balls joined by rubber bands or confined within a rubber bag. In the grav material's rare-earth nuclei we stretch the bands, or bags, until the quarks become 'confused' as to which nucleon they belong. Then—Do you understand virtual particles? No. Well, in order to keep nature's accounts balanced—what you humans call symmetry—every 'real' particle is enveloped by a cloud of virtual particles that continually pop into and out of existence in matter–antimatter pairs. A gross oversimplification; I will give you a reference to Hawking's work later. These overlapped quark bags then 'trap' the nucleons' virtual particles. That is, their gluon fields transmit the energy of the input EM field plus the bond energy of some of the grav crystal's molecules so the virtuals combine into 'real,' relatively stable massive particles. This net matter gain is similar to that which takes place at the event horizon of an evaporating black hole and produces Hawking radiation. But our 'extra' matter particles decay instants later and, along with the decay of some nuclei of the crystal, leave a lot of heat—entropy's cost. In effect we violate symmetry briefly. Meanwhile, an intense gravity field had been created due to the presence of the extra matter. And since the crystal's structure causes alignment of the gravitons thus produced in the rare-earth nuclei, we get a directed gravity field whose strength depends on the strength of the EM field. The whole process is pulsed to several hundred thousand times per second. This is in ordinary application."

Renata and several others looked somewhat hammered, but no one ever successfully stopped Droom once she was boosting along.

"However, this will not work for the ftl translation. We need only one tremendous burst of gravity in a much shorter time. But for total conversion to be done with EM energy input, we would need thousands of liquid-metal MHD generators instead of the tens we have. Rather, we use a method derived from our solution of the unified field theory."

Umar acknowledged her compliment with a weak, self-conscious smile as she continued. "We *cool* the crystal to very near absolute zero, which shrinks the quark bags and crowds them together. Then, at the proper transition temperature, we input the correct kind of energy, and the bulk of the nucleons' intensified, overlapped virtual-particle clouds becomes real. In effect we dissolve the bag confinement—or cause the decay of the nucleons if you prefer—and create a super-dense *quark soup,* just the way intense pressure and gravity does it in collapsing neutron stars. But the input energy has to be uniform, instantaneously applied throughout the material, and of a kind that also will further increase the density of the intensified virtual-particle clouds. So we simply let—"

"Cosmic rays!" Renata exclaimed triumphantly.

Droom displayed a bright ring of agreement, whose quickness also indicated admiration of Renata. "Exactly. Cosmic rays out here are mostly high energy protons, with few antiprotons, so we have a net density gain in 'real' matter added to the virtuals. And their kinetic energy is a free source of the correct energy applied uniformly to the grav crystal plates by space itself."

"And too near the sun, within the heliopause, the variable solar wind debris would mess that up," concluded Renata.

"Yes. Out here, perpendicular to the ecliptic plane, input on our hull is sufficient and exactly calculable. Extreme accuracy is required. Also we can safely turn off our electric-magnetic shields, to let in the rays unabated, without worrying about solar flares or other larger debris. Of course, we must take into account the 2.7 degrees Kelvin background microwave radiation from the Big Bang. Our 10 percent light speed is creating a bow-wave with measurable energy, but we will simply remove that through the refrigeration system. As Krieder knows, we are using the dopplered directional intensity of this radiation as a frame of reference for velocity measurement. Yet we can do without it during the brief translation."

"Sort of shakes one's faith in Einstein, again," A.H. said, smiling, but only Umar glanced at him in recognition of the joke. Special Relativity asserted the lack of a cosmic frame of reference.

"OK, so we get a super-dense gravity field; what's that do?" insisted Renata with upraised brows.

Squeezing his eyes shut, P.C. said snidely, "You really haven't been keeping up, have you?" He too was not altogether happy about her and Umar, and his cut about study time was not lost on her. But he squelched any reply by turning to place his hands against the cool glass of the bay and stare out at the sun's small dot.

This attack on her finally prompted Umar, who dropped his hunched shoulders, took a breath, and quickly said, "We are going to form what is mathematically termed a 'trousers world.' This is an internally consistent space-time structure invented in the early 1900s, I think, long before its use in physics was discovered. Just as group theory was invented two centuries before it was found ideal for describing certain aspects of quantum theory, or the theory of anticommuting numbers was developed before its use in supergravity.

"Imagine a pair of trousers divided into three separate volumes: each leg and the space above the crotch. Call one leg the 'normal cosmos,' the other a 'superspace,' and the above-crotch volume the 'hypersurface.' In a trousers world, events occurring in the normal cosmos and the superspace are never causally connected; that is, they can't affect each other; no leg-to-leg cause–effects are possible. But events in either leg can have effects in the hypersurface, the above-crotch."

Warming up to their quizzical looks he said, "I know this is illogical in *this* space-time, where if A always causes B, and B always causes C, then A always causes C. But not in a trousers world; A will have no effect on C. It *is* mathematically consistent, just out of our experienceable existence, till now. We're certain a sufficiently dense, extremely brief gravity field over a given volume—namely, this craft—will deform its normal space-time into a superspace, connected to the normal cosmos only through a hypersurface, enwrapped by it, so to speak. This will remove us from this universe to one of our own making, temporarily of course. The energy required to sustain the gravity field comes partly from the grav material, which will be consumed in 4.017 quintillionths of a second, or so. The trousers world will collapse; we will return to this universe.

"But during this state, the hypersurface will act as a 'bubble,' being drawn to the largest mass nearest our line of flight and along its vector direction. Otherwise, we'd be right back here at Sol. We have instead aimed for Tau Ceti and will reappear just beyond its heliopause, maintaining our direction and velocity. That is why measurement and timing are vital. Any more grav material, any longer a real-time duration for the trouser world, and we might be drawn into the center of Tau Ceti itself. It is the hypersurface, not the colony-superspace, that reacts to the cosmos and navigates to the objective, like a ball rolling downhill. That is why we will not be harmed by the inward-directed gravity tides when the grav material is converted or by the explosion when it breaks down to pure cosmic rays. Only that which is within its ring will be translated, just ahead of the grav field's inward-rushing bow-wave. This takes place so rapidly that there is no damage to our structure."

The semicircle of faces was suddenly very intense. Then Joan spoke softly. "How long will this take? Uh...in real time."

Umar was hesitant again. "Ordinary cause–effect events cannot pass for us in so short a time span. And there should be no sensation at all, unless it is a feeling of loss. But in a trousers world, the legs are not connected to the crotch by spacelike curves. That means events in the normal cosmos and colony-superspace region are not simultaneous with, nor before, nor after each other." Over their exclamations, he added hurriedly, "I mean there's an equal probability that no time will pass in this universe either...or we may reemerge *anytime* in the past or the future. That was why we warned this might be a one-way trip. Once we have translated, we can use stellar configurations to find the truth and calculate the exact effect, but this initial try..."

It struck them all fully for the first time, even those who had heard the explanation before. They were about to attempt something totally new. When Fermi's group had assembled their pile of radioactive bricks under the stands at the University of Chicago it had been the same. Certain results could be predicted, but others were simply unknowns, beyond even the statistical reach of science. And here no one could stand ready with an axe to spill boric acid and quench the effect.

The voice was a buoy bell on a fogged night: "Captain, we have .01 degrees on the salt bath."

Mowry turned to the visitors with a challenge. "Well?"

A.H. knew the taunt was for the humans not the Hhronka. "We're *all* volunteers, aren't we?"

Even Mowry lost his formal bluffness as he twisted back briefly to nod at the woman. "I suppose something momentous should be said, but I am no Armstrong, and I'm literally too frightened to think of anything."

They all stared at him. The lifeboat syndrome had suddenly equalized them with its sense of imminent danger. From Mowry this was quite an admission, and it released their suppressed gestures. They exchanged brief wishes, chest touches, and handshakes, in which even Umar joined, lingeringly with Renata. Then they pressed to the bay instinctively and watched the tired carousel of stardust, hoping for some sign of the translation.

Joan's back pressed firmly into A.H.'s belly; their hands touched both their children. Contact seemed important. To their right Shree and Droom were side by side; Mowry stood back a pace, visibly sweating. Oddly, Umar appeared to relax for a change, his fingers locked prayerfully together as he stood next to Mowry. Twee moved up to stand close to Renata.

A woman sat watching the refrigeration comp chill them into oblivion. Within the linked units on the rim, a stepwise process took place. An intense magnetic field was applied to the grav material, magnetizing the nuclei and aligning them. Then this heat of nuclear magnetization was conducted away to a bath of paramagnetic salts, which was in turn cooled by liquid helium dilution refrigeration. Finally the magnetic field on the grav material was zeroed, and its nuclei were left at a slightly lower energy state. The cycle repeated, inching down toward the goal temperature.

P.C. didn't turn around as his sarcasm sliced out: "Oh, for God's sakes! Quit with the heavy breathing! I got something 'momentous' to say, and ain't it appropriate that Showboat Sagan said it! 'We have lingered long enough on the shores of the cosmic ocean. It is time to set sail for the stars.' No applause? He didn't get any either. Push the damned button! Let's get into your Cosmic Pants, or whatever, and get this . . . over with."

His last clause was robbed of its surrogate bravado as his father tried to touch him mentally. A.H. had returned the affectionate merges of the two Hhronka. (Their calm wasn't surprising, another benefit of the altruistic approach to their personal lives.) Then, he'd inadvertently brushed Twee's strong merge with P.C. His attempt to join was harshly rejected as the youth clamped his Self tightly within.

If we don't survive this, it won't matter, he thought stoically, and if we do, I'll have other chances to try crossing *this* gulf too. He leaned his chin against the back of Joan's head, and she responded with her own pressure. He smelled her hair and the insulation odors of the bridge and felt the miniscule vibrations crisscrossing its deck. There was no sound but breathing.

It is good to be alive, to know, he reminded himself. But I feel oblivion near, and I am afraid.

"Ready," said the woman at the console, her finger above the switch that would release the last cycle, remove the last pico-Kelvin, and push the temperature down to the transition level at which the cosmic rays would have effect.

Mowry glanced at each of them, his face open and smoothed with the sudden trapped feeling they all shared. Then he shrugged, snorted resignedly, and said, "Go."

Her finger fell . . .

. . . a lurch, a cerebellar muscle spasm that wakes to warn of sleep, a tiny space of void—deep, deep—turned inside-out to spill its nothingness, a collision with a door in the dark, a single frame clipped from the reel of life's film and the free ends spliced. But the breach remains.

The starfield shifted during an involuntary blink (squeeze the lids shut, lest the nothingness flood out and cover me with oblivion).

A few normal days passed. And whether this discontinuity was the memory of a past event, the herald of a future one, or just a self-imposed delusion grew uncertain, then unimportant . . .

Of course, it was P.C. who named it the Van Winkle Rip.

Chapter 6

Tau Ceti. Not surprising that it had proved, according to the evidence of the Kmeaan transmissions, to harbor a planet that had evolved sentient humanoids. Though this main sequence star shines 11.9 light-years away, its G8 spectrum is closer to the sun's G2 than any other star but one, within 17 light-years of Sol. The single exception is the Alpha body in the Centauri triplet. But this, our nearest neighbor system at only 4.3 light-years, has little chance of possessing stable terrestrial planets due to the interactions of gravity tides from its three components. The G8 classification includes a surface temperature only several hundred degrees cooler than Sol's 5800 degrees Kelvin, which also fits Tau Ceti's luminosity, being less than our sun's. So promising were the similarities that it had been a prime target for Drake's Project Ozma in the early 1960s, when he'd aimed a radio-telescope at this star and listened in vain for artificial signals.

A.H. reviewed these memories as he lay spread-eagled face-down on a towel near the stream below their dwelling. Through the roof arch and onto him fell this sun's twice-reflected light. Once the *Wind* was well within the system, they'd redeployed the mirror disc and had instructed a "natural" twelve-hour day. Since it was certain nothing very harmful was getting through the polarization and electromagnetic screens, he'd begun brief sunbathing daily. He was aware of the skin and eye problems prolonged exposure to any stellar radiation could bring, but he also needed the relaxation it brought. And this was the time, perhaps the last time, for such interludes.

Till now, the journey had proved nominal. The translation had rather anticlimactically created the effects predicted, and stellar configuration indicated little if any time shift. A.H. himself had immediately supervised these calculations and measurements. Allowing for Tau Ceti's positional difference from Sol, the constellational alterations were exactly predictable to within an angle of .01 seconds arc. He had felt sure no time had elapsed during their existence in the self-created universe. And twelve-year-old signals from Sol had confirmed it.

The Kmeaan message had described a family of seven planets without asteroid belts but with occasional comets, which the third Hhronkan expedition had verified. They were quickly found, revolving about their primary in an ecliptic plane with nearly twice the angular thickness of Sol's. Fortunately *Wind* had come in at a high incline "above" this, and the seven had been given close scrutiny. The outer four were gas giants, similar to Saturn, but oddly without rings or habitable moons. The innermost planet was Luna-sized, rotating slowly only 15 million km out, a burned crisp of rock and metal. The middle two were terrestrial and at hopeful distances from Tau Ceti. Here was the first surprise. The Kmeaans had identified the third world as theirs. Yet at 190 million km spun an oblate spheroid with an 18,000-km diameter and an atmosphere of 10 percent oxygen, almost 90 percent nitrogen, with a few trace gases. But there were no detectable bodies of water, an essential to humanoid life. And the second satellite was 100 million km out, had a 16,000-km diameter, and an atmosphere of 24 percent oxygen, 59 percent nitrogen, 10 percent helium, 7 percent neon, and traces. This one was 80 percent covered by water. A far more likely spot. Yet both moonless worlds had to be visited, for both held gases indicative of life and industry, and both were totally silent of telltale communication-band signals.

Tau Ceti had long been noted as a "noisy" star, even emitting random EM radiation from that portion of the spectrum useful in high-density communication. Within the system this noise became enormous. They trained the comp's decoding ear to filter this out but still found nothing with a certain artificial pattern. And weeks of sending out greetings in Hhronkan also went un-

answered. When this result had been obtained soon after translation, it had depressed both contingents. This intensified when
the old transmissions from Earth and Mars could no longer be
separated from the growing interference, despite the decoder's
best efforts. It implied they couldn't send back to Sol either and
so were effectively isolated.

This, in turn, deepened the entire mystery. How had the first
Kmeaan message been sent through such interference? Either
the physical environment had altered drastically since then (as
part of the Kmeaans' destruction?), or they'd found the means
to eliminate the problem. Then why hadn't any of the three
Hhronkan expeditions, no mean scientists themselves, done
likewise? Or at least sent back a robot probe?

It seemed Shree's hypothesis could be correct. There were no
radiation belts, but apparently some mutual disaster had destroyed both native and visitor, or at least left them incommuni-
cado. How else explain the additional absence of any planetary
surface output of sensor-detectable energies, the types not
scrambled by the noise, that were the signature of technological
civilizations? If any beings remained on either world they must
be Iron Age savages at best. Or had they come so far to find
only an untended graveyard? There was little choice but to go
on.

Of course, they had months ago decelerated to a velocity
considered safe in these unknown volumes. They had also altered course to pass only ten million km from the arid third
planet. Indeed, it was currently a lifeless waste of vast silicate
sheets, violent storms, and quakes; except for its purple-tan
color, it could have been frozen Wlaata before terraforming.
Low background radiation was inconclusive evidence for a nuclear holocaust, and it was unlikely this globe had ever held an
advanced culture. So another course change had taken them
spiraling in toward the star. They had gathered stellar data and
made use of its gravity well to save fuel and throw *Wind* outward in an Hohmann curve intersecting the orbit of the second
planet, now on the opposite side of the primary. With umbrella
frame reextended, they were now coasting to this watery world.
Rendezvous would be in ten days.

A.H. felt the tickle of sweat streams rolling down his skin,
like ants crawling, from the backs of his knees, the small of his
back, his neck, his hairline. The terry cloth was already wet
with his musty odor, and the tips of the long grass blades had

begun to poke through the cloth and his thoughts. Amazing how this star's photons resembled Sol's. Same white-yellow tint, same scythe heat on his body. His bare buttocks felt tender to his palms, and he couldn't chew his gum while facedown. He rolled over, recentering himself on the towel with a lift from his hands. Now the hot light plastered his front, massaging his skin evenly. Like X rays, Kmeaa's radiations seemed to penetrate him completely, not just down to the dermis. Through his lids it was a glowing, splotchy redness that also itched the lining of his nose. Sunlight, direct or reflected, was like snuff, and he sat upright to enjoy the free release of the building sneeze, followed by the temporary contraction of the nasal membrane that allowed the left nostril to breathe without his having to tug it away from the bent septum (dislodged in a bar fight long ago, and he didn't want to suffer two black eyes again to have it surgically corrected).

With the tremendous explosion of cool sputum particles, the gum shot from his opening mouth and landed, a conspicuous pink pebble on the green grass. Too green, he thought. That's why he reached to retrieve the processed plant sap. No large saprophytes dwelled here to initiate reclamation of the organic gum, not even earthworms or *kwerlli* worms. Only well-controlled soil bacteria and too-green grass. As though it had been spray-painted. The Queen of Hearts's garden without an Alice.

He definitely had begun to miss the unpredictability that only a planet surface could grant. There were few surprises on a world where you knew of *everything* because it either had to be here or you had voted on its presence.

He heard the multiple tomtoms of feet and looked up to see Mowry and some of the crew jogging in file along the knurled grass near the stream's far side. All in shorts, some barefoot, the larger women in halters, their bodies glittered as the captain conducted them like partridges through the curving forest. They came close enough for him to hear their chorused panting, accompanying the tomtoms in a symphony of stress. One of them did wear a player button in one ear, for inspiration. He wondered what the music was. His own heartbeat was always enough. He'd done his lap early yesterday and would repeat it tomorrow; that was also enough, with isometric lifting and R-ball, to keep him physically and psychologically regular. Humans were 55 percent muscle; bruise it or lose it.

Mowry looked over at last and, deciding he couldn't ignore

A.H.'s presence, gave a quick acquiescent nod. A.H. simply lifted his right forearm and flipped up the open palm at just the correct speed so Mowry could never be entirely sure it hadn't been a *sieg heil*.

"Bleep!" said the oblong black box beside the towel. They had all begun carrying the perscomms when they'd entered the system; instant communication might be imperative. Startled he jumped and twisted to flip up the cover with the little TV screen as it came on.

Shree looked up at him, black-white waves of shock and joy combing his face. "Krieder! We have received a transmission originating in space only 200,000 kilometers away and apparently intended for us! It is a combination of both binary encoding and vocal audio. Listen!"

His flickering face remained, but his rasping bass was replaced by another voice, as sibilant, hooting, and multihued as any Hhronkan. A.H. listened for a second before he too joyfully realized it *was* a Hhronkan speaking, though in a rather garbled dialectal form! His elation choked off quickly. It was also very definitely a warning.

They fell through a hot, hissing, violet fog. Like a defensive corpuscle, the cloud of friction-born ions engulfed them, seemingly determined that, since it couldn't prevent their entry, it would attempt to blind the invaders. A.H. twisted against the webbing to look from the snowed-out screens to the starboard port. Beyond and below the shuttle's rounded nose, through the shimmering indigo, Kmeaa-2 was as comforting yet awe-inspiring as any world exploited by life. Just aft, the curving segment of northern hemisphere was a sunlit aqua overlaid by a thin misty rime. Directly below, gray-reefed clouds, underlit by occasional flashes, formed swirling cyclonic and jet-stream patterns. Ahead, dark rifts in this frosting silhouetted sections of ocean made black by the cloud cover and the low angle of the sun that chased them from behind.

Orbital observations had confirmed that water covered almost 80 percent of the planet, broken by two major continents, a minor one, and frequent scattered volcanic island chains. The large mountainous continent traversed the temperate zone of the northern hemisphere, and the other flatter one lay close to the equator in the southern. The lesser, triangle-shaped, appended from near this to stretch toward the south pole.

As instructed, they were gliding in ahead of the sun, counter to rotation, to come down on the north shore of the larger, flatter southern mass as it crossed the dawn line. The *Wind* spun in orbit above, revolving about the world's poles to avoid passage through planet shadow. Still escorting it were three of the five robot drones that had been the source of their first contact with the Kmeaan Hhronka. Within hours of this transmission the fleet of boxy uncrewed torchships had arrived. The original warning had contained instructions to be followed exactly, else they faced attack. Their initial joy had been significantly diluted.

For another day the guard ships, obviously armed with laser and missiles, had englobed them, scanning but silent to repeated queries. They had become nervous enough to discuss destroying the robots. But Shree had countered with simple logic.

"These Hhronka know now who is aboard this craft as well as how to detect repulsor film, and therefore know this craft is without its protection. If they meant to attack us they would already have tried. They want something; let us see what it is."

He referred to the thin layer of special Hhronkan polymer that could be overlaid on a surface. Any force, over a limited range, impinging on it would be spread throughout the entire layer, converted to coherent radiation, and reflected harmlessly back out. It was a sheet laser, an effective shield against photonics, sonics, and the lesser missiles. Only a large nuclear warhead could overwhelm its structure, destroying it and whatever it layered.

Then a live message from the approaching planet had also bypassed the interference on a specially encrypted frequency. Upon seeing the answering visage of Shree, the ordinary-looking Hhronkan at the other end had become nearly ecstatic, and the "rescuers" had again begun to feel a sense of success. But not entirely.

When the *Wind* had slowed itself into orbit at Kmeaa-2, they'd discovered part of the means by which the planet had *deliberately* maintained comm interference. A ring of satellites in geosynchronous orbit poured out continual jamming noise to mask all such emanations leaving the planet. They had all been surprised by them and stunned by the implications.

A. H. had told an executive committee meeting with Mowry on the bridge, "The energy, hardware, and comp management required to coordinate these interference patterns, yet leak through only desired comm, such as the commands to those robot drones, and perhaps even the message to Sol so long ago, is stupendous. Also you realize, since no artificial signals have ever been detected from Tau Ceti, there may be many other such interference devices scattered throughout this system to mask any signals arising off-planet. So far we've seen no evidence of such habitation anywhere else in the system, however. Add to that the shielding needed on power plants, nuclear reactors, and any other energy/particle-producing equipment to prevent local detection near or within the system itself . . . Gentle beings, where I come from we would say this world is 'playing possum.' Before we accept their invitation to land *en masse,* we should find out what they're so afraid of. I suggest a vanguard."

Shree had flashed a white ring of agreement as he took the floor just ahead of Mowry. "News is the oracle. Thirty thousand years is a long time; life here, influenced by the natives, must be very different from that on Wlaata. Before we commit ourselves, or even activate and arm the human shuttles as Captain Mowry wishes to urge, I want to personally meet the Kmeaans and survey the records from the time of their first invitation and the arrival of our expeditions. Mostly I want to know why our people submitted to, and evidently cooperated in, being cut off from Wlaata completely. Krieder and I will go alone. We will be wired with live transmitters working on the same coded frequency as the drones, so you may monitor all that happens."

Even Mowry had failed to protest this plan. After all, A.H. believed that going on this expedition had probably clenched the "living legend" status for both him and Shree. And who argues with legends? Especially ones who are never defenseless, even when entirely unarmed. And Joan sat nodding supportively, acquiescing. How he envied her at times. He certainly would have been anxious if their roles were inverted.

His chipped smile faded as the shuttle entered the cumulus layer and the sunlight clicked off. The soft hiss on the hull became a crackling howl. Instantly they were engulfed in the stomach of a gray-white storm. The craft was rocked and slammed irregularly up and down by gales that machine-gunned hail and rain into the cockpit windscreens. A.H. quickly returned all his attention to the navcomp and its clearing radar screen in the short, tilted panel before him. Shree's supple hands twisted the control grips on his reclined chair's arms to maintain stability with airfoil surfaces only. The altitude reading on the console caught A.H.'s eye as it dropped.

"We're too fast! Can't you keep the nose up higher?" he nearly yelled. If they couldn't slow very soon, the autopilot would take over and the engines would start; they'd use precious lift-off fuel. He could feel his rapid aortic pulse pressing his trachea like a kitten's nursing paws. Finally, he had to recognize his deep excitement.

But he also felt guilt at doubting the Hhronkan's skill. Already the numbers' rate of decrease was back in acceptable limits, and they still followed the ping of the landing beacon supplied from the surface. Visual guidance was impossible, as predicted. Partly in apology for his doubt, A.H. weakly expanded his Self and brushed Shree's.

:: Rough! Eggbeater in a dirty fishbowl!

Though Shree's field was contracted, it was still concentrated enough for A.H. to sense acceptance of the apology and his own emotional set as well. Shree was also responding to their situation, beyond the needs of piloting; his pleasure was anticipatory. A.H. felt his eagerness to greet the Kmeaan Hhronka and join again the two branches of his people. This despite his own doubts and the mysteries they must solve. And the fact that Feeahra's descendants, Shree's own bloodline, were probably among these people was added impetus.

Yes, they were all highly motivated to alter their initial reservations. All now wished to establish normal relations with the planet's inhabitants, were anxious to come and see for themselves the third triumph of Sentience over Nature. They had all convinced themselves this vanguard would find the satisfactory explanations needed for the Happy Ending. All but A.H. His doubts still snagged on one point glossed over by the rest. It really wasn't subject to logical analysis. Somehow he could not erase the queasy sensation he got each time he considered the possible significance of the last expedition's abridged message: "further than life."

"Shree," he cautioned, "remember to keep your Self well contracted and weakened unless we're totally alone. Very probably these Hhronka have *baasa* among them." He stopped short of reference to Shree's own descendants. "We don't want to give anything away prematurely. Rely on speaking English; they may have periodically shut off the interference and picked up some human broadcasts in the last two centuries, but translating these would be next to impossible without human help."

The buffeting had eased, and Shree looked away a moment from the pulsing console above him. "Yes. I agree, as I have said. And I suggest we merely observe—react to nothing. Pretend we are here only to do as they have asked, receive a welcome and determine living conditions for the remainder of our peoples."

White rosettes pulsed across his face. He had, in turn, read A.H.'s emotional set. "But be optimistic! All will be well, I am sure. After all, we have found them, have we not?"

Suddenly the shuttle fell from the storm. They were now three kilometers up, and ahead through the ground haze two lines of yellow landing spots glowed. The haze thinned, and they beheld the city: "Atuum-uleen" the Kmeaan Hhronka had called it, the City of Life.

The significance struck him at last. He was about to contact yet another civilization! One so ancient that when the first Hhronkan expedition had reached it, *Homo sapiens* had still been busy murdering and fornicating the Neanderthal into extinction.

Throughout the expedition he'd maintained an unemotional veneer. In fact, the planning and execution of the trip here had been almost boring with success. Nothing unpredicted had occurred from the very beginning, and the months had passed too quickly. The lulling effect had submerged the high that was gradually building unnoticed within, the selfish motive underlying his genuine support for the altruistic goal of their mission.

At this moment, however, it all ruptured out—as a well-founded fear: Considering what finding the Hhronka had done to human society, and what this Kmeaan world had apparently done to the Hhronka who came here, how could they all help but undergo some kind of massive disorientation? Would they survive it? Suddenly he felt cold sweat. It was all happening so fast; they should have gone more slowly and considered every aspect and its consequence. The ship jolted, and he was recommitted to the scene below.

Sitting at the end of a short peninsula that crept into the slate sea, the city formed a perfect circle. During the first days in orbit they'd learned from visual observation that all this world's cities had circular outlines. But Atuum-uleen was apparently the principal one; they were to be greeted there by some sort of official. Communications had so far been cheerful but quite brief and minimal in information.

Spreading away from the city down the peninsula and back onto the hilly mainland for many miles were quilts of neat croplands. The patterns proved these were mixed polycultures of different food and nonfood plants interspersed for pest control. Probably automated, so little intervention by the citizens was necessary. All very Hhronkan. But the wheel-spoke layout of the city wasn't.

Thirty to forty spoke-boulevards extended radially from a central hub through at least that many concentric ring-boulevards. Most buildings were many-storied, giving the appearance of a hatbox arcology from high above. But as they fell, he saw the stair-step skylines clearly, yet not the details of structures themselves.

His attention went to the hub of the city. There stood a gigantic black pillar with an expanded capital. An abstract toadstool, it dominated all other structures and rose hundreds of meters above them. Myriad yellowish street and building lights winked off in sequential block patterns to announce sunrise. This regularity bespoke an automation similar to that of the croplands. But for the Hhronka, rigid practicality would never be applied to the usual haphazard freedom of their residential areas. This blurring of the Hhronkan utilitarian–esthetic dichotomy was the first probable native Kmeaan influence they'd found.

The landing strip lay tangent to the city's circumference and stretched across the center of its finger of land. Shree finally joined A.H. in letting the navcomp land them and released the control handles to study the scene in the last minute before touchdown. They saw an expected amount of city air traffic, most of it apparently using grav material to aid in slow vertical maneuvering. They guessed only heavy freighters economically used lift surfaces, like this strip, for takeoffs and landings. Now they were only seconds from the wet black strip, the ground details expanding toward them as though on a giant balloon.

Just before the screeching bump of the wheels, A.H. noticed that at least this section of the city's border appeared to be marked by a curving row of tall cylindrical pylons, erected on a bright yellow band between the strip and the city. The poles were identical, one at the end of each radial street, and had some kind of bristling attachment at the top. Giant mechanical sentinels guarding the city, ready to scream alarm upon invasion?

When all the wheels rolled on the tarmac, they felt the planet's .89 g for the first time. The webbing held them back as the compilot steadily braked to full stop in a kilometer. A.H. enjoyed the lighter weight and kept his grav belt off. But Shree sagged in his seat under the increase of nearly one and a half times his normal weight. Then he touched his belt and visibly straightened. In the quiet of the cockpit they heard distant clicking as the hot underbelly cooled. To the left began the farmlands; ahead the eyebrow of dark sea lifted. Across the flat open expanse to their right the skyline of Atuum-uleen humped upward in gauzy specters; the smooth gray sky merged distantly with the ground and the city floated between. Bordering the puddled strip's city side were several low outbuildings, and among them stood a small group of figures. A vehicle sped from there toward the shuttle.

Their eyes jerked to the console screen as it pinged to announce results of atmosphere diagnosis: 16° C   790 mm mercury here at sea level   no toxic chemical levels . . .

"We will have to take their word the microbes here are no more dangerous to humans or Hhronka than those on Wlaata," said Shree as he motioned for A.H. to switch on his transmitter. These were of the wafer variety, powered by body heat and sewn into their clothes.

"Let's still use the airlock, OK?" murmured an unassured A.H.

The inner door clacked airtight, and the outer slid to Shree's touch. A cool damp mist swept in as he lowered the seven-step ladder to the ground. A.H. wished he'd worn more than a lined rain jacket, but Shree seemed comfortable as always with his robe and callused bird feet. They climbed down into the gray light. The city's hum enveloped them, a living breath.

A.H. glanced at the shuttle, which seemed undamaged, its dark underside still radiating enough heat to feel good on his face. Then he looked around and stubbed his toe at the ground. The wet tarmac was like very smooth asphalt, but his plastec ankle boots adhered to it like new tennies to polished wood. Perhaps it had a rubberlike powder added for traction, as they used back home. Yes, .89 g felt just fine, added a spring to his walk. The sky was a bit bluer gray than Earth's when heavily overcast, more like Wlaata's near the poles. He'd like to see it clear, if that ever happened on this watery world of frequent torrents.

He took a deep breath to halt his speeding mind. The air felt the tiniest bit thicker going in, higher air pressure and higher density. Or it could be the wetness he tasted, an after-rain mold that sat in the nose like smoke. The lubricant-neoprene odor of the shuttle's bottled air was replaced by . . . what? It verged on spicy. Then he knew it was the smell of growing plants, the crops.

For the third time he stood on a different planet's surface. Each created its own sensory gestalt. It was similar to the way he felt anytime he went over a thousand clicks from a place he was used to—the unfamiliarity, the otherness. Yet it was more. Lonely, slightly frightening. Exhilarating, the way quick fear heightened perception. In contrast, Shree seemed unaffected and stood peering through the lifting mist at the distant crowd and the approaching vehicle.

It arrived with the sound only of disturbed air and soft tires. A.H. smiled; no wonder Shree had been intrigued. It was a crystal egg five meters long balanced on a squat four-wheeled frame of light blue brushed metal. It was empty except for a small dash plate with an underslung steering wheel at one end and what resembled giant green pillows covering the curving floor.

A Hhronkan monotone slowly said, "Excuse these facilities, but this field is normally used only for cargo. They are waiting. Your craft and luggage will be seen to. Please enter."

A.H. had the sure feeling it was the car itself that had addressed them, not some being speaking through a remote. Well, in some terran cities and heavily mechanized areas on both Earth and Wlaata, advanced robots often interacted with the living. This one was using the familiar form of the Hhronkan tongue, without the dialect they'd first encountered.

Searching for the entry to the perfect surface, he said to Shree, "Courteous to reprogram it in what must be ancient Hhronkan to them."

Shree looked at him in surprise as he forced out the entire sentence despite their mutual display of humor. The gas molecules of the denser air, with a net slower vibration rate, lowered the register of his voice so much he sounded nearly as bass as Shree. He recalled party balloons and how helium squeezed his voice to Donald Duck's. This was an equal but opposite pitch. His laugh pushed back the dread.

"Yes. A true welcome. Let us hope both peoples have also learned to speak it," Shree returned, his own speech a drumming croak that reelicited A.H.'s grin.

He was about to ask Shree if he saw an entry when he let his hand rest on the upper curve. The cool, hard material—it lacked the brittleness of glass—was instantly warm and pliant. Before he could shift his weight and remove the hand, an opening thinned beneath the palm and expanded outward so rapidly that he lost balance and fell through it. He was startled enough to call out; the stuff had responded like living skin! But he truncated the cry when he landed comfortably on his right side on top of one of the pillows. Rolling back upright he looked out at Shree's whitened amusement and muttered, "Apparently one has to knock first."

The Primary bent to join him on the silky cushions, the opening shut, and the car curved around. Suddenly their pillows came hissing to life with the same rapidity as the egg's shell, swelling up and shrinking to pneumatically form-fit them. A.H. felt he was being groped. It was nearly obscene and he felt relief when the adjustments stopped . . . almost. Now he felt like a child, feet unable to touch the carpeted floor of the egg. Shree, of course, had just the right dimensions. Other than size, however, it was the most accommodating and comfortable support he'd ever . . . cooperated with.

From the smooth quiet ride, propulsion must have been electric. He answered his next question himself: they used wheeled transports over short ground distances because it was cheaper and more maintenance-free than floating around at the same one meter on grav mesh. The dash readouts and spoked control wheel were inert, indicating the car was being internally operated as suspected.

They crossed onto the yellow border, and A.H. watched one of the pylons approach on his right. He nudged Shree and pointed to it. The Hhronkan looked from the enlarging crowd to him to register puzzlement with gray circles on his cheeks. Then he nodded in human fashion. They both realized the need for simple distraction from the tension of this moment of first contact. Still, these structures were odd. Even the rectanguloid metallic outbuildings lay within their perimeter, leaving only the landing strip outside. Ten to fifteen stories tall, they tapered up slightly and were not cylindrical but six-sided. The closest appeared to be built of cream-painted metal, like a street flood. There were no other details except for the apical "antenna." It was tree-shaped and had a metal trunk where it attached to the pylon, but the many delicate upper branches were transparent, gleaming like fine crystal. As they passed the column, he saw the pylon's base sat in a wide, deep well. Approach to it was impossible without some walkway being placed across this moat. All the antennae were directed inward toward the city's center along the wide boulevards that began at the pylon wells. They marched out of sight in both directions along the bright yellow road. With such orientation the antennae could not be for intercity comm, and so many shouldn't be needed for intracity duty. In fact they couldn't serve any function he knew of. He twisted back for a final look, and the vague feeling of aberration he'd just noticed became definite.

It was an intrusion of his Self so strong it also manifested at his sense's edge. There was a slight tingling like charges gathering on hairs and a luminescence visible as glowing indigo only to his peripheral eye. Over all palled the distant murmuring of crowds—not from the approaching material one, nor was it his indigenous cochlear buzz. It was the subliminal evocation of restless ghosts, as those omnipresent in a vacant forest or in a shell absconded from its shore. In shock he turned to see Shree's skin hidden! So it was real, and as noxious to the Master, *baasa* as to his Pupil. What could cause such phenomena? Shree held a worm-finger athwart his full lips. Only then did A.H. bargain to resist the tingling, mumbling, indigo fog and accustom himself to it with an act of will. He concentrated on reality beyond and was rewarded with a diminution to tolerable levels.

Ahead he heard Hhronkan music flares begin. This electronically synthesized sound was totally familiar, if not pleasing, to him. Most Hhronka expressed admiration for Tchaikovsky, and their public salutes echoed this kind of swooping scale and rhythm. For him, however, it always resembled action themes from holo operas, the giddy kind for teenies, where characters fought with swords at two paces when they still wore lasers that could crisp each other at a hundred.

The car slowed into a wide turn to bring it beside the irregularly arrayed group. Behind it and above, a huge display wall scintillated with multicolored patterns abstracted to create emotions of joy, triumph, and cordiality as shown on Hhronkan skin. They were being given first-rank honors. The two dozen Hhronka were ordinary in body, but extraordinarily costumed. That was the appropriate term for the spectrum of color and cut they wore. From solid black and gray to abstract pastel swirls, from full trousers and jackets to mere serapes. Many even had four-toed shoes and decorated themselves with jewelry, a rarity among Hhronka. Gone, except for a few variants, were the uniforms of Meethlah and Orrtaan.

When no openings appeared in the egg's shell, Shree palmed one on his side. As they left the car, the music peaked and died at its unseen source. Right on cue, two separated from the crowd and bobbed forward, seemingly well adapted to the heavier gravity, for they wore no grav belts. The male who stiffly palmed Shree's chest was a bit shorter than he, with a brow ridge so slight he resembled a noseless human. The Orrtaan version he wore was more like full-length pajamas, loose and of dark gray silk-smooth weave.

"Give . . . as you require," he said clumsily in a loud, deep voice without display.

He was echoed by the female, who greeted A.H. similarly. Her gender was not ascertainable from her sleeveless knee-length tunic of coarse chartreuse fiber. The Hhronka did not tag sex by color or apparel, and the custom still maintained among the Kmeaan Hhronka. But to his experienced eye, her less angular facial structures, closer-set eyes, lower ear pores, and purring hiss of voice were unmistakable. She stood nearly as tall and broad as her companion and pressed A.H.'s chest firmly enough to make him brace his legs.

He and Shree returned the greetings, and he saw the Primary's skin flatten, then wrinkle, as he struggled to avoid hiding his skin and revealing his deep emotion.

The two backed a pace and the male said, "Primary Shree Shronk, Director Krieder. From the hearts of all the core-families we welcome you and both your peoples to Teffht and Atuum-uleen. I am Durren Gar; this is Baay Liifan. We are to guide you during your orientation to our city and speed the process of enabling the rest of your crews to join you here."

When they both stared a moment at him, he snaked both arms in mild apology. "Please forgive my speech. The language transcription will require further active training between us for fluency in the Hhronkan of our forbearers."

Apparently these Hhronka had made some research progress in the last 45,000 years, A.H. realized. The best that human–Hhronkan encephalearners could do was bolster synaptic circuits to speed the process. There was no direct information transcribing yet possible.

Shree replied, "Your speech is quite adequate. But we are both overwhelmed at truly finding you, the children of our lost Children. Many of us doubted this."

"We are most joyous over your coming," returned Gar without displaying or hiding his skin.

By this time A.H. had sufficiently overcome his excitement and self-consciousness to recognize the scrutiny he was receiving. Although he appreciated that these Hhronka had never seen a human, the intensity of their expected stares was unnerving. Their eyes were brushing every square inch of him. And since they showed no displays, he couldn't tell if it was out of curiosity, fear, malice, calculation, or any combination of these. His gaze drifted back to Baay Liifan, and he saw the same intensity there. The peripheral view of Shree's query circles brought him back.

"Did all three of our expeditions arrive here safely?" he asked Durren Gar.

A.H. sighed within. Shree, abandoning their agreement to merely observe, was wasting no time seeking out Feeahra's fate.

Gar paused only momentarily. "Yes. All three arrived."

Shree's legs straightened up, then sagged back a little in relaxation. He exaggerated his perusal of the onlookers. "And where are the Kmeaans . . . that is, the native Teffhtans? We had anticipated meeting them also."

For the first time they saw a display. Gar's face flecked with a wobbly uneven whiteness that might have indicated humor, but there was no definite Hhronkan pattern. It quickly fled.

"They are here. Now please allow us to give you a brief excursion through Atuum; then we will take you to your residence, where we will speak at greater length."

The two guides moved around them toward the car, and suddenly the official welcome was unofficially over. The crowd casually dispersed without further interest in the strangers, wandering off in several directions toward the city. A.H. and Shree hesitated in startled confusion, then followed their hosts to return to the egg car's rear cushions. Liifan took the role of driver and Gar faced backward as they rolled onto the nearby black radial boulevard.

It was soon evident Gar had indeed meant "brief." The large ovoid fairly raced nonstop in a zigzag path, first inward along a radial, then around a concentric for several blocks before turning in or out again. Ground traffic on the unmarked and unsignaled streets was nonexistent, and the few Hhronka they saw traveled on foot along broad sidewalks. The other comparisons and contrasts with a terran city or the manufacturing districts of Wlaatan towns were inevitable and rather disappointing to A.H. The simplicity made the scene barren: no hydrants, traffic signals, display screens, marquees, ads, waste receptacles, trash, or utility lines. Of course, this only attested to the likelihood of Atuum's total subterranean automaticity. But all the febrile accoutrements of societies that yet desired or required close constant interactions by live fallible beings were gone. Perhaps replaced by an ordered sterility not found even among the termites. He knew too little to judge yet. But passersby were not congregating anywhere; if they took any notice of their car, it was but a look of brief, intense curiosity, then a return to scurrying self-interest. The differences between this culture and Wlaatan grew ever greater in his mind. Had the Teffhtans really been able to influence these Hhronka to this extent or had the change been intrinsic to them all along?

Still no native Teffhtans were to be seen; perhaps they were nocturnal, or they lived in segregated areas or cities as did most humans and Hhronka on Wlaata. The buildings rose as high as twenty-five or thirty stories and were closely bunched, often stretching entire blocks without alleys or any other separation. The few windows or other openings only added to the cliff-canyon effect. Some facings appeared to be stone, some concrete, and one type, interspersed every three blocks, was an iridescent whitish glassy material that broke up the burgeoning morning light like diffraction gratings into cubist rainbows that pendulum-swung down at them as they sped by.

It recalled the confetti cascades he'd been forced to smile through on first return to Earth after helping join humanity with the Hhronka. But this was clearly no parade. If any of the beings they saw even knew who they were, it was of only momentary interest to them. He wasn't disappointed, but quite puzzled. How could they all be as nonchalant about this visitation as they appeared to be?

Overhead, an occasional oblong wingless flyer was occulted by a building roof as it landed. He interrupted Gar's droning description of Atuum's obvious superficial simplicity and invisible supporting mechanization.

"How do the people move within the city?" he managed in simple Hhronkan, substituting synonyms for words he couldn't pronounce.

Gar looked at him for a breath. "There is an underground system beneath the streets, an electric one with grav-flux suspension that also handles nonliving traffic as well. Surface cars such as this are now used only for rapid inspections and repairs at ground level, or for special occasions like this. Massive transport is actually not needed. This is yet another consequence of our total automation. No one *need* work at daily jobs; indeed, such occupation is a privilege earned. Common necessary toil is left entirely to dependable stationary or mobile robots on the lower levels. So no living work force is shuttled back and forth. We are left completely free. This is similar to current conditions on Wlaata. Correct, Shree?"

The Primary flarred open his nasal pore and shut his eyes in an effort to quell mild irritation at the slight in his title. Gar seemed unperturbed by this, and A.H. wondered if these laconic descendants were even aware of "ancient" courtesies and such telltales of display.

Shree said, "We on Wlaata have always felt satisfaction in doing some necessary work ourselves. Also we have found machines to be less dependable than predictable."

Gar's manner, incredibly to A.H., became almost haughty. "I for one would never consent to doing anything a machine can do as well or better. This is why I am a historian; the only one in Atuum, and one of the few on Teffht. Is this not the freedom for which our ancestors left Wlaata and chanced what they would find here?"

A.H. now noticed how taut Gar's skin was. It stretched like parchment over the sharp corners at the ends of his low brow ridge, crinkling when he spoke. And his cat-eyes were lit by a fire whose coldness he'd never before seen in any Hhronkan. It held a focused intensity, the pent energy of a driven mind.

"This is partly so," Shree capitulated as softly as his croaking voice allowed. "They also came to join with the Teffhtans, one sentience to another."

Shree's next statement was cut short as he saw the sudden

change in the cityscape. They'd covered about half the disk of city in a jagged semicircle and had reached the waterfront. The dense rectangularity was now replaced by infiltrating canals, lagoons, bridges, and irregular clutches of low, sand-colored, rounded structures reiminscent of Hhronkan homes. The wild familiar randomness fronting on the water cheered both visitors. Still, the black radial streets sliced through. Out one he glimpsed the ocean and saw a pylon standing in the water like a tall buoy. So Atuum was completely encircled by them. He had an intense need to smell the sea, to compare it with Earth's and Wlaata's.

Gar was lecturing on at high momentum, like Droom. "This is the oldest part of Atuum, built in a combination native–Hhronkan design. These canals supply our water, some of our energy, and much recreation. We hold this area as a shrine to our past; residence here is a treasured privilege. That is why you will be housed here."

These relics proved the natives had been as disorganized as Hhronka. Perhaps the compacted city had simply evolved to save space, A.H. thought.

"How do you open this for air?" he asked, pressing at the clear material without effect this time.

"For safety, it cannot be opened that way while in motion," answered Liifan. She touched a switch on the high dash. At first A.H. noticed no change in the shell. Then hundreds of pinhead bubbles appeared at the rear and nose of the transparency and spread open to admit the odd sweet-salt pungency he craved. He actually chuckled in unexpected delight as the hushed current brought an odor of brackish limestone.

They turned off a radial into a rare dead-end street and stopped smoothly before a large, humpbacked, tan-green stone mass that sat at the terminus. It was isolated far from surrounding building clusters by open land covered with raked white and black gravel. They left the car and crunched over the loose stuff. Without a curb to retain it, the pebbles had spilled in runnels onto the street. A.H. was again refreshed by the sea breeze from the right.

However, the mumbling-tingling, luminescent fog still beckoned with distress—when he allowed it to. He must analyze with Shree at the earliest possible moment.

The residence was externally similar to the Hhronkan, an irregular collection of lumps, at least seventy-five meters long overall and twenty meters at its highest lump, greenish tan except where dark gray weathering streaks netted the sides of the rough surface. He fantasized a multiply pregnant dirigible flopping here bellyup to incontinently deliver its litter of balloons by eruptive caesarian, the whole scene frozen to stone midbirth. As the four entered a high arched opening, the only one visible, he slapped the solid material. It felt exactly like well-consolidated fine-grained sandstone, as if one enormous rock had been placed here, then carved. But, of course, natural sandstone couldn't have resisted erosion for long.

The doorless entry became a dim, eight-pace tunnel that suddenly widened into a large cavernous court, a small perforation above admitting light from the clearing sky. It was supposed to be one big cave! An ancient sea grotto, complete with pools and aquatic plants, stretched erratically left and right, above and below. Several steps from where they stood, a broad, shallow, plant-bearded pond lay in a cupped recess of the floor. The clear water reflected the skylight as it poured over the distal brim to the right into a chain of lesser tarns, each growing deeper and darker. The lowest abutted and flowed under the court's wall. These produced around them a horseshoe-shaped dry floor that was irregular in width but level. Three shadowy ovals exited the court at knee height across the water from them, and two more pierced the wall at he ends of the horseshoe to the right. Another set of openings, in various sizes and aglow with reflected daylight, pocked the sloped wall to their left and three meters up. It was all very Disney, obviously built to look as though it hadn't been . . . and totally non-Hhronkan.

Because the skylight opening was so much smaller than the volume it fed, the court would remain glittery but gloomy. Also, rivulets seeped down the stone on all sides from the apical hole, crossing the worn floor to feed the ponds. Brown chains of tiny plants hung like bead strings from the gray drip tracks etched into the pseudostone. The thick brine smell began to nauseate him. The day had only slightly warmed, and he shivered once inside his damp shell of clothes. If he hadn't been cleaned of all the bacteria and viruses the human body normally carried, he'd probably have pneumonia after two days of this soggy sandcastle. Again he hoped the local bugs were benign as well.

Appraising their wonder and confusion, Gar said, "The Teffhtans are amphibians and modeled their dwellings to resem-

ble the ancestral sea caves where they evolved. Some of us also
find this stimulating, however. Your luggage has already arrived. I will show you your rooms; you may eat if you wish,
then we shall talk. I trust, Shree, that you will enjoy the native
fare as we do. Your food crate is in the kitchen, Krieder. Of
course, you may sample anything you are certain will not be
poisonous."

Liifan went through a port at the court's end as Gar led
them up the wall to the left. Only when they reached the
sloping base could A.H. see the small ledges and niches that
decorated it. He guessed they served the place of the nonexistent furniture. By taking stretched steps it was possible to use
a series of niches as stairs. At the top they ducked singly
through a hole and stood on the perforated tubular cavern's
balcony that curved out of sight both ways. Gar led to the
first room, through a doorless entry to the left off the balcony.
Each lump outside was the roof of a room inside, very practical and saving of materials.

The space was globular, high-ceilinged but rather small, had
a grainy path-worn stone floor, and again was poorly lit by a
small open skylight. There was a total lack of furnishings. A
single curved ledge large enough to accommodate him as couch
or bed filled a quarter of the wall's circumference and several
tiny niches filigreed the rest. Now he understood their hosts'
instructions to bring everything they might need. And the large
white plastec crate sitting there in the center of the floor topped
by his two pieces of personal luggage held an inflatable cot, gas
lamp, small collapsible table, and enough standard camp gear to
make any place tolerable.

Gar proved he could be a sharp observer when he spoke into
A.H.'s staring silence. "It is barren. But we thought you would
prefer your own familiar possessions rather than try to fit into
Hhronkan furniture. Have I erred in this?"

A.H. looked up to shake his head at the being.

"The Teffhtans who once lived here were communal and actually lived and slept in the enclave below. This was for storage.
We have placed conventional Hhronkan furniture in your room,
Shree. And a simple kitchen is on the first floor; a toilet lies at
this balcony's end."

Gar took Shree out, leaving A.H. alone. The room smelled
of wet stone also; it gave him a lonely sensation, reminding him
of a monk's disciplined cell. In fact, the whole house had a

humorless austerity to it. He couldn't imagine the natives ever laughing here, if they laughed at all. But the place seemed to fit Gar well.

"Some privilege!" he snorted.

He was hungry, but had to prepare his own lunch since Liifan had disappeared and the planet's advanced robotics apparently didn't extend to Gar's "simple" kitchen. It was large and lay through the doorway across from the main entry next to the lowest pond. There were a few electronic conveniences for cooking, refrigerating, and utensil washing set into the gray metal counters and cupboards. And two open skylights provided a fair illumination. (What did they do at night in this house, or when it rained ... hard!?) But he had to draw water into a sink through a foot-pedal-operated tap. He'd been informed the water was distilled, and it tasted flatly like it, so he felt safe in using it. He was holding a diluted pan of soup before what he guessed was the heat plate when Liifan bobbed in.

"Do you need help?" she asked slowly.

"Yes. How do you activate this?" he responded in his pidgin Hhronkan, gesturing at the featureless box.

"Simply put the vessel on it. The farther back it is, the hotter it gets."

"Thank you." He placed it midway on the shiny white surface and went back to his food crate on the counter to extract a can of milk and a premade sandwich. She stood watching him carefully, as though she were an engineer trying to understand and memorize the motions of a machine.

"Do you mind doing this for yourself?"

The question was so unexpected, he smiled up at her passive face. "No. It makes me feel"—he couldn't say the overlaid hoot-whistle word for "at home" so he substituted—"welcome and relaxed."

Despite the surrogate, his meaning was taken exactly. She replied, "We prefer to leave the details of living to our machines, but here there is no choice. When you have eaten I will show you the very modern comp terminal where we do historical research."

As he removed the sterile vac-wrap from the sandwich, he realized he might use her new talkativeness, "You are Durren Gar's co-worker?"

She hesitated. "His student and ... assistant."

Hot fog was already unfolding from the soup so he went to slide the bowl-pan to the plate's front edge with a spoon. "Did I understand his description of your . . . decision-making apparatus? It's almost unchanged from the Wlaatan?" He'd never get the grunt-hiss for "government" out correctly.

"Yes. We are a direct democracy with city, regional, and world levels of issues. Emergency committees chosen from the eldest in core-families can be formed when required. Actually, the authority and importance of the cores has lessened greatly during the past few millennia. Today they are more figurative than operative. We have little need; our society has stabilized so that few truly new situations arise requiring voting or disciplinary decisions."

He halted in pulling open the top of the milk. "You mean everyone does what they're—should do?"

"Yes."

Yellow alert, he thought. This was sounding more familiar, but less plausible, and so, less truthful with every dialogue. "But wasn't our arrival thought emergency enough to convene such a committee? Are you and Durren Gar the highest authority available to us?"

"The people who met you at the freighter port were that committee. It was dissolved after the welcome because it was obvious you mean no aggression toward us, and we two can satisfactorily act as liaison."

Logical. But it left no others to deal with or get answers from than these two.

"We have learned very little about you humans," she began, then added hurriedly, "Of course, you are welcome to live here on Teffht along with the Wlaatans. But we are curious. For instance, do you truly sleep nightly? We have adapted to Teffht's seventeen-hour rotation period with such habit to avoid circadian lag."

Wlaatan Hhronka rarely slept unless sick or injured, usually resting in a reduced state for several hours. Although it seemed an odd beginning question, he nodded. "Yes. We sleep three to five hours a night. Tell me, where exactly do the natives—"

Abruptly she cut off his question. "Excuse me; I must go. As soon as you are finished, we would like to speak with you in the enclave."

He decided talking with one of these nearly displayless Hhronka was even more unnerving than doing so with a human who was always deadpanned and monotoned. He couldn't tell if Liifan had become irritated, fearful, discourteous, or simply exasperated by his inept pronunciation. But she was surely gone, and without showing him that research terminal. A highly mercurial person.

He ate quickly and returned to his room, with toileting as excuse, and held a murmured conversation with *Wind* on his wafer radio. If he was being monitored by hidden sensors, the watchers might think he was merely meditating. They could already know both visitors were in constant contact with the colony; detection of their transmitters was easy, if desired. This was fine, too. What their hosts would *do* about it would at least tell them something real about this society. As he explained to the watch officer, he felt they would get no help from Gar and Liifan. They had to seek answers on their own.

After he replaced the wafer into the pocket of his briefs, he sat a minute—a true meditation to tally the day. Novelty had come with such speed he hadn't had time to reflect. Again he recognized an inner prickling of excitement, one with no relationship to the mumbling-tingling, luminescent fog effect, though it too was here. This was endemic to his character, elicited fully by this day, but building ever since their departure nearly a year (!) ago. *This* was what he'd tried to explain to Joan, among other things, that night Shree had come to urge this trip. All his lusts had been reborn! He *needed* this uncertainty, this challenge, this danger. Was it addictive, and had he suppressed the addiction all these years? He didn't care—he was alive! In an odd inversion, his Mr. Hyde was now thoroughly entombed within the good Jekyl. He loved Joan with full intensity again; his children were closer than ever; his mind steamed with power. Nothing was beyond him! His walk was jocund, and he leaped the last two meters into the "enclave" court.

Shree and Bay were still chatting when he joined them, taking a seat facing them in a deep niche near the first pond. He smiled and kept a casual tone as he said in English, "If we don't start getting some sensible readout from these two soon, we'll have to stall them till tonight and do a little snooping on—"

Liifan broke into his warning with her stilted Hhronkan. "Durren Gar has asked that you both speak Hhronkan as much as possible. And, for scientific interest, we would like to

quickly incorporate a working ability of the human language—
Eenglis?—into our translation comps."

Subtlety was not a Kmeaan Hhronkan strength, A.H. decided. Shree explained the structure of human larynx and the
resulting difficulty in pronouncing Hhronkan. "We will be
happy to supply transcomp data as soon as you can give us a
comm channel sufficient to handle it. Now the only frequency
we know gets through your interference blanket is for your
drones, and its signal density is too low for this purpose."

"It will be done today," she replied.

There really was no way to stall on that, A.H. decided. Durren Gar bobbed out of the opening to the right of the kitchen to
join them without greeting. A.H. tensed involuntarily. If Liifan
was mercurial, Gar was calculating, though he did do most of
the talking—and too much of that. They should have brought
Droom along to counterattack. He would like to see the two
slug it out tongue-to-tongue. Now the historian wore a long gray
tunic with elbow-length sleeves like Liifan's green one. A.H.
settled back onto the gritty surface, ready for another uninfor-
mative lecture. At least the niche's curved design fit him as well
as it did the Hhronka.

Gar stared directly at them for several seconds. "We want to
plan with you in detail your move onto Teffht. We have selected
an area near the city and will help you construct—"

A.H. raised a hand; his jocularity was fast waning in the face
of this sudden shift. Apparently it was time for a direct approach of their own. "Durren Gar, before we allow the balance
of our peoples to come to the surface, or even decide we want to
do this, we must understand several things. First, what are the
reasons that underlie your enormous efforts at total concealment? Why do you and the Teffhtans wish to continue to hide
your existence? For that matter, where are these natives? We
have not seen a single one. Originally the Teffhtans themselves
broadcast their message to *attract* attention, at least from Sol
system and all the other star systems on the line between here
and there. Why did your ancestors from Wlaata's expeditions
cooperate in this concealment?"

Shree's white ring of agreement drew their looks. "This silence created a great sorrow that continues to this day."

Gar's face displayed dark bars of so indeterminate a pattern
they couldn't be sure whether it represented regret or umbrage,
but his words supported the latter. "Very well, since you insist. I

will explain fully. There are no native Teffhtans now, nor any of their records, remaining."

Both Shree and A.H. sat up in shock. They felt the immediate loss of the opportunity for new interspecies communication less than the strain of another swift turn from Gar.

Shree protested with definite exclamation bars on his face. "But you told us during the welcome they were here!"

"I meant their memory lives, with historians such as us, through legend and the few surviving records our ancestors made in that time. The last millennia have not been peaceful ordered ones; much has been lost."

His dark waves of depression were the truest display they had seen from the being.

"As you surely know, Shree, when the original expedition from Wlaata arrived at Teffht, they expected to be met by a technologically advanced civilization. But this was only partly true. The natives were capable of creating the interference network, spacecraft, and nuclear weapons, and of course an interstellar transmitter. But they had no control over gravity, and repulsor film was a mystery to them. In many ways we were already far superior."

"How could that be when they sent us the unified field theory message to begin with!" said Shree, gray pulsed bars making the words exclamatory.

"The Teffhtans did send the message toward Sol—because it was most like Kmeaa and gave evidence of having planets. But they were not the message's creators and understood little of it."

They sat speechless at yet another twist in the tale as Gar went stubbornly on. "This was the cause for their deep fear, for the interference network: about a thousand years earlier, this system was invaded from without by a vastly superior species, whose ultimate origin, even their physical nature, remains unknown. In the resulting war, the Teffhtan home world, the third planet, was destroyed along with the ruthless aliens. No doubt you surveyed its barren surface. The remnant people moved to this world, but carried with them the dread this enemy might one day send other forces, large enough this time to overwhelm them. This has not happened, but indeed it may.

"They managed to capture one of the enemy craft with its library, finally decoding the language. But the engineering ability eluded them; it required power sources and materials that still cannot be produced here. They then broadcast the message and invitation at Sol—only briefly revealing themselves—in hopes that, if intelligence dwelled there, it might aid them with its science against the future return of these creatures. It was simply a cry for help. In a tragic sense, the reverse occurred." Gar paused to rasp several breaths and check his audience's reaction; it was completely noncommittal.

"Once the first Wlaatan expedition had come to this world, they were not permitted to send out any communications. After all, the Teffhtans had what they believed they required; further transmissions might only endanger their anonymity. You could say we Hhronka became captives of the natives. Our ancestors were continually guarded, but they and the next two groups of colonists were given huge tracts of their own land here and allowed, indeed encouraged, to live and research as they pleased. In a sense both peoples had most of what they desired. But in time their fear became ours and we have maintained the jamming cover and the robot patrols that you met. When you suddenly appeared at our system's edge, we, of course, did not know your origin. Fortunately we decided to check before destroying you."

"Then what happened to the Teffhtans?" asked Shree.

"Basically, we outcompeted them. They were amphibians, tied to the sea for breeding ritual and spawning, and would not leave it. For a time we tried to help them adapt artificially from direct reliance." He looked around the house's inner walls. "These are trial homes we built for them so they could attempt to wean themselves to mate and breed here rather than in the limited number of caves at the shore. We offered to build whole cities like this anywhere they chose, but they refused. We showed them how to restructure their genes to reproduce artificially without the ocean. They were insulted. Very firm traditionalists, they were. Technology and the culture that produces it, go together. To accept our aid also meant accepting our attitudes, something they hadn't foreseen before our arrival. When they understood survival entailed a certain loss of identity, they balked. And it is a universal law that when two species' niches overlap partly or entirely, one or both either go extinct or evolve into a new form, away from competition."

Or they're mature enough to mingle and derive a new sociologically hybrid "species," A.H. reflected, which was exactly what he'd hoped would happen on Wlaata between humans and Hhronka, though the idea seemed doomed.

"Over the millennia we remained on land and grew into a worldwide population, while they stayed at the shores and dwindled. Near the end, when they realized their fate, several militant groups tried to destroy all of us, but succeeded only in hastening their end, and obliterating most of their own physical culture. I most strongly hope this satisfies all your doubts and we can begin with your people's location here."

They sat in awe of the being's prosaic manner. A.H. could not stop his grin as he said to Shree calmly in English, "That's the rankest compost pile I have ever smelled, not even internally consistent. A fairy tale to coerce children. Real science fiction."

"Agreed," replied Shree, looking back at their host. "But I think we had better make them believe we believe it."

A.H. struggled to quickly find some credible way to stall their determined host from switching to jailer. Only one occurred, disquieting but nearly failsafe. "True. So tell him this: we're satisfied; we want to bring down another shuttle tomorrow with fresh supplies and a small crew to help us begin surveying a townsite. Our peoples have to vote on it, but we're sure they'll want to remain here. And our own families will be this next group." To Shree's glance he said, "We can use their help. And they'll be no safer on *Wind* should real fighting start —a fact I hope he doesn't think we understand, since including our own relatives will ease his suspicions that we aren't really convinced. I'd give anything to tele this one now, but I'm still sure that's a talent we shouldn't reveal. And he could be a *baasa* himself. So give it your best."

While Shree hooted and hissed, A.H. smiled and stared at Gar. What he saw in the being's eyes evaporated the dregs of his euphoria. Tonight; it must be tonight, he decided. Tomorrow the people he loved would be coming into the eye of a storm that could quickly destroy them all.

Over five hours had passed since he had, so he decided to take advantage of the lull as the meeting dissolved and Shree went with Gar to call *Wind*. Hoping the sanitary facilities weren't as parsimonious as the furniture, he went up to the balcony toilet indicated by Gar. It was a three-crapper, typically Hhronkan. Either they had replaced the original native type or those beings hadn't used indoor plumbing. Amphibians would naturally have combined bathing, mating, and toileting in the same enclave ponds. Hhronkan anatomy precluded sitting for elimination; both sexes simply dipped bowlegged over a shallow stool. And they were very casual about it; no stalls separated the row of wide gray metal cups. Across from them were two pedal-operated lavatories with polished crystal mirrors. Each stool also had a pedal at its left and right sides, one to flush and one to create a cleansing spray.

As he leaned over the first stool and tugged open the stikseam of his fly he realized he'd held it too long. His bladder was too full for easy release. He'd have to concentrate and force out a bit at a time until the stinging pain abated and the seized sphincter relaxed. How it had once streamed out; now it only dribbled. With a sigh he felt the tight pressure in his rectum that could no longer be denied either. He had dreaded this from the start of today's mission. No matter how important, exciting, and romantic even a legend's life, he still had to secrete and excrete once in a while. And unlike the Hhronka, he had to sit down. He considered the portable stool in his room, but then the warning signal became acute.

Accepting the inevitable, he hurriedly ripped open his pants and stripped off them and his shorts. Backing up slowly he settled onto the lidless lip. The cold bite of metal made him jump, then he managed to balance there. The rim was so low he couldn't get his legs under him, and he had to spraddle them forward and reach out and back to grip the cup's rounded edge with both hands like an inverted crab.

Naturally he had just begun when he heard feet rasp along the balcony and Shree charged through the door. A.H. had seldom seen him so perturbed. His skin was alternately flickering with dark bars of puzzlement, rippling with distress, or smoothing as he managed to hide it again. He held a small metal jug in one hand as he went without apology straight to the second stool. Lifting aside his robe with an outer palm, he finger-spread his thick genital flaps, freeing his stiff organ to fire-hose the empty cup, and stepped down heavily on the right pedal.

Over the rim flush, he finally looked at A.H. and croaked in English, "More mysteries! I did not come here for more mysteries!"

Evidently Shree's period of joy over finding these offshoot

Hhronka was also past. At least he spoke English; they could be monitoring them here as well. Shree paused to tilt a drink from the flask.

"I can accept their lack of decorum, even of simple courtesy: do not bother to introduce the core-family Judges, if indeed that is who those—I felt like a scavenger *naagli* on display! That first one I spoke with in space was shocked and happy to see us. But these greeters were merely curious, then . . . we were completely ignored! Very well. Have only *two* prepared who can speak to us in our language, effectively isolating us. Very well. Drop our titles before we have touched even twice. Avoid answers to direct questions, or make asking them impossible without rudely interrupting. I can accept the virtual loss of patterned facial display, and the adoption of more individual dress, along with the language changes. All inevitable, perhaps, with the length of time involved.

"But this city! It is truly hideous, lifeless! I could not breathe in that first section. The people are practically rubbing skins, they are packed so closely. And can you imagine Hhronka voluntarily using an *underground* transport? Krieder, I find it difficult even to comprehend the total disappearance of the *ooural,* a fear so deep it has been inherited on Wlaata through over three thousand generations! Yet this concoction of Gar's is surely the finish!"

A.H. relaxed his abdominal muscles as a fart popped and a final soft cigar slid out. "I also noticed you felt the fog effect just after we landed."

Shree's cat-eye smote him balefully. "You had to bring that up, too, I suppose. Of course I did, at the same time as you. As though I had drunk three liters of your abominable scotch! But it is more an itch than a tingle, and I see no fog."

A.H. started. "We don't experience the same effects . . . it might not be a strictly sensory phenomenon, as I thought."

Shree had no patience for this speculation. "Yes, and maybe it is simply an effect of this new environment. Perhaps we will become acclimated. There are more important queries."

A.H. nodded at the flask. "What are you drinking?"

"Leenawah," the Primary answered after taking another gulp. He began pacing the floor as he spoke. "At least they have managed to propagate some of the more worthwhile Wlaatan organisms the expeditions carried. When I told Gar—does *he* have a title other than 'historian'?—I would be sleeping on the

roof of this *dungeon,* he provided the bottle...seemed disappointed you cannot use it, too."

He smiled into the cup rim between his knees. The berry juice was the same as terran tea for Shree; he'd get drunk fast, but it would only make A.H. pee. The thought urged him to tilt up a bit more to ensure hitting the rim inside. Since the Primary was echoing his own doubts, he chose the opposite tack.

"As you once said, in 30,000 years many changes can take place. They've had a new environment and outside influence from the natives. We humans affected you on Wlaata as well."

Shree weaved a path from the middle sink to the stool. "This is also one of my major questions. Look at the results of our union: advancement, growth, a reaching out. Yet here we see withdrawal, shrinkage, paranoid isolation, and a relatively unchanged tochnelogy!"

The *leenawah* was slurring his speech already, and his bob definitely had more swoop.

A.H. remembered the egg car's shell. "Oh, I don't think it's that bad. The people seem comfortable; no one has to work, we're told; there's material plenty—"

"Where will *we* be in 30,000 years, using the complete understanding of the unified field theory! Droom already speaks about limitless energy from ordinary matter conversion, while they still use fusion here. We could have true force screens replacing matter surfaces; personal force fields —what would *that* do to war and crime? Even electronic enhancement of the mind itself to create *baasa* of everyone. Someday anyone may be able to link directly to another or to computers, sentient or not. Perhaps create a colonial sewermind from many individuals. Material wish fulfillment, or even immortality of a sort, if you desire such a thing. All within the foreseeable future. But why not *here, now?* Advanced robots, bubbles in car tops, and data transcription directly to the brain are not fantastic progress! Why no breakthrough like Umar and Droom's? Indeed, as on Wlaata, total automation might have slowed change, but this is stagnation on a far vaster scale. They make us on Wlaata seem wildly experimentive by comparison! If this has been the influence of the native Teffhtans, what kind of creature could they have been? Almost I am glad they are gone...regret we ever found them, or they us...Feeahra's children."

Absorbed by Shree's plaintive if muzzy soliloquy, A.H. started to rise. He pushed off with his hands to get his feet onto the floor, but his right came down on the stool's left douche pedal. Instantly a hard cold corona of water sprayed up at him from the top ring of nozzles inside the rim. The shock made his foot slip off the depressed plate; he lost balance and fell backward into the cup's center and his own cold mushy wastes. As he struggled disgustedly to latch onto the rim and pull himself up like an opening bloom of limbs, Shree seemed to really recognize what he was doing for the first time since entering.

With complete earnestness he asked gently, "Are you not supposed to flush it first?"

Chapter 7

After the incident in their first R-ball game, Umar had tried to ignore Renata, and she'd accepted this, if reluctantly. His naive vulnerability had only increased her infatuation and evoked her rudimentary protective instinct. But in the months since translation, her continued overtures had finally convinced him his guilt was as unnecessary as her forgiveness: she did not feel irreparably soiled by his clumsy attack; in fact, she was attracted to him in spite of this (and in his mind never *because* of it). His cuticle-chewing had ceased, and they had begun playing regularly at both R-ball and those other innocuous games by which friendships are created and often bypassed to more intimate but less loving relationships.

The day the two envoys fell down to Teffht, Renata invited Umar and Twee for a few cutthroat games to still her worry. This would never be completely fair. Hronka were possessed of faster reactions than humans. Add to this their greater average size and extreme suppleness—even without hip and shoulder ball sockets their jointless bodies netted out far more flexible—and they would usually win any brief athletic competition. Their weakness was in their tubular insectlike respiration that could never match mammalian lungs for gas exchange. Once their oxygen debt built up, it took far longer to repay. Without stamina, Hhronka often relied on a languid play pace to mete out energy reserves just fast enough to win or at least gain sufficient advantage to stay ahead when they tired and the human opponent kept on attacking. Hhronka always won the 100-meter dash and always lost the 10,000-meter run. And in R-ball one Hhronka always played two humans in an eleven-point cutthroat game.

Floating on the soft pain from the exercise, they sat ringed by a small circular booth in a dim corner of the "CNS Lounge," one of the two human recreational-substances areas on the rim. Although Hhronka didn't normally use drugs as social lubricants, Twee stiffly sipped cold tea with Umar while Renata went to the bar to tap her third double scotch and water. They were still silent when she returned with the short clinking glass clamped in her hand, trying to figure why there should be tension between the two.

From the first, Twee had been cool toward the Teheranian. She wasn't certain how much Droom's lukewarm opinion of her mathematician co-worker had influenced him—she was such a flap mouth!—but Renata wanted them to become as close friends as she and Twee were. She was yet of an age when approval by those nearest was important, even for pursuance of the infatuation Umar represented.

She bent to Twee and patted his warm chest gently, smelling his new-leather odor. "Oh, come on, Gumby. We had to hone you down first, like always. Don't be a drudge," she said with a smile. It had required more than words to explain the nickname she had given him when they were both quite young. In her cinema collection was a set of tapes of a stop-action 'toon character made of tan clay called "Gumby," moderately popular a century and a half ago and resembling Hhronka in an abstract way. He had never objected to this, even when she'd attempted to explain what "cute" meant.

His skin stayed open, and he droned, "I am not drudging. You won fairly."

She sat next to him and reached up to lock her arm around his warm torso. "Then let's get looser." Already feeling lightheaded because she wanted to be, she said to Umar, "You sure you won't try one of these half-'n-halfs? Pops says it's a great way to unscrew your bolt, and I agree."

He patronized her with a smile. "No, thank you again. We Muslims know God has forbidden us to misuse any food or drink to our detriment. Purity of body and purity of soul are closely related."

Her eyes sought the ceiling. "Umar! Sometimes you make your religion sound like a straitjacket! We also accept the wisdom of 'all things in moderation,' and we say 'cleanliness is next to godliness'!" She lilted her heavy brows. "But as for me: one person's detriment can be another's bolt-unscrewer, and we all need our bolts unscrewed periodically."

Twee, obviously affected by the tea, issued a splotchy, misshapen, white, humor display and then broke into the repartee. "Your father's report does have us all worried. I too had hoped for some quick answers and the meeting of the descendants of my mother and sister. Now it appears these Hhronka do not want to cooperate, and this makes our fathers' task more difficult—and dangerous."

Like P.C., Twee saw through her facades to the whole truth, without *baas* they swore. She stirred her drink with a finger and mused that being nonhuman had the advantage of greater objectivity when judging human actions and motives, and vice versa of course.

The Hhronkan twisted both arms so his "upper" thumbs pointed down and began shoving his tea glass back and forth with his outer palms. "P.C. told me during this shift Captain Mowry has again urged the committee to take the fighters from storage and prepare them—"

"What!" Renata lifted up from the soft brush of the booth's maroon velveteen upholstery. "Wouldn't the Kmeaans sensor that as a hostile act? And what good would twenty-four Rocs do against a flock of those drones, or surface-launched missiles, or whatever they might have?"

Twee halted his play with the glass to look at her. "We have had the axle lasers autotargeted on the two guarding drones and the upper atmosphere since we arrived. Their sensors have surely read this. Actually, from your father's report, I believe they would never attempt to destroy us. No, they seem to want us all on the surface—for some very good reason. Rather, the shuttles could be used to rescue our fathers as a last resort."

Her mouth opened slightly in understanding, and her head nodded into her drink. Umar, who had been staring at Twee since he first spoke, now knitted his brows.

"You feel true kinship with these Hhronka though they are removed from your blood by almost 70,000 Earth years?"

As gray arcs of mild surprise rose on his cheeks, Twee put matching human inflection into his voice, a sign of accommodation Renata noted with pleasure. "Of course! On Wlaata each Thaw generation of Hhronka was separated by periods twice as long as that due to the Freeze. And though these people may be changed socially and psychologically, they are yet Hhronka! They are not merely our first seeds sent to sprout elsewhere, and for me it is not only that my own family was among them. It is a continuity far more important—eternal. There is no English word for this, unless it is part of the idea of *soul.*"

Umar was nodding. "Then your people and mine have more in common than I'd ever thought. We too feel a strong bond within our clans, our families—" He faltered, and his face fractured in its composition. He had no clan; he was without family.

Renata, rapidly becoming what she considered drunk, was feeling satisfaction at the intimacy the other two were exchanging, without actually comprehending its cause. So when she saw Umar's disturbance she was determined not to let anyone's mood wreck her precarious self-fulfilled high. It was distracting her from concern for her father and adopted father, and distracting Umar in turn seemed an altogether pleasant prospect. Tonight the Sheik had returned, with his Valentino eyes. Rhett was back from the "wohaa," and she needed the masculine solace he could give. Downing the dregs of her scotch, she sucked in a melt-rounded ice cube, rolled its cold slickness around her mouth with her tongue, and popped it back into the glass. Spreading out her knees under the table, she casually rubbed her left to his right. Though he started, and her action was obvious to Twee, she maintained pressure. He blinked at her but lacked the will to shift away from the thrilling contact.

She smiled lazily, assuming her most seductive Scarlett O'Hara manner. "Speaking of closeness, I've been wanting to know how you Muslims carry on courtship. How *do* the men ever choose a woman in the first place, when they're hidden in those laundry bags?"

Umar was embarrassed that she spoke of so intimate a subject at all, especially with another present, though he was Hhronkan and was performing the desirable role of chaperon. He glanced at Twee, who calmly sipped his tea and stared at them.

"The . . . choice . . . is initially made by arrangement between the parents or close relatives," he said as he got a running start at the unavoidable reply. "However, the individuals themselves sometimes meet by chance."

"OK. But how does a man decide he wants to court her? Here's one time I see the woman has the advantage; she can at least see what he looks like. What does he go by?"

"For us, physical appearance is of secondary importance. Through conversation we first learn of each other's intelligence, warmth, character, education, vivacity. After all, it is on such qualities that a marriage really will endure and reward both people."

She was genuinely impressed. "That's probably true, or should be, but most of us count looks higher than we should in relationships. Still, doesn't beauty or handsomeness matter at all in such decisions?"

A smile bubbled onto his fine, thin lips. "Oh yes. This is a gift from Allah, to be treasured as any other luxury received without being earned."

She scrunched down one thick brow a moment, then nodded. "An interesting point of view. But exactly what is thought beautiful in your women? Do you prefer them thin or fat?"

Again the coquette, she sat straight, pressing her narrow waist to the table so her grapefruit bosom projected above it.

Umar pretended not to see the bold ploy. "In the middle, I suppose."

"And what other features do you take as luxuries?" She proudly shook her head so her burnished copper hair swept over her shoulders.

Now he grinned openly at her flagrant performance. "Yes, we find long hair of your color, a dusty sunset, to be very attractive."

"And do you find me attractive?" she asked with a barely controlled seriousness.

His dark skin flushed darker as he stared down at the table. "Please, Renata; it is unseemly to ask anyone such a thing so directly."

Having hooked the desired compliment, she bent her head demurely. "Very well, excuse me. So the two people are now interested; what's next?"

"If the woman has never been married before, consent to court must be obtained from the nearest adult male relative. But if the woman is divorced or widowed, they may arrange matters themselves. This trial period may continue as long as both wish, and consists of practically living together. But, of course, they may never be unchaperoned until married."

Pushing out her thick lips, she telegraphed her entire meaning with her eyes. "That could be quite embarrassing to the chaperon at times, couldn't it?"

He was appropriately shocked. "Any physical contact is forbidden till marriage; all else is fornication, a sin against God's Will!"

His knee withdrew, shattering her mood. The fish was off the hook. His seeming hypocrisy was especially frustrating since *he* had initiated first contact himself in a far more overt way. Pithily she said, "What? Not even a little nip and tucker? Isn't sexual compatibility also supposed to be one of the rewards of marriage?"

Umar was silent as he continued to stare at the table, shoulders sagging under her displeasure and his resurging guilt.

Even as she peevishly went on, she knew it was the alcohol talking, vindictiveness growing from her simple disappointment. "You often remind me of my plants, Umar. Their whole lives, as dirt seedlings or hung on aeroponic lattices, they have to have weight. Without it, they grow roots and stems all random ways, and the fruits get misshaped, or bitter, or screwed up somehow. 'Einstein's children' Dr. Hosung calls them. They can't tell the difference between true gravity and centrifugal inertia, yet they need one or the other constantly. But most *people* need guidance in morals only when they're children; once they grow up they can decide for themselves what's correct without having on–off dogma imposed on them in every situation for their whole lives!

"With you and your religion, everything's either right or wrong, yes–no, without the states in between that, believe me, do exist. There's a big difference between being in lust and being in love, with several stages from one to the other. How can you be certain where you are, without what you call 'fornication'?"

Not lifting his head, Umar replied firmly, "This is one function of the courtship. You will know the difference when the need for the physical becomes secondary to the feelings of love."

She leaned back onto the curving bench again. "I'm sorry. That sounds rather...naive, to me. You can have lust without love, but you can't have love without lust."

Suddenly Twee stirred, forcing his torso to bend up from its slouching relaxed position. His skin remained beige, but flattened momentarily, then roughened. He said softly, "Finding someone to love is but a happy accident. Being in love requires a conscious act of will."

He rose quickly, looped his empty glass to the table, and backed into the booth's exit niche as though driven by their surprised stares. "Excuse me. It seems you have defeated me a second time today."

As he bobbed away through the sparsely filled tables, Renata looked at Umar. "Now what in hell did he mean by that?"

Her Gumby was not exactly renowed for volatility, so his outburst left her without a quick response. She fretted in silence for almost a minute as Umar attempted to start, in as subtle a way as possible, to separate them, unchaperoned and excited as they'd become. Then she hopped up and rescued him.

"I'm sorry about my blowout. I'd better go see—"

"Of course! Please!" he quickly responded, half standing in courtesy. But she was already gone.

It took some jogging to catch Twee at the top of the stairs to the tram. The rec center was unusually empty; he saw her coming down the esplanade, the lights of its planted split levels throwing red-reflected spectra from her jostling hair. He had to wait for her; there wasn't a choice. His four-chambered heart rhythmically shook her image in his eyes.

As she stepped left onto the landing, she looked about to ensure their privacy would last. For moments neither needed to speak. "You've grown another decimeter since we left Wlaata, Gumby," she said to acknowledge that her head now came only to the top of his sloping torso. An unusual mix of gray and black snaked across his brow bulge as he bent his head to her.

"We have grown together all our lives, Ren," he responded with human solemnity, his eyes seeking hers intently. "That is why I do not find the human body extraordinary." His left hand snaked to brush back the hair from her right shoulder, an old habit for him, yet he hesitated now before doing it. "These soil-colored filaments, the stick skeleton layered with flesh, the clawed fingers and toes, the acid smell, the nearly mute skin, the face with that inconvenient hump in the center, and the expressions displayed largely by shape rather than color. I no longer even note them as many Hhronka usually do. Yet from earliest memory I have seen your individual qualities. Your white skin that seems a constant Hhronkan display of joy; the studied grace with which you move—despite your long bones; the mixture of intelligence and curiosity that drives you and the education springing from them; your pleasant, giving disposition that tempers your egoistic ambition."

She half smiled in shy awe. He seemed to be both chiding and complimenting her. He'd also done that before, but never with such intensity or intimacy.

"When you were still learning to run, I rode upon your swelling inquisitiveness, sensing its hungry ache and explosive wonder. I have known your delight and terror at first recognizing people beyond your family. I evolved with you from egocentricism to interaction, and shared the insecurity you conquered in choosing your identity. I also suffered your pain, shame, and eventual pride when menarche forced itself upon you."

Finally she blushed with chagrin and surprise. He was confessing to have secretly merged with her all her life, in violation of his *baasa* ethics! She was flattered but confused about his motives for telling her now.

"I am aware of the fuzzy weave of your happiness when free flying or watching a sunset, and the fine-grained images of your loathing when injustice or falsehood reduce the worth of those about you, and the glass-smooth hardness of your determination when challenged, even the billowing ecstasy of your passion. I am not ashamed for invading your mind; I have stolen nothing from you and aided you whenever I could. I needed the love that has grown between us; you are as close to me as P.C. in many ways, even though you cannot merge."

"And you are as much my brother, Twee," she said with a reserved chest touch, fingertips alone, to be in keeping with his growing formal tone and aloof manner.

"And so, I do not remain silent when I see a danger to you. Umar is but another infatuation, none of which have given you the love you want. Tonight he at last began to care more for you than you for him. Still he does not yield to you. Denied your desire, you may choose to ennoble this superficial emotion, but it would be false, borne more of ego than involvement. Eventually you—"

"Aren't you presuming a little too much!" she said hotly, brows joining as she blushed even more deeply. "My whole family, my *real* family, feels the same way. Yet they've kept quiet about it! Why should you have any more right than they?"

His nasal pore dilated wide, skin like ice, as he whispered hoarsely, "Do not throw away joy to this man for whom you hold nothing dear!"

He was gone before she could think of any appropriate rebuttal. A slow smile paved over her puzzlement as she continued to look down the stairs. But then utter seriousness erased both emotions, leaving her empty and anxious.

Since he was a natural *baasa*, Twee was a master of self-control. So his skin remained beige glass until he'd entered the boxy unoccupied tram car. But when it hummed away on its maglev cushion, his entire body erupted with rippling dark waves which gradually ran together, black as dried blood.

Supper had been a stilted embarrassment. Shree had continued drinking from midafternoon, so had been in a sorry state. A.H. had stopped probing the hosts. Instead, Gar had volunteered the obvious: he wasn't qualified to handle technical questions. Their scientists could deal directly with each other. A.H. promised to discuss this with Shree next day. Then Gar had spoken of the great future to be gained from cooperation. Despite his recent learning of old Hhronkan, Gar was an impressive demagogue but had revealed only his ambition and intelligence and had not reassured A.H. in the least.

Again he witnessed the intensity of Gar's stare. Though it was reminiscent of Shree's, there was also a disjointed quality hard to analyze. The best he could do was to behold Gar's face as a mask, hiding all his true features except the eyes—as if the real being peered through foveal holes and worked the puppet face.

The large meal had started at sunset, and soon the historians had excused themselves for bed. Shree had by then dissolved bubblingly into his *leenawah,* and A.H. had carried him upstairs with help from his grav belt.

Although A.H. had been chagrined, the hosts had seemed almost horrified by Shree's increasing condition, as though they were watching someone slowly slicing his own throat. Yet A.H. had not apologized for him. Shree rarely became intoxicated; his behavior simply indicated the depth of his distress over the failure of their mission to this point. He had anticipated too simple a resolution once he'd known living Hhronka were on

Teffht. This was one way of recovering from his disappointment—even if it stank of "human nature." Perhaps A.H. was rubbing off on the Primary again. He also cared about finding the truth, but at present he could be more objective . . . certainly more functional.

At midnight local time, only eight and a half hours since dawn and eleven hours since he'd awakened that day on *Wind,* he again went to the toilet. The shorter planet day had given him a monumental case of lag. Not only was his urination rhythm disrupted, but his sleep reflex had activated early. He splashed frigid water in his face and cursed uncooperative physiology. A Sta-lite would be ideal—except he didn't need the shakes later. Instead of returning to his cot, he turned on his grav belt and balanced himself with the planets' field at .3 g. Leaning out the portal into the balcony tunnel, he held his breath and listened. Not even a mouse. But a glow just at his vision's limits, not the purple tingling kind, oozed into the balcony through one of the small apertures in the enclave wall. On tiptoe he peered down at the chamber. Each of the gray drip streaks on the walls was glimmering with yellowish bioluminescence shaped like bunches of grapes. The plants. By this dim illumination he saw no movement below. He went back to his room. Why was his heart slamming so? He really wouldn't care if they did discover his unannounced departure; as with his earlier report to *Wind,* it might stir up some answers.

Stepping onto the stone bed, he bent knees slightly and hopped straight for the open edge of the skylight. Clutching the gritty outer surface with his palms, he hoisted a folded leg up and through, then hauled up the rest in a rolling motion. He had to throw out his left arm quickly to keep from continuing off the small dome on which he lay. His room was one of the higher stone bubbles atop the dirigible, and its outer wall sloped directly to the gravel below.

His jacket snagged at the shoulder on something. There was a translucent pane in a black oval frame bolted to runners on the dome. All the skylights were so guarded against rains. He smiled, then wondered if he might return to find it closed. Withdrawing a phillips from one of the tool pouches of his vest, he found the leading edge of the frame and jammed it into the runner track.

The ground seemed farther down than it should, so he notched to .2 g, slid on his pants till the wall went vertical, and then feathered onto the thumb-sized rocks with only a light rattle. The sky had cleared up earlier, but it was now clouding from the direction of the sea. All the neighbor buildings were dark; a globular flood lamp shone yellowly from about fifty meters to his left, sufficient to see no one was about. Leaving the belt setting at a light .5 g, he moved away carefully over the shifting pebbles with the salty breeze to his right. The next cluster of residences coiled along the opposite steep, reeded bank of a wide canal extending bridgeless into the dark both ways. Without slowing he touched the belt back to .2 g, took three long strides, and leaped over the star-reflecting ribbon. As his path peaked, he felt null g and had to wave his arms a bit to maintain upright posture. He overshot and came down with too much forward momentum, which tripped and spun him into a tumbling roll. He lay there, feeling light-headed, and looked back over the canal. The crash onto the pebbles had been loud, yet no one cried out or followed. Perhaps these Hhronka were heavy sleepers, now that they'd picked up the habit.

Minutes later he cautiously stepped out onto the next radial boulevard west from Gar's, five blocks from the calm sea. There were no vehicles and no pedestrians either way. He wanted to experience the city up close, not separated from it by a careening vehicle. Maybe he would find some clue so far overlooked or deliberately hidden from them. The city's center lay beyond the black V's vanishing point. Floor globes ticked off every other block. Yes, there was a possibility. Although he'd seen its pillar and open plaza down each radial, they'd gotten no closer than a kilometer or so. Coincidence or deception?

It was warmer with his back to the cool steady sea wind, and soon its organic spice was replaced by brackish staleness as the radial crossed a twinkling canal. Since the wide street was absolutely deserted for its visible length, he stopped worrying about discovery and relaxed. From a distance he might be taken for another citizen out on a walk.

Except for the arrowing mat strip and its seamless gray sidewalks, this ancient area was an amorphous tangle of worn, spackled, stone residences little different from Gar's. There was a pebbled frontage of a few meters between the street and the first buildings; after that, chaos. But what it lacked of Hhronkan style was covering vegetation. Oddly, it reminded him of a coral reef exposed by low tide, with the polyps withdrawn into their rocky foxholes. It was easy to imagine it teeming with the diminutive pebble-skinned Teffhtans, busily pursuing their rigorous, dour lives—never suspecting time itself was against them.

Ahead a few hundred meters, this relic landscape ended and the modern high rises began as a light-splotched wall. Putting himself back under .2 g again, he began taking giant strides to cross the distance quicker. He soon got the rhythm down, coordinating the plop of his tennies with the slap of the hard surface and the power of the next upward thrust. He paused to rest.

Back toward the sea the flood globes on their tall stalks were magic wands hung in gauze. Weather was moving in. Despite the exercise, he felt a wet chill and stuck the top half of his jacket's lapels together about his neck. With the sea fog obliterating everything, he couldn't be sure if the luminescent fog was still present, but the tingle and mumble had certainly receded. He had to concentrate to detect them. Was he getting acclimatized?

He arrived at the border between the two areas. The concentric street divided them like a razor. Across it the cliff of monoliths right-angled, reflecting half-cones of globe light and creating a gun-sight gorge. He slowed to a quick walk and started down the left sidewalk. He noticed more "missing" details. There were no signs, nor any address numbers on the buildings or at intersections. People here might use some sort of portable comm device for location, as the perscomps could be used on the *Wind*. Also there were no openings in the buildings at ground level, other than their entrances. The rare windows started at the second- or third-story level.

It was an Impressionist's view of a city; that was it. Gross shape without functional reality. It *looked* like an ordinary humanoid habitation, but it *felt* like a movie set. The same feeling the residence, and Gar himself, gave. Built to look superficially real, but behind the false fronts they were hiding—What?

He veered to one of the doors and saw only a metal jamb flush with the wall encasing a solid transparency. No handles or touch plates. Perhaps it functioned like the car's shell. But it failed to perforate for him when he pressed repeatedly at its cold surface. Inside was only a dark wide hallway, no lobby. He swore he'd seen some lit lower level windows as well as doorways when back in the old section. But now only a few upper stories held some yellowed rectangles, and not an entrance in sight glowed within. Of course, they might shut down automatically at a certain hour. There obviously was no nightlife. These Hhronka had apparently become completely diurnal.

"Talk about rolling up the damned sidewalks," he muttered.

Suddenly a large drop of rain flicked at his turned collar, spraying his neck with cold. Instinctively he sought an overhang for cover in case of a shower. None of those were in sight, either. Looking up, he caught the tiny, cold punch of a drop in his left eye, shook-blinked it out, and saw the sky had become a bowl of frosted glass, casting back the city's lamplight to silhouette the building tops, which now seemed to be holding up the mists: it would be more than a drizzle. There weren't even any obvious subway entrances. He'd be willing to try a ride back to the beach on it if he could find out how to get on. Were the stations all in the building basements?

These folks were real homebodies. Perhaps street life was nil for them, the boulevard solely for rare local movement. Certainly another difference from the gregarious Wlaatan Hhronka.

The hub was now a visible dot, the giant toadstool cap draped by mist. There was still no movement other than the occasional humming flyer overhead. In the total silence, his own ear buzz forced itself into his awareness. Three concentrics later, he heard the second artificial sound: a soft mix of hum, whirr, scrape, and bump. It was cyclic with a ten- to fifteen-second period, and it was approaching from the left around the next corner. He stood midblock before a building faced with the white glass. His first impulse was flight, avoid being caught by citizens or police whose reaction to an unescorted alien was an unknown. He hesitated. Hide where? The noise peaked at the cusp of the building. There were no alleys in this block and there wasn't even time to race back to the next cross street. His heart ricochetted as he plastered his back to the nearest doorway, pressing his left cheek to the slick, wet pane.

Suddenly the material grew warm next to his cheek and gaped so fast that he repeated his car pratfall into the entrance. The sound enlarged as he drew in his legs and lay at the carpeted baseboard of the dark hall. With relief he watched the transparency reform from a thick rime at the jamb, dulling the curious sound and putting at least that between him and his fear. He lifted his head just enough to see the street.

A large black metal machine nosed rapidly and steadily into view along the near curb in his direction. Initially he was too struck by its form to see what it was doing. Take a small box;

mount it before a larger box with fan housing atop it; put this on two-meter-high tires, and add cow-catcher bumpers all around. The thing had no occupants, for there was no place for them, and it simply rolled against the low curb, uttering its monotonous symphony.

He popped a laugh. Anyplace on Earth or Wlaata, he would have recognized it immediately. The design was totally unlike those of his two home worlds, but it used the same economical technique. An EM field magnetized all metallic and paramagnetic particles (the hum) and removed them first to a separate storage bin for recycle; a vacuum created by the dorsal fan (the whirr) sucked up the balance of debris sent airborne by the rotating underside brushes (the scrape), and a compressor blade (the bump) segmented its final storage in another bin. The paramount street cleaner!

He relaxed from the wall and looked back into the hallway's gloom. Its recess was invisible. But as the sweeper's symphony faded, there was a sound. An echo of his own breath . . . or the scuffling of bare Hhronkan feet? Stopping his chest on the rise, he rotated his head to reduce the interference of the buzz. There. The shy rustle of defense? Just around some near bend in the passage. With instinctive fear of darkness, he ripped open a vest pouch and snapped the IR goggles over his head, then groped out the switch and thumbed it on. Coagulated red light overfilled the hall and cast rusted shadow into its right turn about ten paces ahead. Tempted to send his Self before him, his own caution to Shree cudgeled the urge, and he repressed breathing instead.

The spongy carpet kept his advance silent as he went to the corner. The walls were of the same white diffractive glass as the building's facing but gave back only a splintered dull glow to his coherent light. More rustling, retreating down the corridor branch. Of course, the infrared made him only equal to the Hhronkan residents, whose vision responded to it without adding lenses. He quickly edged an eye around the hall's sharp angle: empty. Wide opaque double panels twenty steps away closed off the hall. Had he seen them shutting?

Going to the panels, he tugged at one of the tulip-shaped handles. Locked. With an ear suctioned against the cold metal, he heard a low grumbling and felt strong steady vibration. For several moments he stood weighing options, then unstuck the flap on another pouch with a sigh. When he'd found the kit untouched in his crate, he had been surprised. That meant either they hadn't searched his gear (improbable), or they'd missed the significance of what the pouch held (very improbable), or they didn't care because they intended to know his every move (most probable). Which in turn meant Gar and his minions (cohorts? bosses? spies?) were aware of his presence here and gave tacit approval—or they would know soon and might object strenuously. Fructify it. Fram the factors in this situation and see what fell to understanding.

The Hhronkan sonic cutter was a fat cylinder with a rotatable wheel at one end; opposite this, a bundle of short tiny pins was affixed. At max power its effective range was only inches into any material, a poorer weapon than some knives. But just then he wanted its designed function. Twisting the wheel, he held the pin bundle up to the seam where the panels met and pressed the stud at the wheel's center. The thin scream was audible only if he listened for it. The smoky flare of the material in the seam proved it to be organic, some type of plastic. Halfway down the juncture his hands wavered as his wrists changed angle, and twin scallops of material were gouged out of both panel edges. Stubbornly, he went all the way to the floor before shutting it off. He pulled at the right tulip quickly to keep any melted parts from rejoining, and the door swung out. It was a kind of airlock, with another set of panels enclosing a short wide space. He snapped his IR eyes off. These doors pushed open at his touch. He ceased to breathe.

Sensory images and their implications conjoined in a maze. The space was gigantic; it went up into darkness—the entire building! He stood on a ledge in a vast version of Gar's enclave, partway up one sloping stone wall. The light came from meter-wide veils of the bioluminescent plants hung around the entire wall. Within their penumbrae lay dozens of ponds, and from high fell a huge cascade of falls on the far side. Lace sheets splattered into a series of rock stairways—the vibration he'd felt that now trembled the floor in resonance with the very air. It masked all other possible sound. The smell of Teffht's sea drifted in the cold mists.

Then he deciphered the black lumps dotting the mega-enclave. Hhronka were everywhere, singly and in groups, all still. The reclosed door was solid at his back, and the cutter now felt good in his hand. Those he'd followed could be as close as the nearest. None of the lumps moved. Was this some kind of communal dormer? Cathederal? Entertainment? Regardless, why would imitating the vanished natives' habitat have become so important to Hhronka? This was not simply another mystery, to be explained away inconsequentially by Gar.

If every rainbow-glass building, one each three blocks, held such a mega-enclave, then a significant percentage of Atuum's densely packed volume was being committed to—what? Some kind of compulsion that forced these Hhronka to crowd their living space far beyond the *ooural* level, yet "waste" the space of these buildings? Why not simply expand the city inland? Or better still, out along the coast, where such cave habitats were natural? It was an internally self-contradictory situation; Hhronka could not have created it sanely. His breath caught. What if *all* the buildings housed such enclaves? The thundering vibration must be invading his reason. He pushed the inane conjecture away with the door and returned to the street.

Still it was empty and silent, so he had Gar's approval or ignorance. That didn't stop his disappointment. So far this junket had merely aggravated first impressions. This was a super-stagnant civilization of Hhronka altered, perhaps incomprehensibly, by their infusion into native Teffhtan society, whose psychology could already be outlined from what they'd learned. And this was no help to their basic problem, verifying the truth about the disappearance of the natives and the trans-planted Hhronkan's continued concealment.

The drops were becoming more frequent and smaller. Naturally he'd left his roll cap at the house; his hair was like a dead five-pound frog on his head. About all he'd get from this was a cold. His determination to continue was nearly washed away when the mumbling-tingling effect forced itself back into his awareness. The real fog must have been masking the peripheral indigo one because as he looked around he—He saw a wobbling glow pulsing from the face of a building across the street and several blocks on. Though it didn't resemble the effect's indigo fog, it was such an extraordinary anomaly in this city-simulacrum that he walked swiftly along the sidewalk toward it.

One of the stone-faced buildings had a deep U-shaped plaza notched into its face at street level. He came to its seaward side and looked in—and was paralyzed. At the open square's center was the most fascinating artificial object he had ever seen. Its placement predicated sculpture, but no art in his experience had so elementally affected him. With iron certainty he knew this was the source of the effect he had first sensed at the landing strip. The tingling (now like itching powder on his skin) and the chorused mumbling were at their most intense, and the fog had swelled to join the glowing display of the sculpture.

The object had three components: a solid centerpiece, the glowing display, and motion. The centerpiece could have been glistening silvery metal or glass. Five meters long, it was vaguely cylindrical with both rounded ends swollen, like a femur corkscrew-twisted a half turn. One trochanter was larger than the other, and both had melon-sized bumps scattered on them. Without edges or angles it was a collage of spheres and ovoids. The display was a variable cloud that enveloped the object entirely. It pulsed and changed constantly in size, color, brightness, and opacity, one instant fitting like a skintight transparent layer to the object, then springing out into a livid spectral sun that hid its femur core. The cloud's apparent motion and speed changed at random. In patternless motion, too, was the object itself: rolling, swinging, then tumbling end over end with, or reversing counter to, the cloud display, yet never leaving position at the plaza's center.

And it floated! It stayed at least a meter above the large rectangle of stone over which it gyrated. Yet he saw no embedded mesh or plate of grav material nor even bronzelike studs of the crystal in the surface, which could have produced the null-g effect. And there was no other way he knew to make an object of perhaps several tons spin in midair.

Then he snorted, deflated by speculative disappointment. It must be a simple holoimage, projected into the space by hidden cameras in the walls. Special-effects comps had been doing tricks like this for half a century. He walked to within a step of the luminescent cloud. It was breezeless, supporting his discovery. But his reaching hand paused in a dredge of doubt; to be wrong meant possible pulverization or electrocution. Taking his nail clippers from his left thigh pocket, he underhanded it toward the object. It passed without effect through the cloud.

Ping! Its contact with the tumbling object was followed by a loud pop that showered sparks in a semisphere luckily excluding him. He lowered his hands from his face to find a small remnant of cooling steel near his foot. Definitely *not* a projection. The sculpture constituted a solid reality that the combined human– Hhronkan technologies could not now produce. Still, there was something else here . . . another level to—

The Shadow fell between Spirit and Action. The Hollow Man was helpless before the patterns. Recognize the emotions and ideas enambered in these abstractions. Never repeating. Kaleidoscopic. Yet so deep, personal . . . roiling through his awareness. The Imprisoning Mirror; Ultimate Mobile, conveying the eidetic *him:* euphoria of alcohol, warmth of charity, satisfaction of good sleep, contentment of high-fat foods, blissful dissolution of ejaculation, excitement of free flying, fulfillment of love, pride of accomplishment, release of laughter. Straw-stuffed headpiece filled with: shrunkenness of solitude, instability of hate, waste of ignorance, void of loss, regret of error, guilt of iniquity, fear of insecurity, price of perfection . . .

The Shadow spoke; the Hollow Man heard: "Some experiences are unique, carried through life to its final moments; so integral a part of identity they never can be revealed to another —yet are constantly near consciousness, reviewed and turned at every possible aspect until familiar as the mouth." [moments of horror and hatred, holding in his child's arms the blood-sprayed corpse of Franklin, ignorance and guilt caging his *baas*]

"Some events are merely rare, the loosely formed base of the mythic homilies bartered with friends or close acquaintants, lies to portray Self as it desires to be, but never is." [denying total loneliness, grazed even as he embraced his children, knowing they too must recognize—broken Golden Bowl—this, eventually]

"The bulk of living is common ignored happenings, endlessly rocking in déjà vu, subliminally contracting the guideposts of subjective time, spiraling the decades to years, years to weeks, days to minutes—collapsing a lifetime into and composing it solely of the rare and the unique—mere months for the less adventurous, the cautious, the unlucky." [the assurance and ambivalent relief he knew on waking each day to find this filmy dissolution had not been the terminal one]

"What would you do to extend this time? What would you do to make it *worthwhile?*"

He wept; he laughed; he discovered. Time collapsed to singularity; he expanded as light. But he did not control, could not turn and walk away. The tight tether on his Self loosened, extruded from him by the sculpture. He let it flow.

Sound! The background mumble exploded into a vast neuronic interference that instantly fedback through his Self as an enormous chorus of a million yearning voices, a hymn of the dead pleading to be returned to life. Instinctively he palmed his ears, bent with tears spasming from his crushed eyes. No! It was contact with the mind of a moronic giant—without thought, only the white noise of its vegetative maintenance. But its power held him inexorably, preventing his withdrawing his Self back into himself for refuge. A thunderclap disturbance suddenly echoed through his mindnet. He was being hammered into a thin veneer, peeled free, crumpled into a ball, rammed into a cannon, and blasted into a billion sintering particles. Singly, the pieces became embers, then ashes.

His propriosensors told him he lay nearly in fetal position, and his skin enjoined that he was slippery wet. The tired fuzziness of his mind gratefully agreed to this return to the womb and its comfortable floating dream. But the rhythm of the tiny stamping feet on his front and left sides denied him this line of least resistance. He opened his eyes slowly and was reincarnated into the middle-aged body of a man reclining on stone with his left hand raised, palming a mirror-smooth surface. Its silvery lumpiness drew all his attention. The rain that struck him and rolled away was also spattering this surface, creating myriad ephemeral water-domes that either slid down over the surface into his hand or were bombarded into oblivion by successor drops. The War of the Aquahemispheres. He would have been content as its eternal observer and correspondent. But a tolling voice called out a name, and he heard it and the deluge's steady roar for the first time.

"Krieder!" it yelled into his left side.

The word recalled a reality in which this was *his* name. It drew him back to the memory of what had happened prior to the womb. He jerked his right hand away from the sculpture in fear of another, electric death. Then he rolled clumsily from the flank of the still object that lay next to his head and into two thin fleshy columns. He looked up through the rain shadow of the bending figure of Liifan.

"What do you remember?" The face dripped the question— not How do you feel?—along with streams of rain. It was as if she'd touched a switch on his sensorium. He began to shiver violently; his skin was a firm shell holding out warmth.

"Cold . . . I am cold," he stuttered through scissoring teeth.

She looped down both hands and lifted him easily by neck and knees. He felt the solid contact change from his right side to his left as she cradled him warmly and skirted the sculpture to go deeper into the plaza. He looked around her beyond the niche and saw only the vertically splintered, moving gray that shrouded the world. Then the sound and the icy splattering ended. He was allowed to slide down onto his feet but was held by both upper arms while he tested himself. In the universal language of bodies in contact—returned pressures, tugs, and pushes—he told her he could stand alone though he still shook involuntarily.

They were in the entryway of the plaza building; it was well lit and empty. He saw the door reform, diking the flood of noise and cold, yet he felt his perception was still filtered through the rain's thick gossamer. This was only his third Teffhtan interior, and he wanted to inspect more closely. But Liifan's firm, warm hand guided him along the pale blue ceramic corridor; he was too weak to resist. Around a turn there was a bank of lifts; they entered one as its door moved aside, and she touched the checkerboard switch panel. His belly spun weightless for a moment as the floor retreated below him. The flickering level indicators looked wrong somehow; he couldn't read them and was too chilled to care why.

They exited onto a wide balcony set flush halfway up the wall of a circular white tunnel, the underground system. Its entrances were in the basements after all. It was the sterile corridor of a pediatrics ward, and he'd just been delivered here newborn from the plaza.

The shakes stopped; he was starting to warm up. His chin, however, continued to tingle as his skin had outside; the lingering sensation had been masked by his chill. The finger he rubbed over it came off with a small, clotted, bloody smear that quickly outlined the cuticle and quick of the nail. Evidently he'd cut it somehow in collapsing onto the stone plaza.

As usual with local structures, there were few details beyond the smooth surfaces, almost as if these beings were embarrassed to admit they lived totally mechanized lives and so abstained from accessible outgrowths of this. Many of the roles of manual knobs, handles, and switches of human and Wlaatan machinery, were here subsumed by invisible "smart" sensors. It ultimately robbed the user of the opportunity to reprogram and lessened freedom of action.

The tunnel must have run beneath a radial street, for it went straight to infinity both ways, lighted by a segmented line of rectangles along the side opposite them. To their left a dot burst into being and strobed through the light gantlet, enlarging at surprising speed. A.H. was certain the car's silent five-second deceleration had pulped anyone aboard. But when the fusiform vehicle arrived behind a puff of cool air and floated a pace from their balcony, he saw it was empty. Both its transparent side wall and the balcony's solid railing folded out and down to couple as a gangwalk.

They entered a single twenty-meter room with many Hhronkan saddle-chairs hung from thick rods. But Liifan clutched one pole on the far side, rather than taking its merry-go-round seat, so he imitated. There was a touch panel nearby on the far side of the car above the window-wall, and she looped up a hand to it. Symbols lit redly on its screen. Again they were totally unfamiliar to A.H., containing no hint of Hhronkan. The car closed and accelerated again, but more slowly, in silence. He recalled Gar had explained it used the mass-driver principle to push or pull it magnetically with grav suspension as backup. He was struck by the juxtaposition of this archaic technology next to the miracle of the sculpture.

Finally she spoke without looking down at him. "You should not have gone alone. You would have been killed if you had touched the *usstaa* while it was active. It is only for looking. What were you seeking?"

He decided not to be defensive; maybe he could bluff her. "How did you know where I had gone unless you were tracing me? So why did you *let* me go alone?"

She stood unmoving, perhaps caught off guard.

"You know that Primary Shree Shronk and I carry . . . voice senders, which is how you followed me. Why did you let me go into possible danger?"

Again she froze until he sighed with recurring exhaustion. "Baay Liiffan, it is obvious we have a . . . circular problem. Neither of us trusts the other enough to freely give the information needed to create that trust."

Her only response was a wallowing light display he feared was a vestigial pattern of amusement.

Chapter 8

His awakening was a resurrection, but he had to roll away the stone himself. Still exhausted, he struggled up around local noon and found Liifan and Shree chatting again in the enclave. Hollow and shaky, he spoke a brief greeting and attacked a huge breakfast. On his first swallow of rehydrated water buffalo, he felt a tight dryness on the upper side of his soft pallet. He tested with more swallows and a few ear "clicks," then threw down his fork in disgust. He had a sore throat for certain.

These were rare enough and serious enough that he was sensitive to the earliest symptoms. The local microbes had got the better of his defenses, weakened by last night's foray. If they created a typical illness, the discomfort would spread around his nasopharynx, down into his throat, and make swallowing like trying to gulp a basketball. Then his leucocytes and their allies would battle the unwanted bloom of symbiotes back up into his nasal cavity, where they would scatter like the cravens they were into the membranes of his eustachians and sinuses. The mopping up operation would create a flood of thin yellow-green mucus, a pharyngeal menstruation that sloughed the infected lining with the bugs. His tubes would plug up and his hearing drop in sensitivity, partially deafening him, when the middle ears couldn't equalize pressure. And no amount of nose blowing could stop the drip from layering his trachea and bronchii with stiff plaques that tickled and brought on coughing spasms to remove the slimy bitter lumps, which he had either to spit or eat. There was usually no fever, but a general weariness of limb and mind, which lowered his IQ about fifty points. He'd be bloated and constipated an entire week or so. This was always the pattern of the illness, and nothing could be done. No cure, no treatment, only mild temporary symptomatic relief was possible.

After centuries of research, neither human nor Hhronkan medicine could totally prevent flare-ups like this. The little devils still evolved along the crest of their parasitic wave faster than the immune system could be stimulated or imitated. Of course, these Teffhtan bugs might be quite different, despite assurances, and kill him outright—but painlessly, he hoped.

He halted his deliberate depression, accepting this as unavoidable and determined not to let it interfere with their crucial mission. But when he shaved after eating and saw the cut on his chin for the first time, his mood returned. It looked like a shaving nick, triangular and neatly sliced; no simple fall could have done it. Yet he was sure this hadn't happened yesterday. Was he truly getting so old as to forget such a thing?

It was past his eight-hour check-in so he said, "Come in, *Wind,* Krieder here," and pressed the back side of the wafer in his waistband to receive. Only the hiss of frying grease. His face smoothed in shock. Now even the old drone frequency had been jammed, no doubt changed to another. He and Shree were totally isolated! Worse, Mowry and crew might do something foolish to attempt rescue. The stalemate must be broken at once! But not by causing the drones above to attack . . . by stalling Gar longer. And *Wind* must be reassured. Then they could continue the search for the truth.

What facts had they? The absence of natives, if they took Gar's word. The interference–concealment screen based on the natives' transferred paranoia (could there be any reality in Gar's wild tale?). Their hosts' reticence and reversals. The rainbow-glass building's mega-enclave, an irrational relic. And the *us-staa,* as Liifan had called it; he'd never heard the word before. Yes, that had been a miraculous experience to him, if a potentially deadly one. But not because these Hhronka had apparently learned how to suspend an object without a visible grav mesh between it and the ground.

He'd given that some clear thought. Almost certainly the

entire surface of the sculpture had myriad tiny crystals invisibly embedded in it, which allowed the motions he'd seen. And bombarding a repulsor-film–coated metal with oscillating microwave could have produced the cloud display. Another day, another miracle explained.

Rather, it had been the emotion–memory elicitation and Self contact, and what it had extracted from him, that still thrilled and frightened him. It had seemed his soul had been sucked out of his body for public viewing. And this mindnet had felt like one enormous yet simple Self field. Was it completely artificial and deliberately designed only for *baas* interference, as the Teffhtan comm and power equipment were concealed and jammed against all observation? Was this mindnet concentrated enough to totally jam his Self near the *usstaa* only?

Easily ascertained. To prevent last night's trauma, he condensed his field just enough to flip it out, then retract it instantly. The "sound" saturating him once more wasn't powerful enough to entrap him, but it was as strong as in the egg car. So the mindnet was a generalized phenomenon, perhaps present over the entire planet. It created an adequate protection against use of *baas,* with intense crippling concentrations at each functioning *usstaa.* Could such a system truly be meant only to counter *baasa?* Could these Hhronka be that paranoid?

Even the spotty sunlight, the first he'd felt on Teffht, failed to cheer him when he entered the enclave. He stood between Shree and Liifan, who reclined in niche seats close to the second pond, and said to Shree, "You look awful."

Actually the Primary was recovering from his drunk rather well. His skin, underlit from the pool's reflections, was only slightly patched with dark gray discolorations, the normally purple irises were not quite black, and his mood was orders of magnitude above A.H.'s. Too bad he would soon have to destroy it for him.

The bulbous face lightened randomly. "Paying the price for a night of true sleep, which I needed."

A.H. kept his tone casual and smiled at both beings as he spoke English. "We've been cut off totally from the *Wind* by the jamming. And I must tell you things about my outing last night, things I'll bet Liifan has never mentioned to you. Don't try to use your Self; there's some kind of inhibitor field everywhere that can trap you."

Shree covered his response well and replied in English despite Liifan's hard stare. "The shuttle landed a half hour ago. They will arrive soon. And Gar has been working on imprinting the transcomp data all morning. Do not be surprised if he and any monitors understand simple English the next time we see him. This will complicate matters. And I agree we must look elsewhere for truth; I can get nothing but generalities from these two."

A.H. was struck by Shree's reversed attitude. No longer a begrudging victim of fortune, the Primary had resumed his more customary decisive role. His spirits firmed as Shree devised.

"Liifan has told me each of the new arrivals will be assigned a guide, but we two will continue with our historians. However, I have little doubt of their ability to locate anyone quickly, even without personal comm devices. Probably a surveillance system exists throughout the city, even beyond. Yet this house, Gar's residence, is excepted, I am sure.

"We must avoid these guides and do more reconnoitering. I suggest we assign our families tasks according to talents, ones complex and lengthy enough to remove them from this house. That should also remove their guides. I have gathered from Liifan there are no regular police, so other guides would have to be recruited to bear on us once we are located by the city monitors. That will take time. Also I believe they may not use overt force at all for now; no risk will be taken that might harm the people they seem to want here so badly. Yet we *are* supplying them with valuable hostages—"

"And I still say they'd be no safer on *Wind*. I'm much more worried Mowry will start something when we don't check in."

"That presents no problem. It is our uncensored communication they wish to eliminate. Once our families are here, I will personally call Mowry, with Liifan watching, to confirm their safe arrival. That should restrain him sufficiently."

A.H. reconsidered the presence of his family in relation to the escalating danger they were all facing. It was definitely a solid stand-off. Even if the human contingent decided to simply exit the situation, and were allowed to do so, the Wlaatan Hhronka would never agree without evidence of their relatives' well-being. He understood this intellectually and somewhat emotionally from his contact with Shree. It went beyond simple tribal cohesion or a sense of responsibility. The yearning went so deep, it could be described almost as sacred fervor.

They heard smothered gasps of surprise, then footfalls, in the house's foyer tunnel. Joan and Droom led in P.C., Renata, Twee, and Umar, followed by six native Hhronka. A.H. missed Joan's special smile when he saw the Teheranian trailing the others as they all stared around the enclave. She came to give him a scented kiss as Droom and Shree exchanged touches; the other humans tossed verbal greetings, all still grinning at their voices' lowered registers. Twee only watched silently as usual.

Joan put an arm around A.H. and pressed a breast to his ribs, whispering huskily, "I missed you last night. First in a while."

He glanced down with a half smile, then darted a look at Umar in a question she chose not to see. Instead, she pulled her head back to scrutinize his face.

"You're ill. Sore throat?"

He nodded with lips pressed in disgust at fate.

Her worry increased. "If it's local, it could be serious. Maybe you should—"

"Not unless it gets worse. I'm needed, remember?" he said softly. "Why Umar?"

Her head cocked with her brow in admonition. "Now, stay slack. When we heard from Shree that the Teffhtans were extinct, he asked to join us to see what he could learn from the old expedition recs. He was surprisingly calm about it all, considering his hopes. And as for his other reason, don't interfere. We've been through this before; give it time. Besides, it *is* her business. She needs protecting like a gestating *traan* beast."

"It's not that simple, not here under pressure. There's something about him I've never—"

"Gentle beings," Shree announced rapidly in English, stepping into the crowd with skin relaxed and neutral for Liifan's benefit. "There is vital information to give you, and it must be done now. Our principal host, whom you will no doubt soon meet, will be familiar with English. Therefore all sensitive talk must pass between us only when alone here, or it should be handscripted and immediately destroyed. Outside we will be monitored continually. When I called yesterday, I pretended we are ready to accept the situation here; such is not the case. We have not been told the truth about the planet's natives and several other matters. Our position remains precarious. Droom, Twee, do not hide your skins."

The sudden loss of elan in the humans' expressions wasn't perceivable by Liifan, but she'd note the Hhronkan one easily.

However, P.C. couldn't resist saying wryly, "So we're here as the acid testicle, right?"

The variety of responding looks agreed to the inappropriateness of the humor, and he was efficiently squelched.

Shree quickly continued: "You were brought down mostly as decoys, that is true, but your observations could be important. Do whatever we ask without question, and also comply with all our hosts' requirements. Lastly, Twee, P.C., never attempt to use your Selfs here. There is everywhere an entrapping interference we do not understand yet."

The two youths fastened each other with muffled and embarrassed puzzlement. Then Twee said hesitantly. "That is . . . not entirely true, Father. Just after touchdown, we were so excited, we merged almost reflexively. There was no such interference."

Ignoring his attempted excuse at their failure in ethics, their fathers exchanged a look without expression but signifying noncomprehension: *yet more mystery!*

Durren Gar bobbed through the left door at the court's far end and came to join them, surveying each newcomer in turn as Shree briefly introduced them by name and relationship. Each studied him innocently, falling into their acting assignments. Gar's face blossomed with a white discoloration hinting a pleasant satisfaction. This increased when Shree explained each new visitor would like to immediately tour the city's environs with an eye to speeding colonization planning.

"Tweeol and P.C. are propulsion and power engineers. They want to survey whatever generation equipment you can give us to supplement what we will transfer down from our craft for our new city. Renata is an agriponics tech; please show her your croplands and the techniques you have found most productive. Joan specializes in community design and management; in fact, she once helped direct the human research settlements on Wlaata. She would appreciate reviewing any plans you have done of our city's site and organization. However, overall administration will be correlated by A.H. and myself, the same roles we held for many years. We would expect to confer with Baay Liifan and you today."

Yes indeed, thought A.H., he *was* in top form again.

Shree's gaze went to Droom and Umar. "These are the codevelopers of the ftl translation method we used to speed our journey here. I am sure some of your physicists are eager to discuss high-density gravity fields with them." He twisted toward the Orrtaan Primary, occulting his face from Gar and Lii-fan. His brow formed a blink-display of a black oval—Droom was to reveal nothing.

"Yes, that is quite true," responded Gar with odd calm.

Though Umar's understanding of spoken Hhronkan was rudimentary, he'd caught the bulk of meaning and raised his hand to interrupt in English. "Please, Primary Shree Shronk. Droom is completely familiar with the translation system. And I cannot pronounce Hhronkan; my contribution would be minimal. I would prefer to accompany Renata; perhaps I could be of real help there."

A.H. felt pressure from Joan's coiling arm and didn't react while Shree translated to an expectant Gar. They both apparently hoped to gain from continuing the pretense of Gar's ignorance of English.

The Teheranian's logic was so faulty even Gar picked out the flaw. "They are mates?" he asked with a drill-eyed stare.

Joan detached from A.H.'s side and spoke firmly in pidgin Hhronkan: "No, they are not. But *we* are. For our accommodations, we'll share a room. The rest want separate rooms, please."

Renata's cheeks pinked slightly; Umar looked at mother and daughter in confused chagrin. And no one challenged Joan's request.

A.H. released one chuckle under his breath before Joan pinched the loose rib flesh. But he couldn't control his mumbled riposte. "Well, well. Save the gestating *traan* beast!"

"I am sorry, Renata. We were both already aware of your father's hesitancy over our companionship. But I did not expect your mother to react like a Muslim! Another surprising similarity between our cultures. Perhaps we should begin again, and I will ask your parents' approval."

Nettled, she said, "I don't need *anyone's* approval but yours." Umar's returned reticence only added to his unattainable nature, combining purity into the exotic mix. Her look broke elfish. "Do you mean our companionship has become a courtship?"

He had no reply but to fumble with the seat webbing enclosing him neck to knee within the large curved chaise. The two-seat local flyer was opulent compared to the utilitarian Wlaatan models. The entire bubble-topped cockpit was padded with deep brown plush; their chairs were similarly piled in black; and the mint green dash was inlaid with filagrees of what appeared to be gemstones.

The screens were inert as the robot craft carried them inland above the city. Its twin dorsal jets created a satisfying vibration in their spines as the tall buildings slid beneath like rectanguloid villi in some gigantic intestine. At first they'd been jarred when it had become clear they were to be allowed out to the farms unescorted. While A.H. and Shree had retired to the comp room with their hosts, the others plus their guides had departed in egg cars similar to the one that had ferried them from the landing strip. But Umar and Renata had waited in the enclave with their two unresponsive guides for several minutes before their transportation arrived. The ten-meter craft had settled leaflike before the residence, empty of passengers. Then the two guides had merely pulled up the gull wings and waved them into the seats. Ignoring or not understanding their questions, one had tapped the dash, and the doors had been locked in place. Locked. They'd tried them anxiously.

"Greetings, Renata Krieder and Umar al-Askari," the flyer had said in flat but comprehensible English. "I am to take you to Food Production Sections 173 and 194. I can answer all queries regarding agricultural procedures on Teffht. Whenever you are satisfied, simply request return to Durren Gar's house. The cabin is locked to protect you. Please attach the seat webs and we will lift."

Voice-ops were common enough; the familiarity had relaxed them. Then they realized the native Hhronka probably considered them such unimportant factors in current matters that guards were deemed a waste. By the time they had decided not to be insulted by this logic, they had been several hundred meters up and moving rapidly toward the lumpy gray hills cresting the ridge of mainland beyond the base of the city's peninsula.

Now as Umar continued wrestling with his binding web and his emotions, the flyer crossed over the city hub. Renata noticed and stretched to the transparent door, angling her gaze to watch the landmark.

"Look—the city center. Just an open plaza around the pillar, like we thought; totally empty."

He also tried to see this juncture of the street radials, a geometric symmetry that pleased his sense of mathematical simplicity, but it and the shiny featureless pillar cap had already passed aft. Looking forward he yelled in terror.

"Bank right thirty degrees!" he screamed instinctively to the flyer. A giant rumble swept over the wind's swish.

Coming directly head-on was a much larger freight transport, its bulbous gray nose blind of windscreens or steering ports, another robot. But neither altered course. Renata popped up her head in time to gasp only once and reach for the half-wheel. The freighter's black, ribbed belly blurred overhead, blotting out the cloud-patched sky for a heartbeat. Then they were isolated again, sweating, looking wide-eyed at each other.

"That was way too close!" she exclaimed at the machine's dash. "Are you navigating properly? Please run a calibration."

"Excuse me, Renata Krieder," replied the uninflected baritone. "I and the carrier that just went by were 1.786 meters apart, well within navigational directives for safe operations. Please pardon my error in neglecting to consider human judgmental senses. I will extend collision parameters ten times. Will this be sufficient for comfort?"

"Your local Hhronka sure do play it tight! What if we'd hit a shear downdraft? Make it twenty times," she said peevishly.

Only then did she see his hand still gripped her webbed forearm—Rhett's bold protectiveness. He hastily withdrew his arm under his mesh covering and looked away. Awash with the camaraderie of shared near-death, an extra intimacy edged her tone.

"I guess that answers my question."

He couldn't look at her probing eyes; his self-possession again wavered between anger and lust as it had that first R-ball game. "Renata, I do care for you. For a long time I have felt you are an exceptional person . . . and woman, particularly for your age. But we are very different kinds of people. To think of courtship, regardless of custom, may be asking too much too quickly."

She saw only his Sheik's shyness, that he really ached to hold her tightly, declare his passion, but needless fears held him.

"I don't think so," she whispered with words. But her eyes, her expression said they should continue the topic without voice, especially these pitch-lowered unromantic ones. And words would only demure, only erect obstacles and facades between them and the potential fruition of their desires.

For the first time Umar returned the dare, and they saw none of the land until the flyer bumped down. The door locks clicked, and they reluctantly severed their new communication to climb shakily out. The craft's extended skids and their tennies sank into the dun, grainy mud.

They stood in a notch of the head-high wall of multicolored plants that crested the low ridge overlooking *Atuum*. A small white geodesic dome centered the notch behind them.

The cloud cover had broken into a flotilla of evenly spaced gray-white spheroids in the gray-blue sky, and the toy city's spectrum-walled glass buildings sparkled with the occasional sun patches that drifted inland toward them over the ruffled hills. The day was almost hot, the plant-spiced air devoid of sea smell, flowing around them slowly, clinging with humid thickness.

Umar shrugged off his damp *chal'at* and flipped it back onto his seat, wishing he'd dressed as Renata: yellow shorts and pullover, which expressed each movement of her pointed bosom. He suddenly realized he could now control yet enjoy his sexual response to her "nakedness," could hold it within like an ember against the cold there. He wondered guiltlessly what New Teheran would be like without the necessities of *purda*. His feelings for her spurred him with many questions he had believed he'd never ask seriously. But her companionship now paid him a compensating warmth that narrowed his former perspective to newly acceptable limits.

Becoming mildly interested in her camouflage mission here, she walked to the head-high wall of unevenly spaced multicolored plants. "How many species are interplanted here?" she turned and asked their inanimate guide.

Her question seemed to activate a packaged segment of its instructions. Nose speakers came on loudly. "There are seventeen native and Wlaatan-derived species and subspecies in this section. All have been randomly placed and genetically structured for max plant and animal pest repulsion, productivity, weather durability, and root spread. The more delicate types are cultured totally below ground with—"

"Stop," she said quickly, not wanting to listen to the entire lecture on foods meant for Hhronka—she even recognized a *leenawah* bush—and therefore essentially worthless to humans.

"Are there insects on Teffht?"

"No, not animals with an exterior skeleton and muscle-attachment layer, but there are those of similar size and niche requirements."

"What are the climatic factor ranges over the past ten years? And give me native soil nutrient averages without supplemental fertilization."

As she listened to the numerical parameters, Umar came near and idly examined several of the tough plants. He tried to remove a pearlike fruit from one low yellow shrub but failed. She smiled distractedly at him while the flyer finished.

"Well, no doubt we could make it go here. Might need some gene juggling. But even in the temperate zones, with less rain, we could desalinate seawater and use full aeroponics as on *Wind.* Yield could sustain any reasonable pop size."

With a shrug he agreed tacitly to play this game and waved around their island of mud. "Why don't they do that here? Why use such archaic ground-planting methods anywhere?"

"You're too used to Teheran, where there's no choice," she chided in a deep contralto. "Actually, from an energy-effective standpoint, open surface farming here near the equator is more efficient. After all, enclosed aeroponics just gives better control over large animal pests, weeds, and weather. You still have to spray the roots with nutrient solutions and provide day-round or at least night lighting to maximize growth rates. That takes a hell of a lot of energy, materials handling, and equipment and maintenance. You can accomplish the same things with selected and artificially mutated strains, and let natural precip and sunlight—falling on plants that can use the wavelengths getting through even this heavy cloud—supplement the little expenditure needed for planting and harvesting. Remember, the only reason 'ponics became prevalent back on Earth was the loss of most of the topsoil in agriareas during the Global Dustbowls."

She was finally intrigued and paused to gouge the pliant tawny soil with a toe. "This is rich stuff, and I suspect they've merged both methods to get the best of each. Correct?"

"Correct," affirmed the flyer.

Umar scrunched his face more in disappointment at the total loss of their former mood than in puzzlement, but she was deep into her professional genre—a habit he well understood.

Taking his elbow, she started toward the geodesic at the notch's center. "Let's take a look."

"Please wait," warned the flyer. "The subsurface areas are not well suited for you. Living visitors never come here."

Renata halted, then became adamant. Shree had urged them to stretch it. If she could browbeat this machine, maybe they could do so easily without looking suspicious. "We want to inspect this entire facility! This is important for deciding how best to proceed with our colonization."

The flyer was silent several seconds, seemingly to consider its various instructions, perhaps conferring with live superiors.

"Very well. But I cannot accompany you below. Instead, one of the roving tenders there will guide you. Please touch nothing without first asking."

From within the opening dark hollow at one end of the hut, a yellow light shone at them. Its circle grew larger as it came smoothly to the edge of the hut's gray floor slab and stopped in the penumbra of reflected day. Renata stifled a laugh; Umar smiled.

"It's an issac!" she exclaimed.

Anthropomorphic robots were rare to them. On Earth and Wlaata the nonmetallic nonsilicon-circuited generation had become so cheap that lower-maintenance built-ins for each usage had almost totally replaced mobiles. Stationary ones could be designed for greater specificity, and that dispensed with the need for the generalized versatility for which humanoid or Hhronkoid symmetry was an efficient template. Yet this chest-high model retained a bi-pedal stance, two upper appendages, and a columnar torso crowned by a movable globe. The four limbs were clustered with retractable tool sleeves. The multiply jointed legs now ended in claws. The flexible skin was a smooth gray integument without detail except for access panels in the torso, a speaker grid on the globe, and several lenses just above this, one of which exuded the light they saw.

"I can hardly wait to see why they need one of these," she said eagerly.

"Please follow me," said the grid, its electronic voice a twin of the flyer's.

The issac led them into the geodesic through airseal doors and down a steep wide incline for about thirty paces to another level. There was total blackness except for the issac's steadily sliding conic section of yellow on the gritty floor, but subliminal hearing told them the volume was huge. They withdrew into their clothes from the cool damp, and olfaction dug at a stratification of moldy soiled odors thick with age.

"There is no mounted lighting in your visible range," explained the issac. "The tenders normally use the shorter wavelengths to operate and locate by sensor grid enmeshed in the decking. The lamp is adjustable, however."

The beam brightened, widened, and floated up and out into the distance.

"Uh-huh," hummed Renata in response to Umar's grasp. "All the crops above are actually aeroponic. Very economical."

Materializing into the sweeping beam ten meters above them were inverted forests of whitish dripping tendrils, hanging down from a ceiling of what appeared to be black felt. This was supported at regular intervals by thick square columns of rust-colored metal that were festooned with equipment and spread away in all directions. Where they could be seen at all through the roots, their perspective overlap hid the vanishing points in the distance. Umar thought of a drowned pre-Muslim Persian temple, freshly reemerged, leaving only seaweed and mystery. Also surrounding the solid concretelike platform on which they stood was a plane of open metallic gridwork linking the columns. The issac took them onto this and aimed its beam down.

"Very nice," commented Renata. "This whole lower section is a huge catch basin roofed over with this black material, which is root-permeable yet structurally strong. It's covered in turn with a thin soil layer."

"Fifteen centimeters," interjected the issac punctiliously.

"Fifteen centimeters. This allows for seedlings to root, as well as insulating the porous roof to create a thermally stable environment here. When it rains, water passes through the roof, wets the roots, and falls down onto those watersheds." She pointed with the beam to the heavily stained and grooved solid plating several meters below the grid. "These divert the flow into cisterns, which can be used as reservoirs for mixing nutrients and spraying the roots when needed. And . . . somehow encroachment of unwanted plants is prevented in the topsoil."

"Crop seedlings produce a tag enzyme at all growing root tips that dissolves the porous support material and enables root growth through it. All noncrop roots are stopped or slowed by it, and these are easily removed by scraping the soil periodically."

"Thank you," said Renata tersely. It was spoiling her chance to impress Umar with her guesspertise.

They started along the grid, feeling its toothed lattice through their rubber soles. Occasionally they had to part longer roots like wet, beaded string curtains. The issac hurried on past to light the way. But once Renata stopped to clutch one soggy clump of strands.

"Light, please," she said peremptorily. The robot reversed and obeyed with a jerk. "See here, Umar?" She placed the straightedge of a polished index nail against a marble-sized root nodule. "No doubt these have modified symbiotes, like our rhiyobacteria, that supply most of the special nutrients needed. And notice how the rootlets subdivide like feathers to create even more total root-hair surface area for absorption."

He fingered some of the finer branches she held, not truly interested, but enjoying the brush of their hands.

The overzealous machine interrupted the moment. "Root hairs have been cultured to be spatulate and upcurving against gravity, like tiny spoons to hold water longer and so absorb more. This reduces the necessity of frequent spraying, as long as humidity is kept high enough."

"Yes," she spat at her competitor to quiet it. "It sure is that," she added, webbing her fingers over her wet face. Both were quite slathered, and Umar was past ready to return. But she pushed on. They'd gone over half a kilometer when a pearly brightening grew beyond the splattered escort light on the grid.

"What's ahead?" she asked.

"One of the subsurface hydroponic sections. Do you wish—"

"Yes, we would," she finished, striding in that direction.

Umar opened his mouth to protest the danger of getting any farther from the entrance, already uncertain of its location. But he realized the futility from past experience and followed quietly beside the issac, which apparently also had learned to respect her dominant nature. The columns in front became silhouetted by the burgeoning pearl. Then they saw rectangular daylit pieces of a large open garden beyond the last picket line of the supports. Stepping around and between two of these, they stood at the edge of a colored maze of plants and supporting equipment.

Some puckish titan had used his straight razor to skin off the top meter of a polyculture orchard along with its spectrum-shaded plants and had suspended this graft midair in the largest greenhouse they'd ever seen. Overhead a transparent griddled roof showed them the cloud flotillas still on maneuvers, and the lowered position of Tau Ceti's eye glaring between two of them reminded that Teffht's short day would soon be over. Below the porous black layer, root masses dipped like bunches of white straws into clear, slow-flowing liquid. Waist deep through this shallow lake trudged several twins of their guide.

"Now, this is a little more familiar," she whispered in admiration. "What plants are here?"

"Those too delicate or hydrophilic for the surface."

Thankfully it didn't continue. The clean-swept black layer rode on pillars at knee height above their lattice plane, and Renata hopped up and led through the variegated glade. Again Umar and the issac deigned to protest. Once atop, the nutrient lake became invisible to them, and, except for the intermittent supporting roof beams and pool-table surface underfoot, they might have been back in the open air. As the stroll progressed, they discovered a larger range of fruits and vegetables than expected, from berries on low shrubs to watermelon-sized pomes on stout trees that brushed the greenhouse roof with broad leaves.

Suddenly the eden stopped. Though the planar substrate and the roof continued for another three or four hundred meters, no plants spread between. And in the gloom beyond the end of the greenhouse, they saw no root forests again descending.

"This isn't used?" asked Renata.

"Not now," answered the machine quickly. "Shall we circle right and start back out?"

"Yes," replied Umar emphatically, avoiding her rebuttal by looking down at the issac's lens.

They followed the border of the planted greenhouse plane to its second corner and came to a large pond of liquid in the shadow on the left, abutting the planted substrate at its level. The issac anticipated her question.

"A water reservoir, once used as a culture vat for simple molecules from which more complex foods were constructed."

Out in the unlit cavern they saw the lips of several other adjacent vats, all empty. Renata turned to Umar and smiled contentedly. Her ponytail was now rusty wet at its end, and droplets of sweat hung at her earlobes to match the crystal jewelry streaked on her face. In the hollow of her breasts the pullover and her shorts' crotch had gone from yellow to tan with wetness. Her smile became contentious.

"I'm going for a swim —a skinny-dip, actually. That means I don't wear any clothes. And I know what that means to you, so if you don't want to bust a few commandments, better not look."

Umar only stared in astonishment and disbelief at her impulse, but when she crossed her arms defiantly over her belly and started to lift the pullover, he backed away quickly.

"Uh . . . perhaps I should wait back on the other—"

She chuckled. "You don't have to run away." Her eyes pleaded with him to stay. "Just turn your back till I'm in."

His look fell involuntarily to the white flat skin of her exposed midriff, and he nodded and turned.

She arched her back again but paused to look down over elbows at the issac. "Well? Any rules against it?"

It rotated a lens at her almost expectantly. "No."

"Then I don't care what *you* do," she concluded. Quickly stripping, she piled her tennies and clothing at the flat edge of the metal pool. Without looking to see if they were, she cupped her breasts against a painful smack from the water and jumped in feet first. It was cool enough to make her come up gasping, but before she'd dog-paddled to the far end, it felt the same temp as her skin. Its stickiness was replaced by a sense of giddy abandonment, matching the release from weight the water also gave.

"Umar! It's marvelous!" she yelled gleefully, starting back.

Only then did he turn to see her bobbing slowly toward him, white shoulders rhythmically awash with each stroke, plastered hair like fresh blood. He began to know a totally novel emotion and why he hadn't left her, as morality demanded. It was not the volcanic cone of simple hominid lust that had pricked him throughout life and overwhelmed him on the R-ball court. It was a hunger so intense it now denied him access to all the disciplines, escapements, and governors a lifetime of training had evolved. Yet the need was not localized in his genitals; it emanated from both his physical and mental self. It was a desire to unite not only physically, but also emotionally and spiritually, to interrupt even momentarily his total solitude and the isolation that had bleached his existence since his mother's last breath. A merging to add another's meaning of life to his own, justifying both.

Renata reached his shore and treaded water, studying his intense face, his black shining eyes. Valentino and Rhett. Suddenly only they and this spot were real; the rest was unimportant memory.

"Join me. I promise to keep at a proper distance," she chided.

She leaned back slightly to show him her buoyant wobbling breasts and long waving legs. Then she rolled fully faceup and backstroked away strongly. Bringing her arms completely to her sides each time, she lifted her body up in the water and alternately pushed her breasts out of her armpits to mound them on her chest.

He saw her dark areolas were large and hardened, nipples like high brown studs and each wave from her hands rewet her sienna pubic thatch back down onto its low rise. Looking only at her eyes, he unbuttoned his white singlet robe and dropped it around him to the substrate, leaving his briefs to cover him. She admired how the dimming overhead light embossed the sharp upper planes of his slender, taut-muscled body. Only his high forehead and straight nose showed above his cropped beard; his eyes were lost in the shadows under his thin brows. Leaning forward he curved into a shallow dive, cutting the surface quietly. He went in deep in response to the cold slap and frogged almost to her before rising.

They both came upright, treading at arm's length. Suddenly close to each other in this new way, they became hesitant. She fell back to playfulness, cupped her hands together, and squirted him in the eyes. Laughing, she gulped air and jumping-jacked underwater. Through the distorting murk, she could see his phallus swelling out his shorts, its tip peeking over the elastic top. She reached around his hips, drove her fingers under the band, and pulled it down.

She heard his startled sputter and felt several of her nails snag on his soft buttock flesh but jerked on anyway, exploding bubbles of forced laughter. As the shorts half slid, half tore from his crotch, his phallus snapped forward and hit her nose a soft tap. His torso flexed forward spasmodically. It just seemed to enter her gaping mouth naturally, without planning. She tried to take in all of its smooth firm sponginess but it proved too long, and she bit reflexively when it gagged her.

Then he reacted, grabbing her painfully under the arms and pulling her up to the air as she released him. Anger, fear, and ecstasy were ill met on his wet face. In the lighter gravity they floated at midshoulder without moving; neither spoke with words, each at a brink once more. She waited for his eyes to lose their wildness, then rubbed her palms on his upper arms, felt the lush slippery warmth of his water-lubricated skin.

"Umar, do you remember what Twee said to us that night after R-ball?" she asked softly. A tiny voice reminded her of what Twee had said to her alone later, but that was swept away by his affirmative expression.

"'Finding someone to love is a happy accident, but being in love requires a conscious act of will,'" he quoted exactly.

"Do you love me in either way?"

Helpless agony twisted his face. "I don't know! I . . . I have never felt either before."

She held a true sympathy for him, for any like him. Orphaned as a child, never knowing love as an adult, even from family. It was her family's caring and closeness that had given her the self-confidence necessary to accomplishment, including that of loving—though in truth she herself had yet to be in love, to make that decision. What did Umar hold as his foundation? Was it truly his religion?

"Don't you at least feel comfortable, deep down, with me?"

He became less doubtful. "Yes. Yes of course."

Her smile was pleading. "Isn't that love enough for a *mut'ah?* Or are you supposed to feel Love Eternal for that too?"

His face opened as though she had unlocked the prison gate of his soul.

"Then marry me, Umar, if that's what it takes for you to give yourself. Let's be married in a *mut'ah,* for I feel the same about you. Isn't that one purpose of the temporary marriage, to keep people as drawn as we are from hating each other out of frustration?"

He was quickly waxing animated to the idea, tightly holding her shoulders in return. "Yes, exactly! Fool! *I* am the one to have thought of it!" He became outwardly serious, holding laughter. "You have asked, however, and I now answer. Yes, I will marry you in *mut'ah.* But first I must know: have you ever been married before?"

Her smile spread out to dimples. "No, I haven't, not even temporarily. How about you?"

A mock officiousness grazed his mouth. "That is not part of the ritual. Merely answer the questions. But, no, I have not been married before, in either way."

"Oh," she said slowly as the import of that registered. She'd have to continue as teacher for a while.

"What about the male relative's permission?" she suddenly recalled.

"That is not necessary for the *mut'ah,*" he replied with a satisfied smile. "What time limit and dower do you desire?"

Thoughtfully she took a deep breath, unintentionally emerging her bosom, to which he shut his eyes and suppressed a smile. She giggled, feeling childlike. "Well . . . how about until we next leave Teffht? That should be long enough. These are renewable aren't they?"

Umar nodded patiently. "And the dower?"

Renata paused a moment, shrugged, then grew sober. "I want this to be a total secret, and when we divorce, I want our separation to be complete, no forever-afters. Right? Neither will owe the other in any way."

He nodded in kind. "That is as it should be."

They climbed from the water and stood dripping, without reaching for their clothes. The issac still watched them.

Renata turned from Umar. "We'd like privacy for a while. Would you wait for us at the edge of the greenhouse where we came in?"

It paused a moment, then rapidly disappeared into the orchard to their right.

Umar let go her hands and said, "Repeat this: 'I marry you to myself.'"

"'I marry you to myself,'" she replied, feeling slightly foolish.

"'I accept your marriage to me,'" he responded quietly, smiling with serenity.

"That's it?" she asked when he didn't continue.

"Islam holds all marriage as a simple contractual agreement. There is no sacramental 'estate' to it, as in Christianity. Ritual is minimal, but there could have been friends, witnesses, a feast."

"Do you at least kiss the bride?" she asked with an embarrassed grin. Even this official simplicity had unexpectedly returned a virginal shyness to her.

"That and more, I'm told," he said earnestly.

They almost stumbled into each other, flinching at the first touch of her nipples to his chest. And the first kiss was very tentative, a diplomatic press of lips to confirm their promises. But the second was unending. She felt his slackened penis stir between her thighs and gently pushed him away and down to the black surface. Kneeling on its felt softness, she repeated her action in the pool but with more intentional skill. When he began to sigh deeply and lift his hips to force greater penetration, she spread herself and slowly sat onto him.

Suddenly he paused, entranced by the wonderful strangeness yet utter familiarity of it. His eyes opened to stare up at hers, to her breasts swaying past his mouth. "So long, so long," he murmured.

He wasn't her first virgin, and she knew how seriously men held this moment. Yet for pleasure's sake it was best to relax him. Love should be fun too.

"Hmmm . . . yes, it is," she said knowingly, then joined his bursting laughter that massaged her deep inside.

His quickly stilled. "No. I mean I've wanted you like this for so long."

Ecstasy overcame all else when she moved above him. He felt engulfed, devoured. Individual sensations fused as he was drawn further into her, joining emotionally, beyond mere physical pleasure. It reminded him of his partial merges with Droom, but this was so much more than increase of intellectual power. And no part of him remained spectator. He was stubbornly slow, and by the time he lost all control, she was triple-spent and quite content. Only at his second surrender did she think of Rhett, overpowering her, carrying her up into the dark at the top of the stairs.

And only then, for an instant, did he smell hot sand and mummy fume and glimpse truth through facade. But it dissipated like smoke as they floated together in the umbra of satiety. He pulled her onto his chest, enfolding her in taut arms.

The greenhouse had become cooler with the setting sun, and each rubbed the other's gooseflesh as they embraced. In near dark she roused and began to dress, reminding him they would have to return eventually.

As she watched his body disappear into his clothes, she at last admitted she had caught a hint of something disquieting in his eyes during their lovemaking, something quite different from his pride, triumph, and tenderness. As mere bedmates, she would have challenged him at once. But they had exchanged too much, were now too involved for her to reveal her knowledge of it and ask its source. A second's break in a seeming eternity of contentment simply wasn't worth the risk.

Chapter 9

A.H. was still puzzled. All afternoon, first Liifan then Gar had sat with them in the partly sunny enclave discussing plans for their colonization. Neither host had offered more than broad generalizations or improbable promises, while they had been forced to reveal far too much about themselves or risk being caught in an obvious lie. And no one had mentioned his escapade of last night. He'd expected at least a moderate chastisement from Gar. When it hadn't come that morning he had assumed the historian had wanted to make a good first impression on the new arrivals. But after a couple of sessions of dump-and-spread with him in near private and still no word about it, A.H. began to suspect something else even more improbable.

As he and Shree sat alone with Liifan again in late afternoon, he became gradually more certain, simply from her nervous manner: Gar did not know about the incident; Liifan hadn't told him! His heart pumped faster. For the first time he saw a chink in the opposition, a flaw that might be used to end their stalemate. When she asked if they had any other pertinent topics, he decided to put his hopes to the test.

"Yes," he replied emphatically. "We'd like to visit the city's center. I was on the way—"

"Of course. I will take you there now," Liifan said for the first time using a poorly enunciated but understandable English.

A.H. met Shree's quick look; apparently he had indeed found a weak spot. Liifan too had spent some time being imprinted in his own language; so one charade was officially ended, another begun.

She led them through the door at the left end of the pool chain by which Gar always entered. Beyond, a long stairway dropped underground to a locked metal door. She palmed it open and went ahead through a bare bedrock tube to a small platform. It was an entry to a private spur of the city subway! More subterfuge. Last night when Liifan had "rescued" him, they had gotten off under the next radial westward, emerged next to that street through a kiosk, and walked back to the residence. Since this indicated an increased level of trust, or collusion, on her part, he said nothing in reproach.

He glanced at Shree as they waited for a car; his white sinusoidal burst said the equivalent of "Nice work!"

In minutes the three of them sat astride saddles, blurring hubward in a half-length car that still filled all but the outer two meters of the tube's diameter. As they shot abreast paired circular openings in the white wall, a full-sized car ripped through left to right only meters from their car's speared nose. After his first ride he had learned from Liifan the system was entirely one-way, with each radial and concentric street roofing a tube. It required some very fancy maneuvering to prevent excessive delays or collisions, but apparently they had the comps to handle it—with hair breadth precision. (How calmly Liifan witnessed what was a heart-skip moment for both of them.)

The other car had been filled with citizens, a large crowd for Atuum. Where were they going so late in the day, especially in a city that died each night? He glanced at Shree to see him register the same question. It was time to ride to the sound of the guns, though of course they could also end like Custer.

He dabbed at his raw nose with a sodden wad of tissue. His native infection had decided to overlap the first two stages of its blitz. His gullet was sandpaper, his lead-lined, achy sinus cavities seemed to be dumping watery yellow secretion in gallon loads, and his hearing was dropping an octave an hour. If they'd asked him, he would have been content to return to *Wind* and treat these microbes to copious amounts of alcohol, at least until his red-mapped eyeballs retreated into their sockets. But no one was asking.

He nodded at Shree to take the lead. However, Liifan showed an unexpected perceptivity. Her arm snaked to the control panel and brushed it three quick jabs. The car started to slow.

"There is no need to go to the central depot; it holds only storage and maintenance facilities," she explained at their looks.

The Primary peeled his curling form off the saddle and onto the floor. He took a step toward her and flashed dark cheek bars to emphasize his resolute inquiry. She almost managed to hide her skin before the dark blotches covered her face.

"You wish to see more of Atuum ... without being monitored," she answered. "Our car is now invisible to Gar's watchers, and it will not be missed. I also would like you to see something; we will go where the car that just crossed is going."

Shree held her with his gaze for a moment, then turned to A.H., who nodded. Looking back at her, the Primary asked, "Why did you not tell Gar of Krieder's excursion?"

"Because he already knew. But tonight will remain hidden to him!"

This was such an interesting admission they both decided to withhold questions. Disloyalty or sham, they saw a new piece to the puzzle. Their sudden deceleration reduced the tube's lighting from two smeared yellow-white lines to a staccato of rectangles before they'd reached the second concentric. A.H. gripped his unpadded saddle's suspender pole, trying to torque his abused groin aloft, and japed that here a higher voice would seem more natural. Then the car turned right into the concentric so sharply that he was thrown sideways to the floor with one hand still dragging at the seat's lower edge. This system was designed for the Hhronka's many-levered slat skeleton, which took forces better than his. Shree had braced to the wall, and Liifan had simply locked legs under her saddle's round belly.

"I'm all right," he waved at their downturned faces. "I'll just stay here where it's safe," he finished in fatigued surrender and lay back spread-eagled on the cold metal for the rest of the trip. Could he ever equate this suffering with their mission's worth? Probably.

They stayed westbound in the concentric only briefly, then turned right again into a radial he guessed would bring them back to the seashore but several kilometers along the coast from

Gar's house. The car slowed to walking speed; he sat up. They passed the outermost tube ring and came to a station at the radial's dead end. Now Liifan seemed anxious and hurried them along the platform to the farthest of its four exit passages.

Their car reversed the instant they disembarked, turning into the outer ring to avoid the next oncoming car. It was also packed with citizens, and Shree and A.H. lingered in the passage's mouth to observe. She returned to the exit in extreme agitation.

"Please! They must not see *you* here!" she hissed at A.H. in English.

He looked back at the approaching group of about seventy and agreed. For they were behaving in an unruly vehement manner, desperately pushing one another, scrambling for position out of the station—and they were stripping nude! From the platform they dispersed into all four exits, and several were bobbing rapidly toward them, only meters away but not noticing them yet as they literally tore off their varied garments.

"Come! We will use a private entrance," she urged, hurrying on again.

They followed her around the sharply curving passage and were startled to see its smooth white lining disappear to reveal rough sepia bedrock. Gone also were the light rectangles, and only occasional dim globe lamps hung from the pocked walls, dappling piles of clothing littering the floor. Just before this juncture she stood gesturing into a small opened panel. Pressing on A.H.'s bent back, she tugged the door shut behind them as they heard the crowd make the turn.

The boisterous yet nonverbal sound was guillotined to silence. At first the space was in complete darkness, and A.H. watched the curtains of aurorae behind his lids as his eyes dark-adapted. How he missed his IR goggles. The relief of finally noticing a purple blur also let him smell: the sea, filtered through damp stone and decaying wet-life. He heard footfalls closeby and felt a new fear.

"Liifan, where are you?" he whispered needlessly. He recalled Shree had better night vision that he and would prevent their possible abandonment here.

"I am here," she replied, her bass echoing briefly.

"Give me your hand," Shree offered.

Leaving the solid anchor of the cold rippled wall, he waved a hand before him till he slapped the Primary's warm one, then took it tightly like a child. At first the uneven floor urged him to toe ahead for safe footing, but Shree's constant tug and the lack of any gross deformities in the stone finally bade him stride on faithfully. Soon the purple mist before them grew, and he clearly saw his vanguards' outlines against it. The nearly circular tunnel went level for a couple hundred steps, then sloped down slightly for a while. He could see the fossil–whipped-cream texture of the tunnel, a sea cave that had known the rise and fall of ocean levels through many ice ages.

Then the muted echoes of constant movement and shouts oozed along the walls. Shree halted so quickly, that A.H. rammed his belly onto the umbilical limb with a grunt. Both Hhronka were breathing heavily, but soon Liifan's voice came around Shree.

"What you will see will surprise you and, I think, shock you. There must be questions. Please hold them until we leave, then I shall try to answer." She paused for several rasps. "Perhaps this will make events more understandable . . . acceptable. But do not let your presence be known. They would resent it."

The gloom brightened to grayness and sound divided into voices and booming splashes. Their narrow corridor turned a hard left and the roof and right wall disappeared. They stood alone on a carved balcony with a solid chest-high rock balustrade. It was three-fourths the way up the vertical rear wall of an enormous sea cave. It was the prototype on which Gar's enclave or the one faked in the rainbow-glass building could have been based. Instead of falls, however, the open ocean poured through three large perforations opposite them. Their upper borders reached level with the balcony, and through them they could see far out onto the dark puckered surface that feebly reflected the dying light from the impasto gray plate of sky. The three entrances' lower edges were submerged, as was almost half the cavern floor. It must have been slack tide, for the slight surf lapped below the watermarks on the stone hillocks and rock piles there.

Native Hhronka were everywhere in the great ovoid, thousands of them. Some swam in and out of the entrances, wriggling their limbs like four snakes tacked to a log in their typical stroke. Others squatted or lay on the little islands in the black cave pools. Most sprawled along the dry edges of the floor back to the curving walls. In the misted distance left and right, A.H. could barely see openings of other side tunnels converging into the cavern and other ledges and niches, all mottled with the motions of new arrivals seeking space. Huge veils of the glowing bead plants lit the space too dimly for shadow.

This was not the gathering of orderly crowds, but the thronging of gregarious animals. These Hhronka had shed remaining propriety with clothing, and directly below him he saw continued restless bobbing to and fro, jostling, casual coupling, even frequent blows exchanged. At the whole scene—but especially these last actions—Shree stared in utter astonishment and poorly concealed dark ripples of shame.

A cold wet wind blew in through the entrances and carried salt rot and the burnt untanned leather smell of packed Hhronka. Feeling sick and soiled (if you smell it, you're eating it), A.H. shivered in his damp onesuit and jacket and was reminded of a sea lion cave he'd once visited on the northern Oregon coast on distant Earth. (Had they left it less than a *year* ago?) This setting created the same atavistic primeval feeling, as though he looked far back through a window in time and was an unwelcome intruder there.

Suddenly wet drooled from his right nostril. He'd run out of tissue so he turned away from the others, bent, clamped shut his mouth, and puffed the bulk of the slime from his nose onto the stone, then wiped the remaining strings onto his sleeve, again craving a jigger or two or scotch to quiet the growing hum in his skull and itch in his throat. If he coughed now...

He studied the groups perpendicularly below the balcony, while being careful not to expose too much of himself over the rail. (Would they have noticed, even if he'd blown his nose on *them?*)

As often happens when observing an entire phenomenon, certain details will be recognized long before their importance. So now he noted two extremely odd features about the crowd.

First, he could see only one child present among the many adults. Initially he'd thought this was an adults-only event, but a little to his left sat two parents with their small son between them. Startled, he realized this was, in fact, the first young Hhronkan he had seen on the planet! Not even on their first tour of the city had any children been in evidence. In Wlaatan Hhronkan this was unthinkable; their young accompanied them everywhere as part of their education. Did these offshoots totally segregate their children, or were they just less fecund?

Either possibility bespoke a second heresy against the basic nature of the species.

The rest of the crowd seemed as impressed by the child's presence as he, but negatively. Each neighbor and passerby stared hard at him, and none offered a greeting or sign of the warmth or shared pleasure that both humans and Hhronka exchanged with parents. The crowd created a moat of isolation around the trio, who were patiently shunned and excluded from the garrulous behavior about them. But they continued to play, ignoring all else. How could their attitude toward children have changed so drastically?

Second, he had lived with Wlaatan Hhronka long enough to distinguish faces and forms, just as a Westerner on Earth finally learns to separate Orientals, or vice versa. These Hhronka displayed an inordinate frequency of multiple identicals. He was certain he saw not only groups of like twos, but also clusters of four, five, even ten! And often these identicals were not gathered together, as families would be, but scattered through the swarm, ignoring each other completely. The zygote-splitting frequency was slightly less for Wlaatan Hhronka than for humans. Had this branch naturally evolved this feature on Teffht or deliberately chosen and incorporated such a reproductive pattern, say by massive inbreeding or gene manipulation? Neither argument could support this broad a result, especially considering the confusion that identicals introduced in the processes of individuation and social recognition. Then, why do it?

Though Shree was rapt, A.H. started to point these facts out when he saw a swimmer, a large male, rise streaming from the water near a large guyot of rough boulders. He held a shiny wriggling fusiform animal clenched in his jaw as he clambered up the rocks toward another lone male who stood expectantly centered on the flat top. Stopping several steps below the peak, the swimmer bowed himself and snapped his head up to fling and catch at the other, who deftly snagged it midair in his own mouth. He held aloft in one hand a short, pointed rod of polished green metal or plastic. His face jerked as he bit into the squirming creature. The wet crunch of breaking live skeleton reached the balcony. The entire audience, engaged in random noise a moment earlier, somehow knew of this instant, fell totally still, and turned toward the guyot. The male on top held up both the rod and the scalloped limp animal, then dropped both to the rock. As one, the crowd trumpeted in a long boom that vibrated their balcony like the reed of a wind instrument.

Then A.H. saw that this leader had an exceptionally flat brow ridge, a face like a noseless human. It was Durren Gar. This gathering was not just for idle association, even on so brutish a level. There was a definite important purpose; seeing their chief host here certified that. It proved impossible to get Liifan's attention with looks alone as she stood on Shree's other side and stared as fixedly as he into the hushed audience.

In a few moments a second swimmer, equally large but female, entered the cave, approached the pyramid on its opposite side, and performed the same obeisance as the first. Again their balcony tuned itself to the audience's resonance. Gar then signaled with his arms at the two where they stood below his summit and backed down the landward slope as they advanced. When they attained the crest of the platform, each bent in a round arch to take objects from a crevice there. They twinkled dully in the low light and proved to be an elongated bracelet or forearm greave that they pulled over one hand to cover the area from wrist to midlimb. This coordinated move ended with a dual leap onto the center of the flat peak. Each performer stretched to clutch one of the short rods left by Gar, then stood facing the other like statuary.

With extreme slow motion they began circling, brandishing both the rod (pike?) and greave. Occasionally each would spin in place, then continue the bobbing carousel. This was some sort of ritual performance; the movements and audience responses were quite stylized, stiff, and rehearsed. The crowd, upon some visual clue he missed, chanted several lines in unison, but the words were not in a tongue he understood. Shree still gave no sign about the proceedings either.

A.H. settled into glancing for a change of action from stage to audience, though they stayed totally quiescent now. Suddenly one of the performers broke from the pattern, leaping toward the other with arms in rapid swinging movement. He couldn't see which one had attacked, but separation and return to the dance was immediate. Then a brilliant lightning flash, distant and without thunder, whited out the three entrances.

A series of parallel gashes like fork marks vertically lined the male's front torso. They dripped blackly in the brief glare. The attack had been real! Another flash showed the greaves ended in curving blades that extended from the wrist to beyond the opened hand. They must have been razor-edged, for the wounds were serious; the male was weaving as he bobbed on around the top of the guyot. This was no mere ritual, but a fight to the death.

Several times he had been an unwilling witness to mortal violence. (Franklin's chest spewing red, his face layered with terror, pain, and the realization of the fatal bullet wound, his body's brief autonomic struggle to overcome the damage, and his final acceptance of it all; his smile.) Now as then, he felt the superiority and guilty fascination of another's pain, and he knew the disgust at the horror he held like a rotting corpse.

He turned away, but Shree and Liifan were likewise entranced. The Primary was displaying horizontal black bars of extreme distress, and she seemed to be mirroring him, the way humans did one another at such times when not sure of a proper expression themselves. Their macabre companionship drew him back to the balustrade. He forced himself to view with near-clinical interest the process of physical destruction.

With the sound of spilling hot grease, blowing rain fell into the cave and splattered its pools. Flashes continued to spotlight the stage. The female sought to pursue her advantage as soon as possible and was repeatedly lunging, spinning, and leaping at her gored opponent. But he parried her with the desperation of the wounded. She was the swifter now, and more accurate; his counters were slower and more poorly placed. The pikes, used more often as saber than as épée, made a thwacking noise on impact with each other or the clawed greaves.

Still the male held on bravely, even periodically taking the assault and forcing her to retreat before his two-handed stab and slash. No. *Bravely* wasn't apt. A.H. would never agree with the rather myopic definition of the brave person as one who knows fear only after the peril and the coward as one who knows it before. Fear is caution's stepchild, and both elicit physiological changes necessary to survival. Any species whose evolved reaction system functioned any less competently would never evolve far. Even so, from his own experiences he knew there were situations, by time or circumstance, where *no choice* was available and "instinct" took over. This wasn't bravery, just successful natural selection, tallying fight or flight. For him, being brave consisted in first knowing *and* fearing you could be hurt or killed *if* you went ahead, and choosing to do so anyway because you felt the objective worth the risk. Any other response or lack thereof was foolhardy, not brave.

And these gladiators didn't appear brave. In the first place, what did they *have* to fight about? Two dead fish? Perhaps this ritual was an imperative for them. But they evinced only an absence of fear, which is not bravery's synonym. They merely seemed rash, fought without the clumsying terror usually embroidering such contests, as though only their bodies tested them, never their spirits.

Both were breathing in swelling gasps that could be heard echoing at the balcony even over the rain, and they had slowed the pace to recoup strength. Cuts from the pike tips laced their bodies with dripping lines. Now the male's first wound had spread a ragged apron of stringy black over the entire front of his torso and legs. If the battle wasn't ended soon, both would simply bleed to death. He heard their rasps become controlled again. Evidently the male felt the end of his reserves near, for he left himself open as he suddenly bounded forward with both arms outstretched. They held their pikes in the left hand, greaves on the right. She countered his slashing left by hooking his rod with her claws, at the same time driving her own pike at his dodging torso and piercing his left shoulder. The wound was near the surface, and as the diameter grew with her thrust, the shaft split out of the skin. In a long flash, A.H. saw the trench and a white flake of bone slat sticking out; blood gushed. While this happened, the male brought his right hand down her back, ribboning it so flesh and bone slats hung in fluttering strips to her midleg. They were literally vivisecting each other. And no one moved or screamed or cheered but sat mute to the final moments of the gory drama.

With his left arm severely crippled, the male had no grip on his pike, which the female wrenched loose with her greave. They staggered apart and stood looking at each other with arms drooping. He thought he heard one of them moan in pain, a buzzing sound. The female was facing their balcony when she used her greaved right hand to retrieve and hurl the male's pike like a javelin at his left side. He barely escaped it by hopping to his right, but she was ready as planned. He landed and sagged to the rock; she leaped forward and used her own pike to spear him in the chest, driving him backward. In the next flash, now joined to crashing thunder, A.H. saw the point emerging from the male's back, a conduit founting ink-blood from his pierced heart as she leaned on the shaft.

A.H. seemed to feel the needlepoint himself, the expanding pressure in his own chest as life was untimely ripped from him. The victim was silent, but A.H.'s cry of pain and relief at the climax of this shared horror also seemed to come from the male. Perhaps a trick of the cavern's topology carried this to the female, or his empathetic jerk above the railing caught her eye. She looked up directly at him, then displayed astonishment with opened nasal pore and mouth at his alienness. He quickly bent back below the railing. With an almost reflexive lunge the male used her distraction to rear against the impaling lance and rake her lower belly with his claws. Hhronkan abdominal cavities are distensible, but possess a thin anterior layer of supportive bone slats as well. The male's dying swat was sufficient to tear away a large section of this wall. Her released bowels spilled out onto him and the ground. A.H. clearly saw the watery sheen of the intestinal mesentery webbing the cascading pink ropes like chains of bursting soap bubbles.

The wind from the entrances carried the odor of rotten eggs up to them. The burning lead in his gut exploded, and he vomited freely, feeling the expulsion of palpable disgust. Shree and Liifan remained fixed beside him, displaying equal black patterns of deep emotion.

When he looked back, the female had fallen onto her back, and neither combatant moved. Gar was next to them, checking each. Curiously, he rolled each over onto their fronts and momentarily placed a small pillbox object to the back of their heads. Both times the bodies jerked and returned to the wrongly twisted limpness of the dead. He removed the weapons from them and lifted the female in his arms to turn and present her to the audience. Then he carried her to the seaward edge of the pile and simply heaved the corpse onto the slope. It rolled a few times but stopped with only the legs in the water. He repeated the casual disposal of the second body; it slammed into the first, and both rag dolls slid from the glistening rocks. They floated like dead wood and were quickly lost in the rippling shadows.

Naked torso ink-smeared, Gar curled arms and said something brief and formal to the audience. Even if the words had been understandable, the thunder and rain were too much competition. At this signal the entire audience returned to life, but now each of the beings expressed themselves individually. A few hooted in jubilation; some keened with a single low note in sorrow; most didn't react at all. They had already begun rousing as from a trance and leaving. The ritual was over.

Again the three rode in Gar's private vehicle, with A.H. supine on the cold floor, heading home in the outer concentric. They had not spoken since rushing from the cave to beat the dispersing crowd. Then the ennumbing mood had isolated each of them. Soon Liifan vibrated as if to shake off remnants of her own depression and began bluffly lecturing.

"You have seen an ancient rite we call the Covenant. Those who fought, always a male–female match, had chosen to end their lives and wished to do so in the presence of relatives, friends, enemies, and acquaintances."

"You mean it was a lovers' suicide?" asked A.H. incredulously.

"No. Although they may know each other, they are not lovers or spouses," she replied, displaying slight dark smears in apparent umbrage that he could think such was possible. "Such a voluntary pact is rare now, so it drew a large group of participants. The act of combat, of being physically torn from life by one's own kind, is considered preferable, for instance, to poisoning oneself at home like some vermin. The place and the method reminds us of our early ties to the original native Teffhtans, just as their language has intermingled with Hhronkan to create a hybrid tongue. As historian, Durren Gar conducts the ceremony. They once lived in such caverns and used such weapons in hunting and settling personal disputes before their technology grew. The combatants train in advance to create a true contest and avoid simple butchery. If one survives, or both become too injured to continue, Durren Gar . . . completes the Covenant for them."

A.H. had been drawn to her face from the calm start of her amazing explanation. Though the local Hhronka no longer showed full display, they did reveal broad emotion. As she finished, her faltering voice, downcast gaze, and dilated nasal sphincter betrayed her forthright but formerly hidden shame at what they'd just seen and that she was herself disturbed by it. Was this then the "something" she'd wanted them to share, to draw them into her influence for . . . what?

If only he had the strength and will to pursue this, he might crack the spine of this standoff now. But the fever's hum in his head had shifted to a roar; he felt sure he'd have to blow his nose on the car floor any second or drown in his own postnasal drip. His throat had been flayed raw, hollowed out like a reed flute through which dry hot winds blew to reduce him to a withered husk, and his whole sweating body quavered with the curiously pleasant, detached ache of bruised muscles. He wanted only to get to his bed and feel Joan's cool hands. If his temperature rose one more degree, he'd have to get real medical help aboard *Wind*.

Shree felt as useless. He still sat woodenly, ignoring his surroundings and simply staring straight ahead. Yet it wasn't a repeat of his first trauma at Gar's house. A sullen loathing bubbled just within his level of control, else he would have hidden his skin to prevent any black displays. He had prompted the entire mission, foisted it on the humans, using his resurrected friendship with Krieder, had come the light-years to find not only his transplanted kind but also descendants of his wife and daughter, true extensions of his own long-fractured core-family. Instead, he'd found a group of beings who, while physically resembling Hhronka, had degenerated into totally alien life-forms—even more alien than the humans had been when he'd first awakened in their midst.

He could not control the utterance of the question: "And does Durren Gar always treat their bodies like waste?"

On Wlaata, as on Earth, funerals were for the living, not the dead. Brief and poignant, they honored the deceased's life and cremated the body during the eulogy so attendees carried away only pleasant memories. The practice of calmly watching two Hhronka kill each other, then carelessly discarding the corpses could be but anathema to Shree.

Now her face exhibited humiliation in irregular waves of brown. "It is a traditional way to return the body substances to the natural cycles and..."

She realized no answer was actually required or could suffice to quell the wrath his query revealed.

Then A.H. remembered Gar's final formal statement, perhaps significant since it had served as benediction for the ceremony. He managed the energy to ask, "What did Durren Gar say to the audience at the end?"

She took a moment to see that he was in earnest and rasped a reply softly in Hhronkan. "It is a tribute to the permanence of life, a way to end the ritual on a hopeful tone. Roughly translated into your tongue it means: 'They are gone, but we remain. This is Life continued further than life.'"

Chapter 10

"So we really wouldn't need to land any of *Wind*'s generators. The engineers we talked with—our guides translated—promised they can have a trunk laid out to our city site in two weeks! Then we could tap into their grid anytime, using our own transformers to adjust current to our equipment, and add auxiliaries for backup as we grow."

P.C. was so genuinely impressed that he found it easy to play the charade of planning for the move to the surface. And they all continued their roles, even though no natives remained in the plant-lit enclave with them. All the assigned parties had arrived back at the house late and fairly close together. When they had explained to the visibly exhausted guides that they wished to meet in the court, the Teffhtan Hhronka had gratefully retired. But eavesdroppers might remain.

A.H. lay back on the niche next to Joan, fondling his third scotch. The medications were having their effects and the immediate alcoholic anesthesia had pushed away fatigue and misery so he was coherent once more and was even beginning to listen to the others' eager reports. Renata's description of the subterranean farms proved there was a greater capacity for food production than was needed, and this implied a shrunken population. Few children, a cultural attitude that made ritual of suicide, and more power and food resources than they could use.

Of course, the gradual extinction of the native amphibians had lessened numbers, but per Liifan they had never eaten Hhronkan food. So this all affirmed that the Teffhtan Hhronkan also had suffered a permanent decline. Another very un-Wlaatan character—given less-limiting conditions they should have exploded in numbers. What could have been the impetus for the evolution of yet another egregious change?

He rolled his neck under the delicious massage of Joan's strong fingers, feeling her nails occasionally scratch, breathing in the night's misty coolness, relishing it on his febrile skin. They had all donned jackets and were snacking on hot drinks and sandwiches. As he stood near the upmost pond, P.C. sipped coffee between sentences.

"These people may be well advanced in compumation, but I understood everything. It's as if no new principles have been discovered for a long time," he said with a brow-lifted query that asked if this kind of comment was safe to make should they be overheard.

A.H. nodded slightly, then remembered the *usstaa* and his guess as to its suspension technique. "By any chance did you take a close look at a Teffhtan grav flyer? I thought I noticed something unusual about one I saw up close."

His son stared back as if to accuse his father of sneaking a merge with him. "Yeah, he did. That is, Twee did when I was examining one of the rooftop solar units. Twee?"

The Hhronkan youth was startled from reverie. He sat alone on a low ledge to A.H.'s left, staring at Umar and Renata. The new plateau of intimacy these two shared had drawn everyone's attention. And each of them, including Umar and Renata, was aware that the others recognized this. Yet, in a common unspoken convention they all conspired to play a charade within the charade. They would pretend not to see this because the alternative public declaration and comment would be too embarrassing and totally incontinent here and now. So thin a line often stretches between self- and societal image.

A.H. also saw that fresh look of sexual satisfaction draped about them. His imagination popped him a vignette of his daughter mounted doggie-style by the Iranian, their faces vertically stacked, sweating, contorted with the unconstrained ecstasy of near climax. Though this was not her first affair, it seemed to be quite special to her. But he quashed the uneasiness he felt, and several imminent scenes of id-violence to Umar.

He'd made his peace with himself and Joan; he would let it go for now, yet watch to see it didn't hurt Rennie too much. And he truly had more important problems.

Twee's summation was concise to the point of brusqueness. "They have developed a technique using null-g to implant minute crystals of grav material throughout the boundary layer of any conductive surface and control wave output to produce the same effect as with a visible concentrated mesh, which is what you missed on their flyer, no doubt. They can maneuver such vehicles at any orientation to the planet, unlike ours, which must stay perpendicular to the opposing gravity vector. I was told these hulls last two to three of their years—that is, one and a half Wlaatan years—before being discarded, and require no more power than ours."

A.H. nodded in satisfaction. Ironically, Joan was having a more difficult time now than he adjusting to Umar and Renata, so he directed his next question to her. "What about our city's plans?"

She forced enthusiasm into her role play. "I was pleasantly surprised at the completeness, the detail. They've made my job easy! With only a few changes I can use their work to begin construction immediately. It will be a lovely place to live, high density and mechanization, yet bucolic, like some wheelies."

Her expression added that, if this was a trick, it was a thoroughly conceived one.

He decided to risk it. "Did any of you tour the buildings with the white refractive glass facing?" When she gave a puzzled shake, he turned to see the others do likewise. So Gar's guides were attempting to hide the artificial enclaves from them, and his discovery last night had been accidental. Which confirmed Liifan had lied about Gar knowing and had managed to conceal this from Gar as well; she too must have greater authority than he'd first thought.

Joan grew admiring. "From what I've seen, it appears that these Hhronka, like their ancestors on Wlaata, have tailored pop size, cultural organization, and technology to a status quo that allows them to thoroughly explore themselves creatively."

A.H. looked at his feet to cover his expression. He hadn't been able to tell any of them about the suicide Covenant or the other facts he'd learned, which would certainly put the pallor on her utopia.

"I was shown two- and three-dimensional art works and

music of totally novel forms, breathtaking in effect. One sculpture particularly struck me." His head came up in surprise. "I'm not sure whether it was real or holo. It was an irregular sphere that spun and glowed within a colored cloud. Absolutely hypnotizing. For some reason I thought of my folks' home back on Earth . . . first time in years."

They had tested one of the *usstaas* on her as well! Her lesser reaction was expected of a non-*baasa*. He hoped the difference had their hosts thoroughly confused.

"Public discussion halls are everywhere; many were active with groups supposedly debating philosophy and ethics. Anyone's inventiveness can be expressed at no cost to them: plays are produced, music performed, experiments carried out. All by loose guilds of volunteers whose memberships change with interest. The products are 'cast for free on the public holo, with plenty of advanced promo. Even sports are handled in this way. One game I watched that's popular now is like a combination of soccer and R-ball, played in an enclosed low-g court with a hollow ball that has a tube of heavy liquid free inside it. Makes the ball gyrate wildly when kicked. It's real fast and exciting."

Reclined on the opposite side of the ponds from the others, Droom had contributed little as she left a wide fallout zone of food debris around the tray she'd slung together before the meeting. Brushing her mouth with a hand, she swallowed and said, "I dislike flawing your admiration, but I am not nearly as smitten by our newfound cousins' abilities. After spending this entire day with some of their best physicists, I am convinced that, though they have a functioning technology that dabbles at the phenomenon's edges, they do not comprehend high-density fields in the least! Not even the knowledge we took to the Sleep before the last Freeze, and that the expeditions here possessed. It is as if they have actually lost ground! How is this possible, especially when the extinct Teffhtans originally sent us the means to create the unified field theory? I spent most of my time giving lessons in advanced physics."

Which was her code for revealing that she had left them as ignorant as before. A.H.'s knit brows and pressed lips denoted she shouldn't pursue this line further; he'd explain the contradiction later. Grudgingly she took the hint. She'd been a little rough on their hosts perhaps, but mixed in with the stick of criticism was the carrot of improving their technology. And if her observation was even partly correct, it was yet another anomaly to add to the mystery list. She was being her natural irascible self, and in the midst of all the adulation this rebuke would also allay suspicion of their charade.

Alone in the group, Shree had failed to participate in any way. Sitting beyond A.H. and Joan by the second pool, he had silently brooded the whole time. Now the ire he'd suppressed since their return finally overwhelmed him. His face blushed with black whirling smears, then hid itself under tan smoothness; he quickly straightened up from the rock and turned to them.

"Forgive me. I . . . I must be alone for a while . . . think and order my . . ." His mumbled apology became inaudible as he began to bob toward the entrance, seeking escape from their gaze. A.H. stepped in front of the large being both to question and offer consolation, though he knew it to be a useless gesture. Still, friendship often demands useless gestures.

"Shree, can I—" he said as he started to palm the broad warm chest. But the Primary quickly intercepted his hand and clutched his forearm so tightly it throbbed in pain.

Bending to his ear level, Shree whispered vehemently, "No matter what occurs now, I cannot, *will* not, live with these—"

His voice snapped in a throat spasm, and he shot erect. A.H. looked up in alarm at the bulging glassy face to see it staring transfixed at the dark entry tunnel. They all twisted toward the tall slender figure standing there.

It bobbed forward into better light and spoke to Shree in good Hhronkan. "I am to accompany you if you leave."

Shree and Droom knew her from living association, Twee from holoimages, and A.H. from Shree's total projection. It couldn't be her but it was: Feeahra! The delicate roundness of brow, the low cheek contours, the deep violet eyes, and full lips were there, all exactly twinned to memory. Powerful transferred emotion pulled at A.H. Her graceful movements under the filmy yellow robe aroused him; the resonant timbre of her voice captured his desire. He almost rushed to hold her. Droom hopped up and spilled her tray's remains; the other four stood frozen, trying to assimilate the presence of a seeming apparition.

The female respected their astonishment and waited silently. After several seconds Twee moved to her with a tormented question.

"Mother?" he hissed in Hhronkan as dark query circles mixed with white joy.

Her stiffness at their undue inspection melted, and she came forward more confidently to Twee. Greeting him traditionally, she revealed an astute mind. "I am Huulall Oont. Do I remind you of someone?" she asked without display, thereby assuming his affirmative reply.

They saw Twee's struggle to control his uncoiled emotions. Each felt his juxtaposed chagrin, disappointment, and bittersweet joy. Shree seemed to recover first, but A.H., still in physical contact with him, could feel the cauldron of emotions beneath the Primary's shell of self-possession.

"I wish to walk to the shore," Shree said peremptorily to her in Hhronkan.

Again she demonstrated acuity by at once abandoning her position with Twee and returning to the entry. "When you are ready," she replied.

Suddenly concerned for Shree's stability, A.H. said under his breath, "Are you sure you can handle this?"

The being looked down and flushed white bars of dry humor up his face. "Perhaps this is what we all need . . . what I need."

A.H. caught both levels of meaning. Why not pump the new native for information and also enjoy the company of someone who at least looked like love to him—a pretense everyone engaged in occasionally. As Shree moved past him, he pressed his hand to the broad robed back in support. Huulall followed him out the mouth, and the others settled back into their charade.

Stroller and trailing escort were silent as they bobbed down the radial toward the sea. By the zigzag rows of yellow-white lamp circles they saw the street was deserted. The low, gray, cottony walls of burgeoning storm was still minutes out on the metallic sheet of water, but its damp carrier breeze swept runnels of fine sand down the sidewalk at their bare feet. The coolness and open roof of bright stars made him expansive, and he became relaxed.

Relaxed, not somnambulant. Although he'd been traumatized momentarily by Huulall's appearance, he wasn't gullible enough to accept it as coincidental. This perceptive female was Gar's plant, sent to him now to confuse his thinking and garner from him whatever they could use to obtain their true goal— whatever that was. Gar probably *was*, among other things, a historian, with easy access to the records of the three Wlaatan expeditions, which he'd so far kept them too busy to view.

Knowing that Shree's wife and daughter had been in the last crew, he had summoned her look-alike.

Her existence itself presented yet another enigma: Hhronkan chromosomes might have a different structure than human, but they functioned the same. An individual's phenotype would probably not cohere without *some* alteration through thousands of generations. Therefore rare coincidence may have played some part in this. Or she could be the result of exquisite plastic surgery—but done so quickly? What was the full truth of Huulall's origin?

He decided not to pursue this dead end. A more emotional path might cull her confidence. It was easy to let fantasy blend with reality, to feel if not believe that he was simply out with Fee, enjoying once again the privacy of being alone together and the release of tension nature's unfettered aura had always given them. He slowed his pace and twisted to look back at her, beckoning her to join him, which she at once did.

"Why did you come to me tonight?" he asked at the street.

Without hesitation she said, "I was assigned your guide duty for tonight. There are many ways by which strangers in Atuum might be harmed. We wish to see to your safety."

She was at least well trained. "Do you find speaking old Hhronkan difficult?" he asked.

"No. As with all imprinted knowledge, it is similar to how one feels when attempting to renew a long-untried skill and finding it gradually returning."

Her display pattern of curling gray smoke suggested complete calm—an expressiveness worthy of any Wlaatan Hhronkan. Yes, well trained. They entered the next hemisphere of light, and he paused to search her face again. She was definitely more slender, less well exercised than Feeahra had been, but as lovely.

"You look exactly like my wife of long ago," he said, nearly performing the automatic gesture of fingertipping her face as he always had, her white pleasure waves pressing back gently.

"You are aware that I assumed so from the young one's question. He is your son?"

"Yes, our son," he answered, playing on the double meaning of the statement.

With sinusoidal brown streaks of empathy, she said, "She must have been very important to your life for you to still think of her in present tense."

Perceptive, intelligent, and emotionally honest—as Fee had been. He felt a need to change the discussion topic. "From talking with Durren Gar, I understand most Teffhtans have lives of total leisure. Do you not find that rather pointless?"

She became thoughtful, then defensive. "I do not believe this is an accurate judgment. Our lives are not spent simply in recreation. We are all productive from time to time, though productivity does not require the creation of utilitarian things or ideas. What we have here is total *choice,* including that of total leisure. Of course many of us are engaged, at any one time, in such nonproductive activity. But also most of us either sequentially or simultaneously pursue other areas—cultural, scientific, educational—to improve ourselves."

This certainly agreed with Joan's observations.

"For instance, Durren Gar has authored some excellent critiques of the early post-native-Teffhtan epochs that have helped us understand how our current society evolved and where it might go. No machine could do this. I myself am now sculpting, attempting to create forms that visually and palpably can evoke the buried emotions of the viewer. Have you seen any of the *usstaas?* I helped design their shapes."

She was drawing him toward a dangerous topic. Apparently they had deliberately tested Krieder's and Joan's reaction to these sculptures, or whatever they really were. Huulall was digging to see if he'd had such an encounter unintentionally. He hadn't, but he had confirmed Krieder's diagnosis of their distant effects. Several times he'd attempted to spread his Self and had been pained by this mindnet. Even his power couldn't overcome its interference. He had a theory about how this could be done, but the procedure was drastic enough to be shelved until truly needed.

"No, I have not seen one, but I have been told they are intriguing. You portray an idyllic life here. I wonder how those two poor people who killed each other last night felt about it."

A daring revelation if it should get to Gar, but chances must be taken to break the stalemate here. They were in the darkness between two globes, yet he could see her black waves of vexation.

"Covenants are a very small part of our world; we should not be judged by these acts either. Those two chose suicide because they felt there was nothing remaining in existence but to repeat experiences already repeated many times. That too is a free choice. No society is flawless; no culture can create an environment satisfying to all. You have no similar events on Wlaata?"

He placed his hand on her chest. She did not flinch. "Are we now being monitored?"

"Only at a distance," she replied so quickly he felt it was so.

"We Wlaatans have been too dedicated to maintaining our survival against the common enemy of the home planet's Freezes. The Children and the Repositories were all our hope and made all individuals important to the goal. Such do not suicide. Now that has changed. The influence of the humans is great. Many of them kill themselves. But they expect so much from living while giving so little—some, at least. I, however, do not understand how *any* sentient being could become so bereft of hope, so . . . *bored,* even in an entire lifetime!"

Huulall also showed dark bars of anguish but was silent. He felt close to her through this common sorrow and let the sensation enwrap them. The radial's black ribbon dived under fine sand, and they stepped onto the beach. The offshore storm was now about ten kilometers out, its cumulus wall textured by periodic soundless lightning. The breeze had quickened to a wind that still felt refreshing. Their four-toed feet sank through the blowing sand mist into the cool shifting grit, which slipped under their full weight and forced them to alter to a shorter gait for better traction. Along the coast in both directions Atuum's high-rise lights pocked its black cake pan—cover skyline, except near them where the old low dwellings merged in gloom splotched by street globes that seemed one with the climbing sheet of stars above.

As they approached the last berm and slid down onto wet, packed sand, the surf's percussion jumped in volume and cold spume began to dampen their skins. The littoral strip was lit only by the globes of the concentric boulevard at the top of the beach and by the crystal starlight. To their right the water past the curling surf lines was a black undulating membrane.

Caught in the transition zone between beach, water, and sky, his depression slowly faded as they went west. He recognized they'd acted automatically in concert to continue the walk farther than his request. Again the fantasy grew in his weary mind. With few changes this could have been any of a dozen places, a dozen evenings, along the shore of the Narrow Sea. And beside him, so near he could hear her exhalations above the wind, was the person who had first helped him learn the power of loving beyond himself. All the escaping emotions he'd snared at the first instant of seeing her in the enclave rushed free in him. All the conscious decades of being without her, and the nonconscious millennia in the Sleep, of substituting only memory and holoimages, seemed to crush him under their enormous weight. Then she accidentally brushed against him, and the weight was gone. Their arms entwined in a spiral that ended with clasped hands.

At first they were stilted in the touching, discomfited by the last vestiges of reality. But as the walk continued along the shiny cool flat, these too disappeared as rapidly as the washed impressions of their footprints. Their 'twined limbs softened together, becoming tactile tongues that spoke a language only the two of them would ever understand. His pace slowed, but she halted them. He turned her until the city lights showed her rounded face clearly. The crosswise slit pupils of her eyes were bowed open until their black discs seemed to merge with the depths of the water behind her, as though he looked through her head, and was drawn into the larger aquatic mystery of which she was a small projection.

"Love always has a high price. Do you believe that?" he asked softly of her sea eyes.

"Yes, I do," her thick dark lips replied, but a striking wave covered the sound. Her exposed skin rippled with a white display of desire that moved against his torso like fingers.

Suddenly his need for her was sufficient reason for existence, to probe her fantasy, physically and mentally, as he always had when they'd been close. By habit he began to strengthen and deploy his Self. But it struck the impenetrable barrier of stinging needles. She moved against him, and her display's ripples combed his body as the surf rubbed the shore. His gential labia firmed, separated to release his phallus as her lower torso hotly pressed his.

"Not here. In the sea," she whispered, tugging him forward by his robe belt into the rushing cold water.

At first he didn't understand. Coupling in water was not a Hhronkan habit, and he had a moment of doubt. When he was slower than she wanted him to be, she stripped both garments from them and fit herself to him again, locking her mouth to his. With the waves surging at his midleg, he felt the warm sponginess of her lips, and his own mouth and thorax filled with her exhalation. Closing his nasal sphincter too, he responded to the love-breathing until his mind spun from the intimacy and carbon dioxide buildup. A sudden covering wave soaked and jostled them. They parted and gasped as she drew him out farther. Very quickly they were beyond the breakers and were lifted off their feet by a swell. Now the fluid seemed to have no temperature as skin adjusted to the cold. Still clasping one hand, they swam straight out with their other wriggling limbs.

The rolling motion lessened as the bottom dropped away beneath them. While they moved, she pulled him to her and coiled her legs around his so they lay sideways in the water. He slipped into her warm, welcoming body; they released themselves to the floating sensation without and within them. Periodically the water broke over their heads and shoulders, but they hardly noticed. The undulating surface thrust them together and apart with a pleasant rhythm. Millennia passed again for Shree . . . but differently.

"Pprring!" yelled a loud voice above them.

He twisted his head up from the water in surprise. But Huu-lall jerked with instant terror, attempting to part herself from him and reverse their drift. Twenty-five meters ahead and to the left, one of the city's pylons rose from the sea like a buoy. But from the way the angle of its tall hexagonal column never altered from the vertical while the slanting water slapped at its base, it was obviously rooted in the sea bottom. The crystal antenna could be seen pointing toward Atuum as usual. The itching mumble he'd been able to ignore since arrival on Teffht bridged his awareness with increased force.

They had stopped swimming but were still drifting seaward. Her struggle had become frantic in trying to free herself from his limbs. He actually wasn't holding her, but they were so entangled that his cooperation was necessary. And he was so startled by her wild fear, that understanding it and calming her were foremost.

"What is wrong? There is nothing to fear!" he called as he tried to hold her protectively.

The waves had been increasing in amplitude for several minutes, presaging the arriving storm. Now they slid down a deep trough and rose onto a high peak as a cannon-shot thunderclap and flicking lightning announced the blowing rain. He couldn't hear her shrieking voice clearly and decided the weather change had simply been too sudden for her. But in the next bolt's glare, he saw her wide eyes gesturing toward the pylon. It was the source of her terror! But how could part of some kind of advanced comm network cause—

The solution gelled as he became fully rational once again. The storm and her fear had shattered the fantasy, and he saw many things at once. Indeed, this was not the strong and selfless person he'd loved so long ago, but a superficial reflection with none of her mental qualities. A brief flare showed her face scabbed with darkling horror. What he beheld within made her an ugly counterfeit. He was not loving a reincarnation of his dead Fee but adultering with her poor copy.

And the pylon circle was not a communications system. Twee and P.C. had found the mindnet effect absent at the landing strip—*outside* the pylon boundary! They were the generator of the mindnet, with the *usstaas* playing some subordinate role! If he took her outside its influence, he could merge Selfs. The Kmeaan mystery might be solved at last; her fear could be the key! Never before, even during the Covenant duel, had he seen one of these creatures show true fear of any kind. This terror would be forcing her now to scream truthful thoughts, easily read.

Leaving his legs spiraled with hers, he coiled his right arm around her neck and pulled at the water with his left. They rose and fell with the waves and gained slowly on the imaginary line that curved between pylons. Then she realized his intent and writhed in his clutch with shocking strength, even briefly biting him with maniac force on the root of his arm and cutting open the skin. But he only tightened their joining and paddled, certain he was correct and justified in his action.

It was difficult to know where the pylon line was since, with the wind-stirred waves' disorientation, he might merely swim a slow circle and put the pylon behind them but actually go along the shore. He glanced back at the city lights for direction. Several of the glowing spots were rising above the skyline level. They were coming for them, rescuing one of their operatives and recapturing a straying prisoner. He must act quickly. Looking from shore to pylon, he plotted a line parallel to that one and stroked along it. Over his back he watched the pylon top with its glassy dendritic antenna at last move toward his feet.

Above the storm's din the voice of the structures keened with a new sound, louder and more final. They were beyond the mindnet. The moving lights already looked halfway to them; he

could see ovals of white rolling on the waves directly under
each one. Huulall's struggles had lessened with her increased
gasping; she had given up screaming at him and now fought
only to breathe through his wooden coil of arm.

He too was winded, forcing the stiff bellows of his bone-
trussed torso to pump at max speed. But he couldn't wait to
rest. It shouldn't require either a deep or sensitive merge to read
her now, so close and exhausted. Focusing his reserve energy,
he squeezed out his Self and enmeshed her with it. Fatigue
skinned her consciousness, and the worm of terror writhed beneath this, nearly obliterating her very sense of identity. He
concentrated his Self and filtered out this chaos . . .

That instant she died. It was to him like the liquefaction of a
metal spiderweb, made molten by an enormous burst of power.
Only his reflex action removed the contact before he too was
consumed. His mind sank into blackness and his body under the
waves. But he had glimpsed her reality, knew she was *no‘*
Hhronkan, and found where the answers to the mystery lay.

Mowry accepted he was having difficulty sublimating his
rancor when he turned away from the observation bay and the
duty officer let the question die on her face as she swiveled back
to the screen bank. Bad for discipline, but—damn it!—that was
a large part of the reason for his continual mood. He knew most
of the nonbridge crews, human and Hhronkan both, thought him
a hard-core militarist. Unfair. It wasn't the aggressive destruc-
tive facet of the Service he found desirable, let alone enjoyable.
It was the order of efficient training and established routine that
imparted survivability in threatening situations—even if that
meant the best defense be used before the offense. (He was no
Meethlah.) The comps executed the actual operations, but some
person had to decide first to execute. That was discipline's
primer, and those now in charge had failed badly.

Perhaps his authority had been suspended when they'd arrived at "Teffht," but this craft and its safety were surely his
extended responsibility. Freight shuttling to the LEO monitor
platform for Eurosov Region (little glory and no promotion) or
majordomo of this brain-drain wheelie (plenty of glory and promotion), it was the same for the captain of any vessel.

It had been an honor to be asked to command the first ftl
mission—his crews by God *worked!*—yet he'd been frustrated
from the very first decision made by the Committee: not to

attack those robot drones. Since they had threatened *Wind* without even knowing who crewed her, they should have at least tried to incapacitate the unmanned craft before they'd rendezvoused. A single fifteen-mega nuke, detonated fifty clicks from the intruders, and they would have learned whether the Teffhtan comps had the circuitry to withstand that kind of radiation pulse. The data could prove vital to surviving a future battle. Now such a test was impossible with the three remaining drones englobing the *Wind*. And its only laser battery was mounted on the tip of the mirror boom to pulverize any dangerous debris while in flight. Those cannons couldn't even be aimed astern, where one drone parked. Their only other defense was the fighters, and they wouldn't even give him permission to fuel them!

Then had come the risky, but admittedly necessary, vanguard. Well, Krieder and Shree Shronk had volunteered—who could understand what really boosted nhumbies or honkers anyway? But to bring down their own families and their two top diamondheads! At least he'd felt somewhat secure with the constant info their wafer transmitters had given him. He'd known what the hell was happening! Now that frequency was deliberately jammed too, and Shree himself had used a native comm to request a complete English transcomp file! Smoothed-out cerebrum, without doubt. How were they supposed to communicate any sensitive data if the locals knew the language?

Those two had played a very dangerous game, and apparently had lost. After twenty-four hours without a report, Shree Shronk had called on the native comm. Behind him had stood that "Liifan." How was he to judge whether the report had been factual or coerced?

And so, what was he supposed to goddamn do? Of course, the Committee had *now* brought him into their discussions of the next move. When he had strongly suggested immediate "minimum preparedness," they'd criticized his "obvious lack of perspective"! What else was there. Bend-over-and-spread-your-cheeks netted only Vietnams!

He turned back into the slightly "downhill" alcove to hide his wrath and anxiety. The decking vibrated more noticeably than usual, and the axis of the colony wobbled several microseconds of arc, enough to set off alarms in increasing staccato.

Now the officer's face held panic. "Captain, sensors show

massive overloads fore and aft, engine and mirror booms! Heavy damage!"

His first leap carried him back into the bay window with an impact that set his head ringing. Looking up through the blister, he saw several black irregular tears in the slanted mirror's surface. A glittering chunk of metal shot down past the hub through the spokes, luckily missing them. The drones had lased the cannon pod beyond the mirror! Pieces were expanding out in a sphere . . . the rim!

"Close all chevron shields!" he yelled at the officer, and watched to ensure she acted immediately.

The engines couldn't be seen directly from the bridge, so he pull-walked around the deck to the next empty station past hers and touched several switches on the surveillance panel. Crew began to enter the bridge and dart to emergency stations; he took grim satisfaction in their rapid response. Cameras on the aft side of the rim swung toward the thrusters. He watched the scene shift from stars to the cylindrical housings.

The enemy beams had perforated each venturi cone and burst away one entirely. That meant some structural shielding, cooling radiator plumbing, and superconducting coils were gone. They carried spares for all of it, or could manufacture the rest. They could still repair on their own. But if they were hit again . . .

For now they were defenseless and immobile. The launch ports in the aft hub were intact, but with the drones on a contain-or-destroy footing he wouldn't order any Roc out to instant vaporization. *Wind* was bottled shut. Whatever happened would be determined by those on the planet, and he didn't even know if they were still alive.

His hand suddenly felt wet; he looked down, surprised to see he'd slashed it to the bone on the panel's edge.

Chapter 11

Above the background thrumming, the loud rasp on the stone floor called them both—wrapped tightly as mated earthworms —from a light doze. They were aware of the rain's deluge slamming against the closed skylight of their room and then of the presence in the doorless entry. They came erect together under the heavy quilt, Joan gripping his arm tightly, but A.H. knew it was Liifan.

"I have brought Shree."

The wording alone connoted injury. They were forced by the night chill to take extra time adding jackets to day clothes, then followed her onto the balcony. The subdued roar became pronounced. The enclave's skylight remained open, and through it a cataract fell, surging the pools into a short river that swept under the far wall. Drips and rivulets glittered in the bead plant light. When they reached the floor, a blue-white flare of lightning placed a spotlight on a body lying facedown among the spindly foliage in the top pond. A.H. bent to it.

"The guard is dead," Liifan said near his ear, her hot breath fogging as she took his arm firmly.

Then he saw the narcosorb pistol in her left hand. The blue metal squirt gun put a measured dollop of somnotizer onto the skin, causing instant unconsciousness. The malevolence chilled him: why use a nonlethal weapon, then allow drowning? She hurried them to the first portal to the pool's left. The large room was furnished completely yet simply with metal and ceramic accouterments that bore no Wlaatan lineage in their designs. No chaises evaginated from the bare stone floor, and only cubed glow lamps hung from the walls. It was as if these Hhronka had thrown away tradition and started again from anatomy alone.

Shree lay on a high stretcher-cart near a huge gray metal table. Behind him stood two natives garbed in Ortaan-like costumes of jet. He then realized Liifan also wore this dress. A giddy thought struck him: mourners? No. The monitor bands girdling the Primary were sending life signs that kept the boxes beneath him chirping and blinking. There was no obvious damage. But the dirty gray of severe trauma drew lines in his sagging skin. Death had come close. Liifan spoke in the native dialect to the bearers, who left with diffident bows.

"Baay has told you?" Shree asked as his eyes opened. Despite his appearance his voice was strong, nearly casual.

A.H. took note of the first name use; it indicated a change in mutual comprehension between the two. "No, nothing." He watched the naked torso fill slowly with air.

"We have been lied to, as we guessed." Liifan failed to respond. "From the start we were watched and guided in action and thought. Our witness of the Covenant was the first and only function not prearranged by Gar."

Of course, it fit: dog and pony show. Even his trip to the city that first night had been allowed to test his response to an *usstaa*. Perhaps finding the communal enclave in the rainbowglass building had been unintentional but he'd learned nothing not already suspected. These Hhronka were not the twin cousins they pretended to be.

"And tonight, the guide... Huulall was killed on Gar's orders."

A.H. felt a surge of desolation for Shree as the being paused momentarily, then continued. "I was merged with her beyond the mindnet when the drones overtook us and somehow burned out her brain."

Suppressing shock, he heard Joan's sharp intake of breath and glanced from Shree to Liifan, fearful Shree had let slip a vital secret.

Liifan said to them, "We already knew from the old records there was a Primary Shree Shronk who was a *baasa*. We confirmed identity your first night here with retinal pattern."

They'd understood this would be an inevitable discovery; Shree hadn't bothered even to adopt an alias. They had merely hoped to find important answers first, which they had and without using *baas*. Apparently A.H.'s power was still unknown.

Liifan resumed: "The pylon's warning told the monitors they were beyond the *usst* field—the mindnet, if you wish—and its inhibition. Durren Gar was fearful Huulall would reveal the truth to Shree so he overloaded her link."

"Our conjecture was not wholly correct," said Shree. "The mindnet exists only in the city, and it is created by the pylons and central pillar; the *usstaa* sculptures act as booster nodes of concentration. Yet I suspect inhibition of *baas* is not its primary function. What that and 'the truth' are I cannot guess." He stared at her. "But you do wish to tell us."

Without hesitation Liifan said, "Yes. In the morning Durren Gar will announce your confinement to this residence 'for your own safety.' Guards already surround us."

A.H. and Joan exchanged alarmed looks, but Shree made no sign.

"He will demand you begin construction of your city at once, and start bringing down the rest of your people. He also intends to continue the lies, telling you Shree has been hospitalized and Huulall drowned to bring pressure on you out of sorrow and guilt. He had drugged and imprisoned Shree in another residence not far from here. Durren Gar takes no chances; he is ruthless."

Her pause and dark display were well done, whether genuine or not. "You have become hostages. This I finally could not allow. I rescued Shree and came here to aid you."

"And in return?" asked A.H.

"There is a fantastic evil here, a lingering crime of such proportion it can no longer be borne. It must be ended! I require your help, and I know you will want to give it."

"Why? What would so concern us?" A.H. replied, becoming galled that Shree was taking this so calmly, regardless of injury.

"I could tell you, but would I be believed? And even if Shree's *baas* were not inhibited by the *usst* field, I understand there is no guarantee of truth in a merge. You are correct, Shree, *baas* interference is only an unsought by-product of the mindnet. There are, after all, no *baasa* among us."

"How can that be?" A.H. exclaimed. "It is naturally evolved in Hhronka!"

"No, of course not," murmured Shree distractedly, not hearing him. "For you are not Hhronka."

"What?" said A.H. and Joan together.

"You did contact Huulall then?" asked Baay hopefully, in turn ignoring their consternation.

"Only enough to know her fundamental nature," Shree said.

"Then it may be easier to accept that the proof I wish to show you concerns the object of your mission here. I wanted you to see the Covenant first, so I lied about the city hub. The truth is there."

Shree blipped a white-ring nod. "That was in Huulall's mind."

A.H. saw loose ends start to join.

Baay grew more confident. "But alone I cannot get us there; many guards and other obstacles must be overcome." She continued cautiously. "Even my loyal associates refuse to enter the pillar—for reasons I accept, as you will see. *Baas* such as you have been recorded to wield would help greatly."

Now Shree became animated. "Yes. But I demand most of us go, as witnesses. Joan, bring the others."

She started to go, but A.H.'s forebodings resurfaced. "Wait! How do we know this isn't another scheme to find our strengths or weaknesses, another experiment?"

"You really have no choice," Baay replied harshly. "Our drones destroyed your craft's thrusters two hours ago. Should you manage the improbable and repair them, you still could not escape our hundreds of patrol drones. Therefore you must find a way to use what I will reveal to overcome Durren Gar. Otherwise, he *will* use the Hhronka as he wishes and kill every human!"

None of them felt much shock or anger; it fit too well with their deepest fears. It all seemed rather inevitable—now.

With resignation A.H. asked, "Why would you turn traitor and help us now, and why didn't you help us before this?"

At the word *traitor* dark smears flitted over her face. "Because Huulall was a friend . . . for a very long time. And because Durren Gar is my father."

Her gaze fell, and she wouldn't acknowledge their silent gestures of disbelief then grudging understanding: truth or trap, they would have to proceed as Baay directed. They had been helpless pawns since they'd landed and still were. Joan went out to get the others without speaking.

Baay became quite businesslike to minimize emotion. Holding up her pistol she said, "This is the only weapon I have; I took it from the guard after she . . . fell asleep."

"Very well. What other living safeguards must we deal with?" returned Shree, his Meethlah ethics making him more circumspect.

She tallied thoughtfully. "I can divert the underway's monitors as I have this house's. They will record nothing extraordinary for several hours. We can use Durren Gar's car once more and not be questioned. Once inside the pillar's innermost complex, there will be no people. And there is no mindnet there. I can nullify the complex's systems from within as well. But getting inside it will be difficult; live-guard patterns in the outer perimeter are constantly altered."

Joan led in a puffy-faced, map-skinned group striving desperately to awaken. Each of them studied the recumbent figure with relief and quickly greeted him. He was recovering fast enough to join Baay in sketching the latest twists and allowed no rebuttal to his orders. The women made little protest, to A.H.'s relief. But, of course, he couldn't keep Droom silent for long, even with a black circle of negation.

"And why am I not going?" she demanded incredulously.

Shree remained unintimidated. "The party is as large as it need be, and one Hhronkan must stay in case we are late in returning. Then you, Joan, and Renata will stir about and speak to maintain the impression we are all here. How long do we have before replacement guards arrive here?"

"Three and a half hours," Baay answered. "We should be able to get back before then."

"We must leave at once," Shree said. He looped a hand to the cart's lower compartments and extracted two stimutabs. After downing them, he rose slowly from his pallet.

"I need some items from the terminal room," Baay said. "And I will have my people remove this guard before they go. The humans should dress warmly; it will be quite cold. And we must all wear grav flux belts; bring one of yours for me. I will be at the underway entrance."

In the dim overhead light of their room Joan pulled a heavy parka from the luggage and helped A.H. try it on. The rain continued above them; thunder vibrated the floor. It reminded him of the night Shree had announced his intention to come here, the new closeness he and Joan had found, the way they'd held hands in that rain.

"I'm sorry it came out this extreme," he said sadly. "This isn't what I was looking for."

She smiled to exonerate him. "It could have gone several other ways too. That's the gamble we both took, remember?"

He nodded and swallowed at a sudden lump. "If the gamble doesn't pay off, I want you to know I still think it's been worth the price."

"So do I," she whispered as she kissed him lightly.

He more admired her than cherished her, and he couldn't kiss her on the face again. Instead, he pressed his mouth to her soft warm palm. "And I think loving you has been worth everything," he finished and backed from her.

Her eyes glinted with unshed tears; she only smiled again. He was the last one through the tubeway portal, and as he looked back a last time he saw her and Rennie still watching him from the balcony.

The car's slowing fractured their detachment and brought attention to the forward windscreen. The radial tube ended up ahead fifty meters beyond the innermost concentric. They floated at the platform as Baay went to the panel and touched it rapidly, then inserted a rec bloc into the slot. Slowly the white terminal bulkhead in front of them split vertically and slid horizontally. The vehicle nosed through into darkness—ingestion by some metallic behemoth.

In the tube light coming past the closing bulkhead, they saw an enormous chamber rising above several stories to a dim girdered roof. It curved away on both sides into a blackly invisible twinkling distance. Many levels could be seen through the grid floor below. Heavy and light machine operations seemed to be occurring everywhere at random. There were no neat rows or clusters of anything, vertically or horizontally; each performance clanked, thudded, and flashed on its own rhythm without relation to its neighbor. Transport cars lay and floated in various stages of dishabille, with mobile metallic spiders and rooted treelike robots in unceasing attendance: army ants dismantling beetles. It was like Mars's lush stratified rain forest transmogrified to machinery. No native Hhronka were to be seen; then the bulkhead shut, their car's lights dimmed, and nothing could be seen.

"This is the maintenance garage beneath the hub plaza. People seldom come here," said Baay, explaining the obvious. "I've programmed a fault into the car that will require attention from a station near the center of this level, where we wish to go. We will be challenged as we leave, but I can cover our presence."

Since the EM lift of the mass-driver tunnel was gone, A.H. assumed they now floated on grav flux. He heard the nearby swoosh of compressed gas between lulls of the other cacophony. Their self-guiding car was using this as propulsion. Like a low-flying blimp, it threaded a three-dimensional passage amid the unlit cluttered space. The repair robots must have been using IR or other EM, sonics, or laser navigation for their tasks, perhaps because these were more accurate than visible light. Periodic red and white sparks of heated material fountained, and in the reflected glows they could barely see mechanical-jungle vignettes, predator attacking prey in unselfconscious frenzy.

The sharp bump on the car's nose slewed them forward like blown grass. He heard clothing rustle near the panel, then the right side wall opened, admitting cold, ozone-metallic odors, and an increased noise level. A small torch came on, putting a circle of yellow onto the wall-ramp, and Baay followed it to leap onto the open decking. They were preparing to follow her when a loud voice erupted, speaking the incomprehensible native dialect. Their guide quickly bobbed away with the torch into the nearby unmoving machinery.

"Baay!" A.H. shouted at her.

Again fearing betrayal, he jumped from the ramp to chase her. The decking proved very slippery, and his right foot slid back under him, landing him painfully on his knees and palms. Some type of lubricant made his hands slick. He stood gingerly and managed to move to a drier surface. Glancing ahead, he saw the torch circle strike a large column; her hands fumbled with a panel mounted on it. He got to her as fast as slipping tennies and machine-barked shins allowed. From the shoulder bag she'd brought, she extracted a rec bloc. As she looped her arm toward the panel's slot, he grabbed it back.

"What're you doing?" he demanded.

She tore free easily. "It is too late for your distrust! I must explain our presence to the garage monitors at once before they report it to the live guards!"

As she proceeded, he almost hit her, then capitulated. She was correct, as before. They had no way to judge her actions, and no other ally on whom to depend. He'd have to ward off further panic and just hope. The panel showed one red eye, and she said a few native words at it. Part of the column at their left swung open.

"Quick! Get the others in here!" she said, jerking out the card and pointing the torch back at the car.

Sixty seconds later the party was inside the reclosed column. Ascending illumination blinded them; they looked at each other. They were tarnished with black sooty filth from the garage, A.H. worst of all, hands and pants coated with greasy film.

Ignoring their fastidious surprise, Baay said, "I have brought us in through a little-used entrance. I told the monitors we are engineering students touring the garage, but that is a rare occurrence and—"

A panel flashed a green light.

"We will soon have need of your *baas,*" Baay said to Shree.

"I will be ready," he responded, casting covert warning at the others.

Umar seemed the least affected by the emotional impact of recent hours, and his question showed cool if short logic. "Why are there guards at all? The monitors should be enough."

"Because they can be compromised by anyone with access to specialized knowledge of their coding, such as myself," Baay said sharply, then added, "And there are rival factions among us whose distrust demands equal representation in all controls to prevent seizure of this complex. I will explain this later."

So there was trouble among the Utopians, A.H. thought. But there always was.

The party stared more questions at each other but were silent as they followed her up the metal spiral stairs that centered the circular room. These soon exited through the side wall. A short passage led to a square door and a curved ledge reaching a fourth of the way across a bottomless, topless shaft. Intermittent yellow spotlamps showed similar ports and cantilevered platforms coiling up and down the smooth four-meter-wide tube till it was pinched off by the two vanishing points. A cold falling breeze soundlessly tousled hair and clothing. To A.H. it reeked of burnt tobacco and chicken ranch, setting off a series of coughs that drew Baay's stare.

He popped in another lozenge to halt the tickle of this final stage in his alien cold. At least the fuzz was gone from his mind, and he actually felt better than before he'd landed three days ago.

Baay stepped out onto the landing. "This is the main vent for the hub tower, which ascends to its peak. This is known to the guards, too, though rarely used by them in this manner. I plan to leave it about halfway up and bypass them. But, Shree Shronk, you must be prepared; they will kill us on sight now."

"I will be ready" was his repeated answer.

P.C. toed the landing's edge. "If we meet any large white rabbits, I'm taking the very next exit," he quipped weakly. Only A.H. smiled in the dim light; his son's jocularity had noticeably lessened since arrival. True change or high anxiety?

Without waiting for further retorts, Baay touched the belt at her waist and bobbed down, then thrust up. She rose more rapidly than they'd expected. Again A.H. was determined not to let her stray too far and looked back at the rest as he quickly followed. Shree, P.C., and Twee jumped together an instant later. But the Teheranian had little experience in parabelting and fumbled with the control buckle as they called down to his receding face.

He hopped too hard and lifted like a missile. With a short cry of panic he passed through the lower group and soared on toward A.H. Feeling the pressure bow-wave of the rushing body below, he spread-eagled himself across the vent and stiffened for the impact of the helpless spinning man. Umar had frozen wide-eyed, *chal'ot* and heavy robe fluttering around his arms like a rent chute, legs bent astride an invisible horse. When he came even, A.H. grabbed the man's belt and hauled them together, then hunted out and jabbed the setting to decrease the grav-nullifying effect. Umar slowed at once, jerking his belt down and out of A.H.'s grasp. Then A.H. readjusted his own net weight to create a drop of about one meter per second. Snagging Umar on the way, he kicked the slick side wall and fell onto the nearest lower platform.

As his gasping decreased he realized he'd been holding his breath the entire time. "Never zero out when you're inside a structure!" he yelled at the crumpled man beside him. Like moving along a ship's passageway in true null-g, it was easy to get sliding forward, or up, so fast you went out of control—with broken bones the result. And mere air drag would take many seconds to brake a speeding bullet body. He shivered at how close they had come to the platforms they'd shot by during wild ascent.

A couple of seconds later, the others, arms windmilling, arced over onto the platform. Bumping slightly, they spread out along the curving ledge. Baay waved at them from the next one above. Ignoring Umar's chagrin, they all launched once again. Several minutes later, the top was still invisible, and A.H. reckoned they had leapfrogged at least five hundred meters so far. They must be inside the base of the pillar; it was much colder. His parka felt good, though he couldn't keep the hood from fluttering off his head onto his shoulders while sailing upward. Minutes, platforms, and lamps passed. The vent seemed truly infinite. As he shot up from the next landing, like a diver from a pool bottom, he reflected: P.C. couldn't be right, even in jest. This wasn't a Wonderland. For him, the last remnant of charm on Teffht had disappeared with Baay's revelation. Something hugely appalling had happened here, moving her to betrayal. Apprehension ate away the rising sense of adventure he had again let himself feel.

Then her torch's circle lit the next landing above them, and they adjusted their belts to halt level with it, floated for a second before the downdraft began carrying them back. They swam onto the landing at nearly the same moment, even Umar, who had improved considerably. The descending cold made the humans shiver despite their exertion.

While they adjusted belts and clothing, A.H. opened the landing's square port. The smooth white corridor was poorly lit, hinting at only intermittent coverage by the patrols. Several paces in, it joined a cross-passage. He was cautiously stepping to it when Umar touched his arm.

"I wish to thank you for my life," he said earnestly.

Perhaps certain terran ethnic groups were right in their belief that after you save someone you become responsible for that person until death corrects your interruption of fate—a peculiar inversion of the European attitude of reversed obligation by the one saved. Inexplicably A.H. now looked upon Umar with an almost protective feeling. Certainly he no longer saw him simply as the fanatic ravager of his daughter. Maybe this had been fostered by the deep vulnerability the man had shown, the rather pitiable way he failed to balance his scientific realism with his fundamentalist religion. True villains always appeared infallible.

"You're welcome," he said diffidently, sensing the weight of another unwanted duty.

Peripherally he saw the dark blue of the Teffhtan guard's short jacket and trousers as he came around the corner from the right. The laser weapon was already aimed at his chest.

"Shree!" he yelled.

Only later were happenings clearly sorted in his mind. Although the four *baasa* present—due to Shree's secret plan—had spent a great deal of time practicing what A.H. had tagged a "blanket merge"—after all, an interspecies opportunity like this was unique—they had ceased the experiment several years ago, before P.C. had passed puberty. In fact, once the sons' disharmonies with the fathers had bloomed, the most they'd accomplished had been a fractionated field with four nodes; it functioned with great power but without direction. The few forced trials over the years thereafter had advanced it little. The way to total merge was clear to each, yet their desire had been inadequate to permit surrender to the required self-emolation.

But when they saw A.H.'s imminent death, followed by their own, and realized the blanket merge was the only sufficiently rapid defense, their Selfs conjoined without hesitation—as Shree had hoped and signaled for earlier. All four fields sprang together instantly. The mindnet was still there to create interference, but their blended power overcame it like a gloved fist punching through plate glass. Twee–P.C. formed the strong cohesive core with their nearly identical Selfs; A.H. and Shree enfolded this, as layers are also part of an onion. And under the emergency's desperation, the other three finally gave identity and control to Shree.

The Teheranian, still reeling from the vent's trauma of terror, relief, and gratitude, also wanted to protect A.H. in return. And for him there was a more familiar source of aid. He leaped in front of the larger man, threw up his hands, and with every force he commanded, screamed, "In the name of Allah, *no!*"

It could have been his alien appearance and wild-eyed demeanor that made the guard falter. The Shree-expanded blanket merge now performed a feat rarely accomplished in either species. P.C. had dreamed of telekinesis, of manipulating EM forces; this rudimentary power blossomed, was tapped in reflex. The guard's hand moved; the coherent beam of invisible photons arrowed at Umar and A.H.—and was refracted upward into the ceiling! The covering panel overhead smoked and showered debris as a fist-sized hole appeared.

The guard stared at it, transfixed. Then Shree-expanded directed the multiple Self to match the native's mind pattern exactly: it was a startling *combination* of a totally alien core embroidered with Hhronkan facets—as Huulall's had been! Together they remembered how good it was to sleep, long and deeply, how wonderful it felt to awaken much later, healed by forgetfulness and intensely alive. The guard's eyes fluttered and he sagged to the floor and was still. The blanket merge twanged apart, leaving each member gasping in shock at the torn sensation.

When opposing emotions vie, they do not dominate consciousness systematically, but exchange prominence by seemingly random processes. These vacillations are so uncomfortable we often choose one and believe we have rid ourselves of the other. The closeness the fathers and sons had just known swung the pendulum strongly toward the love they shared. Each rode the crest of warmth this created, though they made no overt sign of it.

And beneath this, well masked by it, each had felt the stirring of something titanic, an independent nodule of sentience totally unsuspected, mysterious, beyond Shree-expanded.

Umar also rode a crest without sign. He stared at the heaped guard and the hole, then around at A.H.

"My turn to thank you," A.H. mumbled with a faint smile. He meant only that Umar had been brave—in the truer sense— to shield him, but the man took it as confirmation of his own tottering belief: *he* had turned the beam and rendered the guard unconscious! No, not he, but Allah, working through him! He had read of so many such "impossible" acts by the saints, proving God's power on Earth. Now here too! *This* was the evidence he'd sought. Truly He was omnipresent and omnipotent in the universe. Yet...what did it imply of *his* own nature? Of course, he relayed none of these discoveries to the others, taking A.H.'s thanks as the sign of their mutual recognition. To search for any other explanation now seemed blasphemous.

Baay stood to one side with her narcosorb still in hand. "I only partly believed the records, but it is true," she whispered, in her ignorance thinking Shree alone responsible.

The others absorbed the shift of her feeling, and Umar stiffened with accustomed righteousness. He bent to pick up the key-shaped laser.

"Leave it," said Meethlah Shree. "We will not need it."

"No, of course not," responded Umar happily, dropping it.

Baay led them rapidly down the left side passage, then right into a cross-corridor, working inward toward the giant toad-stool's center. Several times they rode up in lifts. She had to use her blocs and "specialized knowledge" to gain entry through sealed doors. It was a maze whose strange wall markings she knew well. Obviously this had been well planned long ago—but not well enough.

They came to another closed passage juncture, and she put a card into the central slot. It popped aside. Ten guards stood waiting. Now that they had trod the virgin path to the blanket merge, the procedure came spontaneously. Again they sensed the alien, Hhronkan-embroidered nature of the Teffhtan minds. All ten fell without word or beam—like Alice's playing cards, A.H. whimsied.

"Praise Allah!" exclaimed Umar proudly, having repeated his divine command mentally. A second miracle!

After one more white door, the invaders came to a bright yellow one. Baay was visibly nervous and was slow and clumsy in opening the barrier. Perhaps they had to eat something and change size to get through this one, A.H. decided giddily as he felt the prolonged tension.

From just behind him, P.C. whispered similar feelings. "This is like crawling through a mine field with a hard-on." The others gave no appreciation of his humor, but A.H. twisted, wrapped an arm along his son's shoulders, and hugged him briefly in reassurance.

Baay became quite reverent. "The final one; beyond, there are no guards because there is no mindnet. It would interfere with the Life Complex's processes."

They stared at her. Her hesitancy was real and not mere drama, yet they could feel no sympathy since they didn't understand.

"Doubts?" Shree asked with gray-circle display. "We cannot go on without your help."

It seemed to reaffirm her. "No, no. Let us go. Remember that none of the remotes and sensors here are comped to take note of or deal with live intruders. Stay out of their way and touch nothing until I scramble the system. Also, Shree, for reasons I will explain, please do not use your *baas* here."

She made a final sweep of the small panel around the card slot, and the door squeaked as it opened. Chilled air rushed out redolent with leather smell. Then it began to reclose at once. Baay dashed in, and they followed just before the heavy double panel clanked to.

Blackness once again and stillness, a thickening silence that counterpointed A.H.'s cochlear buzz into an ocean's roar. Her torch came on and sprayed over a large high space whose shiny black floor held an array of blank metallic boxes. It reminded A.H. of his first view of the Guardian chamber in Shree's Meethlah Repository, except that here the containers were entirely opaque and the bodies inside not visible.

Both Droom and Shree uttered the nasal hum of sorrowful shock. Even in the low reflected light, A.H. could see them blush dark with ire. "Why have you kept them here in the Sleep?" asked Shree in a whisper.

Baay turned back to place the yellow circle in the group's center so all could see her face. "No. These are not your people." She read their disbelief, their refusal to accept. As they gathered expectantly around her, she began to speak just above a whisper, in an almost confessional tone.

"Most of what you were told by Durren Gar and me is true. The beings who originally evolved in this system were amphibians and did become extinct nearly in the manner described. The data message received on Wlaata was sent by them, and they were in turn sent this information from another star system. And though they did manage to decode most of the content, they could never implement it, even with centuries of trying. But there was no war with some invading species. The strife that destroyed the third planet was their own.

"Many tens of millennia ago the Teffhtans' technical ability in almost every area of science was functional but rudimentary. They excelled only in one area, the study of what we call 'mind.' Indeed, in understanding its physical structure, abstract function, and synergistic totality, they were masters of a technology far surpassing even what the Hhronka brought here with them. The Teffhtans were from earliest times a people dedicated not to the physical conquest of nature but to exploring the mystery of interpersonal relationships. This necessitated an under-

standing of the individual mind and development of intense ritu-
alistic formalism."

She turned to Shree with a blurred white display of cold
amusement rendered leprous by the torch's underlighting. "How
ironic that, despite all this, they never evolved, nor were they
able to create, the *baas* you possess. I will soon show you why
this is of great importance to both of us."

They all hid a response to this deferment.

"The Teffhtans were not only staunch traditionalists, as Durren Gar indicated, but also they were beings of great pride, both
for their accomplishments and their very essences."

A.H. was glad she'd chosen English; he could easily hear the
learned sarcasm she employed.

"Why shouldn't they have felt pride? They had none to compare themselves with . . . until the star message and the Hhronka
came. As with all sentients who are driven by ego, their primary
ambition was to survive death. The original motivation of improving mental capability became subjugated to the desperate
need to conquer termination of individual personality.

"Long before the interception of the star message on Teffht,
they succeeded in developing a device that aided or caused the
transduction of mind. This was preceded by the technology to
duplicate their memories and thought processes permanently,
storing them in crystalline metals. But they realized that a set of
static patterns—no matter how complete—is not a mind. When
the being whose pattern-set had been recorded died, the personality died, too. The recorded memory was but a fossil ghost.
They learned organic minds can be held only in living, dynami-
cally changing, unpredictably imperfect, organic nervous systems. This is why computer intelligences have no personalities;
they lack the irrational base required. Finally they were philo-
sophically compelled to admit that, even if they learned how to
reverse the transfer process from machine storage to organic
mind and produce an exact live duplicate, it would be only that.
To everyone *else* the individual would continue to live, but
within that person's own frame of reference, existence would
end. No immortality would be gained.

"And so the successful device they at last perfected enabled
transference of mind from one live body to another, leaving the
first a husk. The *usst* field or mindnet cannot long hold a
mind. It acts as an intermediary, bolstering and guiding the
field-integrated personality during the brief instants required."

Just that calmly, Baay told them death had been conquered here, if her story was true. It was simply fantastic, an example of Clarke's Law, thought A.H.: technology sufficiently advanced becomes magic. He wouldn't bother asking for further explanation. It would be beyond the current level of understanding of any of them and would have to be accepted as a working hypothesis, for now.

"However, two insurmountable obstacles arose. The field is limited spatially in operation; it is similar to your *baas*, which is why it interferes with its use. And it cannot penetrate solid matter without being periodically boosted, through the *usstaa* nodes. Outside a maximum diameter its sphere of function also ceases. And overlapping of the *usst* transduction fields disrupts them entirely. That is why they must be installed singly and separately."

The circle of generating pylons, the yellow stripe of warning, the isolated cities, and their discovery of no mindnet beyond—it meant these people could never leave their cities without losing the protection of the *usst* field, trapped forever ... by themselves.

"Second, the recipient brain has to be itself mindless. One mind could not force another from its home, nor could one brain house two minds. The records of early failures are a source of great horror."

He felt a thrill the equal of her dark display at what this implied.

"Therefore, they had to grow bodies without personalities. This obviously presented them with a deep moral dilemma. They would have to use sensory deprivation and homeostatic, higher-central-nervous depressants to abort the potential mind of an embryo of their own kind. This they found unconscionable."

Shree and Droom hid their skins, but Twee flickered with ebon shock. The others just looked at Baay curiously, as though they didn't really understand what she would next say.

"There was one other possibility: to clone the body of the mind to be transduced. If it could be reproduced and held ready in a blank but youthful state, the original owner's mind could be automatically switched into it upon death, accident, or severe injury, and a practical means for immortality attained."

A neat plan, A.H. conceded, and a trite one, conceived even on Earth more than a hundred years ago. He recalled Joan mentioning an imaginative fiction novel, *Null-A* something, with this as a theme. Of course, in reality there was for humans a technical hitch to it all, mind transfer aside.

"But again a problem arose: despite a united effort by their biologists, no means could be found to successfully clone a native Teffhtan."

Or human, A.H. added to himself. Evidently both species had similar reproductive and genetic structures that forbade the process. With *H. sapiens,* and most higher DNA-based metazoans, there was but one way to attempt the *exact* replication of an adult individual, duplicated down to the gene level of organization: induce an adult cell to dedifferentiate and assume the form of a freshly fertilized zygote with a full set of genes, then begin growth into an embryo.

But adult cells with full complements of differentiated parental genes either had lost forever or had entangled irretrievably vital gene codings and ingredients that their own ancestral zygote had possessed. Even when cells of naturally dedifferentiated tissues, such as teratocarcinomas, were used, only failure had been achieved.

His cold emptiness spread as he saw where Baay was leading. He was certain the Hhronka also realized the truth, but he couldn't force himself to look at them, to share their horror.

"What the Teffhtans needed were hosts, clone-donors, whose forms would be acceptable to them, whose prepared nervous systems could receive their transduced minds, and whose adult bodies could be cloned. Soon after this decision, the star message had been heard and their plan conceived. They would pass this data on toward solar systems most like this one and wait to see who came. You Hhronka were not the first, but you were the only species who met all the criteria."

With their large eggs and resonant-toroidal chromosomes, cloning Hhronka was relatively simple. Shree himself had explained how the technique had been perfected two Freezes ago, but it had also been strictly outlawed at once. Only a small population survived the Freeze to begin mating each Thaw, and genome redundancy through cloning would have acted counter to natural selection, the very goal of core-family organization, narrowing Hhronkan adaptability even further.

A.H. thought of the razor nick at his chin. He had plucked off the cap of scab only hours ago because he couldn't stand feeling the hard itchy discontinuity any longer. It hadn't been a shaving cut but a tissue sample taken by Baay as he lay unconscious in the *usstaa* plaza. Now he understood her prediction that Gar would destroy all humans. They had been weighed for clone donorship and been found wanting.

He asked Baay as she paused, "Are you a Teffhtan?"

She saw his query echoed in all their tortured, confused faces and said proudly, "I am neither a Teffhtan nor an Hhronkan." She swept her torch across the rows of boxes. "Here the clones are cultured and held in mindlessness until needed at the transduction terminal."

She refused to halt for question or recrimination and led a zigzag path through the gray, shoulder-high vats. A.H. brushed along one in the dark; it was ceramic and ice cold. He estimated over five hundred bodies lay in the vault. How many similar rooms were here? Surely each of Atuum's millions couldn't have a fresh replacement ready. The logistics would be overwhelming even on this compumated world. He asked Baay, to still his slamming heart and delay the pain he—they all—knew now must come.

"It all relies on steady, predictable death rates," she began cautiously, her voice detached, floating above the torch circle as they moved. "We know very closely how many will die or be seriously injured from accident or breakdown of bodily function, as well as those asking for voluntary transduction due to attainment of a preselected age. Sufficient clones are kept here for this demand and replaced as used."

Old bodies for new. And the trade-ins? Discarded as Gar had discarded the two after the Covenant. "You mean this is it? What if there's some mass catastrophe?"

"That is extremely unlikely. The largest number of casualties might come from the collision of two filled underway cars, sixty persons. And that is the max number the transduction terminal can handle simultaneously."

He was about to ask, when they saw it ahead. A matrix of the containers ten rows by six, separated from each other by ten paces or so. They lay in a great square transparent box on an open, griddled, white lattice. The group came to the enclosure and peered at the contents within Baay's spotlight. Each container was bracketed by a pair of the same crystal-dendritic antennae as on the pylons, one suspended above and one in a well beneath the lattice-floor. The delicate branchlets reached toward the boxes from both directions, dead fingers to clutch at life eternal.

"Each cloned body is ready to receive any mind captured by the *usst* field. Except that male goes to male and female to female. There is a difference in mental pattern and function recognized by the field which assigns sex correctly—unless a sex change has been designated by the person. This *usst* field is actually a kind of enormous simple mind itself, or rather an amorphous baseline awaiting the impression of one developed sentience. Each of us and every new clone has surgically embedded inside the brain a link that locates the individual and senses physiological condition. Automatically upon death, or upon a special external signal, the link triggers the *usst* field to join as an extension to the mind of the link bearer—much the same process as your *baas* field, Shree, when you match another's mental patterns and read the feedback. However, the *usst* field *becomes* the mind, and vice versa; it propagates through the field to one of these pairs of antennae and in turn sets up a resonance in the receiving nervous system. It is like water running downhill; the patternless brain is the locus with the lowest energy level for the transduced mind, so it settles there. An imprecise description, but the best without mathematics."

"You mean the mindnet can transfer only one mind at a time?" asked A.H.

"Yes. But this happens in only picoseconds," she replied. "The probability of more than one mind needing transduction in that time span exists, but with our cities' populations it is statistically negligible."

He remembered the exploding sensation that had finally snapped his consciousness in the plaza—a mind in transduction?

"Rarely the link fails to create total interaction with the *usst* field due to the current mental condition of the person—such as when they are drugged or insane . . . some have even had the link removed."

She turned expectantly from the enclosure and lifted the torch to expose their faces. "Yes, we have some who choose ways other than the Covenant to die. So we installed the *usstaa* nodes on the surface throughout the city to act also as backup links for last-moment changes of mind as well as to help the *usst* penetrate solid matter."

Incredibly, she didn't appear to recognize the pun, poorly placed as it was. But A.H. saw his son's puzzled look and joined him in not knowing whether to laugh or be offended.

Now he knew why he and any *baasa* would respond to the sculptures; some kind of resonant feedback to their sensitive Selfs was set up. And it explained why their hosts had been horrified by Shree's drunkenness that first night: a seeming act of nonritual suicide to two immortals.

"The *usst*, however, cannot extend to this Life Complex; it would interfere with the final stage of transduction." Baay suddenly became reverently nervous again. "To die here means true death . . . just as beyond the pylons."

Behind her, the blank end of one box within the enclosure went aglow with amber, then red. The bracketing dendrites strobed a pale sky blue but a moment. The opaque substance of the container mutated to the intense white-orange of molten gold. It rapidly became laced with a fine netting of amethyst fire, which roamed over the dulling ember box for several seconds, then unwound itself into separate woof and warp of purple lines. These raced to the opposite end of the box and vanished. The glows faded back to gray.

From beneath it, appeared small wheels as the container rose from the grid. At the same time they could barely hear the sigh-click of disconnecting apparatus, and the box rolled fairly rapidly across the grid. A section of the enclosure developed a perforation as had the car shell; it dilated as the box emerged. Even before the exit was complete, they heard an approaching sound behind them. A replacement container came swiftly past them, entered, and settled itself in the empty spot like a mechanical hen. The entire exchange had taken less than a minute.

As they watched, the first container went beyond Baay's torch range. A.H. whispered, "That was a transduction?"

"Not all," she replied with some amusement dappling her face. "Now the transplanted mind has to go through several days of acclimatization to its new nervous system, and some strenuous physical conditioning must be done to tone the body. It is not very pleasant, but it works."

That would eliminate all frivolous switches, he thought. Before Shree bobbed close to Baay, A.H. sensed the end of the Primary's patience and the strength of his determination.

Looking down slightly at their guide-ally, he said, "Now you will take us to my people."

Again without response she led them along the array until they came to a lift entrance in the far wall. This one opened merely at her touch, and they went down.

"This is also used by the reborn for return to the surface. It will make our exit quick and safe; the security is for keeping people out, not in," she said with aplomb. "Each city on Teffht has its Life Complex at the top of such a broadcasting tower."

Her manner became brusque, as though she were eager to face a necessary but thoroughly unsavory task. Here, then, must be the core of the Kmeaan mystery. A.H. felt they were descending into the heart of darkness.

"However, from the start Atuum-uleen was chosen to keep all the . . . clone-donors in a central location."

The lift halted. It had become so cold all their breaths volleyed like massed cannon smokes, and even the warmer-blooded Hhronka were starting to shiver. The doors parted.

Baay said with almost brutal finality, "Here are the only true Hhronka on Teffht."

They emerged into a dim blue-gray vault that had the pristine frostlessness of a deep freeze. The bodies lay on closely spaced metal shelves, the racks stretching to the low ceiling, ahead and away on both sides. The group slowly dispersed until each was alone, as though merely examining specimens. That was how A.H. was trying to hold them, as objects not beings, trying to withhold any emotional response as they all had been. Each of them had known already what had to be here.

The crinkled bags were transparent; some had even been carelessly left undone. Inside were the freeze-dried members of all three Wlaatan expeditions to Teffht. Of course. Freeze-drying was the perfect storage method for Hhronka; why waste power on impeded animation and allow them to slowly age? Just use the species' Freeze-survival ability. Another reason humans failed the criteria—they couldn't be frozen without tissue disruption. But the Hhronka had naturally evolved the system, far better even than terran fish and frogs.

He peered closely into a nearby bag at chest height. His stomach twisted in disgust and his throat clenched with nausea. A mummy inside was hacked into an unrecognizable mass; huge gobs of flesh and organs had been scalloped from it in a random way. The next two were the same; casually butchered for raw tissue cultures. Most cells beneath the skin could be cloned except for bone or nervous. One was lacking both legs; another missed its anterior torso, exposing the viscera.

Despite an iron control, he felt wetness on his cheek. This wasn't just slavery; it was a heinous form of cannibalism. He heard a rasping sob and found Shree near the end of the rack in the next row. In their twenty-one years, he had never seen the Hhronkan weep. His black-barred face was glitter-streaked, and he supported his sagging frame with his left hand clutching the edge of the shelf. When A.H. approached him, he lifted the hand and gripped his shoulder tightly. Spots of his fingers' flesh adhered to the metal where they'd contact-frozen; his nasal pore flexed rapidly, mouth flapping for control.

"Look what they have done to my people. I knew it had to be so . . . but I refused to *feel* until I saw." The voice was a ripsaw on stone. Then he dark-rippled with new shock. "The Children, those yet unborn on the first two missions! Where are they? Have they suffered this? And Feeahra!"

He lurched back into the long rows of dim racks. A.H. grabbed the corded belt of his robe and one trunklike arm. He might as well have tried to pull a shuttle uphill by hand. As he stumbled and slid in tow he gasped, "We're running out of time! You can't find her now! Even if you could, you can't take her out of here; she couldn't survive. They're *all* like this! We have to find a way for *all* of them!"

Shree stopped and curled back, mingling the fog of their breaths, misting the jet horror on his face. His python legs bowed forward till the loops touched the stone floor. "I cannot lose her again, A.H. I *will* not!"

The massive round head leaned gently onto A.H.'s chest, and he sighed long. A.H. spontaneously wrapped his arms to the thick neck. He felt waves of desperation and regret from this being, his friend.

"I know; I know," he spoke as he lightly brushed Selfs and rocked him childlike in instinctive commiseration.

The others had been drawn by their loud voices and stood on either side of their row. A.H. faced Shree, and from behind him he watched Twee slowly bob toward them, gray-flecked with sympathy. His arm curved up to Shree's back but stopped before the touch. Only then did A.H. feel helpless, foolish in his embrace. With his skin glassed, Twee finished the tableau by palming Shree's back.

"Father, we must plan rationally if we are to save them all," he said quietly.

The Primary quickly rose with huge gasping breaths, conquering his black display and pressing a grateful palm to Twee. Then Baay's morose tones came from the next row of racks.

"Now you understand. When it was discovered that the first Hhronkan group could become successful donors, receptacles of Teffhtan immortality, the pressure to act at once was overwhelming. The death rate was then far higher; thousands were dying each day who could never be saved. It required only the manufacture and installation of the Life Complexes and *usst* field generation equipment, plus the culturing of sufficient bodies, to halt death forever." They had moved around the rack to her and stood together, hypnotically watching her steaming lecture. "But of course, there were hundreds of millions of natives requiring transduction immediately and only 780 adults and 2500 embryos in the first expedition. Their only technical choice was to make repeated copies of each Hhronkan, many hundreds of thousands of each. That is why you see so many identicals today. And the individuality of dress and costume has evolved to express identification. Some new types were created by using fertile eggs from the females and mature sperm from the males. This too was limited, and the fertile strains eventually died out through transduction since Hhronkan clones are sterile. But the decision was made to proceed regardless. And Durren Gar was instrumental in that decision."

Her face showed diagonal black bars of loathing. *"This* was the Teffhtan crime; their total disregard for the rights of these people—and for those of the next two expeditions! The night after the Complexes were functional, the Hhronka were gassed with sleep-inducer, tissues excised from each, and their bodies placed here as you see them . . . like waste. The Teffhtans didn't even consider asking them if they would voluntarily help. They had lived together, lived a lie of promised coexistence, for over a year before, and the natives believed that the Hhronka would never cooperate in creating what they would consider monsters. So they just took what they wanted. Once there were enough transduced Teffhtan Hhronka, the First or *Inna* they call themselves, clones could be made in turn from clones. The Wlaatans were no longer needed. The next two expeditions were also betrayed this way—used simply to introduce variety, new faces . . . as your group of Hhronka will be used.

"By accident, some members of the last expedition did escape the gassing and learned the truth. They posed as citizens of Atuum and attempted to send a warning message through the interference to your homeworlds. But their faces were too unique, and they were caught even as they were making the transmission. They pleaded with Gar to release these unneeded beings.

"And that was the second crime. Instead of restoring their destroyed bodies, giving them back their stolen lives, they just dumped them here and forgot them! You must comprehend the true depth of the ego involved in this action, for it still operates today in Durren Gar and his *Inna*. The Hhronka had shown their superiority in many ways; the most obvious being the free gift of their technology. But this only increased the Teffhtans' envy. To live with them would have been unthinkable. And they could not let them leave either. Secrecy had to be maintained since they wished never to share their immortality. In this way they could always say among themselves: 'All others die, but we continue.' So they would be like gods. Yet even this shabby victory eluded them."

Her display took on fine white spots of irony. "When they performed the first mind transductions, they learned its final truth: those switched were subtly and permanently changed. Even a mind-blanked clone still holds a rudimentary nub of sentience. It is not possible to grow a healthy nervous system without it retaining some elementary characters whose essences lie in the inherited structure and function of that system. When the Teffhtan mind was grafted onto this framework, part of the native character was lost, overlaid by the Hhronkan precursors. And this repeated with each transduction. Piecemeal the Teffhtans became less themselves, a little more Hhronkan. That is why we speak a mixture of both tongues and display some Hhronkan expressions, though such are mere shadows of the pure forms.

"You can guess the Teffhtans' reaction. They were trapped in a dead end. This dilution meant their pure mental nature would also not survive. Already they resented the eventual physical extinction of their kind, the strangeness of the alien body, the loss of natural parenthood due to clone sterility. Resentment became hatred, for the very species that had 'rescued' them from death! You saw one example at the Covenant. Children are almost universally held in contempt here. Each child's mind is Hhronkan but his culture is Teffhtan since the parents order it cloned but not mind-blanked. And it is an insult to the ultraconservative *Inna*, whose hunger for children never quite outweighs their loathing."

"Is that what you meant by saying you are neither Hhronkan nor Teffhtan?" asked P.C.

Irony crept into her display once more. "Long ago an attempt was made to overcome the loss of mental character. A body was cloned and its mind transduced into it. But the mind was also duplicated and returned to the original body at the same time. That is, they tried to clone a mind itself. This was done to see if being replaced into a younger version of the identical body, which the mind had already inhabited, would eliminate the erosion. Both attempts failed. As in all processes, entropy here also played its subtractive role."

She paused to let a gray smear of derision twist her face. "The personality was subtly altered, yet it held all the memory and emotions of the original, which was of course further altered by having been returned to its former body. Over the millennia to this day those two unique persons have had a most beneficial but often rancorous existence. You see, the mind cloned was that of Durren Gar, Chief Provider of the Teffhtans on the original homeworld when the Hhronka first came—and I am his cloned . . . 'daughter.' "

The listeners were too numbed by the chain of shocks to react to this familial treason. Even Umar stood to the rear of the group, staring not at Baay but one of the corpses. She didn't seem to care and continued her history lesson with fog puffing from her thick lips in long streamers like some bipedal dragon.

"One side-experiment was to test whether the two mind-clones would be *baas* linked. We are not. And when Huulall was killed, Shree, you were spared because you are a valuable hostage and experimental subject as a *baasa*. Gar and I are still similar enough that I know what he knows, such as the workings of this Complex, and what he will do . . . what he has done."

So Baay still wasn't aware there were four *baasa* here. Something she'd said snagged at A.H.'s memory.

"Why were you cloned female rather than male? If Gar truly wanted identical minds, wasn't he worried about sexual or hormonal differences?"

Her answer came back like a knife slash. "His ego knows no limits."

He simply nodded, almost embarrassed. It was a good example of the Asimov Syndrome. The ultimate egocentricism would be this: clone a copy of yourself in the opposite sex as mistress. Wasn't it truest incest as well as ultimate narcissism?

"From the first, he knew control of the Complexes would ensure his continued control of Teffht. So did the heads of the Clans who supported his rule then. A struggle began that today continues, although the groups involved are now totally different. Since reproduction was no longer possible, family structure soon collapsed, and the Clans with it. The *Inna,* being those with power and so the first transduced—Gar foremost among them—gained ascendency. They sought to restrict use of the process to the elite among them. But immortality had been sold to the Teffhtans on an egalitarian basis, though there were many who refused it and wanted it abolished. These, of course, died out. Civil wars followed. The species barely survived, and the true homeworld was sterilized by fusion bombs. It was this catastrophe, brought about by Gar's machinations, that tempered the struggle and lessened his power.

"Still, it is the *Inna* who patrol the Complexes, who live in the old part of Atuum near the shore, who attend the Covenants. They enjoy a wide range of privilege that the *Muunaw,* the powerless, never know. Krieder, you stumbled onto a communal replica of an enclave where the *Muunaw* wile away their lives in the drug-induced memory trance, because a fault in a monitor allowed the door to remain active. I hid this, as well as your discoveries of the first night, to keep Gar from imprisoning you any sooner. Such emptiness is for the *Muunaw,* whose immortality also lies at the whim of Gar and the *Inna.* It is with these helpless ones that I have secretly aligned myself."

"Just what do you want, and how are we to help?" A.H. asked.

"I will explain our plan when we get back. We must leave."

They had entered the lift before noticing Umar, who remained where he'd been standing during Baay's lecture. A.H. and P.C. called to him, but he continued to stare at a frozen body. They went to him; he was nearly catatonic, not speaking or responding to them. When they touched him, he fell into their grasp. They had to pick him up bodily and carry him from the vault.

Chapter 12

With the quickness of preoccupation, they returned without event to the residence and the warm relief of the three decoys, whose talents had not been needed. Baay informed them they still had over forty minutes before the monitors functioned normally. The medi-quik gave Umar a normal EEG, with no trace of damage, though he remained in deep sleep. After they put him to bed, they settled around the burbling upper pond in a semicircle of niches. The night's storm had passed inland, leaving damp but refreshing cool. A.H. and P.C. alternately reported their findings. Baay hovered, eagerly confirming her earlier explanations and expanding when asked. Finally they got to her avowed plan.

"The solution is simple: we clone each of the Hhronka, then resuscitate them, using specially designed support equipment for those more seriously damaged, and immediately transduce their minds into their healthy clone bodies, metabolically accelerated to the same biologic age. They would never even know what had happened; it would seem like that next morning so long ago—plus the brief acclimatization time, only seconds for their twin nervous systems. A new Life Complex would have to be built away from all those now in operation, of course. We could actually erect a neighboring city, using those plans for more than a ruse this time. Or we could install the equipment on

221

craft, if you wish to leave eventually. Either way, immortality will be yours."

A.H. could see they were each deeply affected by the implications of her statement. Perhaps it was a good time to air all views; that could become important very soon. "It really isn't, you know," he said softly, almost kindly, deciding to play devil's advocate and draw them out... especially Baay. A last scrape at this latest layer of truth. They stared at him, confused.

"We will all die someday, you Teffhtans included. Your sun will go red giant, or a meteor hit the planet, a fusion generator explode... something. I assume that's why you've never gone into space, too risky compared to planet life."

Her rapid reply was defensive. "There have been several such artificial worldlets of Teffhtans who chose to travel. We lost contact with them all long ago, and if they are destroyed we do not know. There are none remaining who choose to explore."

"Fine. But if some macro-accident doesn't get you, the entropy death of the galaxy and universe itself will. So this really is *prolonged* life, not true immortality. That probably can't exist. And we must all consider if even prolonged life *should* exist, for us. Look what this form of living has done to these Teffhtans."

Joan nodded thoughtfully at him. He saw measured reserve in Baay, understanding and interest in P.C. and Renata, but the Hhronka were apparently ignoring him. He proposed the obvious. "It seems the impact of the transduction method has been to alter but continue internal strife, imprison most Teffhtans in their isolated cities, expand a natural species' chauvinism into a megalo-paranoia, and force many to eventually choose suicide as the only escape from total boredom. Is this what *we* want to be given?"

His children and Baay tried to speak at once and paused together in courtesy. Then Joan's deepened resonance interrupted in turn as she leaned out from her niche to take them all in.

"Do you think humans or Hhronka would respond to long life as the Teffhtans have? I remember the objections to immortality raised last century by O'Neill, the same man who designed our wheelie. One thing he feared was that immortal dictators would hold power indefinitely, rather than dying off of old age. But this is rather specious to me. There is always assassination. And then there would always be another to take his place—there always was, back when one person could hold that much power in a simple nation. It's the presence of the dictator *niche* in the cultural environment that creates the dictator, not vice versa. Of course, assassination wouldn't make any change here. I mean, Gar would be transduced to another body, although I'll wager it's been tried regardless."

Baay held up worm digits. "Three times; all successful. But each time, his well-laid contingency plans defeated those who sought advantage during the brief confusion. He celebrates the dates like birthdays. However, the title *dictator* does not truly apply anymore. As Chief Provider, Gar's opinion is trusted above all others in the *Inna* on important matters simply because his past judgments have been proved so sound—with the one exception during our great Civil War. Otherwise he would have been overthrown by factions in the *Inna.* But the exercise of power here is quite meager. There are so few real decisions to make now. Without crises what does a dictator do? In fact, your coming gave him the first excuse to exercise authority in decades.

"However, the exercise of *privilege* marks each of us: residence, food, entertainment, luxury items, occupations, even available materials for personal pastimes. A caste system exists here with several levels, broken mainly by the *Inna—Muunaw* distinction. You have been allowed to witness only the life of *Inna* here. That of *Muunaw,* as Krieder saw, is far less desirable."

A.H. shook his head in irritation. "That does explain a lot. And any pecking order based on that irrational and petty a foundation has to have developed as the result of massive stagnation. I could see that happening with humans easily! When large differences don't segregate them, they'll settle on small."

Joan smiled. "Big-Endians versus Little-Endians."

Baay tried query circles on her cheeks, but they came out Rorshach blots.

A.H. snorted. "It's a reference to a fantasy written by a human about the tiny people of Lilliput. They fought a war over which end of chicken eggs to break open." His humor evaporated as he recalled some of the equally flimsy bases on which humans had slaughtered themselves for real.

"That was another of O'Neill's concerns," resumed Joan. "He thought a long-lived society *would* become a conservative and stagnant one—through such means as the arts and sciences becoming dominated by undying masters who strangle the new thought and rise of juniors, or the predominance of older people simply being too entrenched for novel ideas. I don't agree that's true in humans, and I've seen the proof myself. Perhaps a couple of centuries ago on Earth, one person could have so dominated a field of culture—surely some did. But now, in our huge Information Age pop, there is room for many such accomplished people. Anyway, it's impossible for only one person, or even a group of people, to become adept at all the facets of even one modern art or science; they're just too complex. So are educated people, whose tastes change with time. It's not simply a matter of age, but exposure."

"Familiarity and contempt," said A.H. with a nod.

"Exactly. That demands more than a single supplier in the cultural consumables. Creative people *will* be heard. As for elders being fixed in their ways—another myth. I know many who are intensely interested in the new, whether scientific discovery, art form, or trivial fad. It's true many are content to simply suck beer and holo, but that's so among people in all age groups. I wonder if they'd stay content, knowing that would be the program going on *forever.* Perhaps they'd find the courage to look within and truly educate themselves. Maybe it's the *closeness* of death that anesthetizes people, not its removal.

"That's what's confusing about Teffht as a test case for stagnation. If the artistic inventiveness I saw was only of the *Inna* caste, then self-expression among the *Muunaw* must be artificially suppressed. There's no sure way to gauge the effect of prolonged life on most cultural areas over this entire society. However, even taking total compumation into account, with its removal of the need for *applied* technical research, it appears the Teffhtans have lagged in *basic* research at least. Yet Wlaata had similar problems and no immortality. In fact, it was the imminent 'death' of the Freezes that stagnated them! Perhaps the caste system has operated here to suppress this kind of progress, too. In which case, the effects of this prolonged life can't be separated from those of the social form over which it operates."

Baay cut in. "Yes! Yes they can! In addition to finding this system personally abhorrent, I intend to pull it down as an obstruction to fundamental change!"

"We couldn't blame you for that," Joan responded earnestly. With a wrinkle dividing her thick brows, she said, "O'Neill's anxiety over children is the one I can identify with. If, indeed, long life were to induce a higher degree of egocentric selfishness, it might preclude the patience and generosity required for childrearing. Young and growing people would disappear, or become as rare and repugnant as they are here. Our society would lose a valuable source of renewal, awe, and wonder at life."

"Or," interjected A.H., "it might mean changing to another form of rearing, such as exogenic birth and communal nurseries, as in Huxley's *Brave New World*. Either way it could be a death knell for the nuclear family, as though it weren't terminal already."

"Or," returned Joan with a hopeful smile, "it might mean a more complex and enriched group family, such as Toffler's 'polyfamily.' That's not uncommon on Earth now."

Baay's deep drone broke into the discussion. "You both forget that unless you find a way to clone human bodies, you must transduce as sterile Hhronka and gradually become more like them, as have the Teffhtans."

They were somber for moments, then Joan said, "There could be worse outcomes. The loss of awe, no matter the source, I think, might contribute to O'Neill's greatest fear: the boredom of the centuries and eventual suicide. It's happened here, in a big way."

"You have seen our disused power and food production facilities," Baay said, looking at a blushing Renata. Only hours ago she had learned from Baay that her wedding and instant honeymoon had been taped by the monitors—revenge of the issac? "There would be no use denying that a large proportion of the early transduced Teffhtans became despondent and killed themselves. This took place over a very long period—the Covenants are rare today. Those unsuited for this immortal environment have been removed. Every species would have such; it must happen with yours."

A.H. stood abruptly, his pretense deeply etched by his beliefs, slicing a hand through the air in emphasis. "You'll never convince me there's not a human or any sentient alive who doesn't at least resent and feel hesitant about personal oblivion! And most would go to great effort to see that moment postponed." He thought of Umar. "How many human institutions, mores, customs, and accomplishments hold as their primary aim continued life, whether in this physical form or another?" He thought of his reasons for writing his book and gave Joan a slight twinkle.

In his rebuttal P.C. was also vehement. "Well, I wouldn't do just *anything* for mere survival! There are limits to what living is worth!" Renata nodded her confirmation.

Arrogant youth. A.H. sighed his disappointment. He'd hoped his children wouldn't share so obvious a lack of foresight . . . but he had, too, once—certain mistakes are everyone's right. "That may be so for you, but don't ever assume it for anybody else. Nearly all people your age feel immortal; death is so far off as to be nonexistent. But the first time something in your body stops working the way it once did, or you feel your mind begin slowing down, memory failing, or that inexhaustible energy of youth just goes—then see how much life is worth when there's less and less of it! But to always have it *and* health? I think that has been the root problem with sentience from its first appearance. As Joan implied, why bother to strive for a moral life, or even to define morality, when death is always close and life is often without a shred of justice, reward, or punishment? In fact, why work for *anything*—wealth, power, or knowledge—when you must lose it all eventually? Many people don't; they shuffle along, stunned by frustration, eking out life based on the barest hope that something beyond themselves will someday make it worthwhile. And yes, some end it for themselves—perhaps not due to the loss of that hope, but only to feel *some* control over their own reality. Hell, *I've* planned suicide . . . at the appropriate time—even a poor player knows when to stop strutting and fretting. Others squander life on self-centered indulgence . . . what utter waste, how incredibly sad!

"But for me, the satisfaction I've found in producing, in making a *difference"* —he glanced at Joan— "and in loving you has at least made the trip worth it so far. As for the rest . . . only the old and the dying can give completely honest answers to what life's worth."

The thoughtfulness and joy in P.C. and Renata's faces made them his two babies again, and he loved them both for it. But Joan's response was solemn as she reached to squeeze his hand.

"'The weariest and most loath'ed worldly life that age, ache, penury and imprisonment can lay on nature is a paradise to what we fear of death.' I agree with Shakespeare. And I believe even potential suicides would be stopped by the fact of an eternal healthful youth promising opportunity and hope as well."

They were all quiet for a minute, considering what was for them still the unavoidable.

Joan released A.H.'s hand as she leaned back again into the runneled stone and stared up through the skylight at pale cloudlets. "I think Baay may have touched an issue central to this. We've almost made the same error that most of the speculative fiction writers back in the 1900s made. While they nonconsciously accepted the near-infinite variety within humanity, they seemed to presume every alien species should display a total uniformity, physically and mentally. That might have made their writing easier, but it oversimplified probable situations. Evolution *must* create wide diversity in any species—unless the genes are directly tampered with. Even the Hhronka, with the great pressures they've had to conform culturally and the small gene pool that survived each Freeze, still show fair diversity. But the Teffhtans seem a contradiction. They've allowed this caste system and Gar to rule their lives unchanged for tens of millennia. Why? Has something truly been 'bred' out of them? Is long life responsible? That would indeed imply immortality perpetuates and homogenizes whatever society it comes to!"

A.H. shot upright with a grin, the final sham ripped away by the discussion. "Of course! Teffhtans show physical uniformity because they were forced to by the transduction procedure. However, psychologically I'll bet they were originally as diverse and dynamic as any sentients. Then long life became a reality. Those that rejected it or suicided are gone; those who could not be content living in this society left it. Who remains? Those whose fear of dying, in space or in rebellion, is greater than their sense of responsibility to change this society for the better. That's the secret of Teffht. The *fear* of death has never been eliminated! True immortality has never operated here! Held back by the *Inna*'s control of the Complexes, this has made it a closed society. Individuals here have stopped searching for the relative truths of their culture, or at least stopped doing anything about it. They've become *resigned* to everything." He looked around at Joan with a nod of emphasis for his unspoken argument.

"When this process was abandoned, the betterment that comes of responsibility and its resultant action also ceased." He stood and turned to them. "Many people surely do assume an accountable behavior in only *one* lifetime. But *this* could be the great benefit of a secure long life: most people would learn to eternally *strive for perfection, knowing it is an unattainable ideal.* This may be the final step in the natural selection process, one that makes mature societies out of mature individuals, who at least try to do what's right."

His audience was still not complete in its attention to his ideas, and were lost in their own. He sat back down. "We've carried this as far as we can. What we've all been saying is that immortality must be an individual decision. We can't predict what would happen to anyone else or to any society. In fact every goal and system would probably be affected! The whole baseline would be altered in ways we can't even guess. Therefore, we surely can't decide for two entire species! We owe it to them to give them the choice."

Baay spoke enthusiastically into the lull. "We *Muunaw* would welcome the sharing of this knowledge with you and any others we meet. We recognize the strength to be gained by joining peoples and want to end the secrecy. If you are correct, Krieder, all the better reason. The only obstacle to this will be the *Inna* and Durren Gar. We must gain control of at least a few Complexes. There are confederates of mine in the guards of seven cities' Complexes ready to coordinate attack. That would leave only planetary communications and the monitors in the Complexes themselves to deal with. That is where you play a part."

She turned her attention to Shree, though he continued to ignore the discussion. "The Complex monitors in all cities can be temporarily eliminated as I did Atuum's tonight. An attack on a Complex during such a time would easily succeed—except for the drones. They are our only police. Seldom required here, they patrol off-planet. Yet minutes after first alarm they will be on the surface, dispatching their *vurkari*—and *them* we cannot stand against!"

Her shudder was visible, and her face actually became shiny and do it right!"

my knowledge of its encryptions. Indeed, this would also give us a way to announce a new leadership for Teffht."

"Baay," said A.H. to her back. "How could capturing only seven Complexes force Gar to surrender?"

"We need only take possession of these few to gain capitulation from them all. No one has ever managed such a coup against Gar. The *Inna* will lose confidence; they will be leaderless. And there is no one better qualified to replace him than I. The *Muunaw* will, gradually, gain equality by my order.

"You have twenty-four fighters that are repulsor-filmed. That makes them invulnerable to the defenses we are willing to use on Teffht. Nuclear warheads will certainly never be employed anywhere near a city. The drones are similarly filmed. At worst it would be a stalemate, each side preventing the other from landing and deploying forces. So we must carefully coordinate the attacks, first on the comm center, then with the fighters, to have a good chance of success."

"So what you really need from us are our fighters?" asked A.H. cautiously, sensing vague alarm.

"Them and Shree's help," she responded pleadingly. "Believe me, it is risky, but this will work. Such coups have been tried many times before, but none had filmed fighters, nor *baas* power, nor my help. And I can think of no other way to free your people and mine!"

The Meethlah Primary came alive like a disintegrating sand sculpture. He stood rapidly, his face eddied with diagonal black bars of disgust. "I will do *nothing* that endangers the life of another! Not again. Otherwise I shall do anything necessary to bring my people back. As for the rest, no Hhronkan will care *what* you do."

A.H. saw Droom and Twee display white agreement, although Twee was hesitant, as if he were deciding just then. He saw Shree notice his puzzlement. This seemed to aggravate Shree's ire as he twisted back to him with a bloom of black on his entire face. "If what you have said is true, A.H., then you humans are closer to these Teffhtans than to us! Humans and Teffhtans as well have *never* understood us! All the Wlaatan expedition members here might very likely have volunteered as clone-donors. So much larger the tragedy. We do not value our physical form so highly as to be jealous of its use. What your Teffhtan ancestors misinterpreted as potential Hhronkan opposition was a simple reverence for *any* evolved sentient life-form.

But the Hhronka have never been and shall never be interested in the pseudo-divinity of personal immortality! We maintain life through our descendants. Each generation is our continuance, yet becomes greater than its bearer because they receive not only their total learning but their total love. Our children become the gods we create!"

A mix of mortification and anger raced through A.H. He was supposed to be the expert on the Hhronka. Yet he found himself totally consternated by Shree's statement. True, they had never discussed at length the topic of physical immortality. Why should they? It was so distant a possibility. And he was certainly aware of the reverent importance placed on the Repository Children to carry on Hhronkan culture. But he'd assumed this was an artifact of the Freezes and the necessity of the Repositories themselves. Supposedly that was now a past era, with interstellar travel feasible.

Apparently this attitude pervaded the Hhronkan character independent of the need for Repositories. A.H. agreed with Joan totally on long life. And they gave their children much, but not *everything*. How any sane being could feel any different was incomprehensible to him. Still here it was—and after twenty-one years of an association more intimate than most people could ever have. Yes, there would always be some unfathomable facets to another species. Somehow the tall Hhronkan looked slightly different as A.H. stared back at him with the others.

From the side of the enclave they heard a sound like a bag of wet sand hit the stone floor, then ragged breathing. Renata's cry for help brought them to her where she knelt beside Umar. He lay on his back, eyes widened and glazed, jaw clenched forward so his lower teeth overlapped, his spittled lips pulled back taut. Every major muscle body jerked in uncoordinated spasm, arching his back off the stone and flailing his limbs. He was fighting to breathe through his clamped teeth, and foamed saliva flecked his beard. A.H. felt an irrational shame for him.

"It's some kind of seizure!" Renata cried tearfully as she tried to hold him flat. P.C. and Twee quickly helped her pin him.

"Droom, do you know of any history of his having epilepsy or attacks like this?" Joan asked.

"Never. This is the first I have ever seen," answered the Orrtaan Primary as she watched in fascination.

Urgently Joan said, "We must get him back to the *Wind*. If it's some kind of neural disorder, the effects can be minimized."

"Will Durren Gar allow us to take him?" asked A.H. of Baay.

"He will not need to," she responded eagerly. "The fate of you humans is already set in his mind so he does not care what you do, as long as his plans are not endangered. I can give orders to the monitors and drones to let one of you take him in your second shuttle. That will be considered safe. But it will also be a fortunate opportunity to get word to your crews to prepare the fighters secretly and plan coordination of our attack."

"I'll go," said Renata at once. "The autopilot can handle the flying, and he may need attention all the way. I can do it."

The desperate pleading look in her face told them arguing was useless. But A.H. still sought Joan's acquiescence. She nodded slightly, and he said to Baay, "Get everything ready— and do it right!"

Chapter 13

The cloud-plaqued surface of Teffht lay half in the planet's penumbra as the shuttle arced up through the stratosphere. Renata watched their streamer of condensation in the rear screens. Like a seed blown from some gigantic dehiscent pod, she thought, then felt guilty. She should be talking constantly to Umar, who lay webbed into the copilot's chair still inert.

His seizure had lasted several minutes, then subsided, leaving him comatose. On the medi-quik his EEG has showed definite trauma signals. Within ten minutes Baay had personally escorted them in a flyer to the edge of the landing strip, where robots had taken over the flight preparation. Just before Renata had slid into the ground car with the stretchered Umar, Baay had handed her a small rec bloc.

"To allay Gar's fears I have told *Wind* only that a human is injured. Give these plans to those in charge. They detail time and places for your fighters to come down, as well as complete data on the Complexes. This will be our only contact. In thirty-six hours we will first reprogram the drones to ignore your fighters, then my people will begin operations to secure those Complexes listed here. I wish you well."

In the contrast of her haste and the predawn calm, it had been easy for Renata to forget Baay wasn't a true Hhronkan, and she had palmed her robed torso in farewell. The Teffhtan had merely turned away and left. For an instant it had reminded Renata of how Twee had reacted to her hurried good-bye—but he'd shown what almost seemed hurt, not like Baay's . . . anger?

The steady beep of the medi-quik standing on Umar's opposite side brought her back. It pumped solution into his right arm and displayed vital signs on a tiny screen. He was still in a coma. And speaking directly to him was the best medicine she could offer now. Enmeshed neck to knee inside her seat web, she could not even reach across to him. Though acceleration was now mild, it was too much for her to stand by him and provide tactile stimulation to help keep his higher neural pathways functioning normally. The medi-quik was handling the brain stem, but only interaction with a live person could reach the cerebrum with its intellectual constructions. If she continued to jog his somnolent mind with personal talk, perhaps any permanent damage could be lessened.

Lying there, still and relaxed, he looked so childlike, but his beard brought back the incongruous image of the Sheik. She must at least let him know she was near, caring and supporting.

The hiss on the outer skin decreased considerably. "We're nearly out of the atmosphere, Umar," she said cheerfully. She stretched her netting to see the lower console. "The engines will shut down in two and a half minutes, then we coast around to *Wind*. It should take only a half hour more. Dr. Mubawe should be ready for you; just hang on, keep thinking, don't let go of yourself."

Her neck leaders were cramping with the strain of twisting her head to the right. Just before she let it roll back against the slick padding, she thought she saw him stir. Perhaps a more intimate topic would have a deeper effect. Staring through the nose ports at the indigo sky, she said, "Remember the night we played R-ball with Twee and, uh, discussed love and courtship? I said I believed you could have lust without love, but not love without lust. Well, I'm starting to think that might be wrong." She added a softer tone. "It might be possible for two people to love each other romantically and never make love."

The vibration in her spine quit before the smooth percussion sound of the engines. Her stomach rebounded a bit from the loss of acceleration like a fish in a net. Below the black, star-sprinkled window, the console screen read out that they were at *Wind*'s orbital-matching velocity, ETA twenty-six minutes. Suddenly she heard a rush of breath in her right ear. She knew who it had to be, but still jerked around startled. Umar hung midair, his face only a handsbreadth from hers. There was no time for relief. Her fear was prescient, for he was exploding with rage.

"Lie to me no more, *harlot!* For Allah has given me a vision, and I know the truth!"

The medi-quik's IV and sensor cuff floated freely with his loosened seat web, and she worried he was about to have some kind of relapse. His rounding eyes were thoroughly bloodshot, his breath corrupted, and his skin the whiteness of a fly maggot. But his speech showed he was coherent, if not rational. He had always spoken with solemn dignity; now his wild voice and manner held the authority of one totally certain of himself.

"From the instant I first saw you I felt your power, dragging at me, dulling my resistance," he said as he studied her curiously, like some lab specimen. "I suspected you could not be merely a young woman; your actions were too sure, your understanding of my weakness too accurate."

At this sign of mental deterioration, she said carefully, "Umar, you've had some sort of seizure, back at Gar's house, remember? You were unconscious for over an hour. I'm taking you up to Dr. Mubawe for treatment because we're afraid you've—"

"Cease!" he screamed through bared teeth as he darted his face at hers like a bird pecking at a worm. "We both know this was not illness but *naql,* the direct revelation of Truth from God! He has shown me what you are and who I am. You preyed upon my loneliness, the price of my uniqueness, and sought to pervert my sexual urges, to betray me to God's enemy, who is your master."

Now the fear came, tearing with sharp claws at her. She saw he truly believed this, that he would act on the belief. She slid her right arm to unhook the bar holding the side of her cocoon. His hand shot to it and clamped it fast. She struggled only once, but was held quite effectively. He smiled in triumph as she stared at him, dry-mouthed with terror.

"Power and knowledge are given me now. It began in the Life Complex, when Baay showed the depth of the Teffhtan defiance against God's plan of natural death. Indeed, they have made a god of it, and thwarted the true way. Their souls, though they inhabit Hhronkan bodies, are those of *kuffar!* So too have I realized, after so many years of their deceit, that the Hhronka themselves are unbelievers. They worship only their descendants; Shree admitted this. It was the sign for my vision to begin. I saw many things clearly for the first time, in this my current memory. Both these peoples as a whole are guilty of *zulm,* and God has willed they be given justice for this breach of the *Qur'an*'s most fundamental law!

"There shall be no other god but Allah!" he screamed.

"It now is my responsibility to bring this justice here, as it is to bring justice and peace everywhere." He expanded with pride, using his grip on her chair to torque himself upright. "As I lay twisted in God's hand, all the puzzles of my life were solved. My mother-custodian knew, and so held me in awe from the beginning. All the clues are there! I am of the House of Askari. My gift of intellect allowed me to comprehend more about the nature of the Universe than any other man. Yet my memory went back only to the age of seven. Now it is complete; all the pieces fit with perfection. I was born of Hasan ibn Ali 'Askari, the Eleventh Imam, in Sammarrah in the 256th year of the Prophet's birth. My father was poisoned by the Caliph Mu'tamid when I was only four years old." Pain showed briefly in his face. "I recall everything; our simple pleasant house with its dirt and tiled floors, the slaves, the scorching days and cool nights, but most, the smell of hot, dry sand. My father sat encircled by the faithful as he revealed God's will or interpreted His law. After his death I was entrusted to his closest companion, Uthman ibn Sa'id Umari, from whom is taken my name in Occultation, which by divine command began in my seventh year and lasted 1,174 years. Like the Prophet Jesus, I was then again made flesh immaculately by an unmarried woman. Can Holiness proceed from sin? I was also allowed to mature as Jesus was, so I might continue my work as a man, knowledgeable of his time. All that was lacking was the knowledge of my true identity. I *am* the Twelfth Imam, *Sahib al-Zaman,* the Lord of the Age, the promised Mahdi!"

She realized Umar had been nonconsciously nursing on these ideas his entire life. He was the orphaned and rejected bastard of a legal prostitute. He desperately needed to believe what he'd just expounded, as an edifice for his fragile ego. As with so many, religion formed the basis of the lie, instead of offering him the courage and solace to face the truth.

And she had made the same error Scarlett had, but with Rhett rather than Ashley Wilkes. She had dressed Umar up in an imaginary suit of clothes that didn't fit. He wasn't a dashing privateer or Arabian prince, but only a frightened child. And frightened children could be very dangerous.

Reviewing her memory of their talks, she frantically sought a weapon, something to buy time to get free of the webbing— Of course! "Umar, I'm not specifically doubting you," she said calmly to his triumphant face. "But I recall you said all Imams are able to perform miracles. Where is yours?"

He grinned in haughty victory. "Demon, struggle to the last! My final proof! Your own father and the others witnessed my first miracle in the Teffhtan Complex. By the will of Allah, I turned aside the laser beam that would have killed us both. Krieder himself acknowledged this!"

Her face contorted in genuine confusion. "I don't recall that even being mentioned; perhaps he didn't want to let Baay know about their combined *baas*. But I gathered their blanket merge knocked out the guards."

His disgust was barely controlled. "Such evil could not occur in my hallowing presence! I now know that all so-called *baas* is the work of others of your kind. The *Qur'an* tells that the *jinn* both aid and plague mortal existence with their supernatural powers."

With a broad grin, she showed amazement. "I'm a *jinni?*"

He shuddered. "Or your body is so inhabited—your soul pushed aside into oblivion...as mine too was, temporarily, whenever Droom and I were partially in contact. Forever they nibble at truth and faith."

His face was sweaty, his eyes shifting as though he spoke only to distract her from what was to come, and to build his courage to the acting point. She became desperate, losing the control required to humor him.

"Oh, Umar! There *are* absolutes in life, but no religion can tell you what these are, for everyone in every circumstance! You must use faith *and* reason to find truth, otherwise we wouldn't have been made rational. That's where choice comes from. Without choice where's the temptation and opportunity for sin or righteousness? You talk as if you have absolutely no doubts about any of this. I believe evil's greatest triumph comes after we cease to have any doubts, and stop searching for what's right."

He said nothing for several deep breaths. Staring above her out into space, he seemed to waver a moment. Then his grip on her web's sidebar tightened so she heard his skin squeak, and he wiped his face with the back of his other hand. She saw the green oxygen bottle from the medi-quik in that hand, held by the rubber mouthpiece. Horror welled within and ran down her cheeks, tasting salty in her mouth.

"Umar, please don't," she whispered, choking out the words through her constricted throat. "Please don't do this to me. I loved you."

The last seemed to calm him. He was suddenly friendly, almost tender, and tears also wet his face. "And as I loved you, I married you. Now our contract is completed as agreed. We have left Teffht's surface, so the marriage period is over. Therefore, I divorce you; I divorce you."

"No! No!" she yelled as she shook her head, trying to stop him before the third repetition.

"I divorce you. Lastly, the dower must be met. We must terminate our relationship permanently. I shall do that as I give you the justice that will also be the Teffhtans'."

He lifted the heavy globe; she was too terrified to scream. She writhed beneath the webbing, hands tearing at the web strands from the underside, trying to free her left arm and get it over her. But she was in too snugly. The look on his face was oddly pleading. It canceled her fear.

"*I* won't give you absolution," she whispered harshly.

The first blow struck her dodging skull on the left parietal area. She heard the bone impact and felt her head bounce down and onto her right shoulder. Then feeling and sight were scrambled; she saw superimposed images, one of the console and one of Umar raising the globe again. There was no pain as the blackness melted over her.

He struck a second time because *jinn* are given great strength. The click of breaking bone both satisfied him and released him from all reservations. He had been correct. It was amazing how clarified his thoughts became, how thoroughly and rapidly his plan emerged. He rewebbed in his seat. The *Wind* was only minutes away, its silver speck already visible through the cockpit windows. Sufficient time to copy Baay's rec bloc. He'd dock sloppily, to show his distraction, and tearfully describe how Renata was injured in . . . a cave-in at the farms. Then he'd put Baay's data into Mowry's hand and explain her plan, urging the immediate flight preparation of the fighters.

And when the first one was ready, he would be, too.

* * *

Again they slept. Atypically he awoke like melting solder. The subliminal sense of danger instantly fired him to full awareness. He jerked upright on the cot and stared at the dark portal. The impression of contact was undeniable. He had evidently freed his Self during uninhibiting sleep. Despite the mindnet's scrambling effect, he'd managed the briefest touch with a nearby mind. A mind whose aura filled him with horror.

It couldn't have been Joan; she was always calm, well ordered, positive, like being in a library containing only the books he loved. Even in dreaming she would never be pondering such violence. There had been a determinedness, a vast coldness, an implacable selfishness that brought him to shudder with a soiled feeling.

He shook her until she moved by herself. After Renata had taken Umar, they had first made sedative love, then lain in bed several hours, finally exhausting themselves to sleep with whispered talk. Her mumbled question was abridged by the bright glare from the balcony as two silhouetted Teffhtans followed it into the room.

They simply stood there with hand lasers pointing at them from either side of the torch. It was the inaction that panicked both targets. There was no way to defend themselves. He hugged her with his arms as she leaned into him, a final sharing. Then . . . nothing. The two intruders remained statues. At last she pulled away, intrigued by the seeming reprieve. It all clicked, and A.H. knew whose mind he'd sensed.

"Durren Gar knows," he said, and she nodded.

Tiredly they got dressed and moved past the guards down into the pastel dawn washing the dewed enclave. The damp added to A.H.'s feeling he had been dipped in his own chewing gum, and he badly wanted a piece to freshen his tacky sour mouth. It had taken them longer to react than the others, who were already clumped around the upper pond. Baay was conspicuously absent, and they hadn't found Shree's hiding place. Ten additional guards, weapons dangling, distributed themselves along the wall outside this inner circle. Like all Atuum's citizens, they wore a variety of costume, reminding A.H., since there were no regular police, these were draftees. Surely they were of the *Inna;* Gar would trust no others.

P.C.'s sardonic smile ill fit his sleep-swollen face as he loudly said, "OK Corral time, folks, and I feel like a Clanton."

They were too despondent to reply but went to brush against him for comfort.

"I'm glad Rennie and Umar missed this," Joan murmured as they nodded.

Droom and Twee were silent and unresponsive. They'd been caught and few options existed in consequence. Perfectly staged, Durren Gar now entered through the comp room door next to the underway entrance. He wore his usual knee-trousers and vest of light blue. Idly A.H. wondered how Gar *could* still be in a power position after all this time. O'Neill notwithstanding, it was a spectacular accomplishment, considering Baay's outline of their turbulent history. Probably Gar was one of the few—and so, Baay another—who had both the disciplined capability to handle the crises successfully and also the obsessive tolerance to endure the tedium in between—a survival of the fittest in this pseudo-immortal environment. The characteristics he'd felt in the brief merge fit such a mosaic, and the Provider's searching eyes, lack of expression, and sure movements now exuded these battling qualities as he circled behind them, raising A.H.'s neck hair with his direct look.

When the tall being passed by the humans a second time, A.H. got the clear feeling that if the two Hhronka hadn't been there, he would have killed them without preamble. Instead, he bobbed on back to stop close to Droom and addressed only her in a patient low voice.

"Fools. Baay Liifan has tricked you as well as me. Apparently you forgot something she never could. When her link no longer registered in the *usst* field, I was soon alerted, of course. Either she was dead and transduced to the Life Complex or she had left Atuum. A check of all newly reborn showed she was not among them. I did not believe she would ever leave the city; that is irrational and Baay does nothing irrational. I know her quite well."

He wasn't giving away anything unnecessarily, such as Baay's true nature or Shree's "disappearance." To keep Gar's suspicions quelled once more, A.H. demanded, "Where is Primary Shree Shronk?"

The Provider paused, studying him intently. "He is in safe hands."

He is that, thought A.H. And for once we have *you* fooled!

"That left only the truth: Baay had not died but had gone into the Complex illegally, with Shree Shronk's help...possibly others of you. This too was dangerous, so her purpose must have been highly rational and highly dangerous to *me*. The city and Complex monitors revealed no intrusion, but I suspect the guards we found asleep were actually attacked by you and her somehow. Only your presence here could have prompted her to such action. Therefore, I must know what you have planned with her. She has disappeared again, and it will take some time to search the Complex. Has she truly left the city? Is she dead or her link deactivated?" He seemed distraught rather than angered. "This uncertainty cannot be tolerated!"

All the captives now exchanged looks, realizing the truth. Baay had used them to get the fighter attack launched on the selected Complexes and no longer needed them. Again they'd been caught in a fabric of lies, of half-facts, to maneuver them once more in the struggle between these two. Since they couldn't communicate with *Wind*, they couldn't countermand the attack, which would proceed in just under twenty-three hours. It seemed Baay had retained if not refined her "father's" ambition and ruthlessness.

Droom was staring steadily back into Gar's cat-eyes. The Orrtaan's skin went glassy with suppressed emotion, yet her deep monotone was somehow heavy with outrage. "We do not care about your petty squabbles over power. We have no desire to disrupt your eternal prison. You and your people have committed a depraved crime against the Hhronka; still, we do not desire retribution." She threw a significant look to A.H. "All we want is to restore the lives of those you have used and to leave this world forever."

She slowly looped up her left palm to Gar's chest. The guards started, but a twist of the Provider's head stopped them. Droom exerted enough pressure to force Gar back a step; it was a sign of unabridged disgust. A.H. smiled openly at this bravado.

"If it requires the total sacrifice of every one of us in the accomplishment or attempt, then that is what will happen—no matter what you do."

For a heartbeat Gar seemed hesitant; his eyes searched all their faces for unity, then he resumed a dominant stance and attitude. "A compromise can be reached; we can both get what we want. After each of you Hhronka has given us tissue samples for clones, we will restore your people and you may leave in peace."

P.C. yelled angrily, "Is that why your drones destroyed our engines!"

Gar's widened eyes and nasal pore signed surprise. "I see Baay has revealed much in order to cull you. Well, no matter. Intentions can be altered; engines can be repaired, and we can still cooperate. Now you have little choice—"

A.H. cut in as impatiently as his son. "We've heard this."

White nebulae clouded Gar's face in amusement. "And so? My knowledge equals Baay's. You *are* helpless."

A.H. nodded at his son and Twee. They could form a blanket merge without Shree; it would lack the great power, but it could function within the mindnet for this purpose. To his amazement, Gar's face blackened, his lips formed an O of shock. Just from A.H.'s confident signal, Gar had recognized attack! He leapt back and motioned to the guards, whose lasers shot up to aim at preselected targets.

"Now!" yelled A.H., throwing out his Self to mesh with theirs in a sunburst merge. All thirteen Teffhtans collapsed to the stone floor. He came around to look down at Gar; even asleep the flint face seethed with his mind's caged malevolence.

"We can't leave him *and* Baay loose; they're too damned clever—though I'm tempted. They make better adversaries for each other than we ever will for either one." He waved at the youths. "Let's tie them all quickly."

Droom was already clutching one guard's laser and regarding Gar as he lay with one arm in the pond. "So, even to such as *this* you give mercy?"

Twee and P.C. turned around from the niche-stairs at her question. Joan and A.H. stopped collecting weapons and stood quietly for several seconds, looking back at her.

A.H. was resigned. "Will the deaths of Gar or these twelve make any difference in what has happened? Equivalent actions don't always guarantee justice, Droom. I wish to God it did; it would make deciding so much easier. But an eye for an eye brings only blindness."

Black waves of distress wriggled down her cheeks like frightened sidewinders, but she was silent.

"When you kill a sentient being, you kill part of yourself. That's from the Meethlah creed, I know, but it's true. I'm sure of it from my own experience." He waved aside her rebuttal. "Spare me Orrtaan rhetoric. Do as you wish with the guards.

Gar, however, will be a valuable hostage—*that* turnabout is fair."

The word *hostage* tickled his memory. "I'll go get Shree!" He plunged through the dark mouth of the tube stairway and risked an ankle taking three steps at a time. The warmer rising underway draft lifted around him. He skidded to a stop before the small access port set waist-high in the left wall just before the opened station door. Rotating both inset handles simultaneously, he yanked the square panel out as he yelled, "Freedom!" Empty. The cell held only a few crates and remainders of a meal. His neck pulse fibrillated and the panel slipped in his grip. He rebounded from fear to anger; he had gone with Baay. It fit too well. She still needed a *baasa* to take the drone control station, but then— The palm-sized black disc caught his eye as he replaced the port. Picking it up, he pressed the battery reserve tab. It lit soft white; he smiled. Shree had left him a message: he was aware of Baay's double-cross. Whether he'd gone with her on his pretext or on hers mattered little. This dangerous adversary was under Shree's watch; that was a relief. But leaving the transceiver said Shree was assuming a very risky but necessary task and A.H. was to do his best to warn *Wind.* With enemies on two sides the outlook was bleak. Then the wafer reminded him of something else. They still had a chance to beat the odds if they hurried!

Running back, he explained what he'd found (how calmly both Hhronka took the news) and then led the way to the comp terminal room with Droom and Joan behind. The walls were coated with display screens, some holo, some TV, with touch panels checkerboarded between them. Saddle seats on rollers stood before them, but otherwise the small room was empty.

He paused as Droom bloomed a black negation circle on her face and pointed to one of several pairs of binocular eyepieces protruding from the panels nearby. "You cannot operate any of this unless your personal retinal pattern has been keyed into the system's security locks and a special code given. That is why Baay or Gar had to be here when Shree was communicating with *Wind.*"

"We could . . . ask Gar to turn it on for us," A.H. suggested with a thin smile.

"Threaten him with *rhetorical* death—here in the city?" asked Droom, employing human sarcasm. "No. Besides, barricading ourselves in this undefensible house is a dead end. We must be free to move at the correct time. Escape in our shuttle is improbable; we are not even sure it is still at the landing strip. Communication with *wind* is impossible with the jamming— you still have your wafer comm?" A.H. patted hand to butt. "Very well. Baay is surely planning to commandeer our fighters with her own forces after they land, completing her betrayal. We must hide until the attack comes and contact our people as they penetrate the interference field. If we warn them all before landing—"

"*If* Atuum is one of the target cities," murmured A.H. "Gar did say Baay's link wasn't registering. What if she *has* left the city for some other?"

"Do you think she would? She seemed very hesitant even to enter the Life Complex," Droom pointed out.

A.H. twisted his palms up. "At least I think *we* should leave. That'll remove the Teffhtans themselves from pursuit. They'll have to send their drones."

"Which might be worse," returned the Hhronkan.

"There's nowhere else to go. The Complex will be sealed like Fort Knox by now. Let's talk to the others," he concluded.

They returned to the enclave to find thirteen trussed bodies and two heavily armed cohorts. P.C. had even thoughtfully grabbed an emergency survival case from A.H.'s crate. Somberly they agreed their optimal plan was to take Gar and leave Atuum.

"The drones must have an independent capability that initiates only beyond a failsafe limit," Droom said. "That may buy us some time. We need to stay alive twenty-three more hours. One of us must warn our fighters, or else we shall lose everything." Her steady look at each of them in turn sealed the group decision each had already made privately. It wasn't an act of bravery this time, A.H. knew. They were trapped in a lethal situation, and if any must die it should count.

Silently they left the house with Droom volunteering to carry the still sleeping Gar over her back. "If they fire at me, *I* will not be the one who kills him."

The neighborhood was entirely peaceful with no one about. The largest flyer parked at the street's end was an unarmed six-seater. Since the cockpit was built for the Hhronkan anatomy, Droom piloted, and A.H. and Twee sat beside her in the front. Droom dumped Gar faceup across the carpeted rear floor and proffered him to Joan and P.C. as a footrest, which proved unavoidable. Even before Droom got the twin jets warmed, Twee looped an arm to their left toward city center. "There."

Seven blue-silver dots moved across the clearing early sky, twinkling in reflected sunlight above the roof line of the high rises. Their formation spread into a line for attack.

Droom's guesswork at the controls was obvious when her first attempt to rotate the engine baffles for vertical lift failed and they were instead pushed over the gravel into the front yard of the house. Their exclamations were drowned out by the screech of the metal landing skids on the stones. Quickly the Orrtaan's hands darted over the dash panel once more, and she hooted with satisfaction when its piloting screen displayed a more probable takeoff simulation. With her left hand gripping the little knobbed joystick on the console, she touched the activate switch. The thrust was far greater than necessary, pressing the tops of their heads like weight discs, and the house dropped instantly from sight. Looking down through the lower curve of his right-hand gull-wing, A.H. saw a fountain of black-white gravel spewing out from the spot.

A second later this fountain became a volcano of exploding steam and rock, which rattled the flyer's underside like hail on a tin roof.

"That was no warning shot!" yelled A.H.

They all looked up at the umbrella of craft now above them. There were two kinds: five were drones like those that guarded *Wind;* the other two were squatter, bigger through the beam, with a notch of cargo bay beneath the tripod of jet venturi at the stern. None had cockpit windscreens, so all were robots.

"They must not know we have Gar with us," Droom said.

Twee reached out and activated the dash pickup. "Do not attack! We have Durren Gar on board."

In answer, a rectangular slice of the clear canopy and side wall of the fuselage between the right front and rear seats disappeared in a smoking pop of laser energy. Most of the material was vaporized, but some molten blobs of plastic splattered the back of A.H.'s chaise and P.C.'s arm and chest, eating black-edged holes through his onesuit. As he screamed in agony, the others watched helplessly, but Joan released his webbing and pulled him away from the whistling meter-long slot and across her lap. Tearing apart his clothing, she picked off the still-hot blobs with her nails.

Luckily Droom had been maneuvering the flyer at random

since lifting, and so they'd missed taking the hit more to the center. They were all swaying and bouncing under their webs from the rapid vector changes, and the disorientation prevented their recognizing Gar's triumphant voice for several seconds.

From beneath their feet came his smug announcement: "The drones know they cannot truly kill me here. But you are all unlinked corpses!" He made a throaty barking noise that must have been the imitation of original Teffhtan laughter.

Joan's right boot closed his mouth with bruising force. "How far *up* does the mindnet extend?" she asked Droom caustically.

Droom responded instantly by sending them skyward at a sharp angle under max acceleration, while still shooting random curves to avoid being outplotted and hit. The EM scan on the central screen showed a pulsing net of crisscrossing laser and particle beams. Several hits crackled and lit like welding arcs on the craft with an irregular staccato, leaving scorched pocks on the hull. A pair of holes burst in the canopy just in front of Droom's head and punched complement holes in the seat between her legs. Then another left a pit of fused components where the screen had been. The burnt smell of ozone and camphor was quickly swept out the perforations in the craft. Through all this, only Droom had maintained an upright position, continuing to steer erratically.

"There went comp guidance assist," she said casually as the passengers rose once more.

A.H. cautiously looked out, then down. Through a skein of thin cloud, the city had shrunk to a dinner plate of lines and blocks. They were above the level of the attack fleet. And now those craft could use all their weapons without fear of hitting Atuum below. One heat-seeker would finish them. They waited. The air grew frigid.

Finally Droom asked, "Are we out of the mindnet?"

A.H. gathered and expanded his field slowly. There was no mumbling, tingling, luminescent fog. As in the Complex he felt he could breathe freely again. But then he bumped into P.C.'s field, expanded in pain. He nodded at Droom and looked back at Joan, who was already dressing the burns with the kit as the youth, mouth clenched, submitted quietly. Again he admired his son.

Under Joan's feet Gar was no longer haughty; he too vibrated with the terror of any mortal faced with instant death.

She couldn't avoid a small needle, if only to vent her own fear. Removing her gag boot, she hissed, "Any new orders?"

His reply was immediate, loud, and pleading: "You must land at once! In only seconds the drones' override commands will decide you are too dangerous and will attack regardless of my presence! I beg—"

Her sole returned roughly between his jaws. "That's what we wanted to hear."

Droom said, "We cannot stay up for twenty-two hours, whether they attack or not. We must find a place they cannot follow."

A.H. had been thinking about that. "We could defend the entrance to a narrow sea cave. Then when Baay scrambles the drones, the ones following us will be affected too, and we can get back into the city during the confusion."

No one challenged this bit of loose hopeful logic. Droom smoke-ringed assent and touched an intact part of the board. The flyer shot level toward the coast at quivering velocity. The wind rushed in through the canopy gaps so loudly they didn't even hear the hit in the stern. There was a jolt; they yawed right; then the craft began to steadily fall. As speed decreased they could finally hear Droom.

". . . left engine only. I can hold it stable by dropping down on grav flux. Find a cave quickly!" she was yelling at them while never looking away from the approaching slate water and readouts.

They sledded out over the ocean and fell even with the tops of the barren cliffs wending west along the coast from the city. The sound and vibration from the stern halved, but they continued to fall as the remaining engine cut out irregularly. The five passengers strained to the left, searching for a black pock in the gnarled tan face of the two-hundred-meter-high ledge. The sun was now almost vertical and light reflecting from the swell-tufted surface of the water underlit the rock like spotlights. Several likely candidate holes near sea level whizzed past as A.H. exclaimed and pointed.

"Can't you slow a little?" he shouted over the din.

Droom merely curled a limb to point backward. They turned and saw first the mangled engine cowlings, then the seven drones only a few hundred meters behind and slightly above them. Bursts steadily erupted the sea in boiling spouts alongside and before their flyer. Droom continued a patternless zigzag course. Still, no missiles trailed exhaust plumes at them.

They couldn't really be trying to kill us, thought A.H. He unhooked his web momentarily and leaned across Twee's lap. "They're trying to capture us alive! Slow down; they will, too!"

She tapped the board after only a second's hesitation, and the half-canyon of water and cliff quit blurring by and began showing detail clearly.

As predicted, the pursuers kept back, waiting for them to crash, firing frequent "encouraging" shots past them. Their failsafe limit for target destruction had not yet been reached. Suddenly there was a sharp pinging sound from behind and dark smoke jetted from both crumpled foil venturi. The flyer dropped to within ten meters of the water before Droom compensated with the grav flux control.

"There!" yelled Twee as he curled his arm. About half a kilometer ahead was a large semidisc of darkness at the water's level. No other openings appeared near this one. The engine quit completely for three heartbeats, then kicked on again with a tortured howl and additional volumes of thick black fume. They had no choice. Droom kicked in the reverse baffles to slow them, then used the steering nozzles to swing toward the yawning mouth. They were over 250 meters out, curving along a path that should have them ingested at right angles to the cliff and at only ten to fifteen kph—if the engine held. It didn't.

With only fifty meters to go, the cliff face above the entrance grew a line of debris mushrooms followed by the crackling thunder of superheated stone. The chase group was trying to seal them out of their refuge. An avalanche of chunks curtained the hole. The engine popped several times in a row, a sure death rattle. At the last instant of power, Droom threw the craft into a straight-line course that would bring them home a second earlier than the first course.

"Brace!" she yelled, and the six pressed back under the webs of the padded chaises. The flyer was only two meters above the rolling crests, coasting on its flux field into the mouth. The avalanche continued; they drifted into it. The entire entry was now clogged by a ridge that had few gaps low enough, but Droom aimed well. Luck did the rest. The flyer was drummed by the rain of debris, canopy cracking like ice as the runners scraped over the reef of newly fallen boulders. The blunt nose entered shadow just as an excised eight-ton wedge of cliff came down like a guillotine.

They all looked up at death silently, realizing timing alone would now determine their fate. A second slower and the passenger compartment would have been at the wedge's impact point. Instead, the aft section and both engines were sheared off and crushed as the boulder bounced, split once on the reef, and settled into the right half of the mouth like a pair of incisors. The flyer's fore section was torqued down into the new pool trapped inside the reef. Its momentum and dying grav field carried it wobbling another twenty meters before friction with the water caught it. As the wave scooped up by the nose stole its kinetic energy and exploded on into the cave, the section slammed to a halt and floated for several seconds. The deafening cacophony of metal, rock, and water was replaced by total silence.

My beautiful hair is all gone. That's what they'll say first, Renata thought as she steadied herself with a palm to the smooth gray corridor wall. She rolled her neck around her shoulders again. She couldn't get used to how light her head felt without the weight of her shoulder-long tresses, even though her skull was completely covered by the skintight tan plastec cast. They had shaved her scalp in order to repair her hairline temporal fracture, and this had alarmed her the most when she'd awakened. After all, she *had* awakened; she was alive and relatively well. That crisis was past. A little vanity could be forgiven.

Dr. Mubawe had come in at once, his black face beaming at her rapid recuperation from the surgery. Before she could ask, he had inadvertently revealed Umar's fiction: the unfortunate ceiling collapse in the farm's underground during Baay's tour, and also the true nature of the Teffhtan Hhronka and their use of the earlier expeditions' personnel for the attainment of immortality—a final layer of truth to explain Baay's plan for revolt.

It had required little persuasion to gain Mowry's cooperation. The Committee was still discussing the situation, but with no engines, there really was no choice but to aid the side opposite the one that had crippled them and promised their destruction.

And *she* was the one in hospital with an extra fissure in her

skull. Anything said against hero Umar now would be taken as
ravings. So she had to stop him, alone. Three things were certain concerning Umar: he was a genius, and therefore capable;
he was utterly mad, and therefore dangerous; and he'd gone
ahead with Baay's plan, so probably wanted to use one of the
fighters to return to Teffht. There was no other way for him to
carry out his threat, though exactly how even he could manage
the total destruction of these creatures she couldn't guess. Regardless, his premature arrival would endanger their plan, and
everyone involved . . . including those she *truly* loved.

It had taken a long time to sort out these facts from the
alphabet soup of consciousness. Her head hurt constantly, despite the pain-doser behind her ear. It wasn't only the worst
headache of her life; it buzzed and throbbed with each heartbeat, and every throb seemed to be squeezing a bit of gray
matter out of her left ear like toothpaste. There was blood oozing from it onto the open-backed white gown she still wore.
Grinding nausea filled her belly so she couldn't hold even water
down. And a cellular weakness dragged at her every move.
Each step was into another bucket of cement. She was actually
grateful that both swollen bare feet were now numb from the icy
metal floors.

Time was the primary factor now. She lifted her head to
study the numerals materalizing on the corridor clock. Only
eleven hours were left of the thirty-six countdown till Baay
launched attacks within the seven Complexes. Mowry's fleet
would be nearing readiness, and that meant Umar might get
away at any moment.

Her own exit from the hospital had been fairly easy. All staff
had finally left her room during the "night" shift, and only ward
monitors had remained. There had been close moments when
she'd removed the sensor cuff, signaling her departure, and
dashed across the corridor to hide in an empty room, and again
when she had stopped in a supply closet to avoid the search. But
it was a large wheelie, and they would never suspect she had the
definite objective of getting to the hangar deck in the southern
hub. A quick ride in the deserted tramway and up the spoke lift,
then lesser weight made the pull-walk to the hangar tolerable.

She avoided the hub's axial tube conveyor when it proved
quite heavily used by the Rocs' loading crews. Instead, she took
one of the curving crawlways that passed between the hull and

inner pressure walls from the spoke junction longitudinally to the engine deck in the hub's south end. Before it came to that level, the crawlway gave access to the fighter hangar. Since the hub's rotation created a mild centrifugal thrust, the flying craft were launched by placing them on double-door sections of the hull-floor and simply opening them, allowing the fighters to be slung slowly outward. Docking was done in reverse, using the belly jets to dorsally enter the hangar, then reclosing the sections. The north-polar, nonrotating lock was more convenient for freight and passenger ships.

The ladder marked "Hangar Deck" led up through a hatch in the floor against a bulkhead. She poked her nose above the metal plates and looked. A fighter stood so close, its wing almost spread over her. It must have been flight-ready because no crew members were around it, and the banging machine noises and shouts were all coming from beyond. Perhaps others were finished as well, awaiting the sleeping crews. She needed a vantage point to see them all. The gray bulkhead behind her held a ladder reaching an overhead catwalk. The climb was long even this light, but she finally dropped her package and lay on the cold grid, wheezing at the susurrus of pain. The doser charge must be completely gone, but along with the pain came greater awareness. In a few minutes she felt better than anytime since awakening.

Her view covered half of the twenty-four ships as they curved up and away in two ranks around the arc of floor. The space resembled the inside of a huge half-drum, gray, festooned with the conduits, cables, anchored and mobile modules, and people necessary to service the Rocs. These were small, light blue versions of shuttles with the cargo space behind the shorter cockpit expanded to fit in larger thrusters and fuel tanks. Missile racks covered both swing-tilt wing surfaces; pits of lasers lined their leading and trailing edges; and several had the bivalve nose cones that opened like clams to accommodate firing the particle beamer within.

The four nearer her were ready; only the farther ones showed any activity. Fueling was complete; several dark splotches stained the plating. Armaments were still being loaded, and cowlings were scattered about as engines were calibrated.

When the lone workman bypassed these, he drew only her attention. Before him rolled the large platform of a gerlinger, piled above his head with white plastec crates. He got closer and his beard and stilted walk betrayed him. It was true that if you behaved as though you belonged in a place you usually could be there unchallenged. Umar had only exchanged his robes and turban for a onesuit and cap, and he was being completely ignored by the same people who had ridiculed him openly for months. He went beneath the fourth Roc from the end of the row to her right; it had already been placed over a launch port.

By the time he'd entered the ship's belly hatch and opened its cargo bay doors above the gerlinger, Renata had returned to the deck and stood behind the thick, right-rear landing gear. As the platform began to grind up on its scissor scaffolding, she heard him moving within the bay and climbed the short, slanted ladder into the blister cockpit. Except for the two pilot stations, side by side behind the wraparound windscreen, the tiny space was only a cramped passage leading aft. Access panels and test readouts dotted the entire inner surface where it wasn't padded.

She bent through the open aft hatch into the unlit galley-san section; both those alcove doors, on either side, were dogged shut. Astern through the next open hatch she saw glimpses of Umar as he rolled the platform and its contents into the right side of the bay. The reflected light from below showed the underplanes of his sweating face, and the anxious look in his eyes as he too raced time.

There would be no more verbal exchanges; he could not be persuaded now. To rush him or wait. She took the surgical kit from her left armpit and unwrapped the sterile packaging. Included in the standard instruments was a twelve-inch bone saw, shaped similar to a pointed keyhole saw with angled handle, all steel with glued-in flint-flake cutting edge.

She wished she'd had the time to find a narcosorb, a surer and more humane weapon, but concern over being caught before she got here had taken precedence. A sharp thrust to his lower abdomen was most certain to do disabling damage that could be healed. All she wanted was containment, not revenge. Coshing him was too risky in her condition, and a backstab would probably skitter off ribs. She felt herself reel dizzily, and her left shoulder thumped against the galley door; her cry of pain found its way out.

Instantly Umar froze, head cocked back toward the noise. Her gut clenched in fear, then she nodded. This was better;

make him come to her. She would strike as he bent to pass through the hatchway. Pressing her bare buttocks to the smooth left door, she let the package drop and held the saw back in her right hand.

His boots scuffed carefully around the crowded space and paused at the hatch. She watched his right hand grip the thick jamb, then his left. His dark curly head swung under the lintel. She brought her right arm quickly around with elbow and wrist locked, hand tightening on the knobbed handle. The tip hit soft resistance, cut, slid through and free! Too late. He'd seen her motion and backed a step so her thrust connected only at the end of the swing, grazing his right side just above the pelvic bone.

Choking off the startled cry, he whipped his right arm down, and the saw was gone. In despair she shoved past him to the cargo floor, hands sweeping to relocate the weapon. Not certain of his opponent's size or his own next action, he fell back several steps more away from her. Then he saw the gleaming cap and profile as her frantic search ended. Her right hand's sudden stop tipped him, and he quickly stamped on it. Her yelp of agony mobilized his attack; he used his left foot to kick her in the midsection as she struggled there on all fours. The wind groaned from her, and she fell forward. He found the saw, picked it up carefully, then knelt beside her.

"Satan has great power," he said more to himself, nodding in recognition of her recovery. "But Allah is stronger! His *Mahdi* cannot be killed!"

Renata was gaping like a landed fish, trying to work her stunned diaphragm and get air back into her emptied lungs. He was without expression as he clutched her gown in his left hand, pulled her over on her back, and jabbed straight with his right. The saw point bisected the tip of her right breast where it spread over her chest and entered between the fourth and fifth rib, puncturing the diaphragm, liver, and lower right lobe of her lung, severing the secondary pulmonary arteries. The entire blade was within her.

Oddly, there was no cutting sensation, as she'd imagined. Rather, it felt like a strong hammer blow to her abdomen, and it burned hotly like a bullet. Her legs thrashed spasmodically for only a second. Her body became limp, a separate entity, but her mind was unexpectedly clear.

Umar grunted in satisfaction, stood, and smiled amicably.

Removing his onesuit, he proudly showed her his erection and the bleeding wound in his side. Then he tore her dampened gown away from her pelvis, quickly entered her, and thrust savagely, like an animal. She only stared up glassily at his ecstatic face, feeling truly sorry for him, not for herself. Other than that, she didn't react at all, as she lay there slowly bleeding to death.

Chapter 14

Seat webbing had held them fast, but nothing had protected them from falling rock. The three passengers in the front were unmoving; Twee had a deep cut along the right side of his head just below the ear pore; a wet scarlet patch crowned A.H.'s hair and grew as Joan looked. Droom had a black bruise on her left arm and several cuts from shards of the dematerialized canopy that covered them like chipped ice. In the rear, Joan had been luckier and suffered only slight cuts and wrenched muscles. But P.C. was simply gone, his web torn free on both sides. Only Gar, cushioned and covered by the undersides of the front chaises and pinned on the floor, was unscathed.

Joan had come out of the daze just after him, and now looked down to see his left foot working at his bonds. They had used spare optic fiber cables to tie his arms the only secure way for a Hhronkan: each arm crisscrossed around behind the upper torso with wrists tied together, and these also joined by a loop through the crotch and around the neck. They had left his hose-like legs free to walk, and with the left curled up to his chest he plucked at the knots with the four nimble toes.

She watched him dumbly for several seconds without reacting. Then P.C.'s absence registered, and her mind cleared in sadness and anger. Both her shod feet came down on his busy bare one. The fury in his cat-eyes instantly became terror as water cascaded in through the hull wound near P.C.'s seat.

"We are sinking! Let me up!" he screamed, struggling to bend up against her feet, fluid already washing the floor's carpet.

The level sloshed over him so quickly she acted without plan. Releasing her webbing she straddled her chair's lower end and lifted Gar from the cold water, ignoring the spasms in her back. He was far too heavy to lug to the closest shore, a rocky rise ten meters to their right. He stood expectantly, waiting for her to free his arms. The gurgling sea was up to her knees.

"Swim over there!" she yelled in the proper direction. His dark display of terror was sharper than before as she shoved with both hands on his resisting back. They were now only a foot out of the water, so he made little splash when he belly flopped. By then Droom stood by her seat, watching but not moving, holding her arm against her torso. The flyer's nose bubbled below the surface; both seated passengers were up to their chests and still inert. Joan shook Droom violently, and she weaved as though about to collapse. Altering the settings on their grav belts, Joan lightened the two Hhronka, then groped under the water and released the two front seat webs. The flyer fuselage disappeared under the roiling surface, leaving only their two heads in the air.

"You take Twee; I'll get A.H.!" she directed Droom.

The flyer belched its last trapped air and quickly sank, conveniently leaving the four of them floating free. Joan clutched A.H.'s collar and towed him to shore. It was a steep, slimy pitch, but the water's chill had begun to awaken him. He helped her drag him out and find a rounded shelf for his butt. Then she looked back at the Hhronkan gamely wriggling with her legs, pulling her charge through the water with her good hand on his robe. In the glittering reflections coming into the cave through the open right half of the entrance, she also saw Gar silhouetted. He clambered out of the opposite side of the pool onto the debris reef. With a gasp of fear she ran to her right around the pool's landward shore, already knowing she could never reach their hostage before he escaped.

She sprinted, slipping, and kept glancing from her shadowed footing back to the struggling figure with its arms still bound. P.C. was lying facedown where the impact geyser had deposited him, and she fell flat over him. Shock, fear, relief, then anger rippled through her when she heard his shallow breathing. They'd all suffered near-death largely due to the machinations of the being now atop the pile of rubble forty meters in front of her. If he got away, they were indeed dead. Calmly, she stood and drew one of the two stubby laser pistols she'd thrust into her onesuit's thigh pockets. Gripping the spongy fluted handle to activate it, she sighted with care, watching the bright red aiming dot glow on the rocks, and curled her index finger around the trigger bulb.

There was a muffled hum-buzz, and the broken surface two paces to Gar's right burst apart once more with a sizzling pop. From a cloud of hot fog, stone shrapnel whizzed, hissing into the pool. Gar screamed in pain as some found his legs. Joan quickly shot to his left with repeated results. Though hurt, her target froze upright and turned slowly to face her, convinced of her marksmanship.

"Swim to me," she called quietly and with total finality.

He bent his neck to watch the red dot glide in small circles over his upper torso. She could hear his deep gasping even that far away; it steadied her hand. With care he picked his way into the pool and swam straight to her with wriggling legs. By the time he was pulled from the water, A.H. had stumbled over and collapsed by his son.

"Well?" she anxiously demanded, motioning Gar to the low, curved rear wall. A.H. sat up and gingerly removed his sandy hands. "Broken left upper arm; from his breathing I'd guess several cracked ribs; probably a contusion or two but no fracture; lots of bruises. Must've rolled up this slant with the water, so the impact was cushioned. Where's the medi-quik?"

"In the flyer," she answered, worried at his disorientation.

"I'll get it," he said. Instead of rising, his eyes rolled up, he turned dead white, and fell backward with a moan.

"Oh, damn!" she cried. Back around the cave both Hhronka lay half out of the water. She pointed her weapon at Gar. "You make one motion I don't tell you to make, and I will burn off both your arms and legs!" she said furiously. She wagged the short glassy barrel toward the Hhronka.

Twee was still unconscious, but Droom was merely winded, her torso ballooning in and out rapidly. Joan stationed her prisoner against the wall again and with one hand jerked the belt-

lightened Droom to her wobbly legs. Shoving her second gun into Droom's good hand, Joan asked, "Can you watch him?"

Droom's eyes were clear as she smoke-ringed and pointed the laser, addressing him in gasping monotone Hhronkan. "I am Primary of all the Orrtaan. You know the meaning of this."

Gar sagged down against to the rock in reply, staring at the muzzle and the face dark-swathed with contempt above it. Joan had to dive twice before locating the medi-quik's plastec case, and when she streamed out of the black pool, Twee was alert. He helped her attach the sensors to her son, and keyed it to human norm. It was a mild brain bruise, and A.H.'s other diagnoses were also correct. She used the spray-skin on Twee's leaking cut and A.H.'s scalp cut and gave her son and husband a shot of anti-shock. They wrapped P.C.'s ribs, then set his arm in insta-cast. While it warmed and hardened, Joan checked Twee; his head injury was not serious either and needed no treatment immediately. A.H. awoke, peered into her eyes, and ordered her to take shock preventative herself, then they checked each other and dressed lesser wounds.

Finally they put an elastic bandage on Droom's arm. The onset of shock in Hhronka can be seen in random dark mottling in the skin along the back of the torso. Since neither of them displayed it, she held back on anti-shock, which tended to make them drowsy. At last there was nothing to do but squat on the cold rock and stare at the entrance.

Joan let herself react by quivering against A.H. and refusing the sedative he offered. The pool was dead calm behind its new bar, but a breeze circled the cave with a thin moan.

"When will they come?" she asked no one in particular.

Droom answered after several seconds. "They know we've lost the flyer and so our equipment and illumination. They'll come after total darkness when the drones can use far IR to see us and not even our Hhronkan eyes can see them."

The light had already dropped to the midafternoon gray of the short Teffhtan day but was still bright enough for them to examine their refuge. It resembled the Covenant cave in color and texture but was only one hundred meters long, fifty deep, with a vaulted roof twenty meters high at its center above the pool. They sat on a sloping rock shelf that curved from the left side of newly blocked entrance, going underwater on their right about twenty-five meters beyond where P.C. had beached. A scum-encrusted tide line indicated that the ledge, now twenty paces at its widest, was never completely submerged. Despite the mild salt breeze, a dirt-dry odor of mold nauseated the humans. Even without moving, they could see no other entrances or exits. It had therefore also become their trap.

A.H. stood slowly; there was no pain. Depression could be as fatal as actual attack. "Damn! Is anybody else hungry?" No one responded; Joan only hugged P.C. closer and shrugged neutrally. "Let's not just sit waiting for execution; let's do whatever we can!"

Without waiting for reply, he waded down into the chilling water. He hyperventilated and dove only once, returning after two minutes with a porpoise's burst of exhalation. Both arms were laden with the ration box, a bag, and several small metallic cubes in a net bag.

Dumping the goods onto the ledge, he shivered miserably like a soused dog. "It's getting my crotch wet I hate the most!" The evening light was failing; it could be the end of their last day, and his attempt at P.C.'s role had little effect. They ate a cold meal without enthusiasm, and Joan fed P.C. intravenously from the medi-quik. When they'd finished, spirits were a bit higher. A.H. stood to face the group.

"Droom, you're relieved," he said, pulling out a length of damp Perlon rope from the bag and tossing it to her. She bound Gar's legs and toes as he continued. "I've found a way to use the *vurkari*'s infrared vision to our own advantage." He held up one of the cubes. "Hhronkan emergency heaters from our survival kit. We'll put them at the other end of the ledge, set on low to match our bodies' heat output, and trigger them by remote as the attack starts . . . should confuse them for a moment anyway. Then we'll hit them with these."

He withdrew a silver egg with a stud in one end, a Hhronkan sonic grenade. With a delay timer they acted like explosive grenades, but emitted several bursts of extremely high frequency sound that would jellify all animal tissue within twenty paces and should disrupt EM circuitry enough to incapacitate the *vurkari*.

"How did you get those past the search they put us through?" asked Droom in surprise.

"Compliments of my wife," replied A.H. with a grim smile.

"Buried in bulk food canisters," said Joan, taking no satisfaction for the confirmation of her pessimism.

"I found two more lasers. How many is that?" A.H. asked.

Joan and Droom each held up one, and the Hhronkan said, "I think Twee and I should use them, while you two throw the sonics." To A.H.'s hesitancy, she continued, "We should all be prepared for these machines. They are nonorganic killing robots, no doubt armored and very fast. Since our reactions are quicker than yours . . ."

Not wanting to dwell on the depressing reminder, A.H. handed the pistols out. "Let's move P.C. around to the left."

Two triplets of lights moved low over the water outside the cave. At first they thought the nightly rain clouds had failed to collect and some stars were being magnified by the thicker air near the horizon. But then the two groups settled onto the water and winked out like fireflies. In the remnant twilight, the two drones with the swollen undercarriages floated grayly about two hundred meters from the cave mouth. They watched intently; A.H. wished again he'd found the binocs sunk with the flyer. The half-round cargo doors folded inward quickly to leave twin black holes at the ocean's surface. The tiny hairs along his spine went erect. Something *slithered* into the water from each.

When still an "orphan" at the experimental breeding camp in Eastern Kentucky, A.H. had done some work with octopods as a biology exercise. He'd found their octagonal symmetry mystifying and their certain intelligence fascinating—it gleamed in their all-too-human eyes, similarly intense but aimed at very different goals. In that way the little cephalopods were more alien than the Hhronka since their body plan forced an entirely nonhumanoid psychology on them. Their movements, seemingly clumsy but in truth sudden and sure, had always left him tingling with an illogical revulsion. There was something innately sinister to them, like the sadism of the cat without the ameliorating playfulness. This glimpse of motion affected him in the same way now, and his belly tightened in dread.

"They are coming," said Twee, stoic as his father.

The dim forms had gone under at once, and only the floating drones remained visible but inactive. Suddenly A.H.'s plan seemed totally inadequate to him, laughable, worthless against these perfect soldiers—and they were sending only *two*.

"Let's forget the heater dodge. They probably read shapes too well for that to have worked anyway," he said feebly. "We *could* use a visible light source; that would even us visually. And we can still use the sonics effectively."

Droom stirred, rose, and went to the nearest heater box. She showed them how to open the base of the metal can and expose the thick red fuel tablet. She put it down and backed several paces, then aimed her laser carefully in the gloom. After a flaring white puff of smoke it began to glow with an orange-white luminance that ate steadily into the substance. "It will burn this way about fifteen minutes," she said.

They rapidly scattered the rest throughout the cave; the resulting light threw their multiple giant shadows onto the walls and roof so that a company of Vahallic ghosts joined the fight.

A.H. knelt beside Joan and P.C. She smiled with determination as he studied their son's sleeping face. "I want you to stay with him over there," he said, pointing at the left end of the shelf. Instead of the strong rebuttal he expected, she merely nodded and allowed him to pick up the youth. When they were settled, he hesitated to look at her again, knowing she would see his insistent tears. But she took the decision from him.

"I'm getting really tired of these good-byes," she whispered with a thick voice. There was nothing left to say, with words. His gaze darted to her streaked face, and his fingers brushed her wet cheek as he smiled gratefully. He lifted P.C.'s tangled damp hair from his face, then turned away—and froze.

His guess at the *vurkari*'s form was nearly correct. The first scudded over the debris reef like a starfish in fast-forward, pressed to the craggy irregularities and rotating rapidly. Before it went into the pool, he clearly saw its pentagonal symmetry. The five tapering limbs joined to a globular central mass, all smoothly covered with an oily blue-black integument. He estimated eight meters from tip to tip. The Hhronka had seen it too and had backed up to the wall next to Gar to avoid hitting each other.

If he could catch it in the water! The sonic pulses would have a much greater effect propagating in the thicker medium. His shaking hands already held two of the cool hard eggs as he dropped the bag and sprinted toward the pool's edge. He pressed in the studs two seconds apart and threw the one in his right to the far side of the water, then underhanded the other only a few paces from shore. The depression it created refilled with a *plunk!*

"Sonic!" he yelled, diving backward and pinning his fingers into his ears. The trace sound beyond the immediate sphere of destruction could rupture eardrums. The others imitated; Gar and P.C. had already been protected with rubber plugs cut from the medi-quik's supplies.

Five seconds later the pool's surface beyond where the flyer had sunk seethed, rumbled, and grew a huge mound of water that erupted into tatters of hot fog, then vaporized in hissing steam. Two seconds later the effect repeated nearer them. They felt the hot spray, and the entire pool surged back and forth as though in a bathtub. Finally it quieted. For several seconds they studied the water; nothing emerged. A.H. grinned over at the Hhronka and stood to retrieve the bag, holding up a finger.

"One down, one to—" He choked off his elation. He was walking at the pool's edge back toward Joan and looked down. The lantern-heaters had begun to flicker, but enough light was left to show a movement beneath the water directly below him. He couldn't quite decide its shape so he bent closer to the surface. A dark round object sat motionless against the shelf about one meter underwater. It moved. A circle of glittering eyes looked at him *knowingly.* He snapped upright in terror, caught a heel, and fell backward. It was too late even to yell a warning.

A fountain jetted up the rock slope through the space he'd just stood in, preceded by a dark blur. His eye muscles could not accommodate fast enough to focus on it. Spasmodically he jerked his head up and around to the Hhronka, following the blur overhead. Two yellow laser beams lit the mist enveloping the *vurkari;* he heard the sizzle of steam and saw the faint dotted lines of coherent photons. Droom and Twee were alternately firing directly into the whirling mass, yet this made little difference: the machine continued to attack the cave wall just to their left! A.H. cried anew in victory. His sonics had scored after all. The disoriented *vurkari* was flailing at the stone like some mad eggbeater, sending chips flying. He saw no marks where the two beams were hitting the shiny skin and looked back at Droom. The Orrtaan now stood still, ignoring the attacker, with both pistols aimed out the cave mouth.

"Shoot!" he yelled in panic, thinking the Primary had frozen. But she proved the clever tactician again. A.H. was advancing on her when the second *vurkari* entered the cave. But this one completely avoided the pool by leaping over it from the top of the debris reef. It sprang up like a closing parasol and glided in a perfect parabola just beneath the cobbled roof. A.H. felt himself go lighter as it passed above him on its grav flux field. Droom was lasing at it the entire time. Not with pulsed beams, but with both pistols issuing steady continual lances of energy. This would drain the power cells in only seconds, but it made it nearly impossible to miss, as if she used a firehose on it. Still, A.H. saw no damage.

It touched down on limb tip like a ballerina, only paces from the three against the wall. And four lasers were striking point-blank without effect! Then he felt a wave of heat roll over him from the combat. He understood. The *vurkari*'s shiny integument was repulsor filmed! It must be some advanced variant on the molecular layer that not only gave the usual protection but also stretched and bent with the surface it coated. Little wonder these machines were so feared; they were nearly invulnerable. Then how had his sonic barrage crippled the first one? Obviously it hadn't. Spontaneous failure? An imperfection in the coating? Such timing would be fantastic luck, but such coincidences did happen in reality. And it showed the enemy wasn't omnipotent!

The logic behind its radical symmetry was demonstrated as it operated in more than one direction at a time. Still floating on its flux field, it pushed itself forward with a tentacle. The other four reached for the laser pistols. Its movements were an incredibly fast blur whose content was sorted by the mind not the eye. Four objects sailed through the air to splash into the pool, and then the three Hhronka were aloft, held in the coiled limbs, but still thrashing, living.

Relieved, A.H. realized the Teffhtans were taking no chances on injuring or killing Gar. The failsafe limit had still not been reached, and all captives were being treated equally until identity was clearly established. But what would it do to humans? Twee yelled something, but it was lost in the deafening chatter. In panic A.H. ran back toward his family with no clear thought in mind other than physical closeness. Forgetting he couldn't use the sonics now without killing his own people, he bent to retrieve the bag as he passed. A blow on his buttocks flipped him into a somersault, and he came down rolling several steps beyond. Totally surprised, he looked up to see one of the pentapus limbs reaching for him like a frog's tongue. At the same time he heard the grenade bag plunk into the pool. The thinning tentacle had telescoped out after him at lightning speed! Despite its tendrilness, it still encircled his midsection tightly and elevated him off his feet in an instant. It felt like the cast-iron strength of a Hhronkan limb and could have been so constructed, but the skin stretched and contracted perfectly to hide the interior.

Suddenly the berserk *vurkari* stopped killing the wall and froze in position with limbs raised. Several voices continued the cavern noise. A.H.'s imprisoning limb drew him in with a clicking vibration. The machine had no apparent interest in Joan or his son and was ignoring the struggles its three captives were making. A loud Teffhtan voice issued from a grid near the top of its globular center. Now that he was held snugly against it, A.H. could see more than its circle of sensor eyes. The sphere was bejeweled with weapon ports, sampling orifices, and a few lidded slots. And the shiny skin covered the globe too. It wasn't oily to touch; it had the dry smoothness of glass and was hard and metallically cold. He saw that each gap in the skin was protected by a connected flap in the continuous integument, giving complete repulsor effect. He seemed to feel the active intelligence within the adamant shell, thinking on its own. But *baas* could not merge with nor control this nonorganic brain. It would do as it was told or programmed, without remorse, he remembered. He forced himself to become rigid.

Droom also dangled unmoving in the next arm, staring back intently at Gar, held just beyond. He couldn't see Twee across the globe. Finally the *vurkari* stopped speaking; Gar answered, and it released him to rush and stand against the wall, his bonds cut so unobtrusively A.H. missed it. The Provider's display was peculiarly both vengeful and indignant. He steeled himself to hear Gar's instant execution order and feel the coil about him tighten until he was pinched in two. But before Gar regained breath enough to speak, ports on the shiny sphere flipped open and a holoimage glowed alive in midair.

There was a narration but it was in unintelligible Teffhtan. Yet its subject was chillingly familiar. Umar was inside the Life Complex and being recorded by a monitor there. He directed a large box-laden gerlinger through an empty corridor. Gar stood looking at the small image with openmouthed horror, now displaying black-white flickers worthy of any true Hhronkan.

Droom recovered first, yelling over the *vurkari*'s narration. "Gar, I know what is in those boxes, and you will have to delay our execution—if you want to save this world from total destruction!"

* * *

Umar's escape from *Wind* was ridiculously easy, but this neither surprised nor delighted him. The moment he'd struck down the demon-possessed Renata, he had freed himself of his anonymous past as a simple but gifted man and truly resumed his mantle of authority as the *Mahdi*. In the role of God's Justice Bearer, he was granted certain rights and powers, beyond wisdom and leadership. These powers could work wonders routinely, but when necessary to ensure success of his mission, miracles could also be performed, as he'd already demonstrated. Therefore, he fully expected to arrive at Atuum's center tower without contretemps. And the concommitant rapture he should feel in doing God's will would surely come after His justice was dispensed to this world. Then he would begin to plan Wlaata's destiny and man's part in it. He could not do there what he would do here, as long as innocent humans lived on Mars, some of whom were Muslims.

The crews in the fighter hangar continued to ignore him and his craft until he fired its engines. Actually, this wasn't necessary to launch, but he had to give them warning he was about to prematurely open the bay and explosively evacuate it. Though confused, they reacted as experienced crew and scrambled into the nearest locks or sealable ships. He had previously learned when the bay-release mechanism would be linked into the fighters' on-board control. One minute after this time, and thirty seconds after the jets fired, he touched on the launch sequence at his console and leaned back between the seat's webbing and pads. Pushed by escaping air, the bay panels burst out from under, and his Roc was blown into space. This had been Mowry's plan for getting six Rocs out simultaneously to deal with the three guard drones.

Through the cockpit bubble he saw the shaking bright cup of the hangar shrink "above" him; his body was lifted painfully against the webbing, then it retracted to pull comfortably tight. He felt various thrust vectors and saw *Wind*'s half-shadowed hub wobble back and forth. The fighter's steering jets countered its roll and then the main engines fired full thrust. On his console the radio-contact button lit redly, but he kept the pickup off. The wheel rim sailed overhead quickly as "up" became his ship's blunt nose, and Teffht's cloudy ball became its target.

As expected, his solitary unorthodox exit had not gotten him through the drones' blockade. The small combat screen began teakettle whistling and flashing with hits and misses. Two of the three drones around *Wind* were pursuing him, leaving the last to continue guarding the now-suspect hangar ports. He let a smile float onto his mouth in mild satisfaction of botching Baay's plans. If any launch doors opened now, they would be instantly blasted by this drone. The *Wind* was effectively sealed.

Repulsor film coated his ship's entire exterior like a skin, absorbing incoming energies, converting them to coherent photons, spreading them throughout the layer, and radiating them harmlessly into space. Its lower threshhold of function allowed small quantities of certain energies through, such as visible light, radio, or sensor probes. This was why the scene outside his windscreen looked normal to Umar. Yet the reradiated energy from the protection layer thoroughly scrambled the filmed sensors, whiting the readout screens for an instant. He understood this and was not concerned. And since the drones were similarly protected, he didn't bother to let the ship return fire.

But if the film's upper threshhold were surpassed, the multivalent resonating molecular bonds of the film itself would be overwhelmed and the material destroyed, along with the Roc. Only a fusion explosion could produce this concentration of energy. So when his combat screen squealed at the approach of two missiles, he became very concerned.

The drones couldn't use nukes on their own world, but till he entered the atmosphere he was an allowable target. Now certain his fighter was filmed, the drones had each fired one missile; they were bright-seekers of course, homing on his luminous exhaust. Umar saw their tail flares clearly in the aft TV screens and decided it was time to give the combat comp its head. He punched at the engage button and was slammed into the chair's pads. The ship changed its angle of planet approach, diving directly at it rather than coming in tangent to the atmosphere. He jerked with alarm, but could not move under the acceleration. At this steep angle velocity would be incredible—no problem with air friction, due to the film, but deceleration for safe landing using the engines alone could become impossible. And even if the enormous impact force of a crash could be handled by the film, the *interior,* including himself, would certainly be macerated by the huge inertial difference. The ship would be transformed into a repulsor film bubble of multiatomic plasms. Gravity was not an absorbable force but a deformation of space-time caused by the size and relative motions of masses. The film had no effect on gravity or its Einsteinian twin.

His combat screen was flickering again; this time with counts of his own craft's laser firings. The cannons in the wings' trailing edges were continuously emitting good hits on both missiles. Not surprisingly, they still closed the distance between them; they too were filmed. Why didn't his ship launch its own missiles? Then he saw the distances involved overlaid on the image and realized that by the time his defender missiles hit the drones' the explosions would be near enough to destroy him. The drones themselves wisely remained behind at a safe interval.

His ship was gaining speed, falling straight into Teffht's gravity well at over Mach 7. The cloudy three-fourths-lit circle already covered most of his sky. Still the ship aimed lases uselessly back at the two missiles. They were only a kilometer away when the Roc's sensors discerned the first wisping of the stratosphere on the hull. Before the engines' increased vibrations reached him, the ship's course alteration pushed him down into the chair so hard he couldn't breathe for several seconds. He spun into darkness. Finally the abdominal pressure cuff let up, he awoke, and his eyes focused; the navcomp showed the ship was back on a tangential landing path. Automatically his right hand pressed the dressing over his wound; there had been no way to explain it to a doctor, so no stitches could be had. Still, the hand came away unbloodied . . . divine protection.

And the two nukes were plunging on toward the planet! He comprehended it all at once. The blanket laser barrage from his ship had acted to totally blind the missiles' own sensors. Having no access to new data, they had flown on a straight course for several seconds toward Teffht after he'd turned in the atmosphere. By then, it was not possible for them to follow; the air offered too much resistance for a fast turn, and they'd run out of fuel. They were now a danger only to the planet, a fact the drones well understood. Two dwarf suns lit and conjoined in the aft screens to burn for over a minute.

So the Teffhtan machines were not perfect after all! The flawed product of a flawed race, more proof of innate sin. They could be fooled—by human handiwork. How great the glory of God! To be so expressed in the superior abilities of His chosen people! He was so buoyed by this exultation, he simply ignored his pursuers as they followed him to the surface without further attack. When Atuum's circular grid appeared through a rent in the late afternoon weather, he released the navcomp and took back manual control. This part he had totally worked out for himself.

As expected, the city sky was filled with a defensive fleet. Wasps about the nest. Several—not drones, since they had viewing blisters—periodically took shots at him. Fools, he thought, they can't accept the defeat of their machines; their pride is too great.

He passed high over the black dot of the tower cap and halted. On screen, the nearby streets were pebbled with masses apparently ignorant of or not concerned about the mind transduction device's capacity. But then, they wouldn't be aware of him—yet. Perhaps this was only the usual crowd of citizens at daily life. If Krieder's suspicions about Gar's ordered pretenses were true, then a whole different pattern of normal behavior might now be shown.

For seconds he considered beaming several blocks of a radial street or two, sending Satan a few hundred souls prematurely. Suddenly, he shook in icy revulsion and righteous fury. This was cruelty, not justice. Indeed, Satan was whispering even to him, even to Allah's *Mahdi* as he began his work! How like the Prophet Jesus' temptations! Thwarting this cunning evil was his ultimate goal now. Besides, he had a better target for the Roc's weaponry . . . and *he* had no restriction about nuclear warheads.

Canting the ship's nose down on its grav flux, he quickly aimed and fired two missiles from under the wings toward the four-hundred-meter cap of the tower. Several drone craft shot into their paths. One actually succeeded in getting between one of the little cylinders and the cap. The concussion and radiation of the tiny sun were brightly repulsed by the other ships' and the tower's films. The small roiling pulse even blotted out his own sensors momentarily. But the other sunlet left a large ragged-lipped hole near the edge of the slightly curving cap's surface. Waves of the pebbled masses far below now surged out the radials away from the destruction. He smiled.

Baay's data bloc had not lied. Of course the precious Life Complex tower would be filmed. And the smallest tactical nuclear warhead a Roc carried would just be sufficient to sunder the polymer with little damage to what lay beneath. She'd planned well, but he'd planned better . . . naturally.

At once the Roc plummeted through the rising dust and thick

smoke directly to the hole. The defenders obviously had not been prepared for his desire to *enter* the Complex. Only as he settled flush onto the cap wound without extending landing gear, so the cargo bay doors could drop into it, did one drone try to head him off. Knowing nonnuke missiles were ineffectual, it rammed.

But this failed too since the collision produced no transferred impact on either vessel. The drone's horizontal motion was canceled, reappearing as a spherical pulse of high-energy radiation that sent a column of superheated air upward with a crack of thunder. Then the drone slid off the cap edge to assume station with the others close to the settled Roc.

When the sensors announced contact, he shut down the engines and leaped toward the canted cargo bay. So far time was on his side. There would be confusion now in choosing the next defensive step. By the time Gar or Baay or whoever was in control realized they must send in the *vurkari* to search, he'd have disappeared. He would get directly into the lift used by the "reborn," and so avoid all live guards, as Baay's plans had indicated. He suspected Baay of some kind of betrayal, not that it mattered anymore. It had been Allah's will that he gain this data to aid him in this mission.

Once inside the transduction vault, he would wreck the monitoring system, making it necessary to search every level. And how would they know where to look, unless they also knew what was in the gerlinger's crates? That they would never guess. All he had to do was set it up in the correct place and leave the way he'd come. The Roc's exterior locks were keyed to his palm and voice code alone. Once reclosed it would be impregnable. As for the rest, God would protect him, His *Mahdi!*

"His will be done!"

As he climbed through the opening bay hatch, his foot struck a soft damp bundle lying still on the floor. He glanced at it in distaste, then went on. It was only the demon-used husk of Renata.

Chapter 15

On previous nights, A.H. had found Teffht's curtained sunsets beautiful. But now, to a prisoner with little hope of freedom, this one seemed as horrifying as some nuclear afterglow. Tau Ceti created a bloated rotten ochre wound in the dirty cloud banks near the western horizon, like a red giant swelling to engulf its luckless family of worlds.

They stood on the black tilting tower cap next to the *vurkari* drone, the rufous sheen painting half of every vertical surface. Atuum's lights already spread away on all sides like ranked premature stars. A warm rising wind still exhaled up and around the tower into the mushroom remnants of the explosions far overhead. Except for the two downed craft, the surface was a sleek sable curve—the event horizon of a black hole . . . staring out from ordered chaos onto random-mattered infinity.

At Droom's ultimatum Gar had relented their immediate deaths, and their drone had taken them to city center, settling next to Umar's impregnable Roc. A total of twenty-five minutes had passed since he had landed, yet no tow vehicles had arrived to attempt removal of the fighter from the breach it neatly plugged. With both Gar and Baay absent and the drones each acting independently, the hierarchy of command had been in turmoil. No robot defenders had even entered the cap in pursuit of the Teheranian. But Droom demanded their party do so at once. She was in fine fettle, assuming complete control, throwing out orders to Gar as though *he* were the hostage.

When he finally balked and merely stared back at her, she made no attempt to hide her skin, openly showing black sinusoidal waves of contempt over every visible centimeter of skin.

"If several thousand Hhronka were not trapped here, I would let *all* of you die!" She looped a hand at her comrades behind Gar. "The deaths of only the few of us here would be well worth the retribution you truly deserve! Unfortunately, we do not have the time to remove my people ... and we surely do not have time for any more of your foolish ego-building—you and Baay have already wasted *eons* on that! You are going to have to undergo some very rapid maturation. I need your full unquestioning cooperation as interpreter and liaison with your forces— and I need it *now!* For that, you must stay by my side every instant. If we do not act with extreme speed within the next minutes, then in a few days this planet will cease to exist!"

All of her audience was stunned to silence. But Gar was stubborn. "How could any one being, especially this human, destroy an entire planet? That is not possible without a stellar deterioration, or bombardment by hundreds of thermonuclear bombs." He paused in a moment of haughty reflection. "Or collision with a sizable body. This human surely does not command the comets!"

Droom's fury drained completely when she stared at him and said almost pityingly, "There is another way. And I suspect Umar has worked it out in every needed detail. From my association with him I have learned he is one of the cleverest and most knowledgeable of humans. Without him the ftl drive that brought us here would never have been successfully engineered. Now he has made use of this expertise. In the monitor image we saw, he was directing a gerlinger that bears, I believe, most of our reserve grav material plates.

"What he intends is a variation on the ftl device. We chilled the material and let cosmic rays provide the correct kind of energy to cause nearly instantaneous, total conversion, creating an intense temporary gravity field. But here he will expose these plates to a different type of energy to effect the material uniformly, converting only part of it to pure gravitons—or to a heavy gravity well, if you prefer that description. This will in turn act on the remainder of the plates' molecules to compact and convert them into super-dense matter, resulting in a pure mass of what you call 'quarks.' "

"Like the core of a neutron star?" asked P.C., wide-eyed with awe. The youth was still shaky, but had recovered so energetically during the flight back to Atuum that they couldn't argue him out of the search party. And A.H. realized his *baas* might be vital.

The Orrtaan smoke-ringed and continued. "This mass will be so heavy it will instantly begin to sink through the planet's crust. As it does so, it will accrete surrounding material, in turn compacting it into a denser state as well. In only hours this will spiral into Teffht, pass through the planet's center of gravity, rebound, and continue accumulating core matter to itself, honeycombing the deep interior—but not for long. The perturbations in the location of the center of gravity will alter axial motion and start a series of tremors throughout the entire crust and mantle that—"

"Will sunder our world to pieces," finished Gar in a tone oddly reverent. The edges of his angular face seemed to sharpen as he studied her for several seconds, then turned to one of the drone's outside pickups and spoke quickly. The group followed him from beside the craft along the cap to its edge. The slope was gradual enough to peer over. In the xanthous light from the plaza floods far below, the tower's sheer wall shone obsidian. No detail marred its surface, a deep midnight river flowing from the city to the sky. Beyond, the boulevards remained deserted.

"There are service ports below the cap's lip," said Gar. "But it will take the *vurkari...* "

They came from behind, skittering on tentacle tips across the great bowl. The two pentapods seemed identical to those that had assaulted them in the cave, but only one could be. Without pause they fell over the knife edge. A.H. assumed they floated underneath on grav flux. Scraping and clashing echoed faintly in the warm convection breeze now bathing the tower. The noises terminated with a squeal from below.

"Set your belts for neutral buoyancy," instructed Gar. He curved over headfirst and gripped the edge, then rolled out like a trapeze artist coming off the net. Each touched their wide buckles and imitated, the swing of legs carrying them down and backward toward the tower shaft. Looking up, they found the mushroom analogy completed. The undersurface of the cap lip, from border to shaft fifty meters in, was thick with the same glasslike dendrites as on the outer pylons. Rather than being ranked into gill lamellae, these more nearly resembled a hyaline vineyard.

The *vurkari* had removed an oval plate from the shaft just where it truncated the clustered receptive antennae. Most of the troop drifted directly into this wide gap, and the others were able to move sideways on handholds, once grounded to the shaft. The breeze soughed in behind them as they gathered at the entrance in deference to the dark interior. Suddenly a dull glow silhouetted a lattice of structural supports stretching away above a solid decking. A *vurkari* moved from one of the supports to their right.

"We are immediately over the Life Complex; an entrance lies nearby," Gar said to Droom with a curled arm.

The second pentapus approached from this direction. It twittered briefly. The Teffhtan flushed darkly. A.H. recognized the deep fear response Baay had shown and was certain it was as much for Gar's own personal safety as for his planet's peril. He was about to leave the mindnet.

"The human is not there now, but has been. The master monitor comp has been wrecked, but nothing else."

"That, of course, is part of his plan," interjected Droom. "With it inoperative, the entire tower will have to be searched. Perhaps I can help narrow possibilities. The only way I can think the required energy could be supplied to the grav plates would be exposure to huge numbers of tremendously accelerated neutrons. Bathed in a cloud of them, the material would convert in seconds."

"Yes! Twenty-two levels down, there is a generator using direct conversion fusion power to provide uninterrupted supply should Atuum's network fail," Gar replied eagerly. "The particle wastes, mostly neutrons, are trapped by an enclosing accrete-metal shell."

"That would suffice. He would have only to gain entrance to the shield and have the gerlinger place the plates close to the reaction. Then he would have to contrive some way to time their exposure to allow his own escape. We must contact our ship and ask for a check on missing items he might have used."

Gar displayed ready assent.

"How did he obtain the data needed for what he is doing?" the Provider said suspiciously.

Joan smothered a cry, clutching A.H.'s arm. "He could have got it from the plans Baay sent back with Rennie!"

With a loud clank, the Roc's cargo bay doors puckered apart, then sighed down fifty meters to their right. They all swung toward the sound in surprise.

"There's not supposed to be anyone aboard," whispered A.H. His expression went from puzzled to panicked. "Unless—" His breath caught; heart slammed. He broke to a dead run. Leaping wildly for the lower edge of one bay door, he snagged his right hand onto its airseal strip and pulled himself up. Standing on the lip of the rectangular hole, he suddenly felt foolish. He'd entered the enemy's domain defenseless and completely ignorant, but if what he feared—

His glance was swinging around the dark, cluttered vault to the gangway of the cockpit. He saw the bare foot shining in the stream of artificial light paving the passage. A numbness born of refusal to believe swept him, and he wasn't even aware of going to her. The reflection from the star-grid floor plates showed a sodden, worm-white horror. He was both drawn and repelled. A lassitude robbed him of action, like the *usstaa's* shadow.

She sat propped against the bulkhead girder below the winking bay control panel, arms at her sides, hands on the deck palm-up, legs spread in a V before her. A dark pool circled her like a moat. The rotted smell tightened his stomach into a fist. Her hospital blouse was thrown over one shoulder, exposing the slack, splotched body. How thin and childlike it looked. The blade handle protruded from under her ruined breast like a spigot, the black stream's now-dry source.

He reached to withdraw it, then stopped. Rational and irrational thoughts tracked each other. If he dislodged the saw, the bleeding might resume—she couldn't have one drop left, so much had been lost already. He felt the coagulated blood he'd got on his hands when he'd knelt to her, black under his nails and tacky between his fingers. He was revulsed and wiped them on his pants, guilty but compulsive. He could not touch the putrid *thing,* afraid as though death itself were contagious.

Then the capped head lifted upright; the pasty face filled a little, and the glazed eyes cleared. It spoke softly, plaintively to him.

"Daddy, my hair's all gone." Her mouth opened into a square of silent, helpless weeping, and blood that outlined white teeth ran out over her lower lip. Only a single tear leaked tiredly from each eye. "Help me, Daddy . . . I'm dying."

He felt every nerve burst aflame. It was his child, his Rennie. She was leaving him, and he could do nothing. Surgery, massive transfusion, total resuscitation were too far away. . .

A gentle but firm pressure shoved him aside, and he looked up in surprise. Joan and Droom were hovering over Rennie with the medi-quik from the Roc. The rest watched silently, P.C. chalk white as his sister, the Hhronka glass-skinned, Gar clinical. Twee started to push past the Teffhtan, but retreated as though embarrassed.

Suddenly A.H. was no longer watching the end of his child's life. He saw her past in his memory: the soft pink raisin he'd first held only seconds after he'd watched it emerge, wondering if she'd develop *baas* like P.C. The seven-year-old pixie in agony with a broken arm from reckless play with a grav belt. The sprouting beauty, gloating at having finally beaten him in free flying. The young woman oozing with guilt after her first sex, her apologetic smile telling him she was no longer "his girl." The uncritical awe on her face when she'd first become infatuated with Umar . . . her murderer.

And now he watched her burgeoning sorrow as she realized her death. Joan's wet face appeared across from him, and her shaking hands inserted the IV into Rennie's right arm. Droom was hastily adjusting the readouts on the box.

"Gar's called for a drone to get her back. This one's been keyed to Umar," Joan said with a pale edge of panic in her lowered voice.

He looked back at Gar with gratitude, enmity lost in the dreamy moment. How he wanted, tried to touch her with his Self, give her his will to live. But the *damned* mindnet frustrated his strongest effort to merge, shouting at him with a million ghost voices.

"Momma," Renata said after seconds of deep gasping. Her voice became bubbly as more blood filled her mouth and gushed out. The gagging spasm was short, and they both gently held her shoulders to the wall to prevent excess movement. She looked back up, bright-eyed, at them and spoke, but only the last word was audible: "afraid."

There was no seizure, no battlefield "death rattle." Her life faded like an echo. She breathed out; the cardiac signal fell to baseline; and the light went from her unblinking eyes.

They were stunned in disbelief. It was Droom who now pushed them both away, gently pulled her flat, and applied the cardiac needle, then activated the pacemaker. No effect.

"Help me!" she prompted, starting CPR.

Her quickness broke their lethargy. They couldn't find the airway or pump in the kit, so A.H. began to breathe her. Bending over on his knees, he slid his left hand under her neck and turned her face to him so all the blood drained from her mouth. He would not let himself see the staring, unseeing eyes. Then he lifted her shoulders with the hand so her head dropped back to stretch open the trachea. Pinching her nostrils with his right hand, he sealed his lips to her cold blue ones and puffed. The abdomen rose slightly and dropped quickly when he rocked back for another gulp of air. Fifteen times, then Joan took his place while Droom continued jolting Rennie's sternum with her lapped nailless hands.

There was the background noise of Gar speaking, but to A.H. none of the words registered. Nothing made sense but the movement and the pain and the pause—the fight to breathe Rennie back from nothingness and convert into awareness the cooling meat he tasted.

Much, much later, the EEG bleeped and another screen showed oxygen level in the cerebral tissues had dropped too low. There wasn't enough fluid, even with polyheme being constantly added, to carry the oxygen they were pumping into the ever-leaking lungs. Brain activity had suddenly ceased.

When he heard the final dull tone, A.H. lifted up from Renata's mouth and wiped her salty fluids from his own, swallowing the rest. He'd just felt . . . something. A gossamer touch, like walking through a cobweb in the dark. He looked over at Joan, who pressed her forehead and hands onto the still chest in a sobbing farewell. He couldn't share her grief; there was no need to bind his flesh to Rennie's in promised memory. It was one of the few times he'd been so close to death, but this was not what he'd felt, for instance, when Franklin had died. Then there had been great loss, a sudden void only to be time-filled, deep regrets for them both. Truly Rennie's life had been full and happy, more so than the vast majority's. But so very short. And still, some knowledge secret even to himself granted him a bittersweetness so true to life it didn't need grief for his acceptance . . . or his resignation. He reached to palm Joan's hot sticky cheek.

"Stay with her till they come."

She nodded and twisted her head to kiss his palm, returning both the gesture and deep admiration he had given her.

He rose from his knees as Gar bobbed forward to stare at the corpse. "I have not seen real unwelcomed death, in contrast to the Covenant's voluntary suicide, for a very long time. It is as horrible, and wasteful, as ever."

Peculiarly, A.H. was able to stifle the fury that welled up, to deny the luxury of finally drawing out the weapon that had killed her and turning it on him in justice. He brushed past the tall being, forcing speech. "Then we'd better find Umar or you'll be very familiar with it again."

Droom looked at him for several seconds as she let a sorrow display ripple her face, then curled her left hand to A.H.'s chest. Yet again he lacked the despair for which such solace was intended.

"Thank you" was all he could say. Responsibility pulled at him, as always. "We must check with the *vurkari,* see if they've located Umar, and split into—"

He halted as he glanced behind Droom at the rest of the bay. P.C. and Twee were gone.

Exiting the lift into the dark generator chamber, Umar used the palm-sized control to halt the gerlinger several meters in front of him. Large wall panels came alight yellowly. It reminded him of power rooms he'd seen in New Teheran, but this one was far larger. Looking down from the platform high above the main floor, he counted ten MHD generators, their fifty-meter-long shafts encircling the central fusion reactor like gray flower petals. The outer end of each joined to the bulky collector ring, completing the spoked wheel design. When needed, the reactor sent a high-speed plasma of charged particles raging through the magnetic fields within the shafts to produce electric current directly. But now the reactor, issuing a barely audible hum, fed only one of the half cylinders.

From the collector ring bundles of arm-thick bus cables carried the extracted DC power straight up to the boxy AC inverters, dimly seen through the open grid floor of the next level high overhead. Auxiliary equipment cluttered the perimeter of the chamber, and an odd odor, like hot tar, was faint but noticeable.

He touched the remote again and climbed onto the wheeled

pallet, clutching a strapped crate with one hand as the gerlinger rolled off the platform and bobbed slightly on its flux field. It stopped falling just above the level of the collector ring. He directed its compressed air jets to boost it over this, then let it fall again into the triangular space between two shafts. Quickly he hopped to the floor and directed the carrier forward to the reactor. The alarm on his sleeve chronpatch buzzed softly, but he spoke it off. Surely God would understand his omission of the prayers. He had only minutes left before an organized search might discover his location.

The reactor itself lay within a rough turquoise globe of accrete and metal, which would trap the bath of neutrons he needed. Since half this sphere extended below the solid floor, only a dome was visible. It stood twenty meters high and fifty across, with the only entrance now facing him. The gerlinger halted several paces from these double metal doors. They were lettered with bright yellow Teffhtan symbols that could have but one meaning.

Umar smiled ironically. "Yes. Danger indeed," he whispered with a nod. At once he went to the small dome console at the left of the doors and inserted a bloc with excerpts from Baay's data. He had preset the series of commands necessary to increase power output to max, in effect calling for an emergency response. This would step up the particle flow to the density required to touch off the grav plates. The vibrations in the floor became less subtle, and he felt a temperature change in the cold air of the vault. The superconductive material of the shafts operated at ambient temperature to remove the electrons from the hot plasma, but there was still an energy loss to the outer air through them.

Working rapidly from one white crate to the next, he touched the maglocks to reverse polarity and pop their lids loose. In his haste to load the smaller boxes, he'd had no time to label them, and now surveyed each. He had to tug aside the end panel on the thick-walled metal box within the large central crate. Only a few of the stacked golden bronze plates had shifted. They still formed a solid wedge; its tip would be pointing toward the reactor to ensure proportional penetration of the mass by the neutrons after the box's end panel was opened.

Eagerly he began to assemble the timer of the mechanism also to be housed within the heavily shielded box. He would direct the gerlinger into the reactor's inferno, and the timer would then open the end panel four minutes later.

It was a most extraordinary sensation. An awakening, yes—but colored with a patina of *otherness,* of . . . difference. After a few seconds consideration, it gelled. It was like waking from a dream of being somebody else. That other persona clung wetly, yet was less than—and more than—*this* being. *She* . . . who was she? No name took shape. She was lost to herself. As fear lanced through her, she tried to sit up from her prone position, but it took more effort than . . . it used to?

Waves of disorientation confused all her senses. Holding completely still, she concentrated, straining for clues from her immediate surroundings. Vision refused to focus; only dim rosette blurs flickered. There were no odors, except for a leathery tinge that belonged. No sound was present but her own hollow rasp of breathing. The surface under her was cold, undulating, yet sharp-edged. She held to its anchorage with both . . . yes, hands, as she continued to strain upright and look about.

She blinked and felt the tiny internal eye muscles tightening. The flowing blurs at last were constrained to definite shape. The room wasn't large and held only a corner sanitary cup, a commplate by an obvious door, and the object on which she lay. By the dim light of the single wall panel behind her she could tell it was waist-high and large enough to act as a bed. Indeed, the reddish surface, though cold, was resilient and fluid-filled like a waterbed. A hard blue metal frame formed the border.

She pulled herself across and off it to stand on the glossy black floor. Then she saw her feet . . . and hands. The almost fluid limbs. Her identity flitted nearby just out of grasp like a twilight bat. Hhronkan. She knew the name. She'd known the sinuous limbs, bird feet, and four-digit hands all her life. Of this she was certain. Then she must be Hhronkan.

Yet all movement was so . . . unpredictable . . . filtered through and mutated by a vast random distance. When she closed her eyes, the sense of freedom in the movement was exhilarating but chaotic. She knew her body was in motion—so lithe!—but she couldn't tell the exact position of its parts without seeing them, as if no skeletal proprioreceptors existed. Her mind spun. *Should* they exist?

Anxiety frothed the dizziness and nausea that threatened her consciousness. She fought against all three by pushing free of the bed and starting to the door. The legs wouldn't move correctly; the right foot dragged, doubled under, and she sagged to the floor soundlessly. Recognizing that her body might look normal but not be working normally, she decided to use her eyes to constantly direct where her limbs went. It was like operating a robot by remote telefactoring. Even then her control was sloppy, like a baby's. Was she ill and these the symptoms? Methodically she rose erect by placing both feet on the floor and squeezing the leg muscles until the bowed limbs lifted her. By alternately stretching out one foot, shifting her weight forward, and then straightening the bowed rear leg, she managed a bobbing shuffle toward the door.

When she saw her face in the dark commmplate, returning fear was squelched by shock. Through the erratic bursts of black and white that rippled the beige skin (such supple, alive skin!), she studied all its details. The delicately rounded brow bulge graded down into the slight cheeks; the finely wrinkled rim of the nasal pore barely flexed open and shut with breaths; the wide-set purple eyes with their slit irises offset the thick dark lips above the small chin.

One voice within her said, "This is not my face." Another countered, "But it is a pretty face."

She played the fingertips of her left hand over her visage, feeling the strangely familiar starred texture and warmth. The looseness of her hands . . . she held both before her and wriggled them like worms, truly surprised the knobbly digits could be curled to both palms of the hand. Delightful.

The ring of white that exploded out from her mouth both startled her and filled her with expected brightness. The balance enabled her to think more pragmatically. Glancing around at the bare room, she knew she must gather information from beyond it. Repeatedly she touched the commmplate's incomprehensibly labeled keys, but it stayed dark. So she palmed the door and it drew aside.

The corridor was long both ways before it turned, and was lit only at intervals by single panels; intervening ones were dark. She could see the shiny reflected patches on the floor and began directing her balky limbs to proceed left. Surprisingly, with each looping step, she felt less disoriented, less dizzy, and the nausea soon faded totally. By the time she found the lobby and the apparent lift bank, her walking no longer required constant visual aid.

Similar corridors led off in three directions. To go up or down? Deciding it mattered little, she watched her left first finger tap the lower stud. It lit; she heard nothing. Seconds later the door hummed aside. Within the large box were two beings. One was Hhronkan like her, but male and slightly larger; the other was a head shorter and hairy . . . human, with bruises and a cast on his upper left arm.

All three jumped in startlement, then the two spoke to her simultaneously. It was the sound of their voices that fractured the barrier in her memory. She knew them both—loved them both! And in a mixture of horror, wonder, and joy, she knew who she was, had been. Stumbling forward with upcurled arms, she tried to speak, to make them confirm or deny the dream. In terror she realized this Hhronkan vocal apparatus was entirely different; it would only gasp and hoot. They backed from her and drew pistols; she jerked her hands up, inner palms together, to plead with them not to kill her. They paused, weapons held steadily on her torso. She forced air out the voice tube, worked her jaw and lips. After several attempts, single word she hoped would explain it all came out as a whisper.

"Gumby."

Their mouths formed O's of disbelief, but the pistols lowered. Twee's flesh went jet. P.C's eyes instantly erupted tears as his face flushed.

"Rennie? It's really you?"

She tried to nod and smile at him, but instead she felt the skin on her face ripple in a widening cloud of white joy. Then she pointed to his head and to her own. "Baa . . . sss."

He nodded and firmed his Self, then briefly merged it to ners. Without the mindnet's interference it was easy to tele his sister . . . yet it wasn't. A distinctly Hhronkan tenor overlay the human psyche like a thin varnish, a dynamic mutation that thickened even as he ended the merge. Intellectually he accepted it then, as only a *baasa* can adapt to such shearing change. But emotionally he knew it would take time to assimilate the storm within both of them.

"How?" he whispered back, taking a step toward her and putting a hand to her chest to confirm her reality. The chance Hhronkan greeting seemed appropriate. "We saw you . . . die!"

She tried to shrug, but the bones and muscles weren't there. Instead a dark amorphous pattern slithered across her cheeks.

His lips trembled up at the ends. "The mindnet! You were

still in and its antennae were only meters away! It must have transduced you just like a Teffhtan. Better, in fact! You're already up. Baay told us it takes days before the newly reborn adjust. Maybe Shree was more correct than he knew. Humans must be closer to Teffhtans than to Hhronka, in mind structure anyway."

His harsh laughter was a release of tension and grief as he swooped his arms around her in a hug. She returned it so enthusiastically at first that he grunted in pain. He spoke with enforced calm.

"We'll both have to get used to your new body."

She blossomed with white again as she let him go reluctantly. He really didn't understand what had happened; she could tell. The embrace had finally cleared her mind and rooted her firmly into this reality, and it was an altered one. She still felt the presence of the other dream persona, but she would never be Renata Kriede again; she was forever dead. An example had already manifested itself. During P.C.'s theorizing, they had all become aware of her nakedness. As a human female, their flitting gazes would have embarrassed her. But her new composite psyche found it simply an inconvenience. Ironically, she held no deep remorse over the loss of her former self; it now seemed to have been only a close acquaintance. Her death was regrettable, but *she* felt no great sorrow. There were new areas within her, exciting and interesting perspectives never experienced as a human. Thus, continued sentience had been paid for with an instantly, permanently changed perception. Wasn't this partial reincarnation better than oblivion?

Twee hadn't moved or spoken since she'd uttered his pet name; his skin remained totally black, signaling emotional devastation. For him too, reality was permanently altered—for the second time in only minutes. He'd lost the central object of his personal love, though unattainable to him, and so the more dear. Now she was miraculously returned—as a Hhronkan female! Yet his fear's intensity paralyzed all action.

He could no longer remain distant nor undeclared, hiding behind, perhaps *allured* by, the fragile ethics of miscegenation. He must deal with their relationship as never before—and one change might be its termination. *If* he continued to love this new being, for she was indeed new, then she would be forced to return his love or reject it. He dared not even tele her as had P.C.

For the first time Renata appreciated his plight. She understood all the thousand little things he had said and done in her regard, especially his speech warning her about Umar. Prophetic and an obvious statement of love. But she'd been—her former self had been—too egoistic to see his true devotion. Always he had been a source of and recipient for affection. But it simply had never occurred seriously to her that she could be in love with Twee, and so the reverse couldn't be either. Daydream lasciviously of mating with him, yes; but love? That was the uncontrollable protégé of the heart. And yet anyone could stifle an emotion by ignoring it, by projecting the emotion elsewhere. Had the human Renata done that all these years? Now a meaningless question. Rather, how did they, would they feel about each other?

She bobbed to him and felt the stirring of spring tides within. For her also the barriers, the silly but so-insurmountable mores, were gone. Nothing was between them but possibilities. She symbolized this by embracing him warmly in human fashion, a final farewell and initial welcome.

Her touch coursed through him, resounding bell-like inside that well-guarded spot where he'd hidden his love to maintain identity. He thought of all the risks they'd taken, pain they'd known, to reach this point in life. Oddly, he thought of his father's courage and suffering in taking many of those same risks . . . and of his love, for all his Children.

Encircling her with his arms, he murmured in Hhronkan, "Let us join our hearts as we do our bodies for between us there is love."

She stiffened and withdrew a bit. All three felt the hesitance come after the rush of joy. It had happened very quickly and couldn't be absorbed in only minutes.

"Umar," P.C. said to remind them.

The two twisted apart toward him. Hot revenge had been vitiated as a motive for pursuing the Teheranian. But cool revenge would serve as well as self-defense. P.C. let the lift door close, but touched the operation switch and rapidly told Renata of Umar's recent actions.

"We don't have time to plan an attack on the generator room; we're only minutes ahead of the *vurkari*. We're going to have to free-fly it . . ." He started to address her again as "Rennie," but that no longer seemed proper; nothing did. He was related to this new entity only by memory. "We're going to have to move fast; you'd better go up. Tell the others what we're doing."

The shake of her head was so emphatic he halted his attempt. "Ooo . . ." she rasped out vehemently, dark waves smearing her face spasmodically.

He felt foolish even before he finished saying it. "If you get killed *here,* it'll be the last time!"

Twee spared them both by drawing out a small sonic pistol from his robe and offering it to her. "If we do not proceed before he activates the plates—"

"So *we* stop him!" P.C. said with a nod. "Even if we have to kill him!" To their stares he spat back. "If you're being Meethlah, stay out of my way! I don't believe he'll let us *talk* him out of this. And we can forget using *baas* with the electric interference in there."

They were unable to reply. Twee had never firmly made his commitment, and Renata was searching her new self for emotions strong enough to justify the act.

Out of respect for their quandries, he added quietly, "We'll each do what we have to do."

He touched the switch, and they felt the lifting sensation as the car shot down. He and Twee gripped their lasers and watched the indicator materialize strange symbols, counting the rest of the twenty-two levels. Renata leaned to the wall, watching them in turn, feeling her new calmness like a warm blanket.

Without moving his eyes from the doors, P.C. said with a slight quaver, "Twee, go right; I'll take left. Renata, you take the nearest cover, get his attention, and keep it."

The steadily increasing pressure on their soles told them the car was slowing. They touched shoulders as they faced forward, tensing to leap out. At the final moment Twee burst a blaze of white affection on his face; Renata returned it. P.C. whispered, "I love you both." The doors slid apart.

Without an audible signal from the lift, Umar was startled by but not unprepared for their arrival. Even so, they were earlier than expected. He saw the motion and looked up to watch Twee, P.C., and an unfamiliar nude Hhronka dive onto the platform. He merely noted it and continued working. Completing assembly of the gerlinger's payload came first, and it would take but seconds more. Meantime God would protect him. He snapped the last component board into the makeup frame, plugged the small continuity cable into its socket, and reached to place the timer into the metal box with the grav plates. The control and its timer also had to be shielded from the particle bath until the moment the end panel of the box slid aside. Then its liquefaction wouldn't matter.

He'd just replaced the heavy metal top of the box and tapped its magseal on when a sonic burst struck it just left of his hand. The tight bundle of hypersonic air waves lacked the force to damage the shield box but the energy dissipated throughout the entire surface. His hand absorbed the lid's vibrations like a hammer stroke, and a high buzzing popped as some energy was reflected as sound. His left palm was burned instantly, blackened blisters erupting clear plasma even before he could lift it. With a scream of unbelieving shock and agony he jerked down behind the box and looked frantically around the gerlinger at the litter of crates and packing. The laser pistol and remote lay on the keyboard of the dome console, ten paces to his right. And his assassin's head, the unknown Hhronka, could be seen poking above the lift platform's leading edge. He was an easy target in the corridor between MHD shafts. And where were the other two?

He rolled backward off the low, wheeled pallet, throwing up a small plastec crate as decoy. Before its arc peaked, the air above him crackled and whistled as it was superheated. Flares of vaporized material pierced the crate, and it fell smoking back onto the pallet with a clatter. P.C. and Twee had him in cross fire from the dimly lit catwalks that zigzagged through auxiliary equipment and encircled the chamber halfway up its wall. He must eliminate at least these two . . . or distract them. He kept tumbling toward the console as puffs of crackling laser impacts and pops of zinging sonic bundles danced on the floor and crating all around him.

He reached the console, which lay close to one shaft and so cut off the line of sight of the attacker on his right. Sweeping up the weapon and remote with his uninjured right hand, he fell into the nook created by the shaft, reactor dome, and console, which cut off the other attacker on his left. His back to the dome, he felt the tremendous vibrating power building within, waiting for him to tap it. There remained only the Hhronka on the entry platform, whose shots still could be heard popping on the concrete all around him. Were their puffs of pulverized material warnings or bad aim?

He red-dotted a series of lases along the platform's thick

edge. The head disappeared as clouds of stony debris and dust plumes obscured the volume completely. It was at last time. He peeked at the console and hooked up his right hand to pull and reinsert his bloc. It now commanded the reactor doors to operate. He held the remote and waited.

The metal creaked slightly as both panels receded a half meter, then parted. A desperate howl echoed in the huge room. He looked up and around for the source. It was Tweeol. He had leaped from the shadowed catwalk to his left and was drifting slowly toward him, using his grav belt to balloon. Umar could see him clearly, an easy target silhouetted against a yellow light panel, holding his pistol with both looping arms.

Two quick lases struck the dome's curve above his head, spraying pieces of stone shrapnel at him, and he ducked back. The third hit the console's top dead center. Its keyboard flew apart in a screeching explosion; several chunks stung his legs. Twee was trying to stop the doors from opening, but it was too late. The automatic sequence had begun and was internal to the reactor. But he might still damage the gerlinger! Umar realized.

He quickly pressed the remote with all the strength in his burned, throbbing left hand, and the carrier rolled forward. Twee saw this and immediately changed targets. The first shots hit the large crate, sizzling holes in it, but failing to penetrate the thick shield box within. His next shot, however, blew the pneumatic tread from the disk of the right rear wheel. The gerlinger shuddered but kept rolling, slightly tipsy, toward the fully opened reactor.

Rather than the roar of a blast furnace, only a lonely whine issued from the strangely dark mouth. Umar started at this unexpected lack of mechanical ferocity, then relaxed as he looked around the ruined console and saw the front of the plastec crate suddenly sag and slough from the metal box like hot taffy. Castoff material on the floor in direct line was reacting similarly. The neutron flow was sufficient.

Twee now hung midair directly above the MHD shaft to his left. His next lase repeated the damage of his last to the front right wheel. In panic Umar saw the pallet falter, list right, then limp on. He rose up in fury and pointed his weapon at the middle of the Hhronkan lunatic who would thwart God's will again!

His left shoulder blossomed in white-hot pain! His left arm fell useless to his side as he smelled his own roasted skin. In terror and abject disbelief he whirled, fell into a sitting position, and looked up. P.C. knelt atop the nearby shaft, staring down at him, his face as dead white as the cast on his arm.

Umar recognized the boy's revulsion to the pain he'd caused, yet saw that P.C. *would* fire again—to stop the gerlinger. Suddenly lases and sonic bursts began to pepper the moving pallet from three directions. Its front end was now only a few steps from the reactor threshold. The large crate grew many holes; chunks of melting aluminum flew smoking from the pallet frame. Finally one of P.C.'s lases blew the last remaining tread from the left front wheel. The machine jumped as it rolled unsteadily over the rubber debris; its metal wheels slipped and scrabbled on the hard flooring.

Umar twisted in a circle, astounded that all three of them continued to attack the gerlinger, the instrument of God's will. He would stop them by trusting in Allah and in his power as the Mahdi, as he had the Teffhtan guard in the Complex! Hazed with pain, but swelling in righteous anger, he rolled over onto his knees, pushed up to his feet with his right arm, lifted it, and shouted, "In the name of Allah, *no!*"

The three saw Umar's hand, still clutching the weapon, swing toward P.C. Twee's lase cauterized a bloodless thumb-sized hole cleanly through Umar's lower right abdomen, just above the ragged wound already there. It pierced his seventh rib, right lung, diaphragm, liver, and small intestine, and exited below his onesuit's waistband in a spewed burst of cooked tissue and singed cloth. Seeing himself as the target, P.C. fell flat to the hot shaft as he fired, but the pain from his ribs made him miss totally, the beam merely superheating the air near Umar's right ear. Renata had aimed carefully from her prone position on the defaced platform. The full sonic burst impacted squarely on his left arm, separating it above the elbow. The force of the shot spun him counterclockwise, and his right hand spasmed. The laser beam punctured the MHD shaft at chest height three paces away. With a shriek, a long finger of white plasma jetted halfway across the space between shafts in front of him.

Eyes wide, mouth open in an effort to scream, Umar fell.

"Stop it!" Renata yelled over the roar, hopping up and pointing. Both P.C. and Twee looked back at the gerlinger. Still slewing from side to side as its bared metal wheels grabbed and slipped, it was entering the reactor doors. They hit the floor together and darted toward the pallet from opposite sides, heedless of the radiation. But they were simply too late. The double doors snapped back into place before they were even in the direct path of the entrance. Renata arrived a second later. All three stood quietly exchanging stunned looks. They had failed. The bomb was ticking.

They heard Umar moan, and turned, unbelieving, to see him struggling to rise. At last he stood, weaving, his wet, bearded face creased in agony and eyes febrile with the torture of his mutilated body. He looked back and forth from their hypnotized faces to the waving heat-sealed stump of his left arm and its flayed remnant on the floor, the hand clenching and unclenching in reflex. His childlike wail and flooding tears let them all lower their pistols.

They couldn't fire again at the innocent victim they now saw. Betrayed by his intelligence, his society, his religion, and his family—one of them might easily have stood there instead, stripped of everything.

Umar cried, "I am not the *Mahdi!* It was only my pride, *always* my pride . . . my sin!"

He reeled backward into the curving wall of the shaft, only a step from the shrieking plasma. His eyes rolled upward to the ceiling, the heavens, his God.

"Quickly I come, my Lord," he whispered. Almost magnetically his eyes were drawn to the white jet, its sharp tang of ozone filling the space as its heat ionized the air.

"Behold the finger of His judgment!" he yelled at them, but they could not hear. With a weary smile, almost rapturously, he stumbled into the plume. A mere flicker, and the top half of his body vaporized, his smoking trunk and legs collapsing backward to the floor.

Twee was inert with revulsion, his skin rippling in black-white shock. P.C. dropped to his knees and vomited freely. But Renata went slowly to stand looking at the remains of her dream being's murderer. That event, and now its retribution, were distant, filtered through a fantasy of her own device.

Calmly she said, "Truly, Umar, I hope you are now with your god."

Chapter 16

The lift door opened and several *vurkari* exited as dark streaks, to comb the chamber like high-speed ferrets. Normally they were as silent, leaving only a rush of air in their path, but now the breached generator hid even this. Seconds later, one took station near them, becoming crisply visible between the smoky console and the closed reactor door. Renata was waving her pistol in alarm, but P.C. shook his head slightly, and she slowly lowered it.

Droom preceded Gar and A.H.; without slowing, they walked off the platform and floated to the main floor. Droom quickly skirted and ducked the leaking plasma, clothes fluttering in the hot wind it created, and gave the corpse a glance. She recognized who it must be and displayed shock-sorrow, skin blinking jet and glassing, but only for a second. Then she saw the stranger and accepted her in the press of the emergency.

Still a dozen bobs from them she yelled above the plasma's howl, "How long ago exactly did the reactor door close?"

"Two and a half minutes," P.C. replied loudly, glancing at his chronpatch.

Gar and A.H. came up in time to hear his answer. The group moved farther from the noise to the closed panels. A.H. stared at the newcomer curiously, feeling a familiarity, but tore his attention away as Gar gesticulated with looping arms at the dome.

"Then we have little time! I assume this human would have the intelligence to permit his own escape by staggering the closure of the reactor and the plates' exposure by only a few minutes. I will send in the *vurkari* to push them out. Let us get away from the reactor!"

Twee snaked arms in unconscious apology as he pointed and yelled back, "I destroyed the controls trying to stop it!"

Gar signaled to the nearby pentapoid. It pivoted on tentacle tips and ports clacked open in its ovoid body. Four spots of gray smoke grew in the left panel; seconds later they spouted into white brilliance, sending sparklers of melted metal curving out onto the dark flooring. They watched the dancing red droplets turn black to the accompaniment of increased hissing. Slag dripped like wax; four incandescent pits deepened, joining at the panel's center as a lobed crater.

Suddenly Droom went ebon, and cream ripples sped over her cheeks as she turned to clutch Gar's arm and roar into his earpore. "Umar was also intelligent enough to booby-trap the device!"

As one of the other *vurkari* swept her into a tentacle, a dark display of consummate horror bloomed on the Provider's face and neck above his vest. He screamed a single word, and all the pentapoids stilled instantly. The Orrtaan stopped thrashing when the immobile limb released her and she fell flat. Gar stared at his former prisoners.

"But if we cannot tamper with it in any way, we are lost." Incredibly the being appeared to withdraw to a catatonic peace. "It is finally finished."

They looked in alarm at him and each other in confusion. P.C. stepped over to the *vurkari* before the cooling door and challenged them all, A.H. last, with a look of defiance.

"This time *I* have a plan! We must use the blanket merge to stop the timer before it opens the shield box. Droom, what did Umar have?"

"A cesium beam clock," she replied thoughtfully.

A.H. caught his son's enthusiasm. "Yes! A standard atomic navigation clock! Perhaps together we could do it!"

Twee turned to face P.C. and A.H. "But that means we would have to control EM fields on an atomic level! All we have done so far is turn aside a macroscopic coherent photon beam. We do not know what the blanket merge can do, even if its Self field can penetrate the dome and the shield box—let alone disarm or delay the timer long enough for Gar's people to shut down the reactor."

A.H. nodded at him in understanding and spoke with reluctance. "With Shree's skill and power added we would have a better chance."

Gar said, "He and Baay are still missing. I am sorry."

They exchanged looks of wonder at this incongruous apology.

Droom broke the rising despair. "Gar, dump the reactor fuel core as quickly as possible!"

She had to shake him and repeat the order. The Teffhtan spoke to the *vurkari* as Renata joined the circle.

"Is it permitted to watch? If you don't succeed, it'll make little difference where I am."

The others stared at her, again noting her unexplained presence. P.C. saw the questions rising in their eyes, questions they had no time for and that might upset the emotional control needed. "We must merge now! If it doesn't work, we can still try to escape the planet."

He accepted their accusatory glances and went toward them. They responded by forming a tighter circle, from which Renata retired a pace. Twee relaxed at once, his skin undulating with cream-colored bands as the three *baasa* concentrated their individual Selfs. Gar stood near Droom, observing them with a smear of dark confusion wobbling on his face.

As usual, A.H. had difficulty in ignoring the recent abuse his body had suffered. His very skeleton ached from the crash, and the cuts on his crown and many bruises had swollen large and tender. The migraine added to the tail-end miseries of his dying cold. He looked at the others: the glued gash in Twee's temple, P.C.'s cast and rib bandage bulking under his pullover. They were injured at least as much as he, and he envied them their control. Only after he forced an encouraging smile of pride onto his lips for P.C. could he himself join. Twee and P.C. fused as one. A.H. enfolded this bright hard kernel in support. Their Selfs slid together.

Exactly sixteen seconds remained before the shield box would open to allow the neutron flow into the grav plates.

Even without Shree, the greater duration of this multiple

merge summoned an entirely new entity, whose nodule of sentience they had barely felt in the few instants they'd maintained the merge in the Life Complex. Then they had suspected the blanket Self might possess a true independence from its components. They knew it had EM-manipulative ability, which was all they desired in the present crisis.

But now, formed completely, it showed powers whole orders of magnitude greater than their own separate Selfs. It was sensitive not only to Self and EM fields and photon streams but also to *other* matter and energy fields. This they knew at once. It was like hearing many different kinds of music being played simultaneously very far away. But could it extend control over these fields? At what scale and with what potency? Their plan, and the existence of Teffht and the lives on it, depended on the answer. The blanket Self could not yet give a reply. They permitted it to subsume their identities and wills.

It experimented. Immediately it was aware of extreme flexibility in form and density, far greater than its members' Selfs. In a nanosecond it expanded to fill the volume of the entire generator chamber, being stopped by the room's surfaces, the MHD shafts, and the reactor dome. It felt the solids as though it pressed against hard rubber. The reciprocally sustaining flows of electric and magnetic currents in the DC cables were hot spinning rivers of molten glass and gold, and the leaking plasma jet was a scintillant thorn in the blanket Self's ethereal flesh.

Eight seconds remained. . . .

It touched the stranger's mind and recognized Renata, transduced and reborn. There was no emotional response to this; the impact was spread out too thinly over the disciplined collective mind. It simply noted.

Next it reversed, concentrated its field's density around the single node of identity, the way the human retina's focusing ability concentrates image reception at the fovea. It shrank its own volume and, becoming smaller and denser, the volume it inspected, and turned its attention to the surface of the reactor door. The thousandth-inch level revealed a rougher texture but gave no help toward penetration; it couldn't tele anything beyond.

Although the blanket mind formed a unique entity, its components simultaneously held separate thoughts, as does any individual mind. Within the component minds this sensing of nonmental fields by the blanket node registered abnormally in their individual brains' upper cortices, and so affected usual sense perception in unusual modes. The merged mind interpreted accordingly. The node smelled the metallic surface's brushed texture like a sweetness, saw its bright hardness, touched its velvet blue color, and heard the stern bass presence of tantalum, carbon, and iron, singing chorouslike in its alloy. Beneath this the muffled musics of other fields played on.

Seeking passage, the node shrank its perception zone ever farther, until it smelled the door's brushed texture go from sweet corrugation to a fetid reek of deep pitted valleys down into which it sailed birdlike. The flow of perceptive apprehension appeared as motion to its member minds. When it reached the floor of one valley, the node again distilled and diminished itself; the sides of the valley rushed away to form a giant chasm. Now the light gray color was felt as terry cloth; it saw hardness become chains of ember remnants; and it heard not tantalum, carbon, or iron chorusing en masse, but separate groups of these atoms, whose voices it could distinguish. Still the distant musics sounded.

The node was perceiving at the molecular level! Indeed, it smelled a sour lumpy texture, the ember chains forever in motion, the vibrational flexure of the alloy's molecules as their van der Waals bonds responded to local energy fluctuations. Like incandescent worms, they writhed unceasingly about the node.

Thus it knew: as its perceptive diameter shrank, subjective time sense dilated to "slow" physical events, a Lorentzian transformation rendering the speed of molecular motion palpable to it. The reverse might also be true: perception might be relativistically accelerating and macro-time unchanged, but the result would be the same. Split seconds in the macro-world could take nodal centuries to pass! This could gain the time needed to effect their objective—given it could be accomplished at all. Though it recognized the long subjective passing of time between events, again no emotion attached to this. No anxiety, boredom, or frustration. It simply perceived.

Since it gauged separate molecules, the node should be able to locate voids from which molecular matter was temporarily absent. The material of the door had become a layered mesh, a lattice of odorless dark intermolecular holes, forever shifting. Now one of the musics had grown clearly audible, a syncopated beat with forever-altering rhythm. The EM field conglomerated from those of the metals' atoms. But, though the node was tiny, it carried no electric charge and was unswayed by this rhythm. It sniffed and smelled, looked and saw, nothing . . . there! The node zigzagged through the lattice until it entered a vast blackness and smelled only occasional, musky, erratic islands of gas molecules. It was inside the reactor.

In addition to atmospheric gas, it realized it was sensing effects of the radiation output but not the individual particles or fields themselves. It felt periodic bursts of contact, like hot matches touched to skin, each with a tiny musical cry, as the neutrons and other by-products whizzed through its zone of perception. Still at the molecular level, its zone was too large to sense atomic or subatomic structure directly. And it hesitated telescoping downward farther till it had located the cesium heart of the atomic timer. Being smaller would only waste subjective time in moving. And there were real dangers here as well.

The blanket mind was apprehending a level of nature never explored before in so intimate and direct a way. Its three component sentiences were becoming mesmerized by the overstimulation of this shimmering, darting, palpable, odoriferous, singing, musical microcosmos. It could feel its nodal center drifting apart, its control lessening. It pulsed out a warning :: Beware the loss of total concentration and effectiveness!

The parts responded and resolidified. The node enlarged until it perceived the reactor door, oriented thereby, and shot across the interior to the gerlinger's cargo box. Using the same lattice-penetration technique, it quickly navigated through the dense metal of the shield box and encountered the timer's circuitry.

The low-amperage current was only a weak glimmering trickle compared to the torrent created by the MHD generators. The node hovered near a three-way branch of a printed circuit within a programmable ceramic chip, sensing the bilateral coursing of electrons through and dimly outlining the conductive roadways that stretched off to infinity over a plain of endlessly repetitive, shifting light-point molecular patterns. Why not divert this flow, one component thought, and break the timer circuit? So smeared were identities that only separate thoughts were recognized, not their thinkers.

Another component reminded that Umar might have rigged his failsafe trap to account for this. Direct tampering with the circuits *anywhere,* including the circuitry of the entrapment itself, might cause activation immediately rather than at the end of the set time. The only sure method was to attack the cesium clock as planned. It was a separate module, which could not have been altered by Umar.

Six seconds . . .

The node zoomed along the grids, pierced lattice-walls, searching for the juncture with the clock. Finally it heard the strong baritone singing of tungsten and followed upstream the warm electron flow arising from this source. It was the detector plate of the resonance chamber in the clock. As the beam of cesium atoms struck the plate on the opposite side, electrons were ejected off this side to form the timer current's headwaters. This flow in turn set the quartz crystal timer, and the timer would soon open the shield box. It was this flow of cesium atoms they had to alter.

Quickly the node shrank and plunged through the bright lattice of the plate, and the clear pure contralto of cesium echoed 'round. Again it sensed only the speeding touches and dopplered cry of the steady stream of atoms, which were yet too tiny to be perceived separately. All else, except for the musics, was unending, eventless void. It traced the voice backward through the resonance chamber.

The magnetic field that carried and directed the cesium atoms created a saline taste for the node. Very soon a second, brackish taste was periodically sensed. It had to be the oscillator magnetic field that fed extra energy laterally into the beam, causing the cesium atoms it met to undergo transition to a higher energy state. This hyperfine change in the spin orientation between the outer electron and the nucleus was independent of the oscillator's strength or the apparatus, being solely a property of cesium's atomic structure. The excited atoms, being more massive, were deflected off target, away from the detector, by the carrier field, thereby temporarily lessening the number of impacts and the resulting quartz timer current created on its opposite surface. By using these current fluctuations as a feedback control to set the oscillator's exciting frequency, the brackish taste, a resonance occurred. The oscillator frequency became exactly equal to the hyperfine transition frequency of the cesium atoms, setting up a repetitive physical event whose determination was extremely accurate.

Time itself was still measured as 9,192,631,770 of these cycles occurring in each second. The atomic clock using this system lost only one second in three million years. Thus its continued use in the modern era, though invented over a century ago.

It was here the clock was potentially vulnerable to the node. It considered approaches. If it could intermittently increase the absorption rate of the oscillator's excitatory magnetic energy by the cesium—i.e., increase the number of excited atoms missing the target detector plate and thus lessen the number striking it—it could artificially lengthen the frequency of the timer itself. Literally, a "second" would be stretched in clock measurement. The whole device would in turn be slowed, allowing the *vurkari* time to get to the floor below and remove the fuel cells sustaining the reactor. After all, Umar's "bomb" might be set to go off almost immediately.

Five seconds . . .

Could the node affect individual atoms? To test, the perception zone had to be shrunk to near-atomic diameter. Steadying in the stinging euphony of the cesium stream, the node contracted. It began to "see" dim pinpoints floating by in a vast darkness, each singing its contralto identity. The node observed one such point coming head-on and quickly constricted farther so the point enlarged, slowed, and drew next to it. Subjective time was now dilated until the stream of atoms looked like the ice pebbles in Saturn's rings, merely creeping through the resonance chamber.

Other interpretations of perception were altered. Touch—color was gone; the node felt no visible photonic radiation since the reactor's interior was dark. Vision now seemed to sense shape and movement rather than hardness, a molecular characteristic nonexistent at the atomic level. Smell brought no information concerning texture. The carrier field still tasted salty. Hearing registered that the former group contralto was now only a flat monotone for the single cesium atom. But the distant musics of the many fields had swelled to join the EM syncopation in an insane medley, as if all a radio's channels played at once. Their nature and source was yet unknown to the node.

Suddenly one component mind started. Since in truth the node was employing no actual sense organs—had no eyes, ears, tongue, nose, or skin receptors—with what medium *was* it perceiving reality? It had to be more than the Self field each possessed separately. What was its nature? The ode deigned no reply, enforced its dominance, and returned them to the immediate goal.

Before the node, the cesium atom's electron cloud thrummed its rhythm and shimmered rapidly, constantly changing in response to the enormous forces tethered within. Indeed, individual negative electrons, confined in motion at over 900 kilometers per second, were not seen even at this increased time dilation—only the seething totality of this energy trapped as matter within this volume .000000001 centimeter across. But the fifty-five discrete quanta must be there, each one's set of quantum states repelling the others per Pauli exclusion to prevent atomic collapse and maintain a graded structure and function, all held together by the nucleus and its positive magnetic field.

The particle–wave duality of electrons, and all other subatomic particles, had long ago replaced the billiard-ball, solar-system analogy of structure. The node now perceived the standing-wave aspect of the electrons, the harmonic field oscillations, a shape and movement, exactly fitting around/within each quantum level like Kekulé's benzene snake, tail in mouth. Freed from atomic entrapment, the electron's particle aspect would no doubt dominate where that aspect best fit observation, regardless of whether or not it was the observatory act that gave that aspect existence.

In truth, the electrons were *neither* particles *nor* waves, but four-dimensional energy disturbances within their EM fields. Even now, when perceived directly, they were "slithy toves" spread out around the nucleus and through time, thin throbbing mists of true uncertainty.

The elongated ovoid shape of the cloud indicated its continued interaction with the carrier field, being magnetically polarized and distorted by it. Some shape change must occur when the oscillator energy impinged on the cloud and excited it. Then the node did taste the magnetic brackishness again crossing the chamber and saw the electron cloud pulse, round up, and seemingly *solidify.* Like Hhronkan skin when hidden, a boundary surface became glassy smooth! The node could sense a gelling within the cloud; the flat contralto tone went sharp like a struck gong. The hyaline integument took on a grainy texture, as if millions of eyes glittered. Instantly the void about the atom filled with radiance! The magnetic energy of the oscillator was causing the reorientation of "spins"—a Newtonian label tacked on to the unknowable, but fitting quantum reality no better than "particle" or "wave."

The node reminded itself that it comprised minds evolved at the macro level. It couldn't magically circumvent interpretations of these events on that level. Indeed, it might be, almost surely was, totally missing many nuances of this quantum world simply from inexperience and/or ability to comprehend. A blind person seeking color in the shape held.

At over nine billion events a second, the microwave photon quanta released by the returns of the electron and nucleus to spin ground states were smeared in the node's perception as a spherical glow slightly brighter than the electron cloud and without its syncopated rhythm.

This was the excited heavier state in which this atom would be deflected away from the tungsten plate. On this very effect lay its hope of slowing Umar's clock.

The EM manipulation of the blanket merge had worked at the macro level only with the common exertions of its components. It took energy, pumped through the multiple-Self field, to effect change—though apparently the nature of this mechanism was as unknown to the node as was the nature of the field itself. But at this atomic level, the mere meeting of the concentrated node and the electron cloud should cause an energy transference that would elicit an excited state. It might take much subjective time to create enough excited atoms in this way, but the goal would be accomplished.

The node enlarged itself and moved ahead of the glowing apparition, back toward the detector plate, hunting atoms that had escaped the oscillator's touch. It passed many others in the radiant state, then overtook an unexcited segment in the moving cesium stream. The node chose, contracted, and moved toward one misty nebula.

Pain! There was a convulsion like lightning within the cloud and the node, whiting out its perception. The node felt a literal electric shock that nearly ripped its member minds apart, but they rebounded just before the breaking point. And the electron cloud writhed wildly with a tonal change of identity that was almost a scream. The cloud *sharded* like a light bulb bursting in slow motion, yet the wisps remained in place for an instant. A narrow cone of brightness stood out of the ragged cloud like a searchlight, then disappeared into the surrounding void.

This was not a cluster of microwavelength photons; the reaction had involved only a sector of the electron cloud. No spherical radiation had been elicited. The altered cloud hinted at the nature of the change. Now its rhythm had quickened, and it swirled with bands of thickened brightness like planetary weather patterns. The atom had completely lost its outer electron and become an ion, the most alkaline of all, its cloud incomplete until another electron conjoined. Nevertheless, the node's disruption had been successful; the positively charged ion would be magnetically deflected by the carrier field, in the direction opposite the excited-spin atoms, but still missing the detector.

However, even the durable blanket mind was stunned. And the node dare not risk another such shock to its compositional integrity. Each atom's EM field theoretically extended to infinity—indeed, the node had "heard" its syncopated beat everywhere continually once it had contracted sufficiently. (Thus the impossibilty of absolute zero. To remove *all* temperature from any thermally isolated volume meant creating a perfect energy–matter vacuum. And even though all particles might be excluded from such, there would always remain the background EM flux—if only that of the Big Bang. Only infinite energy could impose such a true vacuum.)

Evidently there was a threshold density within which the node interacted with the electron cloud. And it had very nearly been disintegrated. It felt certain if its member Selfs totally sundered to isolation, reassembly or return of individual consciousness to its owner was doubtful. Their Selfs might become lost, trapped at this perception level without orientation or power to reenlarge—slowly eroding into oblivion, leaving their bodies empty, withering to death without the higher purpose thought gave.

There was no need for regret; the attempt had been made as agreed. The node must expand back to molecular size and exit the reactor at once. If it couldn't interact with the atom, then it saw no way to alter the processes within the clock. The only chance remaining was for the *vurkari* to remove the gerlinger from the neutron bath . . . in time.

Four seconds . . .

:: There is another possibility!

Power surged within it! The node's cohesiveness and strength zoomed exponentially. A fourth component made itself known: Shree! In a gestaltic flash the Primary disclosed he'd arrived in the generator chamber, had sensed their aborted mission here, and had followed the trail of their blanket merge's peripheral bourn to join it.

And they/it was correct. This atom-by-atom approach must fail, even if this new power and enlarged capacity permitted it. There was too little time, even dilated-subjective. A far quicker way must be found. Shree-component allowed itself to be merged completely with them.

The blanket mind was granted the ability to comprehend what had been incomprehensible; it graduated from bright to genius. It fed upon its novel insight. The cesium source for the timer was a heated microgram pellet of the nearly pure element. If it could be properly disrupted, all at once, the detector count would also drop and slow the timer. With Shree's added power the node's control should be finer; it might be able to act without being destroyed in rebound. All components understood the new objective and dangers.

The node expanded to near-molecular size and journeyed up the dopplered cesium flow to its source. When it saw the number of luminant pinpoints suddenly escalate to assume a lattice formation and heard the contralto chorus become a titanic roar, it knew it had entered the delaminating pellet, its boiling surface constantly stripped away by the carrier field. Soon the atoms were packed so closely that repulsive interactions kept them vibrating ceaselessly within their metallic crystal—a gigantic arcology in an earthquake. A thin glowing mist filled the voids, whose cause the node could not guess.

Disoriented momentarily by the cosmic three-dimensional array, the node paused to choose a target. Since all were identical, the nearest would do. To lessen the chance of disruption, the node contracted far below the level at which it had caused ionization. For the first time, it felt a definite *resistance!* Maintaining the compression required constant exertion.

Once it compressed itself into this state, the node was surprised to find no separation between neighboring electron clouds. Then it recalled that in pure congregations of such metal atoms the single outer electrons were loosely shared between atoms to become a "sea of electrons." This was the mist it had perceived at the molecular level and was the basis for electrical conductivity, allowing the free movement of electrons and establishment of current.

A similar state was attained in superconductive materials, but through quite different means. Near absolute zero, the fermionic

character of their atoms' outer electrons took on a more bo-
sonic, less exclusive nature. They became lazy and shared so
willingly they offered no resistance at all to electric current,
would therefore carry it indefinitely. Now a dull thump took the
place of the faster beat of the nonshared cloud. Although the
node was within this luminescent sea, there was no shock due to
the reduced energy density.

It chose the closest bright area, a distant bonfire in fog,
which must be an atomic center, and thrust itself into the now
planet-sized shifting outer layer. It was reminiscent of recs of
Venus probe landings, but here there was no passivity. It felt a
momentary stir throughout the deeper portion of the cloud; it
quickly settled back to a quiescent state. The node pushed on
into the inner mist, the negative magnetic field cloyingly sweet.
Bathed in honey, it passed a great deal of subjective time within
the shimmering, straining substance.

Steadily the honey taste and mist thinned inwardly as it had
outwardly, never quite fading completely. No exact boundary
existed, yet the node had a new compass and milepost to the
nucleus. The taste of the positive magnetic field at the center
was like the tinny bitterness of boric acid. It overlapped the
negative sweetness and grew stronger as the node approached
the origin. Fortunate, for here deep within the atom no other
sensed events were occurring to gauge the passage of the huge
amounts of time subjectively needed to cross the vast space to
the nucleus, one hundred thousand times smaller than its atom,
yet holding most of its mass–energy.

All around lay stressed space-time devoid of anything but the
fading electron fog and the opposing tastes of positive and negative magnetism. If the node remained in this near vacuum sufficiently long, surely some temporary visitor might pass close
enough to sense. But being in this one atom held within the
dense magnetic shield of the clock within the metal box of
plates, such events would be exceedingly rare. Perhaps only
neutrinos could enter here. What would it be like in the unpro-
tected open?

Shree's added component was making the blanket Self more
curious, subtle.

Ahead, in the direction of increasingly bitter taste, the node
saw a lustrous speck. It grew slowly brighter in movement until
it was a sparkling furnace. Still it possessed no shape. Did it
have any, or was it merely very far away? The latter proved true

as the brilliance escalated. With tremendous effort the node forced another reduction of its perception zone to permit other possible fine-structure data to be sensed as it moved closer. This was the most compact energy-matter it had yet perceived.

The node was finally halted in both approach and size reduction when the radiant body grew to apparent moon size. It was as if the node sought to squeeze incompressible water; an adamantine wall stood between it and further contraction. It studied the planetoid as it strained to hold itself within this least zone. Information now seemed to come to it only as vision, and all other "senses" were quelled. Density—number of energy quanta per volume at this level—was registered as a brilliant glare composed of a glowing, ceaselessly moving blur without discernible point—masses, as with the electrons but enormously intenser.

There was no hint of the classically neat bag-of-marbles nucleus, no fifty-five protons to neutralize the charge of the fifty-five electrons smeared into the cloud, no seventy-eight neutrons packed in tightly with the protons to balance out the atomic weight. But then, their confined velocity was over 67,000 kilometers per second, 13 percent of light speed! Yet the node was sure this too wasn't just a blurring of individual particles' motion. There seemed no hint of nucleons nor their theorized component quark triplets. It was more like a boiling fluid than a granular froth. It was the cyclic harnessing and diverting of titanic power by the fluid in a hypnotic, rhythmic way.

It was so very comfortable, so...familiar. Why? The node was lulled into the rhythm, feeling ever more an integral part of it and the power...and gradually, over centuries of subjective time, it began to lose its purpose and then its identity. Its member minds began to drift separately.

Three seconds...

:: The apparently solid matter of our senses has given way to an insubstanial world of transitory particles and the shifting complexity of their unending interactions; a world in which strange laws of conservation compete against quantum randomness and chance to prevent undisciplined descent into chaos and annihilation. CHAOS...ANNIHILATION!

With a start, the node broke itself out of the trap. One of its components had recalled an appropriate quote from the twentieth-century human, Davies, and after considerable struggle had got the others to remember with it. Framing the nucleus's coruscating sensorium into the hard words had robbed it of its hypnotic effect and allowed escape.

However, there was no pulse of relief or gratitude, only shock. The node now realized what it was observing. Of course! It *couldn't* be capable of apprehending individual fermions, subatomic or subnuclear particles, electrons or nucleons. This meant discerning exact momentum *and* position, time *and* energy states in them—which violated the conjugate-pair complementarity of the Uncertainty Principle! That was not possible in this universe, at any perception level. The genius Self eliminated possibilities, reconsidered the evidence it had sensed... the familarity it felt with the nuclear entity—for this was its nature: the meeting of an old but forgotten cousin. Understanding whispered. The node was apprehending the nucleus with its Self field in exactly the same way one *baasa* apprehended another, through merging and feedback of interference. And this implied the deepest truth about the very nature of the mind itself.

For millennia the Hhronka had sought to learn the physical basis for *baas* since it occurred rarely but naturally in their people. Shree himself had been subjected to extensive research into his abilities and their control. But results had always failed to demonstrate anything other than that only living organic minds could possess and manipulate the mysterious Self fields. Now the node comprehended why.

Experiment and Umar–Droom's theory showed color fields, by gluon exchange, exercised the greatest force in the current phase transition of the universe. So potent was its effect that free quarks could never be detected. Whenever quark-composited hadrons, including protons and neutrons, were bombarded with any form of energy, no matter how large, only more hadrons were found. The color force was actually pulling new quarks into being, instantly *creating* them, in the same way that other virtuals burst in from the ambient energy of the surrounding background vacuum, but joining them with the separating quarks to composite new hadrons. Here was a force that manipulated energy and matter at the most fundamental level. And it spilled over, a mere short-range vestige, from the neutron and proton quark triplets in the nucleus to in turn bind these together as the strong nuclear force. At least, this was the particle-exchange interpretation. What the node perceived bore no resemblance, due to uncertainty.

All matter beyond the nucleus was shaped by electromagnetic and gravitational fields. But the node saw that a farther step in the hierarchy of organization of color fields took place within organic nervous systems. Carbon-based life—and perhaps other biochemistries yet unknown—formed an environment in which the nuclear color fields conjoined between atoms in nervous tissues to produce a *megacolor* field. When this structure became dense and organized sufficiently, mind and sentience evolved. Some plants had a little; dogs had a moderate amount; cetaceans had much; and humans, Hhronka, and formerly Teffhtans possessed huge and well-defined megacolor fields.

A *baasa* took this another rung up by having the ability to detect its own and other fields, and interference with them, and to manipulate core parts of them, the Self, consciously. The chemical-electromagnetic metabolism of neurons supplied the raw energy to maintain both the megacolor field and its Self, whose structure was unique to each individual and whose functions were localized, arising from and overlaid onto that of the individual's brain and central nervous system anatomy. When this sustenance was withdrawn at death, the megacolor field–mind–Self collapsed back into the separate nuclear color fields from which it had sprung... perhaps. The node didn't know every aspect of its nature.

This indicated how the Teffhtan mindnet worked. It was an artificial megacolor field, enormous in extent but only a shadow of the structure of a *baasa,* the idiot compared to the genius, without perception or control. As such, it had interfered with the sensitive Selfs of A.H. and Shree since they'd entered Atuum. Yet, it could act as a temporary copy for a unique individual megacolor field, using the field's higher organization as a template by simply merging with it, and then reversing the process with the blank, less-organized field of the clone recipient.

Except it wasn't a true clone—ever. Even if the recipient body and nervous system were grown from tissues of the donors, microchanges would occur during development. This was so even with identical twins split from the same zygote. Absolute congruity was impossible. Therefore, the transduced mind-field was always altered to fit its new home. The greater the difference between old and new, the greater the eventual alterations. So had the Teffhtans been commuted through the ages into something else . . . a hybrid of minds such as P.C. and Twee each was.

Long ago A.H. had seen the parallel between the Self and the ideas of Eastern mystics: the "enlightenment" of consciousness, the joining of an individual's mind with the underlying oneness of all things, and the perception of the interconnectedness of minds with reality. All these philosophy-religions had affirmed that such a mental state was beyond conceptual thought; reality was infinitely complex and to be apprehended only through the intuitive process.

Yet, perhaps here was a rational explanation of Hindu *Brahman,* Buddhist *Dharmakaya,* or Chinese *Tao,* as well as the perception of it. The liberation of individual consciousness to the broadened awareness of nirvana might be a partial merging of the Self with one or many other megacolor fields, as Droom and Umar had enjoyed. Years of practice and effort may have yielded a skill not up to the *baasa* level, but one of low manipulative ability. Perhaps some of the more renowned yogas, and psychics of all mien, were actually self-trained *baasa*. To A.H., merging with even one non-*baasa* gave the sensations often described by such seers.

Finally, the blanket multiple-Self represented a fourth huge step, blending several Self fields tuned to function synergistically as one. However, this *multimegacolor* field was sensitive to *all* other lesser fields, organic and inorganic. It had heard the wild melange of their musics. Therefore, it had to be compounded from the same raw stuff as all of them. The node's field was a re-created relic, a low-energy iota of the Primal Quantum Field created by the Big Bang, before lowering temperature from expansion broke symmetry and caused the phase transitions and other fields to appear. This blanket primal field also carried the qualities of consciousness—the Eastern and other religious views would perhaps hold that all minds were indeed splinters from the Primal Mind—and it could be concentrated back down to its very origins, yet retain its sentience. So the node could sense its idiot-cousin color fields within the nucleus. All fields were in effect phased extensions of the node's own field—thus the feeling of familiarity and belonging.

And the control *could* be extended over these fields. Thus the blanket Self had deflected the laser beam and saved A.H. The node had acted as the primal field's force-carrier "particle," interacting with the photon stream to scatter them coherently.

Now it saw it could interact similarly with all particles to impart energy.

And it saw the possibility of alteration: how to accomplish its goal.

But first it must contract farther. Now it also realized the source of the adamantine resistance to this. Uncertainty affected the node itself! As a "particle" in the primal quantum field, it too was subject to conjugate-state relationships. When it contracted, the energy density it held in the smaller volume increased, and therefore its momentum increased. So its position must become more uncertain as its momentum grew with decreasing perception zone. Now, since it was controlling its position exactly, it had reached the minimum size limit for its total energy.

In order to place itself into a smaller definite position, it must lose energy. How? By removing one of its components? Then it would also lose ability and control. More than ever, it would need both inside the nucleus. Moreover, the node sensed a weakening of its power as its components began to tire. This too would only lessen its control; it must act before they were exhausted.

It thought. Yes! And *thinking* was itself a form of energy within this sentient field. The more it processed consciousness, the more energy it exhibited. It would have to reverse this, relax, become blanked . . . ironically, to meditate and attain what the Hindus termed *samadhi,* mental tranquility.

A dangerous state for the node. If it lost orientation, contracted too far, it might surpass the Planck length. Using the three fundamental constants of physics—the gravity constant, Planck's constant, and light's speed—it was possible to extrapolate the smallest volume that could be meaningfully described: 10^{-35} centimeter. Such a tiny volume of matter–energy–spacetime, perhaps too small even to hold a single quantum for a relativistic instant, constituted a fundamental unit of reality. To perceive useful information at or below this level could prove impossible. Within such a region, reality could break down into total quantum randomness. The node could simply vanish from this universe like a virtual, or even attain the Schwarzchild radius for its density, and transmute into an ultra-mini black hole. But something akin to this latter was its very goal.

Deliberately it pacified its components, orchestrated a symphony of silence, then rested. It retained only its goal and its perception. It pushed through the adamantine resistance and shrank. The nucleus swelled from planetoid to sun, and still the node drew inward upon itself. It fell into the seething surface and was not consumed. It swam in hellfires that sang in long-dead languages ... shrank and fell ...

Suddenly, all around it and even through its ghost presence exploded virtual particles of many kinds. They popped into and out of existence like bursting artillery shells—white, black, white, black—with a wild susurrus that drove the node in-downward toward the zone of Great Calm below.

:: No! There lies the trap!

But the node was unafraid, calm ...

It saw no end to its collapsing journey, but sensed a cusp of action that permitted no easy access. A smooth curve wound upon itself ... a silhouette black-on-white, foreground receding to become background to become foreground to be— Curious, it let itself in-down to the brink. Subjective time had continued to slow. But *time* itself couldn't be separated from *space-time*. Was this cusp the diameter at which space-time events halted sequencing totally? Would the node then in effect become a *photon,* which always moved at light speed and so experienced no passage of space-time events? All of reality through all of time compressed into one instant of present? Must cease questioning ... thinking ... the energy ...

Again it felt resistance, a great turbulence just beyond the calm, as if its hand lay on the thick casing of a high-speed well-anchored machine. To proceed meant not death but eternal change—a transference as absolute.

The nadirs of this cosmos *had* to abut those of others—a foaming Einsteinian sieve of infinite conjunction, meshing reality into reality. Many worlds or splitting worlds—did it matter when control or influence was not possible?

A great mystery lay beyond. Chaos and reason? Surely. Infinitely many near-twins to this? Perhaps. Was that *another* nodal eye performing its own investigation or the mere reflection of this one's desires? That would have to be another story.

Two seconds ...

The node directed its attention from the calm, back up-out to the violent nuclear maelstrom of tumult. It had not *become* a gluon, yet it could sense and interact with space-time over parameters similar to this color-force carrier. This galaxy was thickly nebulous, filled by the anarchy of its moronic quantum-field cousins. Gone was the comfortable familiarity, to be replaced by the inexorable belonging of the mindless hive. *Duty! Perform!* its fellow color fields commanded. The giddy titanic chorus demanded conformity. Despite its enormous power, the node's cohesion faltered, its becalmed will sapped before such termite seduction. It began to disintegrate. With its final thought it responded to both old and new goals: it flung through the nucleus at relativistic speed.

Supreme joy! Once immersed among its idiot cousins it performed its duty; it carried the color force through currents of fire; it imparted energy born of the vacuum and born of itself. It would be ecstatic doing so throughout eternity—or trying to. The happily insane node zipped along in broken erratic lines and curves, merrily distributing energies of creation like a quantum Midas. The ghostlike virtual particles ceased popping like flak in and out around the node–gluon and remained to join the general condensation taking place along its path. In effect it was doing to this nucleus what the cosmic rays had done to the grav crystal's nuclei to create the ftl translation.

A quark soup curdled through the nucleus after the node. The average density rose until its entire diameter fell inside its Schwarzchild radius. It collapsed into a pico-mini black hole; the raging conflagration was softly gone . . . elsewhere. Just before this took place, the node passed beyond the nucleus and the event horizon. It felt cast out for an instant, then full coherence returned and it started to flee from the globular nothingness.

One second . . .

Had the miniscule gravity well of infinite depth remained, it would have quickly ingested the atom's electron cloud, then devoured every atom that collided with it. The entire cesium pellet—and the node—might have been removed from this universe (into the great mystery below the calm?). But it was not quick enough. Even before the node could begin to escape, Hawking evaporation transformed the nothing into an expanding sphere of high energy radiation.

The node had been saved by accident and coincidence. Now it used its new knowledge to preserve itself. As it sensed the onrushing pulse, it simply absorbed the impinging energy and expanded to compensate for the brief flux. So it survived, but the cesium did not. The wave rushed outward through the pellet, exploding it into ionized plasma that melted the detector, stopped the oscillations within the clock, and froze the timer ... a half second from detonation.

The node felt its field and the immediate continuum expand, and was drawn out with it. At molecular size it heard the shout of the bright wave of destruction moving around it, carrying bites of matter, subatomic remnants of the pellet, and packets of radiation.

Englobed within this maniac region it rode out the wave, waiting for it to expend itself and dissipate. Node-weeks later it saw, through a reverberating echo of destroyed matter, the scarred sparkling lattice-wall of the shield box. It had contained the explosion, still held the plates unaltered. As quickly as it could, the node retraced its entrance path to the exterior of the reactor.

Blooming up to macroscopic dimensions, it became saddened. Whole vistas of new knowledge and possibilities had been opened to its investigation. Yet these would have to wait. Reluctant but satisfied, it allowed its member minds to disengage and pull it asunder. Its job was done, but it knew it would exist again.

Chapter 17

His legs failed, and A.H. dropped gasping to a seated position on the solid hot chamber floor. During the entire time (less than two minutes on his patch!) that he had helped give the blanket mind, the "primal quantum field," its existence, his own thoughts had been buffered from insanity by those of the merged mind. But the physical strain filtered through. He'd recorded each thought of the node and remembered every event of the incredible, stupefying journey that had taken subjective eons to complete. He was again a stranger to this tiny ancient dull-surfaced room, to the other oddly fleshy beings near him, and even to himself. It seemed most of his life had been spent as part of the protean node, wandering through a surreal candescent cosmos—subjectively it had.

A glance at each of the others showed they were equally stunned, struggling to recall what place this was and who they were. P.C. was on one knee rubbing a palm over his dripping face, and Twee had turned a mottled ash gray and swayed in place above him. Shree, just outside the original circle, matched his son. Behind him was Baay, coming back to life within the spiraled tentacle of a pentapoid. Gar stood watching her intently.

The chamber had become silent; the plume of plasma was gone; the generators and the reactor were off. They'd succeeded, survived; but he was too exhausted to care, or even to acknowledge the wonder of Renata's new life and form as she bobbed to help him up. When Gar's clone stirred, he ignored everyone else and started to harangue her. Gradually Baay accelerated her responses. Their hostility was self-evident from exaggerated gestures, voice tones, and muddled displays; but no one understood the Teffhtan words till P.C. began to tele them on the subverbal level and translate, whispering to the collapsed circle of *baasa* and Renata.

A.H. was amazed at his son's stamina; he himself hadn't the strength to blow his nose, which had stubbornly begun to drip once more. Gar's manner waxed precise, and P.C. translated him.

"I admit it was very clever and daring of you to use the Complex as hiding place. But depending on these . . . aliens! And giving them access to such vital information! That was inexcusably stupid! You nearly destroyed everything and killed both of us!"

To his limb-weaving tirade, Baay calmly replied, "How was I to predict one of them, especially one with such talents, would become suicidally insane? Otherwise, it would have worked. By the time you would have discovered the plan, I would have had control of seven Complexes and you would have been forced to—"

Gar's Teffhtan bark of laughter accompanied the white Hhronkan blotching of his face. "Do you really think I would use comp codes that could be so easily stolen? I set that up even before they landed! I was certain you would not pass up the opportunity to use them. I knew your every move, until your link disappeared. That was reckless. And to draw the creatures into your plans so intimately . . . even coaching and sending that clone of Shree Shronk's wife to him! You are getting desperate these days."

P.C. halted momentarily in translating to look at Shree, but the Primary was unchanged. Baay's face showed the pinched nasal pore and open mouth of chagrin, but her words sprang from a different emotion. "I am becoming better able to devise your removal each time I lose, *dear Father!* Eventually I must best you!"

The Chief Provider bobbed close to his near-copy and spoke in a deep whisper, having heard the ongoing translation and mistaking Shree as the eavesdropper. But P.C. was reading his thoughts, not hearing his words.

In contempt and triumph, Gar said, "Even then, as always, *my* ultimate superiority would still be proved. Regardless, it will be much more difficult in the future. You are completely friendless now. The *Muunaw* will not follow you after this debacle, and the *Inna* remain convinced of your subordinate ability. Remember this—and our mutual needs—when we resume."

His hand went to her cheek tenderly. "I will see you at the residence shortly. How I've missed you these few days!"

The expression/display on Baay's face riffled through hate, acquiescence, lust, and finally cunning. The observers were as speechless with shock as P.C. when the two "opponents" bade farewell with an arm-twining embrace and the *vurkari* scuttled away with her.

When Gar at last granted them his attention, A.H. said wearily, "This has happened before, hasn't it?"

Gar became expansive, generous, switching to English. "Many times. In fact, Baay has often been Chief Provider of the *Inna*—but only in the far past. Once our judgment was considered interchangeable. But that ended with her chain of decisions that precipitated our homeworld's destruction." He paused somberly at their shocked, dubious looks and displays. "She still refuses to admit that, still projects her guilt to me. One of our enduring tragedies. Even with a near-perfect replica, love is often difficult."

A.H. felt lost again within a maze of falsehoods. "And, of course, there won't be any punishment for Baay, no further action by either side?"

"That would spoil the game! Without the unique challenge, thrill, and sharpening effect of worthy competition—namely myself in another form—plus the other amenities, I would have contracted Covenant long ago."

The malignancy in this being sickened him. It wasn't mere life extension that had rotted Gar from within; he'd seen such decay in humans not yet one hundred. Rather, the weakness of spirit had allowed purpose to wither while leaving appetite vigorous. Another curse apparently shared by both species. That two (they *were* distinct) beings could live solely to play some eternal chess match with their very civilization, and any other unfortunate enough find them, was so unconscionable to him, he was saddened, not infuriated. Perhaps humanity's only true hope lay in evolving naturally into something far better balanced in desire and need. Would long life promote or thwart this?

Unlike him, Shree's fury gave him strength to speak. With dark-streaked face he rumbled, "Could you find *nothing* better to do with immortality than dissipation in this pointless rivalry?"

Gar was highly indignant. "Surviving, emotionally as well as physically, is never pointless!"

"But beings, of our peoples and yours, have *died!* That is counter to your very objective! Irreparable damage may have been done to your society. Surely there is a better, more productive way?"

The Teffhtan stared a moment beyond them. "This time it did get out of control a bit more than I'd hoped. But that was only because I was totally distracted from a closer watch on Baay by your presence and the historical research required to prepare for and eliminate the threat you imposed, *uninvited,* on my world!"

Moving to the *vurkari* at the dome door, he looped an arm at the shut-down reactor. "But that is now a past issue, as are you." He passed behind the pentapoid just as they all responded to his pronouncement. Even Renata pointed her weapon at the frozen robot. Gar's voice echoed around its globe. "If you fire, the sum total of your weapons will still not penetrate to me. Then the *vurkari* will incinerate you. Although I am not certain of the nature, or even the existence, of the 'blanket merge' you spoke of, I believe neither it, nor Shree himself, was effective against Umar's device. It was simply a delaying ruse. The *vurkari* managed to shut down the reactor before it detonated. And I am sure Shree cannot use his power now, or he would have done so already. So I must have your surrender *at once!*"

Two ports opened in the side of the globe. They looked at each other, unbelieving, furious. To have endured so much to learn the truths they had, only to be betrayed again. Gar was correct; they were all too exhausted to use their Selfs. And if they couldn't get control of the situation now, Gar would incapacitate them and that would end it.

P.C. threw down his pistol so hard it bounced and struck the reactor door with a loud clang. Then he looked at it and smiled. The rest copied seconds later, the pentapoid uttered a low grunt, and Gar bobbed back into view. The sharp planes of his face seemed almost crystalline as his nasal pore flexed in disgust at their easy defeat.

With the tone to be used on a stray pet, he said, "You will all now join those you sought to free, even the humans. One day our science may enable you to also be clone-donors. We Teffh-tans can always use a change. Such ugliness would take getting used to, of course, but we did it once. As you yourselves say, variety, spice, and all that."

He motioned to them, signed to the *vurkari,* and began to turn away when P.C. spoke coldly: "Again there is something important that you'd better know before you act, Gar. Shree isn't the only *baas* here, we *all* are. That's how *we* stopped Umar's device, not you. In using the blanket merge we joined our powers and fused the timing mechanism inside the grav plate shield box. But the plates are still there, and now that we know the method, any *one* of us can mentally set them off as Umar intended. And we can do this faster than you can kill us. I, at least, am sure *I* can do it at this moment. Proof?

"Do you remember how we captured you and your guards in your enclave? Of course not! One instant you had us . . . the next you awoke bound in the flyer. Correct? The blanket merge has the ability to make you sleep and forget—as we did the guards in the Life Complex! And in your enclave, *Shree* wasn't even there!"

The realization and astonishment on Gar's dark-blotched vis-age turned to flickering, willful disbelief. Yet he stood unmov-ing for several seconds, weighing the possibilities and consequences. Then he picked up a pair of lasers and spoke to the pentapoid.

"It had better *not* touch the plates!" cautioned P.C. threaten-ingly, adding more proof.

Gar amended his command reluctantly. The *vurkari* rose higher on limb tip and went to the double panel. Bracing three tentacles to the floor, it shoved the other two through the foil-thin base of the melted cup of the left door, keeping its force level below the threshold of its own repulsor film. With a rend-ing screech, the door bent and ripped free of the dome on the third pull, sending dust and debris flying. While it was inside, the antagonists stared tensely at each other.

A.H. barely managed to get his field condensed enough to allow contact from his son's. This time there was no flinching or reticence.

:: That's some bluff you're running, son. Even if Gar doesn't buy it, it is well played.

The reply held warmth layered with satire.

:: Thanks, but *you* taught me how to do it.

The robot stilted back in seconds; its loud voice spoke briefly.

"Very well," whispered Gar, his face a pulse of black-white. "Name your conditions." His shock display remained visible throughout P.C.'s demands.

"You and the tin squids will leave the Complex at once. It can continue functioning normally, but only service robots are allowed with prior permission. As quickly as possible, your people will repair our craft's engines. Then you will construct and install a complete transduction complex in the *Wind,* along with the necessary resuscitating equipment to allow rejuvenation of all the Hhronka held prisoners here. Then you will ferry up their frozen bodies, aid in their rebirth, and allow us to leave this system!"

A.H. gave his son a smile and wink of encouragement, but P.C. pretended to ignore it, obviously enjoying his imperious role, as the white-bedecked Hhronka surely were.

"To ensure your performance, at least one of us will remain here with the plate box at all times until the day we go." He began advancing a step at a time toward the taller being, his voice growing louder and more aggressive. "And to demonstrate the thinness of our trust for your kind, we are going to have you shut down your interference network long enough for us to send to Sol system a complete description of your weapons capability and your history with regards to us. Then if we don't send a second coded message after we leave this system, four months later, the next Sol expedition here will be *your* last!"

By now P.C. stood close to Gar, his head only to the other's midtorso. But there was no timidity in the youth as he poked an index finger hard into the blue vest. Through his teeth, he said, "Is all this getting clear with you?"

Still Gar failed to react, except for the continued black-white splotches of shock.

His own loathing flickering darkly on his face, Shree came forward. "Have no worry about further contact with us. We shall quarantine this system and alert any other civilizations we may one day discover."

A.H. looked around, surprised and delighted.

"We have already gained more than hoped: the recovery of our lost people and the means to prolong life, if it is wished.... and something else, perhaps even more important.

After these expeditions disappeared, we Hhronka made the same choice for societal stasis you have made, though for different reasons. But the results were similar. Unless any species pushes out beyond its own world, it will eventually cease to be productive, cease to offer its kind the best way of life possible. I think this is what has happened on Teffht. Our intermingling could have changed that, just as the human arrival on Wlaata saved *us*. Now you will remain as you are, forever. Slowly shrinking in number, your lives will shrivel into the Covenant —a prolonged species suicide. I am truly sorry, but the most just retribution for what you have done is to condemn you to that complete isolation you so fanatically crave."

In silence Gar stared at the Primary as his own display faded to broken glass. The moment had come. Either Gar was successfully convinced, or they would at least be killed fighting the *vurkari,* not meekly frozen for eternity.

The round head notched down to P.C., and the sharp facial planes seemed to shift and melt like a cracking ice flow. They recognized triumph and then a sad defeat in his face.

Softly he said, "Travel in safety."

Chapter 18

Through the unshuttered roof glass, the starfields slid past the giant's striding legs. Twisting his head over his right shoulder, A.H. tried to locate Tau Ceti, but it had finally blended invisibly with the other yellow-white background suns. Now Sol stood out more clearly. P.C.'s warning cry brought his attention back to flying, and he concentrated on again lining up his glide path to follow Joan and his son through the checkerboard bulkhead between the human and Hhronkan sections.

The emotional memory of Teffht had also diminished, and it seemed impossible they had been fighting so hopelessly for life only six months before. How easy it was to put aside pain, consciously at last, and return to any peaceful and contented mode of living.

However, *The Breaking Wind* and its life-style would never be the same as before. Now it was bursting with the reborn Hhronka, all of whom were yet stuporous with the attempt to internalize what had actually occurred to them so long ago on Teffht. They had been intrigued by the ftl translation of the craft, and absolutely fascinated by the humans aboard. Crowding had forced them to share the human residence areas, with effects ranging from mere nuisances to culture shock in the extreme.

His smiling cheeks bulged against his helmet's faceplate as

he thought of the large female who had literally cornered him in a spoke lift about two weeks ago, stripped herself naked, and gestured openly for him to imitate. Astounding her with his elementary Hhronkan, he had choked back laughter and explained where to obtain recs on human anatomy—and that her behavior was considered inappropriate. He'd left her apologizing for her curiosity. *That* was something he had never gotten from any Hhronkan in twenty-four years.

As the three of them swooped in over the Hhronkan agricells, A.H. watched his son's forceful movements. P.C. had changed, too. Only occasionally did remnants of boyish doubt crop up. Teffht had catalyzed the youth into a confident young man. Although A.H. was a little wistful over the loss of the child, he was also proud of the man and quite happy about the reclaimed warmth between them. It was a closeness more important than in P.C.'s childhood, since it was consciously returned and more intimate because they shared a greater portion of understanding.

They flapped and glided to the edge of the poly-crop area, then spiraled down into the lower cooler air of the first Hhronkan residential section. Its native-designed vine-coated homes produced the minor wonder of fusing a densely forested exterior to an open airy interior. The scene reminded him of another day, over three years ago on Wlaata, when they had all flown together above the yellow-blue-green forest. A simple happy day, without hint of the future. Such days were forever gone, no matter how prolonged their lives, for truly they were no longer together. He pulled his thoughts away from sorrow.

Between the trees scattered about the rolling ground, they saw many of the reborn Children playing in the fading artificial day. P.C. led in to back-flap and land standing in the open strip by the rim's stream. Joan followed quickly to stop several paces to his right, but A.H. used his grav belt and wings to halt a few meters up in midair and lower slowly, luxuriating in the relaxing parachute effect, recovering from the moment's depression.

After doffing her gear, Joan said breathlessly, "Hope we aren't too early for Shree. It has to be a chore to get even Hhronkan kids quieted when there's over fifty of them."

A.H. nodded back. "Let's go see how Droom's doing first."

A total of 2,417 young had been reclaimed from the crypts on Teffht. Most of them had been nonsentient embryos. These had been placed in the growth tanks provided by Gar and set to gestate out just after they reached Wlaata. A few of the rest were the natural children of the expedition's crews and so were housed with their families. But the remainder were intentionally created orphans whose parents could not or would not join the first two expeditions but who wanted to give their offspring a last chance for life, as Feeahra had sought to do for Affeel. Ranging from two to five years of age, these children could have been simply stowed for the trip in impeded animation, along with the embryos. But the general Hhronkan consensus was that they had also been cheated of active life as much as the adults and equally deserved consciousness at once.

Since Shree and Droom were Guardians, the job of caring for the "bouncers," as this age-group was called, had become theirs; indeed, both had volunteered before being asked. The two had commandeered this section of homes, partitioned the hundred-odd young, and initiated the peripatetic form of education formerly used during Rebirth in the Repositories. But when the three visitors wandered through clusters of staring, tadpole-quick young, looking for the Orrtaan, they saw an activity they knew had been completely absent from this ancient training.

Within a gentle, treeless swale stood Droom, surrounded by and *covered* with affectionate hooting bouncers! A dozen of them, naked skins erupting with huge white blossoms of joy to match her own, were each trying to be enwrapped by one of her looping arms. Two were held already, and she nuzzled them and hugged them as if no others were present. But two more dripped from each arm, one rode her back, clinging to her neck, and the others were piled around her legs like reeds sprouting beneath an oak. As she gently lowered the lucky two, the rest hooted in high-pitched frustration to be next, some even hopping straight up in the air to snatch for a hold on her vest and trousers.

Just as Droom noticed the visitors watching with mouths agape, one of her charges made a tremendous arcing leap and landed belly-down on top of her head like a frog on a lily pad. She clutched the female bouncer by one leg, pulled the wriggling creature down into a quick embrace, and set her on the ground. Then she fended off the pack long enough to grasp a whistle at her neck. The low musical tone brought instant order to the chaos; all twelve hopped and bounced away to resume play.

With face dropping back to calm beige, Droom joined them, completely out of breath. "Thank reason . . . for Pavlovian . . .

reinforcement!" she hissed as she rearranged her torn soil-stained clothing.

"Droom, what were you doing? I thought that kind of body contact was never allowed between Children and Guardians?" asked Joan with a smile of apology for the probing question.

But the Orrtaan showed no abashment as she ushered them slowly through the nearby glade. "This is admittedly a trial experiment, but I am certain results will be positive. There have been doubts among our psychologists regarding the standard noncontact procedure during Rebirth. And many have asserted there is a provable difference between the psyches of the Reborn generation and those that follow, those reared in closer personal, innermost-family situations. Your own terran behavioral scientists have done work showing the importance of physical contact in early mammalian and human life to ensure normal emotional development and general health. Perhaps we Hhronka are similar."

Only now did she reveal a subtle emotion of her own, other than curiosity. A trace of sorrow flickered across her cheeks during a brief pause. A doubt she would always live with? They did not ask.

"Anyway, the exigencies of Rebirth itself are in the past. *These* Children will all receive contact, at least until we reach Wlaata. By then I shall know the effects of the treatment and if it is worth continuing. I have divided our outside area into, shall we say, 'contact' and 'no-contact' zones. During free play, whenever I enter a contact zone, which are specific spots such as the swale back there, the Children may approach me for contact affection; otherwise, no. And if things get uncontrollable, I simply blow the tone and they know the period is over."

A.H. literally poked his tongue into his cheek to "hide his own skin," and peered sideways at P.C. and Joan. "And of course *you* get nothing from this yourself?" he asked broadly.

Droom halted and looked openly at them. "I am a Guardian, now and always. Naturally the health of those I train concerns me, and healthy Children are a reward in itself."

Losing patience, A.H. barked good-naturedly, "Oh, Droom! Why can't you admit you enjoy it as much as, or more than, they do? Afraid the human resemblance might denigrate Hhronkan superiority?"

She was puffing up for a reply when they heard movements in the nearby hedges to the left. Light whispers rustled with the leaves and fronds, and then a few small round heads cautiously peeped above the crest of the rise they were climbing. Droom's face rippled with black terror.

"Oh no," she said, so hushed they could barely hear her. "They are doing it *again!*"

Suddenly the rise and the bushes sprouted rushing bouncers who attacked like wild rabbits as they honked and hooted loudly with glee.

"Run for your lives!" screamed Droom as she turned and leaped back down the hill. "Every being for herself!"

Startled, the three humans were rooted and watched in confusion as the living tidal wave bypassed them and caught Droom at the base of the rise. She was bowled over by twenty-plus sailing bodies and came down in a wriggling heap.

P.C.'s laughter exploded uncontrollably when the whistle's tone issued repeatedly without effect from the writhing, hooting clump of snakelike limbs.

"It seems Droom has yet to learn the delicate balance between discipline and love," he said sardonically.

"Come on," returned A.H. through his chuckle. "We're outnumbered here."

He threw an arm over each of their shoulders and, bidding good night to the still-whistling pile, steered through the winding openings in a patch of corkscrew trees. By the time they'd reached Shree's headquarters-house, twilight had been turned off to night. But the elongated hexagon door panel glowed translucent blue to guide them in the last steps. As they mounted the low porch, P.C. spoke softly.

"Remember, we agreed no one's to start up about Ren's living with us again. OK?"

A.H. felt his throat tighten in a spasm of anxiety at the mention of the topic he'd just successfully buried. He could only nod, and Joan committed with the same sign. The porch sensor registered their presence and opened the door, adding in English, "Please come in."

They entered a house mirroring their own back on Mars, except that most of the randomly placed furnishings were Hhronkan. This meant a lot more fabric-covered surfaces; even the walls were carpeted up to the ceilings. Fortunately they could fit into the cradling Hhronkan seats more easily than vice versa, for there were only two terran chairs in the wide living room to the left. It was empty at the moment so the guests sat,

A.H. preferring one of the carpet-covered cups evaginating like mushrooms from the floor. He lay back with a sigh onto the soft nubbiness; it was as sensual and relaxing as good wine. He studied the dim stalactite globe lamps overhead, thought about the vote tomorrow—and tried to avoid thinking about an even more personal decision he must make.

In a few minutes Shree and Feeahra came out onto the balcony from the upper bedrooms and down the spiral stairs at the left. Both wore robes of bright colors and white rosette clouds of smile.

"Good evening, my friends," Shree said.

"Well wisses tu uu," added Fee, her English still slurred. They separated and reclined onto seats bracing the humans. A.H. reflected again that to him Hhronkan manners were generally superior to human ones. There had been no formal standing or chest-touching between old acquaintances, no necessity on their hosts' part to apologize for being late when the reasons were well known, no offer of food or drink since the guests knew they could ask for such or get it themselves at any time. No falseness, no hypocrisy, no forced courtesy existed in Hhronkan mores or folkways; just the simple greeting full of good feelings toward them, the main cause for their coming tonight. It imbued an openness so comfortable that if something were wrong it could easily be discussed without rancor. Indeed, P.C.'s warning had been given to spare their own anguish, not that of the Hhronka. He was sure he preferred this to human manners, designed not to smooth social interplay but plaster thickly over all reality, to present a perfect, average, model person who never existed. Yes, becoming a Hhronkan could have compensations.

That led him to study the Hhronkan pair as a couple. Fee was as beautiful now as in Shree's Total Projection; A.H. could feel that way even from a human viewpoint. It wasn't only her well-proportioned, evenly curving facial and body lines, nor the extreme grace with which she moved. Her intelligence and warmth, reflecting her loving attitude toward life, engendered each movement, word, and display with an almost narcotic effect on him. It was obvious why Shree cared for her as he did, and why they always seemed to have a linkage pulsing between them, even when they were apart, as now. It seemed they were holding hands . . . as he and Joan were. That was the way he often felt about her too. Being one of a Hhronkan couple would have its rewards as well.

Shree's reunion with Fee had been private. Together, they had all watched the Teffhtan technicians rouse her butchered, thawed body to consciousness in the support tank, then transduce her mind to the prepared clone. But alone within the enclosed recovery cubicle, Shree had used *baas* to help her become aware and settle into her "new" nervous system. She had become active faster than any other reborn expedition member, as had their young daughter, Affeel.

"What do you think of Droom's addition to the group training procedure?" he asked Shree to escape where that thought led.

A white blip of humor crossed his face. "I cannot say it is doing much for entraining discipline. And I have never been convinced of the theory of close physical contact being needed beyond close psychological contact for a Hhronkan child's emotional growth. Still, they all seem to enjoy it, and perhaps Droom's experiment will prove something. But I will hold to the traditional way this one last time."

"Last time?" said Joan with brows lifted in surprise.

The deep purple cat-eyes searched all three of their faces, ending on hers. "I have finished my duty as Guardian and Meethlah Primary to my people. It is time for a successor to be found. And it is true that teachers will always be needed, despite the improvements of the Teffhtan imprinting technique. This will but speed up the accumulation of data; it cannot help either in comprehension, or in application to developing behavior. Only experienced guidance can finish another's education. Droom wishes to continue in this role.

"However, for the second time there is an innermost-family with whom I belong. We have all been fortunate beyond our desserts. I do not intend to lose contentedness again."

Fee beamed a pallid burst of pleasure at him, which he returned. A.H. had expected this announcement; he'd seen his friend's attitude changing ever since Shree had learned his wife might still be alive. And his comment to Gar in the generator room about other civilizations had prepared A.H. for Shree's next statement.

"Also, when the vote is taken tomorrow, I will choose to immediately return the *Wind* to exploration, and we intend to join the crew. We believe the lesson of Teffht and our own past is clear. That is why I proposed emigration off-world as the only antidote to eventual stagnation. We must urge laws that force emigration on all those who partake of the transduction system to prolong their first lives."

"That would also control overcrowding, which will be a big problem very soon," added P.C.

Shree displayed a smoke-ring. "Yes, that too. Regardless, for me the future is out here. I want to help lead in this expansion, to be of the vanguard searching for habitable systems and planets, for those who cannot be satisfied with life in a craft such as this. Perhaps we may indeed find other civilizations more worthy of association than the Teffhtan."

Dark bars of repugnance sifted down his face. P.C. mumbled just loud enough to be heard, "Where no man, or Hhronkan, has gone before—or would want to go again!" To their quizzical glances he just shook his head to indicate the remark's unimportance. "From *Star Trek.*"

His son may have quantum-jumped in maturity, but he retained his youthful sense of humor—a rare and good thing. Suddenly he caught a subtle expression on Shree's bulbous face, a certain set of the mouth and nasal pore that in a human would have been a prompting for him to speak. He knew then why Shree had expounded at such length on this topic. Apparently he might be surrendering his Guardianship but not his intrusiveness. Well, he was again a friend, and here a friend's help was especially welcome. He hadn't yet dared broach the subject with Joan.

He took the lead, but spoke lightly, not looking at her. "This is what I've wanted to explain to Joan. It's one other reason I first wanted to come on this mission. As explorers we could be making a real impact back on Earth and Wlaata. And here on *Wind* I sense we've already created a microcosm of our peoples very different from that on either home world. We're an integral part of this world and its crew. I like it and them. They obey *all* the rules . . . or at least know the right time to break them."

With a grin he twisted on the spongy chaise to Joan, who sat unsmiling in the deep easy chair. "Joan, here we'd each have what we want. You a stable home life and I—"

"You don't have to sell me on that," she said sharply, looking at both conspirators to denote her awareness of their collusion. "And that's not my prime need anyway; it never was. I do like sleeping every night in the same bed, with the same man, in the same house, with the same neighbors. Even as interstellar gypsies in *Wind,* we'd have that. I only want to be sure *you'll* still be content with this, years down the road. If that's the case, then I'll be more than satisfied staying on."

A.H. pressed his mouth into a thin line and raised both hands. "Well, there's never going to be any guarantees on happiness for any of us. Change is one of the few inevitable facts of life, even of prolonged life, for which we should be thankful. There may be many years of life to come; either of us might want to try something else."

Realizing he'd veered into an area neither wished to discuss, he quickly added, "I only hope whatever we do, we do it together."

"Yes," said Fee in Hhronkan with happy rosettes on her face. "That is a most important thing."

A.H. suspended the topic by saying softly to Joan, "At least it's a life I can both accept *and* be resigned to."

Her answering smile was not unconditional, but compromise was another factor he'd finally yielded to without resistance. It was also necessary to do that many times in life.

There was a hoot of greeting from above, and Twee, Affeel, and Renata came down the stairs to join them, the older two taking seats. Renata addressed the visitors by their first names, and the child bobbed slowly around them for a closer look, still wondering at their strangeness. A.H. saw Joan stiffen, and P.C. went to the kitchen as soon as he'd greeted them. Shree and Fee preferred a less automated center with cabinets, and when the doors started sliding, Affeel followed him.

Conversation died. With Hhronka this wasn't usually an undesirable or insulting lull; mere companionship was enough. But A.H. felt the universal stress of Renata's presence. It was a unique and disquieting situation, more so for Joan than for him and P.C. as *baasa.* Since her transduction, Renata had become steadily less their daughter and more a Hhronkan. This change was of course directly sensible to him whenever he tele'd her. The human mind that had belonged to his child was there, but distorted and crazy-quilted in its patterns of thought, diluted with Hhronkan tones. Often when talking to her now, he could close his eyes, ignore the deeper rasping voice, and it would be his Rennie back again. Yet he and P.C. were always aware of the mental overlay that truly made this Renata a different entity. *Baas* enabled them to get past the flesh mask and become accustomed to her. But Joan could never directly sense this crystallizing mind and knew only the often-perfect memories and behavioral mannerisms this Hhronkan Renata would display juxtaposed to novel ones in an entirely different body. The dichotomy was periodically maddening to her.

Renata was aware of this and had presented it as one motivating factor when she'd calmly announced she was moving to live with Shree's family. No doubt her growing relationship with Twee had further enhanced her decision.

Not surprisingly, Shree had never revealed a single thought about the situation and remained stubbornly neutral. After all, he would not express feeling sorry that Renata had died but happy she lived again as a Hhronkan, which was true, A.H. was certain. They had been anguished at first but now were *logically* seeing the inevitability of it. And he knew P.C.'s love for his sister's memory and for Twee would soon end his resentment of the changes. Could he and Joan say the same?

He studied Twee where he sat next to Renata. There at least was one positive result no one could begrudge. The youth's entire attitude had reversed toward Shree. Having found the human psyche he'd loved for so long suddenly within a Hhronkan form must have indeed seemed a miracle to Twee. He was no longer constrained by real or imagined ethics. His love could be expressed openly, and seemed to be returned. And so it had multiplied many times, with surplus left for his father and his "new" mother and sister. It was downright human, but then Twee partly was.

When the visit was over and they were leaving, Joan forced Renata to let her kiss her on the cheek. To A.H. it had the feeling of a good-bye to the human still remaining within the Hhronkan. Later, they stood together in one of the spoke's observation lounges, pressed against a cool port. The stars swept toward them, dividing their unending flow to either side of the rim, on an ever-turning galactic wheel themselves. He was behind her, bracing her hard shoulders with his hands, smelling the spice of her hair, when she trembled.

Softly she said, "Will you have the mindnet link implanted?"

Now he felt they were both ready to speak of making this decision. "Should we wait? There'll be lots of impetus now to find a way to clone humans. I'm sure before we die of old age we will have our own young bodies to move into."

"And if we die of accident before that?"

He breathed out deeply. "Then we'd become Hhronkan."

"Like Rennie . . . like *Renata,* " she said quickly, correcting to keep them separate, the memory and the flesh.

"Yes. Would that be so horrible?" He turned her to face him as he smiled apologetically. "I'm afraid I'm a very weak human after all. I want a very long life—with you. But being bored to death is not one of my worries. This is an unimaginably vast universe. We can never live long enough to know and understand even a tiny part of it. But I have a hunger to see this galaxy, enormous as it is. That would be sufficient for me. I want to investigate its structure, understand its physical laws, know its peoples and their cultures. There may not be time even for this, but I want us to try. Partly it must be simple simian curiosity. Perhaps every sentient born has the destiny to do this, and every time any one of us dies it's a failure of that natural evolution. Can't you feel that ache to *know* inside? Haven't you felt that ecstasy each time it's so wonderfully but temporarily satisfied? I'm willing to pay any price for that. That's what children have that most of us lose or bury as we get older. So, if we can't *have* children as immortals, we'll just have to *be* them!"

Suddenly her tears spilled out; the ones from her right eye trickled down her nose as she grinned in bittersweet contrast and laid her head against his left arm. Then her belly spasmed with silent weeping. He rubbed at her hot damp cheek with the back of his hand.

"Our Rennie's gone," she said between gulps of air.

He swallowed the thick glob in his throat and nodded. "Yes. But I love Renata all the same."

She smiled up through the tears, her own acceptance and resignation at last revealed. "So do I."

For several minutes both were quiet, watching the starstream and holding tightly. He thought of the whole adventure, tallied its victories . . . and costs. He remembered what he'd learned at the *usstaa* about himself. There was still a gulf between them, deeply buried in Joan; he knew it could remain there. For their long, long future with each other, he felt he should try again to close it.

"What I said about our exploring is true, but there's something else . . . more basic than that."

She turned in his arms to look up, already realizing his attempt, trying to tell him with her eyes it wasn't necessary, but he spoke over her silent objection.

"You're quoting habit has finally rubbed off on me. Though I'd rather contrive my own 'immortal' conundrums, here's one that says it better than I ever could. It's from Morris West's *The Shoes of the Fisherman:*

> It takes so much to be a full human being that there are very few who have the enlightenment or the courage to pay the price... One has to abandon altogether the search for security and reach out to the risk of living with both arms. One has to embrace the world like a lover. One has to accept pain as a condition of existence. One has to court doubt and darkness as the cost of knowing. One needs a will stubborn in conflict, but apt always to total acceptance of every consequence of living and dying.

"I'm sure I am a victim of that kind of courage, a chronic bravery of sorts. I'll never be content to just wait for something beyond me to make my living worthwhile, no matter how much of it there is."

As she smiled, her tears collected in the corners of her lips. "Not me either. Never again, A.H."

Their embrace bridged more than space, a conjunction different from but as meaningful as any merge of his life. This one would not be broken again; they would never again feel isolated. Wasn't that the truest measure of love? Then she pulled away and asked, as though she'd just thought of it for the first time, "After we go home and visit for a while, then where will we go?"

He grinned and shrugged, waving his hand casually at the starfield of infinite size and infinite possibility.

"Out there."